THE
LAST
NAMSARA

Also by Kristen Ciccarelli
The Caged Queen

THE

LAST

NAMSARA

KRISTEN CICCARELLI

HARPER TEEN

An Imprint of HarperCollinsPublishers

For Joe:
comrade, beloved, champion of all my dreams

One

Asha lured the dragon with a story.

It was an ancient story, older than the mountains at her back, and Asha had to dredge it up from where it lay deep and dormant inside her.

She hated to do it. Telling such stories was forbidden, dangerous, even deadly. But after stalking this dragon through the rocky lowlands for ten days now, her hunting slaves were out of food. She had a choice: return to the city dragonless or break her father's ban on the ancient tales.

Asha never returned without a kill and she wasn't about to now. She was the Iskari, after all, and there were quotas to fill.

So she told the story.

In secret.

While her hunters thought she was sharpening her axe.

The dragon came, slithering out of the red-gold silt like the treacherous thing it was. Sand cascaded down its body, shimmering like water and revealing dull gray scales the color of mountain rock.

Three times the size of a horse, it loomed over Asha, thrashing a forked tail while its slitted gaze fixed on the girl who'd summoned it. The girl who'd *tricked* it here with a story.

Asha whistled for her hunting slaves to get behind their shields, then waved off her archers. This dragon had spent the night burrowed beneath the cold desert sand. With the sun only just rising, its body temperature wasn't warm enough for it to fly.

It was stranded. And a stranded dragon fought fierce.

Asha's left hand tightened on an oblong shield while her right hand reached for the throwing axe at her hip. The rough esparto grass rattled around her knees as the dragon circled, waiting for her to let down her guard.

That was its first mistake. Asha never let down her guard.

Its second was to blast her with flame.

Asha hadn't been afraid of fire since the First Dragon himself left her with a vicious scar running down the right side of her body. A sheath of fireproof armor covered her now from head to toe, made from the hides of all the dragons she'd killed. The tanned leather buckled tight against her skin and her favorite helmet—one with black horns mimicking a dragon's head—protected her from dragonfire.

She kept her shield raised until the blaze ceased.

The dragon's breath was now spent. Asha threw down her shield. She had a hundred heartbeats before the acid in its lungs replenished, allowing it to breathe fire again. She needed to kill it before that happened.

Asha drew her axe. Its curved iron edge caught the early morning sunlight. Beneath her scarred fingers, the wooden handle was worn smooth. A comfortable fit against her palm.

The dragon hissed.

Asha narrowed her eyes. *Time to end you.*

Before it could advance, she aimed and threw—straight at its beating heart. Her axe sank into flesh and the dragon screamed. It struggled and thrashed as its lifeblood spilled onto the sand. Gnashing its teeth, it fixed its raging eyes on her.

Someone stepped up beside Asha, breaking her focus. She looked to find her cousin, Safire, thrusting the butt of a pointed halberd into the sand. Safire stared at the thrashing, screaming dragon. Her dark hair was sheared to her chin, showing off the bold slant of her cheekbones and the shadow of a bruise on her jaw.

"I told you to stay behind the shields," Asha growled. "Where's your helmet?"

"I couldn't see a thing in that helmet. I left it with the hunting slaves." Safire wore tanned leather hunting gear, made hastily by Asha, and her hands were protected by Asha's fireproof gloves. There hadn't been time to make a second pair.

The bloody dragon dragged itself across the sand, intent on Asha. Its scales scraped. Its breath wheezed.

Asha reached for the halberd. How much time had passed since its last breath of fire? She'd lost track.

"Get back, Saf. Behind the shields."

Safire didn't move. Only stared at the dying dragon,

mesmerized, as its beating heart slowed.

Thud-thud.

Thud . . . thud.

The scraping sound stopped.

Rearing back its head, the dragon screamed in hate at the Iskari. Just before its heart stopped beating, flames rushed out of its throat.

Asha stepped in front of her cousin.

"Get down!"

Asha's ungloved hand was still outstretched. Exposed. Fire engulfed her fingers and palm, searing the skin. She bit down on her scream as pain lanced through her.

When the fire stopped and the dragon collapsed, dead, Asha turned to find Safire on her knees, safe and sound in the sand. Shielded from the flames.

Asha let out a shaky breath.

Safire stared at her cousin's hand. "Asha. You're burned."

Asha pushed off her helmet and lifted her palm to her face. The charred skin bubbled. The pain blazed, bright and hot.

Panic sliced through her. It had been eight years since she'd been burned by a dragon.

Asha scanned her hunting slaves, all of whom were lowering their shields. They wore no armor, only iron—iron in their arrows and halberds and spears, iron in the collars around their necks. Their eyes fixed on the dragon. They hadn't seen the Iskari get burned.

Good. The fewer witnesses, the better.

"Dragonfire is toxic, Asha. You need to treat that."

Asha nodded. Except she hadn't brought supplies for a burn treatment. She'd never needed them before.

To keep up appearances, she moved for her pack. From behind her, Safire said very softly, "I thought they didn't breathe fire anymore."

Asha froze.

They don't breathe fire without stories, she thought.

Safire got to her feet and dusted off her leather armor. Her eyes dutifully avoided Asha's as she asked, "Why would they start breathing fire *now*?"

Asha suddenly wished she'd left her cousin behind.

But if she'd left Safire behind, there wouldn't just be remnants of a bruise on her jaw. There would be far worse.

Two days before Asha had set out on this hunt, she found Safire cornered by soldats in her own room. How they'd gotten in without a key, she could only guess.

As soon as Asha entered, they panicked, scattering in the presence of the Iskari. But what about next time? Asha would be hunting for days, and her brother, Dax, was still in the scrublands, negotiating peace with Jarek, the commandant. There was no one to keep a watchful eye out for their skral-blooded cousin while Asha hunted. So she'd brought Safire with her. Because if there was anything worse than coming home empty-handed, it was coming home to Safire in the sickroom again.

Asha's silence didn't dissuade her cousin in the least.

"Remember the days when you would set out at dawn and bring a dragon down before dinner? Whatever happened to those days?"

The searing pain of her blistering skin made Asha dizzy. She fought to keep her mind clear.

"Maybe things were too easy back then," she said, whistling at her hunting slaves, signaling them to start the dismemberment. "Maybe I prefer a challenge."

The truth was, dragon numbers had been dwindling for years and it was getting harder to bring their heads back to her father. It was why she'd turned to telling the old stories in secret—to lure them to her. The old stories drew dragons the way jewels drew men. No dragon could resist one told aloud.

But the stories didn't just lure dragons. They made them stronger.

Hence, the fire.

It went like this: where the old stories were spoken aloud, there were dragons; and where there were dragons, there was destruction and betrayal and burning. Especially burning. Asha knew this better than anyone. The proof was right there on her face.

Sighing, Safire gave up.

"Go treat that burn," she said, leaving her halberd upright in the sand as she started toward the hulking form. While the slaves advanced on the dragon, Safire walked a complete circle around the body, scanning it. The dragon's dusty gray scales were perfect for blending into the mountain, and its horns and spines were flawless ivory, none of them broken or cracked.

In Safire's absence, Asha tried to flex her burned fingers. The sharp pain made her bite down hard. It made the lowlands around her blur into a smudged landscape of red sand, pale yellow grass, and a gray speckle of rock. They were on the seam here. Not quite in the flat desert to the immediate west, nor in the dark and craggy mountains to the immediate east.

"It's a beauty!" Safire called back.

Asha strained to focus on her cousin, who was starting to blur along with everything else. She tried to shake her vision clear. When that didn't work, she reached for Safire's halberd to steady herself.

"Your father will be so pleased." Her cousin's voice sounded thick and muffled.

If my father only knew the truth, thought Asha, bitterly.

She willed the landscape to stop spinning around her. She clutched the halberd harder, concentrating on her cousin.

Safire navigated through the slaves, their knives glinting. Asha heard her grab the handle of the embedded axe. She heard Safire use the heel of her boot to brace herself against the dragon's scaly hide. Asha even heard her pull the weapon out while blood glugged onto the sand, thick and sticky.

But she couldn't see her. Not any longer.

The whole world had gone fuzzy and white.

"Asha . . . ? Are you all right?"

Asha pressed her forehead to the flat steel of the halberd. The fingers of her unburned hand curled like claws around the iron shaft as she fought the dizziness.

I should have more time than this.

Hurried footsteps kissed the sand.

"Asha, what's wrong?"

The ground dipped. Asha felt herself tilt. Without thinking, she reached for her skral-blooded cousin. The one who, under the law, wasn't allowed to touch her.

Safire sucked in a breath and stepped back, out of reach, widening the gap between them. Asha struggled to regain her balance. When she couldn't, she sank onto the sand.

Even when Safire's gaze slid to the hunting slaves—even when Asha knew it was their judgment Safire feared and not *her*—it stung. It always stung.

But slaves talked. Her cousin knew this better than anyone. Gossiping slaves had betrayed Safire's parents. And right now, they were surrounded by slaves. Slaves who knew Safire wasn't allowed to touch Asha, wasn't even allowed to look Asha in the eye. Not with skral blood running through her veins.

"Asha . . ."

All at once, the world settled back into place. Asha blinked. There was the sand beneath her knees. There was the horizon in the distance, a red-gold smear against a turquoise sky. And there was the slain dragon before her: clear and gray and dead.

Safire crouched down before her. Too close.

"Don't," Asha said more sharply than she meant to. "I'm fine."

Rising, she bit down on the scorching pain in her hand. It didn't make sense for the toxins to set in so fast. She was dehydrated—that's all. She just needed water.

"You shouldn't even be out here," Safire called from behind her, voice laced with worry. "Your binding is seven days away. You should be preparing yourself for it, not running from it."

Asha's footsteps faltered. Despite her scorching hand and the steadily rising sun, a chill swept through her.

"I'm not running from anything," she shot back, staring straight ahead at the mantle of green in the distance. The Rift. It was Asha's one freedom.

Silence fell over them, interrupted only by the sounds of slaves sharpening their skinning knives. Slowly, Safire came to stand behind her.

"I hear dragon hearts are in fashion these days." Asha could hear the careful smile in her voice. "For betrothal gifts especially."

Asha wrinkled her nose at the thought. She crouched down next to her hunting pack, made of the tough leather of dragon hide. Reaching inside, she drew out her water skin while Safire stood over her.

"The red moon wanes in seven days, Asha. Have you even *thought* about your betrothal gift?"

Asha rose to growl a warning at her cousin and the world spun again. She kept it in place by the sheer force of her will.

Of course she'd thought about it. Every time Asha looked up into the face of that horrible moon—always a little thinner than the day before—she thought about all of it: the gift and the wedding and the young man she would soon call *husband*.

The word hardened like a stone inside her. It brought everything into sharp focus.

"Come on," said Safire, smiling a little, her eyes cast toward the hilltops. "The gory, bleeding heart of a dragon? It's the perfect gift for a man without a heart of his own."

Asha shook her head. But Safire's smile was contagious.

"Why do you have to be so disgusting?"

Just then, over Safire's shoulder, a cloud of red-gold sand billowed in the distance, coming from the direction of the city.

Asha's first thought was *dust storm* and she was about to give a frantic order, but rocky lowlands surrounded them here, not the open desert. Asha squinted into the distance and saw two horses making their way toward her hunting party. One was riderless; the other carried a man cloaked in a mantle, the rough wool dusted red with sand kicked up by his horse. A gold collar encircled his neck, winking in the sunlight and marking him as one of the palace slaves.

As he galloped closer, Asha thrust her burned hand behind her back.

When the sand settled, she found the elderly slave reining in his mare. Sweat soaked his graying hair. He squinted in the pulsing sunlight.

"*Iskari,*" he said, out of breath from riding so hard. He fastened his gaze on the tossing mane of his horse, obediently avoiding Asha's eyes. "Your father wishes to see you."

Behind her back, Asha gripped her wrist. "He has perfect timing. I'll deliver this dragon's head to him tonight."

The slave shook his head, his gaze still boring into his horse. "You're to return to the palace immediately."

Asha frowned. The dragon king never interrupted her hunts.

She looked to the riderless mare. It was Oleander, her own horse. Her russet coat glistened with sweat, and a smudge of red sand covered the white star on her forehead. In the presence of her rider, Oleander bobbed her head nervously.

"I can help finish up here," said Safire. Asha turned to her. Safire didn't dare look up into her face. Not under a royal slave's watchful gaze. "I'll meet you back at home." Safire undid the leather ties on her borrowed hunting gloves. "You never should have given me these." She slid them off and handed them over. "Go."

Ignoring the scream of her raw and blistering skin, Asha pulled on the gloves so her father's slave wouldn't see her burned hand. Turning from Safire, she took Oleander's reins and swung herself up into the saddle. Oleander whinnied and fidgeted beneath her, then sped off at a gallop when Asha's heels gave her the slightest prod.

"I'll save the heart for you!" Safire called as Asha raced back toward the city, kicking up swirls of red sand. "In case you change your mind!"

In the Beginning . . .

The Old One was lonely. So he made for himself two companions. He formed the first out of sky and spirit and named him Namsara. Namsara was a golden child. When he laughed, stars shone out of his eyes. When he danced, wars ceased. When he sang, ailments were healed. His very presence was a needle sewing the world together.

The Old One formed the second out of blood and moonlight. He named her Iskari. Iskari was a sorrowful child. Where Namsara brought laughter and love, Iskari brought destruction and death. When Iskari walked, people cowered in their homes. When she spoke, people wept. When she hunted, she never missed her mark.

Pained by her nature, Iskari came before the Old One, asking him to remake her. She hated her essence; she wished to be more like Namsara. When the Old One refused, she asked him why. Why did her brother get to create things while she destroyed them?

"The world needs balance," the Old One said.

Furious, Iskari left the sovereign god and went hunting. She hunted for days. Days turned to weeks. As her fury grew, her bloodlust became insatiable. She killed mercilessly and without feeling and all the while, her hate swelled within her. She hated her brother for being happy and beloved. She hated the Old One for making it so.

So the next time she went hunting, Iskari set her traps for the Old One himself.

This was a terrible mistake.

The Old One struck Iskari down, leaving a scar as long and wide as the Rift mountain range. For attempting to take his life, he stripped her of her immortality, ripping it off her like a silk garment. So that she could atone for her crime, he cursed her name and sent her to wander the desert alone, haunted by stinging winds and howling sandstorms. To wither beneath the parching sun. To freeze beneath the icy cloak of night.

But neither the heat nor the cold killed her.

An unbearable loneliness did.

Namsara searched the desert for Iskari. The sky changed seven times before he found her body in the sand, her skin blistered by the sun, her eyes eaten by carrion crows.

At the sight of his sister, dead, Namsara fell to his knees and he wept.

Two

Normally after a kill, Asha bathed. Scrubbing the blood, sand, and sweat from her body was a ritual that helped her transition from the wild, rugged world beyond the palace walls to a life that tied itself around her ribs and squeezed like a too-tight sash.

Today, though, Asha skipped the bath. Despite her father's summons, she slipped right past her guards and headed for the sickroom, where the medicines were kept. It was a whitewashed room smelling of lime. Sunlight spilled through the open terrace, alighting the flower pattern mosaicked into the floor, then painting the shelves of terra-cotta jars in yellows and golds.

She'd woken in this room eight years ago, after Kozu, the First Dragon, burned her. Asha remembered it clearly: lying on a sickbed, her body wrapped in bandages, that awful feeling pressing down on her chest, heavy as a boulder, telling her she'd done something horribly wrong.

Shaking the memory loose, Asha stepped through the archway. She unbuckled her armor and gloves, shedding them piece by piece, then laid her axe on top of the pile.

One of the dangers of dragonfire—besides melting your skin to the bone—was that it was toxic. The smallest burn would kill you from the inside out if treated poorly or too late. A severe burn, like the one Asha suffered eight years ago, needed to be treated immediately and, even then, the victim's chances of survival were slim.

Asha had a recipe to draw the toxins out, but the treatment required the burn to be covered for two days. She didn't have that kind of time. Her father had summoned her. News of her return had probably reached him already. She had a hundred-hundred heartbeats, not days.

Asha opened cupboards and pulled down pots full of dried barks and roots, looking for one ingredient in particular. In her haste, she reached with her burned hand, and the moment she grabbed the smooth terra-cotta jar, pain seared through her and she let go.

The jar shattered across the floor in a burst of red shards and linen bandages.

Asha cursed, kneeling to pick up the mess one-handed. Her mind was so hazy with pain, she didn't notice when someone dropped to his knees beside her, his fingers picking up shards alongside hers.

"I'll get this, Iskari."

The voice made her jump. She glanced up to a silver collar, then a tangle of hair.

Asha watched his hands sweep up her mess. She knew those freckled hands. They were the same hands that brought out

Jarek's platters at dinner. The same hands that served her steaming mint tea in Jarek's glass cups.

Asha tensed. If her betrothed's slave was in the palace, so was her betrothed. Jarek must have returned from the scrublands, where he'd been sent to keep an eye on Dax's negotiations.

Is that the reason for my father's summons?

The slave's fingers went suddenly still. When Asha looked up, she caught him staring at her burn.

"Iskari . . ." His brow furrowed. "You need to treat that."

Her annoyance flared like a freshly fed fire. Obviously she needed to treat it. She'd be treating it now if she hadn't been so careless.

But just as important as treating her burn was securing this slave's silence. Jarek often used his slaves to spy on his enemies. The moment Asha dismissed this one, he might go running to his master and tell him everything.

And once Jarek knew, so would her father.

The moment her father heard of it, he'd know she'd been telling the old stories. He would know she was the same corrupted girl she'd always been.

"Tell anyone about this, skral, and the last thing you'll see is my face staring down at you from the top of the pit."

His mouth flattened into a hard line and his gaze lowered to the tile work at their feet, where elegant namsaras—rare desert flowers that could heal any ailment—repeated themselves in an elaborate pattern across the floor.

"Forgive me, Iskari," he said, his fingers sweeping up terracotta shards. "But I'm not supposed to take commands from you. My master's orders."

Her fingers itched for her axe—which was on the floor against the wall, with the rest of her armor.

She could threaten him, but that might make him retaliate by spilling her secrets. A bribe would work better.

"And if I give you something for your silence?"

His fingers paused, hovering over the pile of shards.

"What would you want?"

The corner of his mouth curved ever so slightly. It made the hair on her arms rise.

"I don't have all day," she said, suddenly uneasy.

"No," he said, the smile sliding away as he stared at her raw, blistering skin. "You don't." Her body was starting to shake from the infection. "Let me think on it while you treat that burn."

Asha left him there. In truth, the shaking worried her. So while he finished cleaning up her mess, she returned to the shelves and found the ingredient she needed: dragon bone ash.

Alone, it was just as deadly as dragonfire, only it poisoned in a different way. Instead of infecting the body, dragon bone leached it of nutrients. Asha had never seen someone killed this way, but there was an old story about a dragon queen who wanted to teach her enemies a lesson. Inviting them to the palace as honored guests, she put a pinch of dragon bone ash in their dinners every night and on the last morning of their stay, they were all found dead in their beds, their bodies hollowed out. As if the life had been scooped out of them.

Despite its dangers, in exactly the right amount, with the

correct combination of herbs, dragon bone was the one thing that could draw the dragonfire toxins out—precisely because of its leaching qualities. Asha popped off the cork lid and measured out the amount.

The mark of a good slave was to see what was needed before it was asked for, and Jarek only purchased the best of anything. So as Asha gathered her ingredients, crushing and boiling them down to a thick paste, Jarek's slave tore strips of linen for fresh bandaging.

"Where is he?" she asked as she stirred, trying to hasten the cooling process. She didn't need to say Jarek's name. His slave knew who she meant.

"Asleep in his wine goblet." He suddenly stopped ripping linen to stare at her hands. "I think it's cool enough, Iskari."

Asha looked where he looked. Her hands shook hard. She dropped the spoon and lifted them to her face, watching them tremble.

"I should have more time than this. . . ."

The slave took the pot from her, perfectly calm. "Sit," he said, motioning with his chin to the tabletop. As if he were in charge now and she had to do what he said.

Asha didn't like him telling her what to do. But she liked the violent trembling even less. She hoisted herself up onto the table one-handed while he scooped a spoonful of blackish paste and blew softly until it stopped steaming. She held her burned hand still against her thigh while he used the spoon to spread the grainy paste across the raw surface of her blistered palm and fingers.

Asha hissed through her teeth at the sting. More than once, he stopped, concerned by the sounds she made. She nodded for him to go on. Despite the horrible smell—like burned bones—she could feel the ash at work: a cool sensation sinking in, spreading outward, battling the scorching pain.

"Better?" He kept his gaze lowered as he blew on the next spoonful.

"Yes."

He coated the burn twice more, then reached for the first linen strip.

When he went to wrap it, though, they both hesitated. Asha pulled away while he hovered, frozen, leaning over her. The off-white linen hung like a canopy between his hands while the same thought ran through both their minds: in order to wrap the burn, he needed to touch her.

A slave who touched a draksor without his master's permission could be sentenced to three nights in the dungeons without food. If the offense were more severe—touching a draksor of high rank, such as Asha—he would be lashed as well. And in the very rare case of intimate touch, such as a love affair between a slave and a draksor, the slave would be sent to the pit to die.

Without Jarek to give permission, his slave wouldn't—*couldn't*—touch her.

Asha moved to take the linen to try to bandage her hand herself, but he pulled away, out of reach. She watched, speechless, as he returned to wrap her hand—slowly and carefully, his nimble hands cleverly avoiding contact.

Asha looked up into a long, narrow face full of freckles.

Freckles as numerous as stars in the night sky. He stood so close, she could feel the heat of him. So close, she could smell the salt on his skin.

If he sensed her looking, he didn't show it. Silence filled the space between them as he wrapped the linen around and around her salved palm.

Asha studied his hands. Large palms. Long fingers. Calluses on his fingertips.

A strange place for calluses on a house slave.

"How did it happen?" he asked as he worked.

She could feel him almost look up into her face, then stop himself. He reached for the next strip—a smaller one—and started on her fingers.

I told an old story.

Asha wondered how much a skral would know about the link between the old stories and dragonfire.

She didn't say the answer aloud. No one could know the truth: after all these years of trying to right her wrongs, Asha was still as corrupt as ever. If you opened her up and looked inside, you'd find a core that matched her scarred exterior. Hideous and horrible.

I told a story about Iskari and Namsara.

Iskari was the goddess from which Asha derived her title. These days, Iskari meant *life taker.*

Namsara's meaning had also changed over time. It was both the name of the healing flower on the floors of this room as well as a title. A title given to someone who fought for a noble cause—for his kingdom or his beliefs. The word *namsara* conjured up the image of a hero.

"I killed a dragon," Asha told the slave in the end, "and it burned me as it died."

He tucked in the ends of her bandage, listening. To get a better grip, his fingers slid around her wrist, as if he'd completely forgotten who she was.

At his touch, Asha sucked in a breath. The moment she did, he realized his breach and went very still.

A command hovered on the tip of Asha's tongue. But before it lashed out at him, he said, very softly, "How does that feel?"

As if he cared more about her burn than his own life.

As if he weren't afraid of her at all.

The command died in Asha's mouth. She looked to his fingers wrapped around her wrist. Not trembling or hesitant, but warm and sure and strong.

Wasn't he afraid?

When she didn't respond, he did something even worse. He raised his eyes to hers.

A startling heat surged through her as their gazes met. His eyes were as piercing as freshly sharpened steel. He should have looked away. Instead, that steely gaze moved from her eyes—black, like her mother's—to her puckered scar, trailing down her face and neck until it disappeared beneath the collar of her shirt.

People always looked. Asha was used to it. Children liked to point and stare, but most eyes darted away in fear the moment they settled on her scar. This slave, though, took his time looking. His gaze was curious and attentive, as if Asha were a tapestry and he didn't want to miss a single thread of detail.

Asha knew what he saw. She saw it every time she looked in a mirror. Mottled skin, pocked and discolored. It started at the top of her forehead, moving down her right cheek. It cut off the end of her eyebrow and took a chunk out of her hairline. It stretched over her ear, which never recovered its original shape and was now a deformed collection of bumps. The scar took up one-third of her face, half her neck, and continued down the right side of her body.

Safire once asked Asha if she hated the sight of it. But she didn't. She'd been burned by the fiercest of all dragons and lived. Who else could say that?

Asha wore her scar like a crown.

The slave's gaze moved lower. As if imagining the rest of the scar beneath her clothes. As if imagining the rest of *Asha* beneath her clothes.

It snapped something inside of her. Asha sharpened her voice like a knife.

"Keep looking, skral, and soon you'll have no eyes left to look with."

His mouth tipped up at the side. Like she'd issued a challenge and he'd accepted.

It made her think of last year's revolt, when a group of slaves took control of the furrow, keeping draksor hostages and killing any soldats who came near. It was Jarek who infiltrated the slave quarters and ended the revolt, personally putting to death each of the slaves responsible.

This skral is just as dangerous as the rest of them.

Asha suddenly wanted her axe again. She pushed herself off the table, putting space between them.

"I've decided on payment," he said from behind her.

Her footsteps slowed. She turned to face him. He'd folded the extra linen and was now scraping the remaining salve from the bottom of the pot.

As if he hadn't just broken the law.

"In exchange for my silence"—the wooden spoon clanged against the terra-cotta as he scraped—"I want one dance."

Asha stared at him.

What?

First, daring to look her in the eye, and now, demanding to dance with her?

Was he *mad*?

She was the Iskari. The Iskari didn't dance. And even if she did, she would never dance with a skral. It was absurd. Unthinkable.

Forbidden.

"One dance," he repeated, then looked up. Those eyes sliced into hers. Again, the shock of it flared through her. "In a place and time of my choosing."

Asha's hand went to her hip—but her axe was still on the floor on top of her armor. "Choose something else."

He shook his head, watching her hand. "I don't want something else."

She stared him down. "I'm sure that's not true."

He stared right back. "A fool can be sure of anything; that doesn't make her right."

Anger blazed bright and hot within her.

Did he just call her a fool?

In three strides, Asha grabbed her axe, closed the distance between them, and pressed its sharp, glittering edge to his throat. She would slice the voice right out of him if she had to.

The pot in his hand crashed to the floor. The line of his jaw went tight and hard, but he didn't look away. The air sizzled and sparked between them. He might have been half a head taller than she was, but Asha was used to taking down bigger prey.

"Don't test me, skral," she said, pressing harder.

He lowered his gaze.

Finally. She should have started with that.

Using the butt of the axe handle, Asha shoved his left shoulder, sending him stumbling. He hit the shelves full of jars, which rattled precariously.

"You'll keep this a secret," she said, "because not even Jarek can protect you if you don't."

He kept his eyes lowered as he steadied himself, saying nothing.

Turning on her heel, she left him there. Asha had better things to do than drag this slave before Jarek and list his offenses. She needed to find her silk gloves, hide her bandaged hand, and pretend everything was fine while she spoke with her father—who was still waiting for her.

She would deal with Jarek's slave later.

Dawn of a Hunter

Once there was a girl who was drawn to wicked things.

Things like forbidden, ancient stories.

It didn't matter that the old stories killed her mother. It didn't matter that they'd killed many more before her. The girl let the old stories in. She let them eat away at her heart and turn her wicked.

Her wickedness drew dragons. The same dragons that burned her ancestors' homes and slaughtered their families. Poisonous, fire-breathing dragons.

The girl didn't care.

Under the cloak of night, she crept over rooftops and snaked through abandoned streets. She sneaked out of the city and into the Rift, where she told the dragons story after story aloud.

She told so many stories, she woke the deadliest dragon of all: one as dark as a moonless night. One as old as time itself.

Kozu, the First Dragon.

Kozu wanted the girl for himself. Wanted to hoard the deadly power spilling from her lips. Wanted her to tell stories for him and him alone. Forever.

Kozu made her realize what she had become.

It scared her. So she stopped telling the old stories.

But it wasn't so easy. Kozu cornered her. He lashed his tail and hissed a warning. He made it clear if she refused him, it would not go well for her.

She trembled and cried, but stood firm. She kept her mouth clamped shut.

But no one defied the First Dragon.

Kozu flew into a rage; and when the girl tried to flee, he burned her in a deadly blaze.

But that wasn't enough.

He took out the rest of his rage on her home.

Kozu poured his wrath down on its lime-washed walls and filigreed towers. He breathed his poisonous fire as her people screamed and wept, listening to their loved ones trapped within their burning homes.

It was the son of the commandant who found the wicked girl, left for dead in the Rift. The boy carried her burned body all the way back to the palace sickroom while his father saved the city.

His father rallied the army and drove off the First Dragon. He ordered the slaves to put out the fires and repair the damage. The commandant saved the city, but he failed to save his wife. At the sound of her dying screams, he rushed into their burning home—and did not come out.

The girl, however, survived.

She woke in a strange room and a strange bed and she couldn't remember what happened. In the beginning, her father hid the truth. How do you tell a girl of ten she's responsible for the deaths of thousands?

Instead, he never left her side. He sat with her through the pain-filled nights. He sent for burn experts to restore her to full health. When they said she would never recover her mobility, he found better experts. And, very slowly, he filled in the gaps of her memory.

When the girl made her public apology and her people spat at her feet, her father stood by her side. While she promised to redeem herself and they hissed the name of a cursed god, her father took their curses and turned them into a title.

The old heroes were called Namsara after a beloved god, he said. So she would be called Iskari, after a deadly one.

Three

The throne room, with its double arcades, soldat-lined walls, and precise mosaic work, was built to draw attention to one place: the dragon king's throne. But whenever Asha stepped through the giant archway, it was the sacred flame that commanded her attention first. A pedestal of polished onyx stood halfway between the main entrance and the gilded throne. Upon it sat a shallow iron bowl, and in that bowl burned a white and whispering flame.

When Asha was a child, the sacred flame was taken from the Old One's caves and brought here, to keep the throne room alight. It struck such awe in Asha then.

Not anymore.

Now the flame seemed to watch Asha as much as she once watched it.

A colorless flame burning on nothing but air? It was unnatural. She wished her father would send it back to the caves. But it was his trophy, a sign of what he'd overcome.

"I'm sorry I interrupted your hunt, my dear."

Her father's voice echoed across the room, snapping up her attention. Asha scanned the gleaming white walls, broken up by tapestries bearing the portraits of dragon kings and queens of old.

"You didn't interrupt. I killed it just before your message arrived."

Dressed now in silk gloves that came to her elbows and an indigo kaftan that swished when she walked, Asha made her way across the room while the eyes in the tapestries watched her. Her steps padded softly on the sea of blue and green tiles as sunlight slid through the skylight in the copper-domed roof, lighting up specks of dust floating in the air.

The man waiting for her looked every bit a king: embroidered over the right shoulder of his robe was the royal crest—a dragon with a saber through its heart—and from his neck hung a citrine medallion. Gold slippers with elaborate white stitching hid his feet.

It was this man she woke to in the sickroom almost eight years ago. The sight of him now brought on a memory.

Kozu's red-hot flames engulfing her. The awful smell of burning hair and flesh. The barbed screams snagging in her throat.

It was the only part Asha remembered: burning. Everything else was lost to her.

"That was your longest hunt yet," he said. Asha stopped before the gilded steps of his throne. "I was beginning to worry."

She looked to the floor. The shame of it made her throat

prickle. Like she'd swallowed a handful of cactus spines.

Her father had too many things to worry about without Asha adding to them: war brewing with the scrublanders, the ever-present threat of another slave revolt, tension with the temple, and—though her father never spoke of it with Asha— the growing power of his commandant.

Asha's bandaged hand throbbed beneath the silk glove, screaming of the crime she'd committed that very morning. As if it wanted to betray her. She held it against her side, hoping her father wouldn't ask about the gloves.

"Don't worry about me, Father. I always find my prey."

The dragon king smiled at her. Behind him, an ornate mosaic was etched into the golden throne, a pattern of shapes within shapes and lines crossing back over lines. Just like the city's labyrinthine streets or the palace's maze of hallways and secret passageways.

"Tonight I want you to publicly present your kill. In honor of our guests."

She looked up. "Guests?"

Her father's smile broke. "You haven't heard the news?"

Asha shook her head no.

"Your brother returned with a delegation of scrublanders."

Asha's mouth went dry. The scrublanders dwelled across the sand sea and refused to acknowledge the authority of the king. They didn't agree with killing dragons almost as much as they didn't agree with keeping slaves. It was why her father had had such trouble handling them in the past—that, and the fact that they kept trying to assassinate him.

"They've agreed to a truce," her father explained. "They're here to negotiate the terms of a peace treaty."

Peace with scrublanders? Impossible.

Asha stepped closer to the throne, her voice tight. "They're inside the palace walls?" How could Dax bring their oldest enemies into their home?

No one had expected Dax to succeed in the scrublands. If Asha were honest, no one expected Dax to *survive* in the scrublands.

"It's too dangerous, Father."

The dragon king leaned forward in his throne, looking down at her with warm eyes. His nose was long and thin and his beard neatly trimmed.

"Don't worry, my dear." His eyes traced the scar marring her face. "One look at you and they will never cross me again."

Asha frowned. If they didn't fear the chopping block—which was the punishment for attempted regicide—why would they fear the Iskari?

"But that isn't why I summoned you."

The dragon king rose from his throne and descended the seven steps to the floor. Knotting his hands behind his back, her father made a slow tour of the tapestries up the left side of the room. Asha followed him, ignoring the soldats standing guard in between each one, their eyes hidden by crested morions and their burnished breastplates gleaming in the dusty sunlight.

"I want to talk about Jarek."

Asha's chin jerked upward.

When the people of Firgaard lost lives and homes and loved

ones in the wake of Kozu's fire, they called for the death of the wicked girl responsible. The king, unable to put his own daughter to death, offered her a chance at redemption instead. He promised her hand in marriage to Jarek—the boy who saved her. The boy who'd lost both his parents in the fire that was her fault.

Their union, he said, would be the last act of Asha's redemption. When they came of age, Jarek would bind himself to Asha and in doing so, prove his forgiveness. Jarek, who lost the most because of Asha, would show all of Firgaard they could forgive her too.

Furthermore, in exchange for Jarek's heroism, the king groomed him to take over his father's role as commandant.

It was an act of faith and gratitude.

In the years since, that heroic boy had grown into a powerful young man. At twenty-one, Jarek now held the army in his fist. His soldats were completely loyal. *Too loyal,* thought Asha. Once he married her, Jarek would be in very close proximity to the throne. A throne that would be very easy to take by force. It worried Asha.

"He mustn't know about this conversation. Do you understand?"

Asha, who was lost in her thoughts, looked up to find them standing before a tapestry of her grandmother—the dragon queen who conquered and enslaved their fiercest enemy, the skral. The artist chose deep reds and maroons for the background and luminescent silvers and dark blues for her hair. The dragon queen's eyes seemed to peer out at her granddaughter with deep disapproval. As if they could see straight into Asha's heart, beholding all the secrets hidden there.

Asha held her injured hand closer to her body.

"You mustn't tell anyone what I'm about to tell you."

Tearing her gaze away from the old queen, she looked to her father. His warm eyes were on hers.

A secret? Her every allegiance was to her father. She owed her life to him twice over. "Of course, Father."

"A dragon was spotted in the Rift while you hunted," he said. "One that hasn't been seen in eight years. A black dragon with a scar through one eye."

Lightning flickered up Asha's legs. She nearly reached for the wall, in case they gave out on her.

"Kozu?"

It couldn't be. The First Dragon hadn't been seen since the day he attacked the city.

Her father nodded. "This is an opportunity, Asha. One we must seize." He smiled a slow, bright smile. "I want you to bring me Kozu's head."

Asha suddenly smelled burning flesh. Felt her throat choking on screams.

That was eight years ago, she thought, trying to fight off the memory. *Eight years ago I was a child. I'm not anymore.*

Seeing the war waging inside her, the dragon king raised his hand, as if to touch her—something he never did. But a look flashed in his eyes. The same look that flashed in everyone else's eyes, all of the time, whenever they looked at her.

Her father didn't like to show it, because he loved her.

Because he didn't want to hurt her. But sometimes it slipped through the cracks.

The dragon king feared his own daughter.

A heartbeat later, the look was gone. Her father's hand fell back down to his side, resting on the gilt pommel of his ceremonial saber.

"If you can hunt down the First Dragon, the religious zealots will no longer have a reason to challenge my authority. The scrublanders will be forced to concede that the old ways are no longer. All will submit to my rule. But, most of all, Asha, your marriage to Jarek will no longer be necessary." He looked back to the tapestry on the wall. To the image of his mother. "*This* will be your redemption."

Asha swallowed, letting those words sink in.

The raconteurs—sacred storytellers from days gone by—warned of the death of Kozu. Kozu, they said, was the wellspring of stories. As such, he was the Old One's living link to his people.

If Kozu were ever killed, all the old stories would be struck from mind or tongue or scroll—as if they'd never existed. The Old One would be forgotten and the link between him and his people broken. But so long as Kozu lived, the stories did too, and the yoke keeping Asha's people shackled to the Old One remained.

Even the most godless of hunters wouldn't dare hunt Kozu down. Her father knew this. It was why he was asking *her*. Asha had more reason than anyone to kill the First Dragon.

It would be the ultimate apology. A way to set things right.

"Did you hear me, Asha? If you bring me Kozu's head, there will no longer be a reason to marry Jarek."

Drawn out of her thoughts, she looked up into her father's face to find him smiling down on her.

"Tell me what you're thinking, Asha. Will you do it?"

Of course she would do it. The only question was: Could she do it before the red moon waned?

The Last Namsara

Once, the draksors were a mighty force. They were the wingbeats in the night. They were the fire that rained from the sky. They were the last sight you saw.

No one dared come against them.

But a storm was sweeping across the desert. Invaders from beyond the sea, a people called the skral, had conquered the northern isles and were hungry for more. The skral looked to Firgaard, the shining star of a desert kingdom. A bustling capital that straddled a seam dividing leagues of white sand from a mountainous mantle. If they could conquer Firgaard, they could rule the world.

Hoping to take the draksors by surprise, the skral came beneath the cover of darkness.

But when darkness falls, the Old One lights a flame.

The Old One heard the enemy coming. He cast his gaze out over dusty villages and desert dunes until he found a man suited for just his purpose.

A man by the name of Nishran.

With that single whispered name, the Old One woke the First Dragon from his slumber. The First Dragon flew fast and far, over the desert, seeking out the owner of it.

Nishran was a weaver. He sat at his loom when the First Dragon found him. The treadles stopped clicking and the shuttle stopped clacking as the weaver looked up into scales as black as moonless night.

Fear filled his heart.

But the Old One had chosen Nishran to be his Namsara, and there was no refusing the Old One.

To aid him, the Old One gave Nishran the ability to see in darkness. Unhindered by the cloak of night, Nishran led the dragon queen and her army across the sand, beneath the pitch of a new moon, straight to the camp of the skral.

The northern invaders were unprepared for the arrows and dragonfire they woke to. They were overcome by those they intended to conquer.

When it was over, the dragon queen did not drive the enemy out of her realm. If she let the skral loose, they would only wreak their havoc elsewhere or return, stronger, for revenge. She refused to be responsible for another people's destruction. So, with the Namsara at her side, the dragon queen ordered each and every skral locked into collars as penance for the horrors they'd unleashed on the northern isles.

With the skral bound in iron, peace fell over the draksors. News of the conquered invaders traveled fast and far. Rulers of far-off nations crossed desert and mountain and sea to pledge their loyalty to the dragon queen.

But the jubilation was short-lived.

Darkness fell once more over Firgaard as dragons suddenly and without warning turned on their riders, attacking their families and burning down their homes. Instead of being lit with celebratory song and dance, Firgaard was lit with dragonfire as terraces and courtyards and gardens blazed. In daylight, smoke clotted the air and black shadows fell over the narrow streets as dragons flew into the Rift and never returned.

Chaos tore Firgaard apart. Some draksors ran to align themselves with their queen, who cursed the dragons for their betrayal; others ran to align themselves with the high priestess, who blamed the queen for the destruction.

Draksors turned on draksors. More homes burned. Firgaard fell into ruin.

That was the first betrayal.

The second came in the form of stories.

Four

There was a long-standing tradition in Firgaard: whenever a dragon was killed, its head was presented to the dragon king. It was Asha's favorite part of a hunt. The triumphant entry, the awed spectators, and most of all her father's look of pride.

Tonight, though, a bigger, older dragon roamed the wilds beyond the city walls and Asha was restless, itching to sink her axe into its heart.

Soon, she thought as she and Safire stepped into the arching entrance of the palace's largest courtyard. Music drifted out like smoke. The sound of a lute whispered beneath the brassy trumpet and the quick, driving beat of the drums.

Before entering the courtyard, out of habit, Asha checked her cousin for fresh bruises and found none. Instead, Safire seemed to glow in a pale green kaftan embroidered with honeysuckle flowers.

"I thought you hated those," Safire said, gesturing to Asha's silk gloves. They were a foreign style. Jarek bought them almost a year ago for Asha's seventeenth birthday.

She did hate them. They made her hands sweat and always fell down her arms, but they kept her burn hidden.

Asha forced a shrug. "They went with the kaftan."

A kaftan that had been waiting in a lidded silver box by her bed. Yet another gift from Jarek.

"Right," said Safire, guessing at the real reason. "Just like the boots."

Asha looked down to her feet poking out from under her hem. In her hurry, she'd forgotten to exchange her hunting boots for her gold slippers. She swore under her breath. Too late now.

Bronze lamps blazed along the galleries of the courtyard, their colored glass drenching the dancers in glittering light. In the center, a wide basin full of water stretched across the court, its calm surface glimmering beneath the starry black sky.

Normally the galleries were boisterous and the lush low-lying sofas full as people sipped sweet tea and gossiped in luxury. Not tonight. For a celebration in honor of the heir's return, after a month away, the galleries were abandoned and the courtyard was crammed with draksors talking behind their hands and glancing toward the empty sofas.

Safire spotted the reason first.

"Look." She pointed to where strangely dressed guests clustered together beneath the gallery, eyeing the draksors out in the court as if they expected an ambush. The draksors beneath the open night sky wore brightly colored kaftans or fitted knee-length tunics, decorated with complicated embroidery and delicate beading. The guests beneath the gallery wore much plainer garb. Cotton sandskarves were wrapped loosely around their shoulders, and their curving blades were sheathed at their hips.

"Scrublanders."

Enemies in the heart of the palace. In the home of the king they'd tried to kill on three separate occasions.

What was Dax *thinking*?

For a group of people as committed to the old ways as the scrublanders were, they seemed surprisingly willing to defy their own god and ignore the age-old law against regicide. It was one of the only ancient laws her father allowed to remain. Rooted in the myth of the goddess Iskari, who'd tried to kill the Old One, the law declared that anyone who dared take the life of the dragon king or queen was condemned to death. Which meant every scrublander who tried to assassinate Asha's father was knowingly committing suicide the moment he acted.

Safire called her name, drawing her out of her thoughts.

"Yes?" said Asha, turning.

"Hmm?" Safire was drinking in the scene, counting every scrublander and estimating which were the most highly trained and which were the most likely to have extra weapons hiding in their clothes. It was the first thing Safire did whenever she entered a room. It was second nature. A survival instinct.

"You just called my name," said Asha.

"No, I didn't."

Asha looked back through the archway and into the shadowy corridor beyond, then to the soldats standing straight as spears along the walls. There was no one else nearby.

Before Asha could question it further, a chilling hush fell over the celebration. The music ground into silence. Asha knew the reason before she even turned back.

The Iskari had been sighted.

Best get it over with.

She stepped out from under the arch and into the court.

Every pair of eyes fixed on her. Asha felt the weight of their stares like she felt the weight of her own hideous heart beating in her chest. Some as angry as sharpened daggers, others as frantic as cornered animals. Asha stared back.

One by one, gazes dropped to the floor. One by one, people parted for her, carving a silent passage straight to her father, who met her dark gaze from across the court.

At his side stood a young man dressed in gold, an *almost* mirror image of the dragon king: curly hair, warm brown eyes, and a hooked nose that had been broken twice. Both times were his own fault.

The young man was Dax, Asha's older brother.

But something was wrong.

After a month in the scrublands, Dax looked far less like his usual lighthearted self: eyes full of mischief, a smile that melted girls from across the room, and fists that seemed to *find* fights. That boy had been replaced by someone else. Someone tired and thin and . . . muted.

Asha left Safire behind. This was as close as her cousin came to the dragon king. As the child of Lillian, the former dragon queen's slave, and Rayan, the former dragon queen's son, Safire's survival was a miracle. She had been allowed to *live*, never mind grow up in the palace where the forbidden union had taken place. The king's grace alone allowed her to set foot inside this courtyard, but his grace only extended so far. Safire would forever stand outside the circle of her own family.

Asha stepped up to her father's side. She threw Dax a concerned look before the trumpeted arrival of four of her hunting slaves. They brought forward the dragon's head, displayed on an ornate silver tray. The yellow, slitted eyes were lifeless now, and the tongue lolled out the side of its mouth. It was a mere shadow of the fierce thing it had been.

Asha's injured hand blazed at its closeness. She gritted her teeth. To combat the pain, she imagined the head of Kozu on that platter. Which only made her long to be free of the court walls, hunting him down.

And then: someone called Asha's name again.

She turned, searching the crowd. Everyone she made eye contact with looked away. As if looking Asha full in the face would call down dragonfire.

She listened and watched, but the caller kept silent.

Am I hearing things?

For a half a heartbeat, panic sparked inside her. Maybe her treatment had been too late. Maybe the dragonfire's poison had already found its way to her heart. How mortifying that would be, to die of a dragon burn before her father's entire court.

Asha shook her head. It wasn't possible. She'd treated the burn in good time.

Maybe the stories are finally taking their toll. Poisoning me the way they poisoned my mother.

But Asha was meticulous about checking for signs. And so far, there hadn't been any.

Her father commended his Iskari on her kill. He gave his usual speech on the danger and treachery of dragons, who had once been their allies before turning against their riders during his mother's reign. He gave this speech after every kill. Which was why Asha was only half listening until he reached for her gloved hand—her *burned* hand—and she nearly cried out at the pain of it.

With his grip firm, the dragon king drew a flinching Asha out before him, giving the visiting scrublanders an example on which to feast their eyes.

"You see what they did to my daughter? This is what happens when you treat with dragons." He let go, no doubt thinking of the day the city burned. Of the day Jarek brought back Asha's charred body. "My Iskari has devoted her life to hunting down these beasts, and she won't stop until the very last one is dead. Then, and only then, will we have peace."

He smiled down at her. Asha tried to smile back, but found she couldn't. Not with her burned hand right under his nose, flaring up in pain, proof of the old story she'd told aloud.

When the dragon king dismissed her hunting slaves and the music rose once more, Dax stepped up to Asha, smelling like peppermint tea.

"My fearsome little sister." He grinned at her and Asha noticed the deep creases beside his mouth. Creases that hadn't been there before he left. "Did you see what I brought home with me?"

He nodded in the direction of the scrublanders. As if anyone could miss them.

"Not *quite* as impressive as a dragon. . . ."

He wore his favorite tunic, one that came to his wrists and ended just above his knees. White scrolling embroidery lined the collar and the buttons down the front, offsetting the shimmering gold silk.

Gold for a golden-hearted boy, Asha thought.

Normally this garment fitted Dax perfectly, showing off his strong shoulders and tall form. But now it hung loose off his wasted frame. His normally starry eyes were dull as stones.

The stress of the scrublands, not to mention the long journey back across the desert, had obviously worn him out. The sight of him, so thin and tired looking, reminded Asha of someone, but she couldn't think who.

"You missed the introductions," he said, studying her the same way she studied him.

"I had things to do." *Like hide the evidence of my treachery.*

"Do you want to meet our guests?" he asked, taking the cup of wine offered him by one of the serving slaves.

"Not really," Asha said, refusing a cup from the same slave.

"Great!" said Dax. "I'll introduce you. . . ."

Warily, Asha followed her brother through the throng until he stopped abruptly in front of someone. When he stepped aside, a young woman stood before them. She wore a finely spun cotton dress, the color of cream. The girl pushed back the sandskarf hooding her face, revealing clear, dark eyes and the proud lift of an elegant chin. On her gloved and fisted hand perched a hawk as white as the mist that gathered over the Rift in the early morning.

Asha stared at the bird. It stared back with eerie silver eyes.

This girl was a scrublander.

Instinctively, Asha stepped back. The girl didn't notice. She was too busy staring at Asha's scar.

"This is my sister," Dax told the girl. "The Iskari."

As he spoke, he stroked the hawk's white breast with the backs of his fingers. They were clearly acquainted, because the bird nuzzled his hand with the crown of its head.

"Asha, this is Roa. Daughter of the House of Song. Her brother couldn't be here, but he so wants to meet the infamous Iskari. I promised I'd bring you with me next time."

He winked, knowing how she'd feel about *that*.

Asha had no desire to ever set foot in the scrublands. They were flat, dull, and impoverished—or so she'd been told. Worst of all, scrublanders were still devoted to the old ways. It made her wonder how in all the skies Dax enticed them here, to the secular capital they hated.

Asha loved her brother, but he wasn't exactly a diplomat. The only reason he'd been sent to the scrublands in the first place was to get him out of the city. He'd picked a drunken fight with Jarek's second-in-command, who fell from the roof and broke his spine. It caused a huge scandal and increased tensions between the king and his army.

But Dax collected scandals like trophies. He was always

picking fights. Or gambling away money from the treasury. Or flirting with the daughters of all their father's favorite officials.

The heir was an embarrassment, and the king's patience was wearing thin. So he sent Dax to deal with the scrublanders, and told Jarek to accompany him. The king knew his commandant—who was furious at the loss of his second-in-command—would keep his son in line.

Roa pressed a tight fist over her heart in scrublander greeting, but her gaze remained fixed on Asha's scar.

"The Iskari herself," she said, in a voice like honey and thunder. Her fist uncurled and fell back to her side. "Dax says you can take down a dragon with your bare hands."

Asha would have laughed—but the arrival of a young man interrupted her. As his shadow fell across them, Asha's stomach clenched.

Jarek.

It was he who'd caught and put to death all three scrublander would-be assassins. He who'd ended the last slave rebellion. He who Asha would bind herself to by the time the red moon waned.

Unless she killed Kozu first.

In the presence of the commandant, Dax was reduced to a mere boy. Jarek towered over him. He stood square and strong, like the foundation of a mighty fortress. His silk shirt stretched across his broad chest, revealing just how solid he was.

Asha looked to Roa and found her eyes narrowed on the commandant.

It wasn't the usual reaction. Usually, Jarek's flawless

physique made him impressive and alluring to women. But Roa seemed . . . on edge.

While Jarek eyed the heir to the throne and his new scrublander friend, his arm snaked around Asha's waist, tucking her against him like a dagger or a saber, squeezing her hip until it hurt.

Jarek was one of the few who dared to touch her.

"Making friends, Asha?" He smelled sour, like alcohol.

She knew better than to squirm away or give any hint he was hurting her.

"Dax was just introducing me to—"

"We've met." Jarek's attention turned to the cut of Asha's kaftan, his gaze consuming her. Like she was a goblet of wine. "You found your gift, I see."

Asha stared into the space between Dax and Roa, her gaze settling on a collared slave serving tea beneath the gallery. She held the brass teapot high in the air, letting the golden liquid arch elegantly as the cups filled with froth.

Jarek leaned in close. "Tell me. Do you like it?"

He knew the answer to his own question.

Compared to all the other kaftans in the courtyard, which were elegant and modest, Asha's was a spectacle. Oh, it was finely made. It probably cost a soldat's monthly wage—which was nothing for Jarek, whose father left him a bulging inheritance.

This kaftan was a luscious shade of indigo. Its thin layers shifted around her like sand, contained only by a wide sash tied tight and high around her waist. If Asha had to guess, she'd say he'd bought it in Darmoor, her father's largest trading port. But the kaftan was made for beautiful, desirable girls. Not scarred, horrifying ones.

It was the neckline, which plunged, and the translucent material that insulted her most. It allowed Jarek to see too much of her. But the last time she'd refused a gift, Safire got hurt. So Asha wore it.

"You look like a goddess."

Asha went rigid. His gaze made her want to disappear. She longed to move through this crowd unseen, gather her armor and her axe, and hunt Kozu down this very moment.

Instead, she said, "You should have seen me earlier: covered from head to toe in dragon gore."

Jarek was not put off. He stepped in closer, careful not to turn his back to her brother and the scrublander. The commandant never turned his back on a threat.

"Dance with me."

Asha stared once more at the slave pouring tea. "You know I don't dance."

"There's a first time for everything." Jarek's grip tightened, allowing him to easily maneuver her away from her brother and his scrublander friend.

"Hey. *Sandeater.*" Dax grabbed the sleeve of Jarek's shirt. "She doesn't want to dance with you."

Jarek's eyes flashed. He shoved Dax. Easily.

The heir stumbled into Roa, spilling his cup of wine over them both. Roa's lips parted in shock, her hands fluttering to the maroon stain seeping through her creamy linen dress.

"Excuse us." Jarek smirked, forcing Asha into the crowd, toward the music. As he did, Asha glanced back over her shoulder and caught a glimpse of Roa's narrowed eyes.

"I haven't seen you in a month," Jarek said in her ear. "I buy you a dress three times the price it's worth. Now it's time for you to do as I ask."

Asha was about to repeat her refusal—more clearly this time—when that voice returned, calling her name. She didn't look. She knew she'd find no one there. And besides, *where* would she look? The voice called to her from a hundred directions at once.

Asha. Asha. Asha.

It reminded her of a story. . . .

She forced the thought out of her head as Jarek dragged her onward, closer to the music. He pulled her into him, locking his arms around her waist so their bodies aligned. So she could feel his desire—hard and prodding.

Feeling sick, Asha turned her face away. She shouldn't have. It was dangerous to show weakness in front of the commandant. But after ten days of hunting in the Rift, Asha didn't have any energy left for games.

"I don't dance," she said again, pressing her hands firmly against the black silk of his shirt, trying to force space between them.

"And I don't take no for an answer." His hands tightened around her. His eyes seemed too hungry tonight. Like a starved animal.

Asha looked away, over Jarek's shoulder, right into the

freckled face of his slave. The skral stood in a semicircle of musicians at the center of the courtyard, their backs to the calm water of the wide basin.

While Jarek spoke, Asha watched, spellbound, as the slave's fingers moved like spiders across the strings of his worn, pear-shaped lute. His eyes were closed in concentration, as if he'd gone somewhere else entirely, somewhere far away from this courtyard.

Sensing her gaze, the slave opened his eyes. At the sight of the Iskari staring him down, his fingers fumbled the strings. He recovered quickly, then looked to the man holding her captive. That dreamy, faraway look vanished, replaced by a scowl as dark as a storm cloud.

"Are you listening to a word I'm saying?" Jarek asked.

He sounded so far away.

For the last time that evening, the call rang out. Her name on the wind. Only this time, it echoed through the whole courtyard.

Surely, everyone can hear it, Asha thought.

But when she looked around, draksors danced and laughed and sipped their tea, oblivious.

Something was wrong. Asha could sense the wrongness buzzing in her bones. She needed to get out of here.

Asha wrenched herself from Jarek, who wasn't expecting this kind of answer and let go more easily than usual. She stumbled, tripping over dancers as she did, and the music screeched to a halt.

The call drummed in her ears. Beat in her blood. Pushed out everything else.

Asha, Asha, Asha.

It made her dizzy. When she looked up, the eyes of Jarek's slave were staring into hers.

Look away, she warned. But the sunset sky was rolling down now and the courtyard floor was rolling up and when Asha closed her eyes to make it stop, she felt herself sway . . . and then fall.

The slave caught her before she hit the ground.

With the room spinning around her, Asha pressed her cheek against his chest, willing it to stop.

This is what happens when you tell the old stories aloud.

It made her think of her mother—whom the stories killed. But as the darkness seeped in, it wasn't her mother's death that Asha remembered. It was the way it felt to be held by her.

It felt just like this.

"I have you," said his voice at her ear. "You're all right."

The last sound she heard was the steady thump of a heart beating against her cheek.

The Severing

Before the great Severing, raconteurs preserved stories. These sacred story-tellers told the old stories aloud: hallowed tales of the Old One, his First Dragon, and his heroic Namsaras. The raconteurs passed these stories down from father to son. They traveled from city to city, spinning words like thread before crowds of people in exchange for coin or a room or a meal. It was an honor to host a raconteur under your roof and serve him warm bread, for he was a holy man with a holy task.

After the dragons fled, the raconteurs sickened and died. The old stories began to poison their tellers, eating away at their bodies, turning on them just as the dragons turned on their riders.

But the raconteurs continued telling their stories aloud. And as they did, they continued to die. As more and more of them sickened, fear rooted itself in the heart of every draksor. This time, they didn't turn on their neighbors. This time, they shuttered themselves in their homes to keep safe. They feared what would happen if the old stories fell on their ears. They feared whatever plague the Old One was unleashing now.

Which is when the dragon queen stepped in.

She renounced the Old One, who'd betrayed them. She outlawed the old stories and declared that any raconteur continuing to practice his craft would be imprisoned. When it didn't stop the raconteurs, when the high priestess herself convinced them to keep telling the stories, it fell to the dragon queen to protect her people from the Old One's wickedness.

She did three things.

First, she stripped the high priestess of power.

Second, she amended her law. Standing in the public square, the dragon queen announced to all of Firgaard that speaking the old stories aloud was now a criminal offense—one punishable by death.

And the third thing the dragon queen did?

She instilled a new sacred tradition: dragon hunting.

Five

Smoke hovered around Asha, clinging to her hair and stinging her eyes. Her breath hushed in and out like the ebb and flow of Darmoor's tide, and with it came the bitter smack of ash.

Darkness enveloped her. The wall beneath her hand was cool and creviced. Made of rock. Just like the ground beneath her feet.

I'm dead, she thought.

But if that were true, was it the dragonfire that killed her or the stories?

Asha thought she'd been impervious to their poison effect. Ever since she first started using the stories to summon dragons, she checked—almost obsessively—for signs of detriment: rapid weight loss, unnatural exhaustion, tremors . . . But for as long as she'd been telling the old stories, Asha suffered none of those symptoms. The stories simply didn't affect her the way they had affected her mother and the raconteurs.

Maybe it was because Asha and the old stories were made of

the same substance. Each's wickedness canceling the other's out.

But maybe she hadn't paid enough attention. Maybe they *had* been killing her slowly, all along.

If I'm dead, I'll never bring my father Kozu's head.

If I'm dead, I'll never have to bind myself to Jarek.

They were bittersweet thoughts.

Asha followed the smoke and ash. The deeper into this cavern she went, the more familiar her surroundings became. It wasn't that she'd been here before. It was more like she'd been dreaming of this place all her life.

After years of keeping the stories down, this place unearthed them easily. They surged to her surface, humming and alive, whispering of the First Dragon and the holy Namsaras and the Old One himself. It made her teeth ache to hold them all back.

Her steps led her to the shadow of a man, crouched behind a small, crackling fire. When he rose, the firelight lit up his face, revealing eyes like black onyx, a bald head, and a gray beard that came to a point just below his chin. A white robe shrouded his body, the hood flipped back.

The breath flew out of Asha at the sight of him.

She knew this man. An image of him graced the walls of a room she never should have been in. As a child, she'd heard his name spoken into the dark, always in her mother's voice.

"Elorma." The name was a snarl in her mouth.

This was the First Namsara. The man who brought the sacred flame out of the desert and founded Firgaard. A messenger of the Old One—who had betrayed them.

"I've been waiting for you." His velvet voice echoed off the cavern walls. "Come closer."

Asha didn't dare.

The fire blazed up between them and she lifted her hand to shield her face from its heat. Elorma smiled at her. It made her uneasy. Like the smile of a slave plotting rebellion.

"As you wish," he said, plunging his hands into the white-hot flames.

Asha gasped, sure the fire would eat the skin from his bones. But when his hands emerged, they were unsinged and gripping two shining black blades, curved like half-moons. White fire danced up their edges and went out.

"Sacred slayers from the Old One." He held them out to her. "Take them."

Asha knew better than to trust him. She knew better than to accept gifts from the Old One. She kept her hands at her sides.

"I have more weapons than I'll ever need."

"Ah," he said, "but these were formed just for you, Asha. They'll settle in your hands like no other. They'll bend to your will and cut down your enemies faster than any axe."

How do you know about my axe?

But if he knew her name, why shouldn't he know her weapon of choice?

"Once you hold them, you'll want nothing else."

Asha thought of how satisfying it would be to kill dragons with weapons like this—quick, sharp, lethal. She shook her head. It was terrible enough telling the stories aloud. But dealing directly with the Old One? That would be much worse.

She could imagine the look of horror on her father's face if he ever found out.

She took a step back.

"Are you not called Iskari?" Elorma asked. "It's an ill-fitted title, in my opinion. Iskari was fearless and fierce. But you are cowering and afraid."

Her gaze snapped to his. He looked godlike in the firelight. His skin shone as if with inner light, and his eyes seemed ancient. All-seeing.

She looked back to the slayers.

How rewarding would it be to stop Kozu's heart with weapons like these. How perfect to take the tools the Old One gave her and use them against him. Just like he'd used her against her own people. Her own father.

We must take great pains to steel ourselves against wickedness, her father told her all those years ago.

True. But this time, her eyes were wide open. This time, she wouldn't let herself be used.

Her father wouldn't have to know until it was over. Until she'd dropped Kozu's bloody head at his feet. By then, he would understand. He would praise her for her cleverness.

Asha reached for the slayers. Elorma smiled a slow smile. As their inlaid hilts slid against her palms, Asha's blood crackled and sparked. White fire flickered up her arms, sealing an invisible bond. Like a bolt locking into place. He hadn't lied. They melted into her hands, perfectly balanced, light as air.

"The gift comes with a command, of course."

Asha looked up into grinning white teeth.

"These slayers can only be used to make wrongs right."

"What?"

Still grinning, he said, "You and I will see each other again soon, Asha."

And then he melted into the darkness.

Asha called after him, but Elorma was already gone. The fire flickered out. The cave was fading fast now, twisting away until the walls of the cavern rushed in to swallow her.

Asha stood alone in the dark, with stories buzzing in her ears and the hilts of holy weapons gripped hard against her palms and a bad feeling prodding at her ribs.

What have I done?

She dropped the sacred slayers into the dirt.

Six

Just before dawn, Asha woke to the smell of orange blossoms.

The night's chill lingered. Gathering her wool blanket around her, Asha sat up and pushed aside the sheer veils of her canopied bed, squinting through the twilight that cast her room in shades of blue. She scanned the wall opposite, where her favorite weapons hung in neat rows from floor to ceiling. Mostly axes and knives. The occasional hunting dagger. And her wooden wasters—weighted weapons for sparring with Safire.

There were no curving, night-black blades.

Asha closed her eyes and exhaled.

Just a dream.

Asha held up her bandaged hand. She pulled back the linen to reveal blistered skin. She could still flex her fingers, though the pain of it made her dizzy. If she could flex her fingers, she could wield her axe once the skin healed. And until then, there was always her other hand. Because all that mattered now was finding Kozu as quickly as she could.

Once she killed him, she wouldn't have to hide anything anymore.

"Tell me one thing . . . ," said a familiar voice.

Asha's gaze snapped to the sill of an arching window, where a shadow perched.

"*Why* did that dragon breathe fire?"

Safire jumped down from the sill and shoved aside the sheer veils of the bed. She didn't bother avoiding Asha's eyes. Not here, in private.

"It's been fifty years since the Severing," said Safire. "Fifty years since the stories disappeared."

Fifty years since the dragons stopped breathing fire.

Except for Kozu, the First Dragon, who was the wellspring of stories. Who didn't need one told aloud in order to set a city ablaze.

Safire grabbed a match from the bedside table and lit the candle there. Instead of answering her cousin, Asha deflected. "Have you been here all night?"

"I'm asking the questions," Safire said, turning and grabbing Asha's wasters from the wall. "Now get dressed. We're going to the roof."

"Saf, I can't today. My hand . . ."

She lifted her bandaged hand, realizing as she did that someone had slid off her gloves. Fear jolted through her. Whoever had done it would have seen the bandage.

Did they see what was beneath it?

"Do you think Jarek will go easy on you because you have a burned hand?"

Asha looked to her cousin. Safire met the Iskari's gaze. Her eyes blazed in the light of the candle.

Safire would know what happened. She would know who undressed Asha.

If Asha sparred with her cousin, she could discover who, exactly, knew about her burn. And then, after determining whether her secret was safe, she could hunt down Kozu.

Tossing aside the covers, Asha slid out of bed and shivered as her bare feet touched the cold marble tiles. She glared at her cousin as she undid the buttons of her nightdress. It was times like these Asha was grateful she'd dismissed her house slaves years ago. They always trembled in her presence, which made everything take twice as long.

Holding both wasters in one hand, Safire tapped the ends of them impatiently against her boot. When Asha was fully dressed, they stepped out onto the latticed terrace, where narrow steps led to the rooftop. Below them stretched a garden of dusty date palms, blossoming orange trees, and hibiscuses. It once belonged to Asha's mother. Date palms always reminded the late dragon queen of her home in the scrublands.

Asha breathed in the sweet smell.

But the night was waning, and with it, her time. She had only six days to hunt down Kozu.

"Let's get this over with," she said, taking her waster from Safire and starting up the steps.

At least her cousin would beat her quickly.

✦✦✦

When Asha wasn't hunting, sparring was their early morning routine: practice for Safire and helpful for Asha—who was a hunter more than a fighter—to learn how to defend herself. Mainly from Jarek.

Safire shrugged off her hooded saffron mantle and threw it down to the pebble-laden rooftop. Asha noticed its fraying seams and ragged hem. Her cousin shouldn't have to wear something so tattered.

I'll order a new one from the seamstresses and pretend it's for me.

All around them, the rooftops of the palace stood empty. Over Safire's shoulder, the horizon glowed a hazy gold and the sky shifted from dark blue to purple. With the sunrise came slaves going about their daily chores. These rooftops would be full of activity soon.

For now, though, there was just Asha and Safire.

"Why didn't you tell me the dragons are breathing fire again?"

Safire swung her waster hard and Asha caught it with her own, the thud of wood on wood vibrating through her.

Her cousin might be useless in the face of a dragon, but she was far better than Asha at hand-to-hand combat. To survive in a world that preferred she didn't exist, Safire had to be strong. And she was—her arms were knotted hard with muscles, and beneath the sheer force of her, Asha was buckling.

"Because . . . you'd worry . . . over nothing," Asha said through gritted teeth.

Unable to hold her stance any longer, she ducked away,

spinning her wooden waster out of the fall of her cousin's.

"It seems I have reason to worry." Safire recovered, then settled back into her fighting stance. "Considering you fainted in the middle of your father's court. Don't tell me it had nothing to do with your burn."

Asha's grip tightened around her waster's smooth hilt. She'd hoped the fainting was part of the dream. "Did my father see?"

"Of *course* he saw."

"What did he say?"

Safire circled Asha, planning her next attack. "Nothing. Jarek did all the talking. Or rather, the screaming—at his slave. Who caught you, by the way. If he hadn't, they might still be scraping your brains off the tiles."

Asha rolled her eyes. It wasn't *that* far of a fall.

Suddenly Safire was there, her waster whistling through the air as she brought it down hard and fast. Asha barely had time to raise her own, barely managed to catch the blow—which still sent her backward.

"And if I hadn't convinced the physician you were just dehydrated, he would have insisted on taking a closer look, and then he would have seen that burn." She nodded toward Asha's bandaged hand. "So you owe me."

Asha lowered her waster.

Her father didn't know, then.

Asha wiped the sweat off her forehead, relieved.

"Thank you."

"Why does it need to be a secret? No one thinks you're weak, Asha. You're the Iskari. You *killed* that dragon. Like hundreds of others before it."

But the burn didn't mean she was weak—at least, not in the way Safire meant. It meant she was corrupted.

With her cousin's waster lowered, rendering her vulnerable, Asha saw her moment. She took it, charging.

Safire's eyes flashed as she blocked and blocked again. Like lightning.

The clack of wood on wood cracked in Asha's ears as she circled, battering her cousin's defenses, looking for a way in. But Safire was always there, like a door slamming in Asha's face.

"And anyway," said Safire, panting as she blocked, "who would I tell?"

"Dax. Obviously."

Her brother would be horrified to learn his little sister was telling the old stories aloud, preserving the very things that killed their mother. And while Dax and their father weren't exactly on good terms, out of worry for Asha, he might go to the king.

Dax couldn't know. *No one* could know.

A gap opened up. Asha took her chance, driving hard at her cousin with her weapon.

She got nothing more than a swift kick in the shin before the gap closed up again.

"Arrrugh!" Asha lowered her weapon. "Just once! I wish you'd let me beat you *just once.* . . ."

"Wishes." Safire shook her head. "*I* wish I knew why the dragons are breathing fire. And why you insist on keeping secrets from me." She stepped back, surveying Asha, who was walking off the stinging pain in her shin. "And also how your brainless brother could bring those scrublanders home with him." She rested the tip of her waster in the roof pebbles and leaned on it. "Speaking of Dax, what did you think of his friend? The quiet one."

"Roa?" Out of breath, Asha spied the water skin Safire had brought up with them. She made for it. "Jarek interrupted before I could properly form an opinion."

While Asha panted and wiped the sweat from her hairline, Safire now stood fresh as the dawn.

"Did you see what she was wearing?"

Asha took a long drink of water, then stoppered the skin. "The knife?" Roa had been the only scrublander without a weapon at her hip. But Asha had seen the bulge of a hilt strapped to the girl's thigh, hidden beneath her dress.

"No. The pendant."

Asha hadn't noticed any pendant.

"It was a circle, made out of stone. Alabaster, it looked like."

Asha frowned at her. "So?"

"It seemed like Dax's handiwork."

Aside from his looks, this was the one thing Dax inherited from their father: a love of carving. When their mother was still alive, the dragon king used to carve all kinds of things for her out of bone. Combs, tiny boxes inset with jewels, rings. And Dax, in an effort to make his father proud, taught himself the king's craft.

"What are you saying?"

Safire came to stand before Asha, reaching for the skin. "I'm saying it's interesting. That girl—Roa—she's a daughter of the House of Song. Isn't that the house Dax used to spend his summers in? Before—"

The words halted on her lips.

But Asha knew what she'd been about to say.

Before your mother died and the scrublanders turned against us.

As a child, Dax was quiet and curious, but also slow to learn things. It took him longer to walk and talk. And when it came to reading and writing, no matter how determined he was or how hard he tried, he couldn't manage it. His tutors had no patience for him. They convinced the king there was something wrong with his son. Dax was simply unintelligent, they said. A waste of their time.

So their mother sent Dax to the home of her childhood friend Desta, the mistress of the House of Song. For years, Dax spent summers in the scrublands, learning alongside Desta's children, whose tutors were more patient.

But then their mother died. Peace between Firgaard and the scrublands shattered and the House of Song turned against them. Instead of their honored guest, Dax became a prisoner. Asha didn't know the whole story, because Dax refused to talk about it. But she knew it was a hurt her brother carried within him to this day.

"I'm just saying," said Safire, tilting back her head to drink. "It looked"—she gulped water, then swiped when it dribbled down her chin—"like a token of affection."

Those words slammed into Asha like a rockslide in the Rift. "Dax?" she scoffed. "In love with a scrublander?"

Safire made an arching swoop of her hands, as if to say *I'm just telling you what I saw.*

"Even if he *did* carve her that pendant, you know how he is," Asha said. "Dax flirts with everyone. It doesn't mean anything. And Roa seems"—*regal, graceful, proud*—"like the kind of girl who wouldn't put up with that."

"It's not Roa I'm worried about."

Asha frowned, hearing what Safire didn't say.

It *was* strange that he'd brought the scrublanders back with him. It didn't seem like something Dax could manage alone. What if he *was* smitten with Roa? And, if so, what if Roa knew it and was using it to her advantage? Using Dax's affection to get within striking distance of the king?

Asha's heart squeezed at the thought. Because underneath all of her brother's ridiculous bravado beat a selfless, golden heart.

The real reason Dax got into the fight with Jarek's second-in-command? It wasn't because he was drunk. It was because it was the second-in-command who'd beaten Safire so badly, she could hardly get out of bed for three days.

Asha's brother might be a reckless fool. But he was a reckless fool who would do what it took to save the ones he loved from pain.

She looked to her cousin. "I need you to watch him. Stay close and make sure he doesn't get himself into trouble."

"We can both watch him."

But Asha couldn't. She had a dragon to hunt.

She walked to the edge of the roof, pacing as she stared out past the city walls to the ridge of the mountain range towering above them. The morning mist gathered in its gray crevices and green valleys. The fading red moon clung to the bit of sky above.

Six more days until the moon disappeared completely. After that, Asha would belong to Jarek.

If only she had more time. . . .

"There's something I need to do first."

Turning away from the sight, Asha gathered up the wasters. She felt her cousin's gaze on her back. This time, Safire didn't put a voice to the questions burning inside her.

But that didn't mean Asha didn't hear them.

"As soon as it's done, I'll tell you everything," Asha said. "I promise."

She knew Safire wouldn't betray her secret. Knew it better than the old stories buried in her depths. But if the dragon king found out Safire knew his daughter was perpetrating criminal acts, it would be the end for her. Asha couldn't put her cousin in a situation that would require more grace from the dragon king—because there wasn't any grace left for Safire.

The less her cousin knew, the safer she was.

A Tale of Caution

Once there was a slave named Lillian. Like all well-trained slaves, she kept her head down and did as she was bidden. She waited on the dragon queen with patience and care, dressing and bathing her, plaiting her long hair and sprinkling her neck with the finest rose water. Like all well-trained slaves, Lillian was invisible.

The second son of the dragon queen was named Rayan. Like most young draksors of high rank, he wore only the finest clothes and drank only the finest wine. He bet on the strongest dragons in the pit and broke in the most unruly of stallions. Like any handsome son of a dragon queen, Rayan caught every woman's eye.

One day, returning early from a desert ride, Rayan strode through his mother's orange grove and stopped short. Someone was singing. Someone with the voice of a nightingale.

Rayan paused, unseen, beneath the blooming trees. He watched, transfixed by the sight of a barefooted slave as she spun on her heel, her plain dress twirling around her as she danced to the tune of her own voice.

Every day after, Rayan returned to the orange grove to wait for his mother's slave. He only ever meant to watch her. He never meant to be seen.

But Lillian saw. Her dance paused midstep. Her song broke midtune. Lillian fled.

Rayan pursued, trying to explain: he hadn't meant to find her that day beneath the blossoms. He hadn't meant to return every day since. He only liked to watch her dance, to hear her sing. The sight of her was like a still pool. Like a calm and soothing place.

Lillian stood with her back against the wall, trembling and wide-eyed, refusing to look him in the face. She fell to her knees, begging. It confused Rayan, who kept telling her to rise.

And then, all at once, he understood.

She thought he'd come to take her against her will. The way a stallion takes a mare.

The thought struck like a blow.

This time, it was Rayan who fled.

When Lillian looked up, she found herself alone. She picked herself up from the marble floor of her mistress's salon. She looked and looked for the son of the dragon queen—but all trace of him was gone.

The next morning, Lillian woke to a bouquet of orange blossoms—delicate white petals in the shape of a star—and a note that said, I'm sorry.

Lillian returned to the orange grove. She found Rayan waiting, his back to her, looking up into the dark green boughs above. She could have left right then. He never would have known.

But she didn't.

Lillian said the name of the second son of the dragon queen, and Rayan turned. His face changed at the sight of her, filling with light. When he stepped toward her, she didn't run. She let him look. And as he looked, Lillian reached to touch his hair, his cheek, his throat.

After that day, their eyes met across courtyards. In dark and narrow halls, their hands brushed. Beneath the cover of night, in secret gardens and forgotten alcoves and tucked-away terraces, Lillian and Rayan gave themselves to each other.

It wasn't long before a child grew within her. But such a thing was *not permitted for a queen's slave.*

Betrayed by a fellow skral, Lillian came before her mistress, begging for mercy. When Rayan found out, he was beyond the city walls with his stallion. He raced back through the narrow, cobbled streets. He ran through the palace corridors. He burst into his mother's throne room.

"I love her," Rayan confessed. "I intend to marry her."

Perhaps it was his youth. Or perhaps it was the foolishness of love. His mother laughed in his face.

Rayan tried to defend himself. What he felt for Lillian was not infatuation. It wasn't even love—it was something more. Love happened between a man and his wife. But the day he found Lillian in the orange grove, Rayan felt like the First Namsara laying eyes on his hika—his sacred mate, his holy match, fashioned for him by the Old One.

Lillian was his hika, Rayan declared.

His mother told Rayan to get out of her sight.

The dragon queen waited for the baby to be born, but no longer. She dragged her slave to the heart of the city and burned her alive in the public square while her son watched, held back by soldats, helpless to stop it.

Three days later, Rayan took his own life. He left behind a wailing baby girl. A girl who bore the name her mother gave her: Safire.

Three days after that, the queen was found dead in her bed. Some say she died of shame. Others say she died of grief. But whatever killed her isn't the point. The point is this:

The son of a dragon queen dared to love a slave, and it did not end well for anyone.

Seven

Asha took the fastest route to the north gate: through the new quarter, past the temple. She moved quickly through the narrow streets. After Kozu's attack, when this quarter burned for three days straight, her father ordered it rebuilt. The effort took almost six years and the labor of thousands of slaves.

Now, as Asha walked, a sea of green surrounded her. Green, the color of renewal. Slaves painted the walls green as a tribute to those who'd died in the flames.

The streets were no wider than a donkey cart, and while she was nowhere near the city's largest market, merchants' stalls clustered along the walls. Mountains of saffron, anise, and paprika rose out of rough canvas bags. The pungent smell of leather wafted from sandal stalls. Brightly colored sabra silk rippled in the breeze.

At the end of it all the white walls of the temple stretched toward a blue sky. Asha was halfway to it when a woman stepped in front of her and fell to her knees, blocking her way. The tang of iron hung around her, and from the way soot gathered in the creases of her skin and the edges of her fingernails, Asha guessed she was a blacksmith.

"I-Iskari." Her head bowed low. Thick, blackened hands trembled as they clutched a long bundle of dyed cloth to her chest. "Th-these are for you."

Slaves running errands for their masters slowed all around her. Asha felt their watching eyes. The blacksmith kneeling in the middle of the street drew too much attention.

"Get up."

The blacksmith shook her head and raised her hands higher.

"Please take them."

Asha glanced from the top of the blacksmith's head to the shape of the long bundle wrapped in soot-smudged linen and secured with rope. A familiar shape. The hair on the back of her neck rose.

Asha took the bundle, burned hand and all. The moment the weight of it sank into her palms, she knew exactly what lay within.

"I worked through the night and finished at dawn," the blacksmith said. "The Old One himself told me how to fashion them."

Asha went rigid. She looked to the doorways and second-story terraces on the walls around them. When her gaze fell on any watchers, they withdrew behind teal or yellow curtains or wooden lattices.

Asha pulled the bundle close to her chest. "Did anyone hear you forge them?"

The blacksmith kept her eyes on the cobbles. "I often work

through the night, Iskari. If they heard, it would not seem unusual."

"Don't speak of this to anyone."

Without raising her eyes, the blacksmith nodded. Stepping around her, Asha left the woman kneeling behind her and clutched the bundle tight all the way to the gates.

The soldats at the gate didn't give her trouble, but Asha heard their grumbled words as they unlocked the heavy iron door.

Where were her slaves? they wondered. *And hadn't she just returned from a hunt?*

The Iskari always hunted with an entourage of slaves. Today, though, she was alone and heavily armored, with her hunting axe at her hip. Going into the Rift on her own, merely a day after her return, sparked suspicion.

They may have wondered where she was going, but the soldats didn't stop her. Because Asha was the Iskari.

That wouldn't keep the news from reaching Jarek, though.

Let it. Asha hardened against the thought of him as she moved deeper into the trees, following the hunting paths. *When I return with Kozu's head, Jarek will no longer be my concern.*

Still, she moved quickly. In case anyone meant to follow her.

Asha hurried through the rattling esparto grass. The cedars croaked and hushed around her. If she was going to call a dragon—if she was going to call the most dangerous dragon—she needed to put as much space as possible between her and the city. She needed to right the wrongs she'd committed, not repeat them.

✦✦✦

In the late afternoon, she climbed the sun-bleached cliffs of the lower Rift, looking back the way she'd come, ensuring the walls of the city were far and small in the distance. She laid the blacksmith's bundle on the rock before her, untying the cords and pushing back the fabric.

Twin blades greeted her: black as night, elegant as slivered moons. Their hilts were made of bone inlaid with iron and gold. And there was a second bundle. Asha unwrapped it to find a shoulder belt and scabbards. She strapped on the belt and sheathed each slayer, one after the other, so they crisscrossed against her back.

Now for the treacherous part. She had only six days to track and kill Kozu. Asha couldn't afford to waste time. Kozu had been seen in the Rift. If she told an old story here, it might draw him to her.

But which one would the oldest and wickedest of dragons want to hear? One about himself? One about Elorma, the First Namsara?

Asha broke away from the hunting paths, heading into the pines and hacking at clinging vines that blocked her way. As she pressed on, Asha drew a story up from her depths. Like a bucket hoisted from a well full of poison instead of water.

Asha opened her mouth to tell it when she stumbled out of the trees and onto a rocky outcropping.

A lean beige dragon lay curled around itself, blending into the shale as it soaked up the heat of the sun. Beyond it, the Rift dipped into a valley of lush green growth around the river snaking through it.

Asha froze as the dragon swung its head to look at her. The smoky stench of it hit her in the face. Its horns had barely come in, making it an adolescent. Judging by its muted coloring, it was female.

This dragon clicked dangerously as it curled its body around to face her. Younger dragons were more prone to aggression. More prone to fighting than fleeing. This dragon was no exception.

It spread its wings wide, like a fowl displaying its plumage to appear bigger and more frightening in the face of an enemy. Its wings cast a shadow over Asha. The sunlight sifted through the translucent membranes, revealing interlocking bones that worked to keep its huge body in flight.

The dragon hissed.

Asha's fingers wrapped around the handle of her axe. On any other day, stumbling across a dragon would have thrilled her.

Asha gritted her teeth. *The sooner I slay it, the sooner I can summon Kozu.*

Slamming her helmet down over her head, Asha gripped her axe, then changed her mind.

Using her unburned hand, she tucked her axe back into her belt and drew one of the slayers from the scabbards at her back. The moment her palm connected with the hilt, her blood hummed.

These slayers can only be used to make wrongs right, a warning clanged inside her.

I am righting a wrong, she thought.

Asha swung the sacred blade, throwing sunlight into the

dragon's eyes, and then lunged. The dragon slithered out of her way, circling back around her. Its scales whispered against the rock. Asha barely had time to duck and roll before it could slam its spiked tail into her back. This was a hunting lesson Asha learned early: always know exactly where a dragon's tail is.

Before Asha could climb to her feet, the dragon lunged, its venom fangs out and ready to bite. Asha rolled again just as it struck, missing her by a fingerbreadth. She rolled again, right beneath it, her back to the cracked rock, her face to an underbelly as pale as an egg.

Asha thrust her slayer up into soft flesh.

Two things happened. First, the dragon shrieked, flapping its thin wings, trying to scramble away. Second, pain like no other raced up Asha's arm and her screams joined the dragon's.

She let go of the hilt. The dragon broke free, dragging itself toward the cliff edge.

Asha sat up. Her arm hung limp at her side. Her breathing came sharp and fast. The pain had vanished, replaced by a horrible numbness.

She couldn't feel her arm. Couldn't flex the fingers of her hand. It was as if the limb didn't exist.

These slayers can only be used to make wrongs right.

Again, she tried to move her arm. Again, it didn't respond.

Elorma had deceived her.

Enraged, Asha screamed her hate at the Old One. "Deceiver!" The word echoed all across the cliffs until the wind whisked the sound of it away.

Asha looked to the cliff edge, where the young dragon lay

silent and still. Maybe it wasn't dead. Maybe she'd just injured it.

Maybe she could fix this.

"Please be alive," Asha whispered, moving toward it. But when she grabbed the hilt with her scorched hand and pulled the weapon out, blood pooled around her boots.

Asha sank to her knees before the dead dragon's head, resting on the rock, its eyes closed.

Her left arm was useless, her right hand burned. How was she supposed to hunt Kozu now?

The bloodied black blade lay across her knees. Asha wanted to throw it off the cliff.

If the Old One thought he could stop her through trickery, then the Old One had underestimated her. It was Asha who, at the age of ten, summoned the most wicked of dragons and nearly destroyed an entire city. It was Asha who had more kills to her name than any other hunter.

Asha was dangerous. She was not to be trifled with. Because, maimed or not, she was hunting Kozu down and bringing her father his head. She was putting an end to the old ways forever—if it was the last thing she did.

Eight

"Would you hold still?"

Asha leaned her head back against the cool plaster of the alcove wall, obeying her cousin. Her knees were drawn up and her limp arm hung in a sling wrapped tight to her body. She'd come straight to Safire's room upon her return from the Rift, where Safire—clothed in a brand-new mantle—proceeded to growl at her.

Despite being in the women's wing of the royal quarters, the room was cramped and dreary. The plaster walls were cracked and yellowed; there was no terrace; and despite the glassless windows, very little light reached in. Before the revolts, the dragon queen's slaves lived and slept here. Now they were confined to the furrow each night, under lock and guard.

"I wish you would tell me how this happened." Safire's eyebrows crept together as she frowned over Asha's limp arm. She was trying to pad her burned hand with extra linen to see if Asha could use it—at least a little. Asha watched her cousin fold the linen, then tie it around and around her hand. She thought of long-lost days when they would hide in the garden under the honeysuckle plants, watching Asha's nursemaid frantically call her name, their hips and elbows touching as they held in their giggles. She thought of late nights lying side by side on the roof, putting names to all the stars.

That was before Asha's mother died. Her mother had been more lax about the laws governing those with skral blood.

"There," said Safire, tying off the linen. "How's that?"

Asha's hand was a bulge of white, completely swallowed by the bandage. She reached for the axe lying on the floor of the alcove. Her skin protested as she picked it up, but she could bear it. She wouldn't be able to hold it long, or even well, but it was better than nothing.

Asha was about to thank her cousin when a loud banging at the door interrupted.

"Saf!"

At the sound of Dax's panicked voice, Safire and Asha looked up.

Safire leaped to her feet and crossed the room.

When the door opened, Dax stumbled inside, looking haggard and ill. Sweat dampened the curls around his temples and made his skin gleam. Blood stained the front of his pale gold tunic.

And that was all it took: Asha suddenly knew who he reminded her of.

Mother.

In those last days before she died, her mother's bones jutted out and her eyes were dark hollows. Asha remembered the sound of her coughing through the night. Remembered all the blood she coughed up at the end. . . .

Whole cups of blood.

Asha got to her feet—a difficult task with a badly burned hand and a useless arm in a sling.

"What's wrong?" Safire demanded. "Are you hurt?"

"I've made a terrible mistake." His eyes were hollow. Haunted.

Seeing the look on Asha's face, he glanced down at the blood on his shirt. "It's not mine." And then he caught sight of her sling, her bandaged hand.

Before he could ask about them, Safire interrupted. "What's happened?"

He met Asha's gaze. "I need your help."

Had the scrublanders done something? Had they hurt him?

Asha rose to her full height, ready to take down whoever had done it.

"It's Torwin."

Asha didn't know that name. "Who?"

"Jarek's slave," Safire explained.

Asha remembered him. Eyes that pierced. Freckles like stars. Long fingers plucking the strings of a lute.

Torwin.

"I thought I could stop it." Dax's hands slid behind his neck, gripping hard. "You know how Jarek is. As soon as you show him you care . . ."

"He hurts the thing you care about," Asha finished.

Dax's arms fell to his sides. He stepped toward her.

"I need you to help him."

Asha shook her head in disbelief. "You're the heir to the throne, Dax. You don't *need* to do anything for him. He's a slave."

Safire looked at her.

"What?" She met her cousin's eyes. Here, with Dax, it was safe. "*You're* not a slave, Saf."

If Dax had a weakness, this was it. Worse than his reckless fighting and flirting and gambling, Dax didn't think like a king. He thought like . . . a hero. He was too kind. Too good. Too soft on the inside. It was going to get him hurt.

"Asha." Dax stepped toward her. "I'm begging you."

Kings don't beg.

"If *I* ask Jarek to spare Torwin's life, he'll kill him for sure. But if *you* ask . . ."

"You're seriously asking me to get a *dangerous* skral out of a punishment he deserves?" Asha studied her brother. Dax had spent the past month in the scrublands, eating and drinking with religious fanatics who refused to take slaves.

What if instead of winning over the scrublanders, the scrublanders had won over her brother?

"He's not—" Dax shook his head, curling his hands into fists. Then uncurling them. He looked like he wanted to grab her by the shoulders and shake her. "He's being punished because of *you*, Asha. Because he touched you in front of Jarek. In front of everyone." Dax breathed in, nostrils flaring elegantly. "If he didn't catch you, you would have been hurt."

"He did more than catch me," she growled, thinking of

the way he raised those steely eyes to hers. *One dance,* he'd demanded. *In a place and time of my choosing.*

"He'll go to the pit tomorrow and never come out," Dax said. As if a slave dying in the pit was supposed to elicit her sympathy. Slaves died in the pit all the time.

Asha shook her head in disbelief. "That is where criminal slaves *belong.*"

But even as she said it, she thought of the beat of a heart, thrumming against her cheek. Thought of the way it felt to be cradled in strong arms.

It had been eight years since she'd heard the beat of someone's heart. Eight years since anyone held her with such gentleness and care.

"It costs you nothing, Asha."

She hated the way Dax was looking at her. As if her very existence disappointed him. As if he was just realizing now that Asha was a horror.

It reminded her of a story of two siblings: one formed out of sky and spirit, the other out of blood and moonlight.

Where Namsara brought laughter and love, Asha thought, *Iskari brought destruction and death.*

Safire stepped up to Dax's side. "I agree with Dax."

Asha glared at her cousin, feeling betrayed.

"Jarek is the *commandant,*" Asha reminded them. "He's obligated to carry out the law, and that slave is his property." She suddenly thought of the skral's hands, carefully bandaging her burn. She quickly shook the memory away. "There's nothing I can do."

"Horseshit," said Dax. "You can *try*."

She scowled at him.

"Please, Asha. How much more can I beg?"

The last time she remembered her brother begging was when, as a child, she'd stolen Jarek's favorite sword and dropped it in the sewer. Before Jarek could punish her, Dax took the blame. Jarek forced him to beg for mercy. As Jarek pinned Dax to the floor, hurting him, Asha watched with tears in her eyes, not brave enough to confess.

Dax must have sensed he was getting to her, because he went on.

"You're his weakness, Asha. Use that. Charm him. Entice him. Do what . . . what every other girl does to get what she wants."

At those words, Safire stepped away, horrified.

Asha's lip curled. The thought of *enticing* Jarek made her stomach prickle.

"Or . . . not," Dax said when he noticed the looks on their faces.

"I don't have time for this," Asha said, thinking of the waning red moon. She had a dragon to hunt down and only six more days to do it. She needed to get back to the Rift.

Asha moved past her brother, heading for the door.

"Wait. . . ."

She didn't.

"What if I gave you *this*."

Asha stopped at Safire's door. The wood, rotting. The brass handle tarnished with age. If someone wanted to hurt Safire, they could easily break down this door. It needed to be replaced.

"It belonged to our mother."

She turned as Dax tugged something off his too-thin finger, then held it out to her. A ring carved out of bone lay on his palm. But it wasn't the ring that caught her attention first. It was the calluses on his fingertips. They looked just like the calluses on the fingers of Jarek's slave.

"Father made it for her."

Jealousy dug its claws into Asha's heart. Their mother's possessions had been burned after her death. Why was this one missed? And why should Dax get to keep it?

"Father gave it to me just before I left for the scrublands." Dax stepped toward her. "If you get Torwin out of this, I'll give it to you."

Asha thought of her mother, dying in bed. Poisoned by the old stories.

She didn't have anything of her mother's. Why had her father given their mother's ring to Dax?

Because I don't deserve it. Because if it weren't for me, she never would have told the old stories aloud. If it weren't for me, she'd still be alive.

Asha might not deserve her mother's ring, but she wanted it.

And while she would never admit it, while she didn't even understand it, she wanted something else. Wanted a certain heart to go on beating.

"Fine."

Dax smiled one of his bright smiles. It didn't make her feel better. Instead, it highlighted just how thin his face had become, how much weight he'd lost.

What happened out there? she wondered.

She shoved the question away and made for the door.

Safire went to follow her, but Asha threw a warning look. No way was she taking her cousin with her to barter for the life of an insubordinate slave. If Asha were going to interfere with a lawful sentence, she would do it with Safire far away. Asha would not remind Jarek of the most effective way to punish her for crossing him.

Just before Asha stepped into the dimly lit corridor, where torches threw eerie shadows across the walls, she heard Dax say, "What happened to her arm?"

"She won't tell me," Safire said.

Asha shut the door tight on them both.

Nine

Jarek's front door opened on the first knock. A gray-haired slave knotted with age hunched in the archway, her dark cheeks glistening with tears.

The presence of a skral startled Asha. The law dictated that all slaves be in the furrow by sundown.

"I need to see the commandant," she said, pushing the door open and entering a turquoise corridor smelling like rose water. Finely woven carpets cushioned her feet.

An angry shout echoed through the halls, followed by an unmistakable sound: the sharp smack of the shaxa—a piece of cord knotted with shards of bone. Asha heard it hit and tear, again and again, at the flesh of someone's back.

The elderly slave whimpered. Asha made her way past elaborately carved cedarwood doors inlaid with ivory and brass. She passed room after room after room until she came to the small court at the heart of the commandant's home, where the heady smell of moonflowers enveloped her.

And then she saw the slave.

He slumped in the shallow fountain pool. The lanterns hanging in the galleries cast him in shadow, but she could see his hands bound and tied to the fountainhead. Blood streamed down his back and into the water of the pool, turning it pink.

Jarek stepped into her line of sight, severing her view of the slave. He'd taken off his tunic. His back glistened with sweat and his muscles rippled as he rounded on his property.

"Well, skral?" His words slurred together. "Was it worth it?"

Asha retreated, pressing her back against the wall, heart pounding in her chest.

She might be the Iskari. She might hunt dragons and bring back their heads, but Jarek held her father's army in his fist. He had the loyalty of every soldat in the city. And for reasons she'd never been able to figure out, he'd never been afraid of her.

She could turn and leave. She didn't have to do this. It was the slave's fault, after all. He shouldn't have touched her.

"Please, Iskari." The words broke up her thoughts like an axe. Asha opened her eyes to find the elderly slave wringing her wrinkled, liver-spotted hands. Her hair was gray and bound in a thick braid. Her anguished, heart-shaped face beseeched Asha. "Please help him."

A crash resounded, followed by a low grunt. Asha dared another look around the corner. One of Jarek's low-lying sofas lay broken, its leg snapped off beside the purple daturas, whose petals opened in the moonlight. *Charm him,* Dax suggested. *Entice him.* But Asha didn't know how to do those things. She was a hunter. She knew all about killing things and nothing about seduction.

Asha thought of the way the slave touched her in the sickroom. The way he caught her in her father's courtyard, holding her carefully against him. As if he wasn't afraid.

It shamed her. If *he* wasn't afraid—of Asha, of the law, of his own master whipping him up to Death's gate—how could *she* be afraid? She was the Iskari.

Jarek spat. His back was still to her. He reined in the shaxa, getting ready for another round of lashes. The longer Asha waited, the more of the slave's life trickled away.

The shaxa lashed the air, ripping at flesh. The heart-wrenching sound echoed around the courtyard and through Asha. She squeezed her eyes shut. With her left arm strapped uselessly to her torso, she drew one of her slayers with her burned but padded hand. It shook with the pain. She gritted her teeth and held on.

The next time Jarek reared the shaxa back, Asha stepped into the courtyard, catching the whip across her blade. When Jarek went to lash again, the shaxa snagged. Asha held on tight, despite the pain.

Jarek stumbled. He spun, squinting through his drunken haze. His face contorted with anger and shone with sweat.

"Who's there?"

The fountain pool was filling with blood. The sound of the gently cascading water seemed out of place.

"That's enough," she said with more courage than she felt. "I'm cutting him down."

Jarek's face darkened. "I'm well within my rights." He tugged on the shaxa, willing it back to him. But it didn't budge.

"You're killing him."

At the tremble in her voice, a tremble Asha couldn't control, Jarek's features settled into an icy calm. "Since when do you take an interest in the health of my slaves, Asha?" He looked from her to the skral and back, his mouth twisting. "You think I forget that it runs in your family?"

It took three slow heartbeats for her to realize what he meant.

Rayan. Her uncle. The draksor who fell in love with a skral.

"Should I expect this when we're married?" He stumbled a little, then steadied himself against the trunk of the lemon tree. "My wife carrying on with my slaves, in my own home?"

She tried to sound calm. "That's the stupidest thing I've ever heard you say."

He looked to the half-slain slave. "It's disgusting." He dropped the shaxa, drew a double-edged dagger, and started toward the fountain. "I won't tolerate it."

Panic sparked inside her. Asha threw down the slayer wound with the shaxa and drew her other one, making her burned hand sting anew. She clung to it and moved for the fountain. Sobriety and swiftness got her there first.

Asha spun to face Jarek and raised her slayer, keeping herself between him and his slave.

Jarek may have been drunk, but he was much bigger and stronger than she was. And she had only one barely usable arm.

So when he lunged with no weapon but his hands, Asha did the only thing she could think of. As he smashed into her, she rammed the butt of her slayer as hard as she could into his temple.

Asha hit the floor with such force, the breath went out of her. Jarek, knocked out from her blow, pinned her to the ground. He was all muscle and weight. Like a boulder pressing down on her.

Asha lay beneath him, one side of her face pressed to the cold tiles, the other against the hot, sweaty skin of his chest. When the room came back into focus, she tried to breathe but couldn't.

He's suffocating me. . . .

She kicked and bucked, trying to shove him off. Her slayer rested only a few steps away, yet entirely out of her reach.

Her lungs burned. Her vision blurred. Gasping for air and getting none, Asha struggled harder, pushing with her legs and hips in one last burst of strength. Before the room darkened around her, hands reached down. Hands spotted and knotted with age. They tried pulling her out, and when that didn't work, they rolled Jarek off Asha with a startling strength. Air rushed into Asha's lungs. She gasped, gulping it in like water, letting it fill her up.

The commandant lay on the floor in a bedraggled heap. Blood matted the hair around his temple, but his heart still beat. She could see the pulse of it at the base of his throat. She had no idea how bad the injury was or how long he would be out, so she stood, grabbed her slayers, and sheathed them. Snatching up Jarek's dagger from the floor, she went quickly to where the slave still slumped in the pool.

Sloshing through the bloody water, Asha sawed his hands free of the binding cord. When the cord snapped, the slave collapsed into the water.

Asha threw down the dagger, which plopped into the water

and sank. She crouched to help him, trying to take hold of his arm to throw it over her shoulder, but with only one hand, it was too difficult.

"I need you to help me."

His gaze lifted to her face, but he didn't answer. His eyes closed slowly. As if he were slipping toward unconsciousness.

"No. Stay with me."

His eyes opened but wouldn't focus. "Iskari?" His lips were dry and cracked. "Am I dreaming?"

"Put your arm around my shoulder."

He did.

"Now hold on tight and stand up."

She didn't wait for a response, just wrapped her good arm around him, helping him rise. He wobbled as they waded through the bloody pool; and when Asha tried to get him down from its edge, he nearly fell. She caught him hard around the waist, her burned hand screaming in pain.

"Listen to me," she said through gritted teeth. "If you're going to get out of here alive, you need to walk."

He nodded. Air rushed across his lips as he breathed in, gathering up his strength. He leaned on her heavily and stiffened with every step, a sharp intake of breath between his teeth.

They needed to get out of here before Jarek regained consciousness. And more than that, dawn was coming. Once the sun was up, Asha couldn't walk through the streets of the city carrying her betrothed's half-slain slave. People would see. And they would talk.

She needed to move faster.

The elderly slave appeared with one of Jarek's hooded mantles. A crimson one. She threw it over her fellow slave's head and shoulders, tying the hood's tassels around his throat.

"Where will you take him, Iskari?"

Asha didn't know. She couldn't hide him in the palace. Nor could she take him to the furrow, which was locked now and swarming with soldiers. As they moved carefully down the corridor, toward the front door, Asha tried to think of someplace safe. Someplace no one would think to look for him.

She thought of her own secrets. Of the places that hid them.

There was the Rift, but that was too far. And Asha had no intention of adding *freeing a slave* to her list of crimes.

"The temple," murmured the slave.

Asha stared at him.

The temple had been antagonistic toward the dragon king for years now. But Asha doubted the guardians would go so far as to harbor a fugitive slave.

"Iskari," he whispered between shallow breaths. "Trust me."

She had no reason to trust him—except for the fact that he wanted to live more than she wanted him to. So Asha did as he suggested.

She hauled him out into the silent street. The salty smell of his sweat mingled with the sharp tang of his blood. The sooner she got him to safety, the sooner she could tell her brother she'd done as he asked, collect their mother's ring, and get back to hunting Kozu.

She focused on that thought as she half carried the slave toward the pearl-white temple rising out of the gloom.

◆◆◆

The temple was once the highest structure in the city, built into the sheer face of the mountain. The palace had long surpassed it. What had once been the center of power in Firgaard was reduced to an empty shell. An obsolete relic.

On the way there, it started to rain. If Asha believed in prayers, she might have sent one skyward. The rain washed away the trail of blood in their wake.

And then, her paralyzed arm began to tingle. As if someone had stuck hundreds of needles in it. By the time they arrived at the temple, Asha swore she could wiggle her fingers just a little.

She thought of her slayers strapped to her back.

They can only be used to make wrongs right.

Asha studied the slave clinging to her. Beneath the mantle's hood, his jaw clenched and his forehead crumpled in a severe frown. His eyes clouded over with pain.

Watching him struggle to stay upright, to keep walking, Asha thought that maybe her own argument didn't make sense. Yes, he'd broken the law. Yes, he'd touched the daughter of the dragon king. But he'd done it to stop her from getting hurt. Had he done nothing, would he not have been punished just as harshly? Wasn't it *better* that he caught her?

"It's all right." Asha's arm tightened around him. "I won't let you fall."

As the slave cast a look her way, the frown in his forehead smoothed out and he relaxed against her.

No soldats stood guard outside the temple walls, with its chipped white paint and faded, crumbling friezes. The streets that bordered it were empty and silent.

Asha helped the slave up to the front archway. Inlaid in the cedarwood doors was the symbol of the Old One: a dragon cast in iron except its heart, whose blood-red glass mimicked a flame.

With one hand trapped in a sling and the other fully occupied, she couldn't knock. So she shouted instead. When no one came, she shouted louder. The effort took all her remaining strength, which had been sapped by the weight of her load.

Finally, the doors opened and a hooded figure holding a candle looked out. The woman wore a crimson robe. In the candlelight, Asha couldn't make out her face. But the robe marked her as a temple guardian, one of several women charged with performing the sacred rituals: bindings, burnings, and births.

When the guardian realized who stood on her threshold, she stepped quickly back.

"Iskari . . ."

"This temple was a place of sanctuary once," Asha said, starting to buckle. "Please. He needs sanctuary."

The woman looked from Asha to the slave, trying to decide what to do. Just before Asha collapsed, the guardian made her decision: she ducked beneath the slave's other arm, lifting most of his weight on herself, then helped them both inside.

The massive door closed behind them with a thud.

Within, it smelled like old and crumbling plaster. Candles burned in their alcoves on the walls, casting long shadows through the darkened corridors. Their footsteps echoed loudly as together Asha and the guardian helped the slave deeper into the temple.

"This way," said the guardian. She led them past archways

and down hallways, then up a narrow flight of old stairs.

At the top of the stairs stood a small, plain door made of cedar. A seven-petaled flower had been carved into the wood. A namsara. The ancient marking for places of healing. Sickrooms especially.

The guardian unlocked the door. Darkness cloaked the area beyond, but the woman moved easily through it, the dim flicker of her candle always just a little ahead. She lowered the slave until he was sitting on something soft and flat.

"What happened to him?" the guardian asked, setting the brass candleholder down beside the cot. She untied the mantle's tassels. The slave cried out in pain as she gently pulled the woolly fabric from his lacerated back.

"The commandant," said Asha, sinking to the floor.

The woman surveyed his wounds, the blood pooling and dripping. Sweat rolled down the slave's face as he gripped the side of the cot, shaking with pain. His arms and chest were bare and streaked with blood.

"I'm Maya," she said, pushing back her hood to reveal strong cheekbones and bright, wide eyes. "I'm going to boil some water and fetch a disinfecting salve. I'll be right back."

In her absence, the slave fixed his gaze on Asha. He stared at her, unblinking. As if the sight of the Iskari was the only thing keeping him from slipping into oblivion.

What use was it now, telling him to look away?

"Why?" The question scraped across his cracked lips.

She frowned at him. "What?"

"Why did you do it?"

Asha thought of Dax offering her their mother's ring.

"My brother asked me to."

His brow furrowed. "You never do what your brother asks."

Asha's lips parted. *How does he know that?*

He leaned forward. From the way he blinked and squinted, Asha knew his vision was blurring. "What's the real reason?"

She stared him down. "I just told you."

His gaze dropped to her arm.

Asha looked where he looked: down at the sling. She tried to flex her fingers. To her surprise they did as she directed—but only barely. While the slave watched, Asha untied the sling. Her arm fell limp into her lap. But if she focused, she could move her hand little by little.

The door creaked open and the slave straightened, eyes darting away from the Iskari sitting on the floor beside his cot. He focused on Maya instead, who held a bowl of water. Clean linen draped over her arm.

Asha meant to leave. To return to the palace.

She shouldn't be here.

But her body felt heavy as stone and the thought of rising overwhelmed her.

So as the guardian washed and dressed the skral's wounds, Asha curled up on the floor at the foot of the cot, her limp arm bent against her chest. She only meant to rest.

She didn't mean to fall asleep.

Ten

"Iskari. It's nearly midday."

Asha opened her eyes and found Maya crouched over her. Her hood was pushed back and the light of a lantern illuminated the soft curves of her face.

Asha's body groaned in protest. She was tired and sore, and it took considerable energy to push herself up into a sitting position. She tried with her burned hand first, and the pain jolted her to full wakefulness. Without thinking, she resumed the effort with her paralyzed hand.

Asha froze. Sitting now, she lifted the hand to her face, flexing her fingers one by one. The arm was no longer numb. No longer limp.

There was no time to marvel, though. She had a more pressing concern: her clothes were covered in dried blood. She couldn't leave the temple like this. Not in broad daylight.

"There's a spring," Maya said, "where the guardians bathe." She held a blue bundle tucked beneath one arm. "I have a clean kaftan you can wear."

"Why are you helping me?" Asha asked, pushing herself to her feet. "I broke into the home of my own betrothed, drew a weapon on him, and stole his property. That makes me a criminal."

"It's like you said." Maya smiled a little. "This temple is a place of sanctuary."

Asha looked to the slave, stretched out across the cot, fast asleep. Wrapped around his shirtless torso were linen bandages, already bled through. Beyond him rose shelves full of scrolls, their carved wooden handles peeking out.

Asha remembered Maya turning the key in the lock. Remembered how deep into the temple they'd gone to get to this room. What in these scrolls warranted keeping them so safe?

"You need to wash and then leave. The entire city is assembling at the pit."

"Is there a fight scheduled?"

Maya nodded.

Her brother would be there. Asha needed to tell him she'd done what he asked. And then, at last, she could return to hunting Kozu.

She took the blue bundle. "Show me the spring."

At the opposite end of the city, near the south gate, sat the pit. Built during Asha's grandmother's reign, the walls of the arena rose up like jagged teeth. Its front entrance gaped open like a mouth, and—as usual—draksors stood just outside, protesting the fights. Just a few months ago, a protest got so out of hand, the soldats couldn't control it and the fight had to be canceled.

Now, the protesters threw rocks at the soldats. They shouted in the faces of the attendees. By the time Asha arrived, more than half of the protesting draksors were clapped in irons. One of them glared at Asha as he was hauled off by a soldat.

Draksors like these, those who thought the skral should go free, would be enraged if they knew Asha was hunting Kozu for her father. They believed the old ways should be returned to, not snuffed out. They were no better than scrublanders.

But everyone knew what would happen if the skral were free: They would turn on their former masters and finish what they had come to do during Asha's grandmother's reign. They would take Firgaard for themselves.

These draksors were fools if they thought any different.

Inside the arena, Asha stuck out like a scrublander, dressed as she was in a simple blue kaftan, absent of beading or embroidery and years out of fashion. Worse than the kaftan, though, was her lack of armor and weapons. Asha had left both her slayers in the temple. She'd go back for them later.

Asha moved deeper into the arena, surrounded by roars of applause. It stank like too many men standing too close together. The arena bowled out and upward, half full of draksors watching matches play out in the pit below.

But news of the Iskari's arrival traveled faster than a windstorm and soon the roars turned to nervous whispers. The clapping hands became clenched fists. As everyone turned to look at her, the crowd dispersed, not wanting to be anywhere near the girl who'd called down dragonfire on their homes and stolen the lives of their loved ones.

"Hey," came a voice at her shoulder. Asha looked up into her cousin's face. Safire dutifully kept her gaze on the ground at their feet, littered with olive pits and pistachio shells. The hood of her new mantle hid her face, helping her blend in. "Where have you been? We were worried."

"I'm fine," Asha said as they passed cages full of criminal slaves behind bars, waiting to be sent down to the pit. She wondered what their crimes were. "Where's Dax?"

Safire nodded to the crimson canopy at the top of the arena. The pit was ringed with benches, like the ripple made by a stone dropped into a pool, and the dragon king's tent rose high above these ripples. It had the clearest view of the fighting down below.

They made their way toward it, up the sloping path, away from the slave cages. When they were surrounded by cheering draksors on all sides, Safire stepped in close, keeping her voice low, her mouth near Asha's ear.

"There's a rumor going around." Safire cast quick glances around them, checking for eavesdroppers. "People are saying *someone* broke into Jarek's home, attacked him, and made off with one of his slaves."

A prickling fear spread across Asha's skin.

She thought of her brother, pinned to a brightly woven rug in one of the palace salons. Remembered Jarek's thick hands around his throat and the way Dax's legs kicked as he fought for breath.

Jarek didn't like people taking his things.

Asha's eyes fixed on the tent up ahead. Its red silk walls billowed, straining against the wind. All she had to do was give Dax the information, and then she could leave.

More spectators parted as the two cousins approached the crimson canopy. Asha stepped into the tent while Safire stayed behind.

Her father sat in a gilt throne. He nodded to Asha as she entered, a question in his eyes. *Why aren't you hunting?*

I'm trying, she wanted to tell him. Instead, she looked to Dax, sitting with his scrublander near the front of the canopy. Roa wore that blue sandskarf wrapped loosely around her shoulders and head. In the desert, sandskarves were worn to protect from the wind and dust, the cold and heat.

Asha watched the way Dax leaned toward the girl, his hand gripping the bench behind her. He kept glancing at her, then away, chewing his lip, bouncing his knee, frowning hard.

When it came to girls, Dax was usually all confidence and swagger. He knew the right things to say. Things that would make a girl glow, then pine for him as she fell asleep at night.

But this . . . this was something else.

Roa seemed tense. Her back was rigid and her hands were gripped firmly in her lap, as if she were not enjoying herself. She didn't even seem to notice Dax. Instead, she stared straight ahead, out over the pit, her white hawk perching on a leather patch on her shoulder. Like she was thinking of a hundred things other than the boy at her side.

Perhaps plotting to kill all of Firgaard in its sleep, thought Asha.

It was dangerous, bringing her here. So close to the king.

Suddenly, someone stepped in front of Asha, blocking Dax and Roa from view.

She looked up into the face of her betrothed.

Glossy hair. Strong, severe jaw. Freshly shaved cheeks. The only thing out of place was the black bruise blooming across his temple.

"Asha." The way his hands clasped hers—like a snare—said that despite his drunkenness, he remembered everything. His saber was sheathed at his hip. "Where have you been?"

Sweat prickled along her hairline.

"Sleeping," she said, matching her voice to his. "I had a rough night."

He leaned in close. Her body tensed the way it did the moment before a dragon struck.

"Give him back." His lips brushed her unscarred cheek. "And we can forget it ever happened."

Asha tried to pull her hands free, but his grip tightened. He spoke so softly, anyone standing nearby might think he was whispering words of love.

"If you don't, when I find him—and I *will* find him—I'll make you watch everything."

He thought she felt about his slave the way Rayan felt about Lillian. It astonished her.

"Go right ahead," she said.

When her father looked over at them, Jarek released her.

Asha saw the troubled look in her father's eyes. She shook her head, telling him not to worry. Stepping around Jarek, she took her seat next to Dax and wiped her sweaty hands on the scratchy fabric of Maya's kaftan.

Jarek had nothing to gain by bringing her offense to light. Jarek wanted Asha. He wanted her the way he wanted the most lethal of sabers or the most hellish of stallions. He wanted to conquer and own her. And, if the whispers were true, if he really was planning to take the throne, their marriage would make it that much easier. He wasn't about to sabotage his chance by exposing Asha's crimes. Not when there were other ways to punish her.

Jarek followed her to the bench and sat down, pressing his leg against her own.

Seeing it, Dax tensed beside Asha, then met her gaze.

Before she could tell Dax she'd done as he asked, Jarek leaned in, interrupting. "My soldats tell me you went out hunting yesterday."

Asha straightened.

"They said you went out *alone*."

If Jarek suspected the truth, if he discovered what her father promised in exchange for Kozu's head . . .

"Perhaps she only needed to breathe," a honeyed voice interrupted. Asha looked to the scrublander on Dax's other side, who stared at Jarek's leg pinning Asha's.

Jarek's eyes narrowed. "Did I ask for your opinion, scrublander?"

Roa's hawk puffed its white chest. Its silver eyes glared at the commandant.

"In the scrublands," said Roa, "no one needs to *ask* for a woman's opinion. It's expected that she gives it freely."

Asha looked to Dax. He should have warned Roa about Jarek and what happened when he was challenged.

"And that," Jarek sneered, "is why your people will never rise above the dirt they live in."

Roa's eyes darkened. It was the only outward sign that his words affected her. Dax, on the other hand, oozed anger. His thin frame buzzed with a dangerous, reckless energy, reminding Asha of all the times he'd stepped into Jarek's path as a child. All the times he'd turned himself into a target to protect others.

Before he could do it again, Asha bent her head toward her brother's.

"He's in the temple," she whispered so only Dax could hear. "Ask the guardian called Maya."

It worked.

That buzzing energy dimmed as Dax looked into Asha's face. From this close, she studied her brother's thinning cheeks. She could see too much of the bones beneath his skin. Just like she could with their mother, in those last days.

Thank you, he mouthed. And then, remembering their deal, he tugged their mother's carved bone ring off his finger. His hand shook slightly as he held it out to her.

Asha took it and slid it onto her fourth finger.

It wasn't a beautiful ring. But its presence held a kind of power. The same power as her mother's voice in the darkness. Or her mother's hands, cupping Asha's face as she told her not to be afraid.

The ring was a reminder: people hadn't always been scared to touch her.

Or love her.

The weight of her mother's ring on her finger comforted Asha.

Dax rose. Roa glanced at Asha before rising, too, then disappeared with him into the crowd.

Jarek nodded to two soldats standing just beyond the canopy, who turned and followed the pair.

Asha was about to go after them, to warn them, when the crowd roared. Draksors got to their feet or hopped up on benches, shouting down into the pit. Jarek rose, one hand going to the pommel of his saber, the other lifted to block the sun from his eyes.

Asha didn't need to look. She knew what was happening: a slave was about to be killed.

Asha had lost all interest in the pit fights when they'd stopped fighting dragons. After the hunting began, there simply weren't enough of them left to keep the people entertained. The spiked metal bars ringing the pit acted as a gate now, keeping drunken draksors from falling to their deaths. Back when dragons fought below, the bars were lowered to keep the beasts from flying away.

"You might be interested in the outcome of this one," Jarek said.

Another roar rippled through the crowd. Chilled, Asha stood. In the depths of the pit below, a young skral forced an elderly skral to her knees. Her gray hair was bound in a thick braid and her hands were knotted with age.

Asha went rigid at the sight of her.

"Last night an intruder came into my home, knocked me unconscious, and stole my slave." Nodding at the skral with gray hair, Jarek said for everyone to hear, "Greta let the intruder in."

Asha couldn't breathe.

"All she had to do was tell me where they went, but she refused," Jarek explained. "So I'm afraid I have to punish her."

Asha's hands balled into fists in her borrowed kaftan.

"It's not too late." He turned to look at Asha. "Even now, she could tell me where my slave is, and all would be forgiven."

Asha should give up the truth, right here and now. She should declare the skral below innocent and she herself the culprit. Tell them the slave they sought was hidden in the temple.

But even if she said all that, Greta would still die—she was complicit in Asha's crime. Despite his words, Jarek was not a forgiving man. And the moment Asha admitted the truth, Jarek's steely-eyed slave would die along with her. And probably Maya, the temple guardian, too.

Asha pressed her lips together in a hard line.

She looked back to the pit.

The combatants knew one another. It was why this fight had gone on so long. If they were strangers, it would have already been done.

But the young slave knew Greta, which made it hard to kill her.

Greta tossed her knife away as she knelt. Its shining edge lay in the red sand, far out of reach, and the boy sank to his knees before her. His free hand cupped the back of Greta's head and Asha saw his lips move, asking a question.

Greta nodded.

The boy slashed his blade across her throat.

Crimson blood spilled over his hands. He pulled Greta tight against him until the life in her winked out.

Cries of victory or defeat, depending on how the bets were placed, went up all around the pit. Draksors hopped down from benches. Those who bet correctly moved to collect their winnings. Others lingered behind, staring somberly down at the bloodstained sand.

Asha stood frozen, her throat burning, watching the slave press his face into Greta's neck as her blood soaked his shirt. He kissed the top of her head and murmured some kind of prayer, until the soldats pried her body out of his arms and took it away.

Which was when he turned the knife on himself.

Eleven

One thing Asha was sure of: she would not be marrying Jarek. If she died hunting Kozu, so be it. She would rather be dead than married to a monster.

Asha slipped through the horde of draksors and fled through the streets, needing to sink her axe into a dragon's heart. The walls crowded in too close. She wanted the Rift beneath her feet and the desert wind on her skin. Most of all, she wanted to hold the First Dragon's head up before the entire city and see the look on Jarek's face when her father declared their wedding canceled.

So while everyone was at the pit, Asha raided the palace kitchens for food. She had five days left before her binding. She needed to pack enough to last.

A lidded silver box waited in her room. When she opened it, a gold necklace studded with rubies winked out at her. Another gift from Jarek.

Asha slammed the lid closed.

She changed into hunting clothes, grabbed her armor and pack, and set out for the temple. Inside, she slipped through the shadows, passing guardians murmuring prayers in candle-lit rooms. She moved silently down the corridors. As she did, she heard the faint sound of a lute being played somewhere in the distance.

As she walked, the gray-haired slave lingered behind her eyes. Her blood spilling over her combatant's hands. Her body slumping forward. Greta had protected a fellow skral, and it had gotten her killed.

Soon, Asha found herself at the bottom of the narrow stairway she sought. The song was louder here. She climbed the steps, stopping before the carved door at the top, about to knock, when the sound within the room made her fist pause in midair.

This was where the song was coming from.

On the other side of the door, someone was plucking the strings of a lute. A voice wove through the notes. A voice like rain falling softly on sand.

A story swelled within her, pushing at her seams. She thought of Rayan watching Lillian dance in the orange grove. . . .

The sight of her was like a still pool. Like a calm and soothing place.

No. Asha forced the story down into her darkest depths and banged her fist on the door. The song abruptly stopped.

When the door opened, Asha looked up into a face flecked with freckles. The skral's eyes were shadowed by dark half-moons.

"Do you have a death wish? I could hear you playing half-way through the temple." She motioned to where his hand gripped the neck of his pale, worn-looking lute. "Where did you get that?"

The moment she stepped past him, she stopped. Dressed in gold, her brother, Dax, rose from a crouched position near the shelves full of scrolls.

The slave shut the door. "Your brother brought it."

Asha looked to her brother, expecting some kind of explanation.

Dax simply studied her, then went back to reading his scroll.

What is going on? she wondered.

But asking questions would only delay her. So, deciding it was better not to, Asha eyed them both warily as she moved for her slayers beneath the cot.

Dax watched Asha put her armor on over her hunting clothes. "Where are you going?"

She ignored him.

The fireproof leather hide curled like parchment around her legs and arms, overlapping in places. She buckled each piece into place before sliding the breastplate over her head.

"Looks like she's going hunting," said the slave, sitting down on the cot. He began to play his lute again, and this time Asha noticed the name *Greta* elegantly engraved near the bottom. The slave winced every once in a while until whatever pain it caused him was forgotten in the joy of playing. In between plucking, he tapped out a rhythm on the belly of the instrument. He let the song build and build until Dax started tapping his foot to the beat, a small smile tugging at his mouth.

Asha stared at them, speechless.

She didn't know what angered her more: her brother's disregard for his own rank or his lack of concern at the noise—noise that would put this slave *back* into the danger Asha had just delivered him from.

She wanted to shake her brother. This was not the behavior of a king to be. It was the behavior of a *fool*.

She couldn't abide it.

"Is this the plan, then?" Asha towered over the skral. "To lead Jarek right to you?"

His fingers silenced the strings. He looked up at her.

"Someone's prickly today."

Her temper flared. Before she could respond, he went on.

"*Are* you going hunting?" He looked her up and down. "Because the law says your hunting slaves have three days of rest before you can take them out again."

Asha frowned. Why would a house slave know dragon-hunting laws? And anyway, Asha always gave her hunting slaves five days of rest. Well-rested slaves made better hunters.

"I'm not taking them."

The slave set aside his instrument and rose, stepping toward Asha, his eyebrows drawn together in that curious look of his.

"You're going alone?" His gaze flickered over her face. He stood so close, she could have counted all of his freckles if she wanted to. "Tell me again, which one of us has the death wish?"

She narrowed her eyes at him.

Dax put the scroll back on the shelf before stepping up beside the slave.

"Asha." Her brother's smile was long gone. "It isn't safe to hunt alone."

"Because stealing Jarek's slave was safe?"

She thought of the shaxa. Of the jealous rage in Jarek's eyes. Of being trapped beneath him, unable to breathe.

The room went quiet.

Once the memory started, Asha couldn't stop it from unraveling completely. She saw Greta's hands pushing Jarek off. Saw Greta giving her murderer permission to take her life. Saw Greta's blood in the sand.

"Iskari? Are you all right?"

The slave's eyes came into focus first. There was something tender in his gaze. Something worried. Out of habit, she almost told him to look away. But the truth was, no one looked at her the way this slave did: carefully, as if bandaging a wound; gently, so as not to hurt.

Asha looked back. She studied the straight line of his nose, the bumps of his cheekbones, the curve of his jaw. He was sharp and sure. Like her favorite axe.

And just like her favorite axe, he was dangerous.

Dangerous . . . but comforting.

No.

Panicking at her own thoughts, Asha pushed past him. She grabbed her helmet off the floor and lifted it over her head. It blocked out everything but the door, which she opened and stepped through, then shut behind her.

On the other side, Asha leaned against the wood, waiting for her racing heart to slow. When it did, she took the stairs two at a time, swearing to stay as far away from that skral as she could.

Twelve

There were officially two ways out of the city: the north gate, which faced the wild and rugged Rift, and the south gate, which faced the ruthless desert. Both were heavily guarded by soldats.

In truth, though, there was one more way out.

A secret way.

Deep below the temple lay a crypt that led to the Old One's sacred caves. In the walls of the crypt were the ashes of the dead, sealed up in ceramic jars. But in one wall there was something else: an alcove small enough for a curious child like Asha to find on trips to the temple with her mother. Hidden in the alcove was a tunnel leading straight up into the Rift, far away from the walls where soldats stood and watched.

It was the tunnel that started the trouble with the dragons.

After Jarek made his suspicion clear, she decided not to use either of the gates. Instead, she took a vaulted stairway down into the temple's depths. At the bottom, she pushed open the old and rotting door. The light from behind her slipped into the crypt, making her shadow stretch and grow.

Without torches to light her way, Asha kept her hand on the crypt walls, letting the cold rock guide her through the darkness. She'd spent so much of her childhood sneaking around beneath the temple that she remembered exactly how far her tunnel was: ninety-three steps through the dark and the damp.

And just beyond her tunnel? The sacred caves.

No one had set foot in them for years. Not since Asha summoned Kozu and he burned half the city to the ground. Before that, the caves were a holy place. And the sacred flame was the temple's beating heart.

A draksor could only enter the caves after she fasted for three days and washed herself in the sacred spring. Even then, she needed to go in barefoot and she could never, ever, set foot in the inner sanctum. It was forbidden to anyone but the guardians.

It was the sanctum where Asha first saw the image of Elorma's face. She hadn't cared then if the Old One struck her down for her disobedience. In fact, she *wanted* to be struck down. That day, Asha came angry. She came to rage and scream and break things. To hurl her hate into the heart of the Old One's holy place.

Her mother was dead, killed by the old stories, just like the raconteurs before her.

Asha's grief made her easy prey that day. It left a fault line running through her. The moment she set foot inside the inner sanctum, the Old One found the fault line. He broke it open and buried a wicked, insatiable hunger within her. One that would turn her against her father, her people, her realm.

From then on, the old stories lived inside Asha, brimming just below the surface. It was how Kozu found her, lured by the old stories buried in her heart. Stories needing to be let out. It was how she almost destroyed the city.

Now, though, the sanctum sat empty and its flaming heart beat elsewhere.

She didn't like to think back to the days before the fire. She didn't like to think about how enslaved she'd been to the Old One, sneaking out of the city night after night at his bidding, to slake Kozu's endless thirst for stories. She might not remember much of what happened the day he burned her, but she remembered the days before it. Waiting for the sun to dip below the mountains. Slipping silently over the rooftops. Taking the tunnel up into the Rift.

As she climbed through the tunnel now, Asha forced herself to remember it all. How she'd betrayed her father night after night. How she'd let herself become corrupted.

When she emerged into the Rift, surrounded by cedars and birdcall, she forced herself to think back further than she had in years as she retraced her steps to the plains where Kozu had burned her.

Asha could see that barefoot child inside her. She could hear the stories spilling from her lips as she ran through the moonlit Rift. She could feel that butterfly heart as her steps brought her closer to an ancient evil.

Asha hated that girl; but she needed her now. There was no room for mistakes this time. She feared if she told an old story aloud, it would summon whatever dragon was within hearing distance. And Asha didn't have time to deal with another dragon. Asha needed Kozu and *only* Kozu. Remembering was the best way to find him.

By the time the sun started to go down, Asha hadn't yet reached the plains. It was getting difficult to see, so she found a small clearing, unrolled her sleeping pack, and stripped off her armor.

She didn't dare light a fire. Instead, she pulled a thick wool tunic out of the pack she'd brought from the palace and donned it to keep warm. The days might be blistering hot, but nights in the Rift could freeze a hunter to death.

Asha wasn't afraid to close her eyes. Over the years, she'd taught herself to sleep lightly and to wake at the slightest sounds. Even if something did find her sleeping, Asha was the most dangerous thing in the Rift.

There was nothing to be afraid of.

The cavernous darkness of sleep melted into dreams. Asha dreamed of a cave where smoke stung her throat. She heard the crackle and snap of fire in the distance, felt its heat sink into her skin. Louder than the fire were the stories, bright and swarming. They were so loud, it was difficult to block them out.

Asha knew exactly where she was. And she knew before she saw him exactly who awaited her.

Elorma stared into the flames as she arrived, as if reading something inscribed there. When she stepped into the firelight, he raised his eyes to her face and pushed his hood back.

"I thought I made the Old One's command perfectly clear," he said gruffly. "The slayers were to be used only for righting wrongs."

"I *was* righting a wrong," Asha said, thinking of the young dragon she killed. "What greater wrong is there to right?"

His lip curled. As if he tasted something sour. "Really, Asha. All this dragon hunting is eroding your imagination."

Asha's temper flared. She didn't have time for nonsense.

"The Old One can try all he likes to stop me, but I'm going to find Kozu. And when I do, I'm going to kill him."

"You're right about the first part," he said. "But we'll have to see about the second."

A loud *crack* broke the silence. Like a branch breaking beneath the weight of a heavy footstep. But it must have been the fire, because there were no trees here. Trees didn't grow in caves.

"The Old One bestows his second gift tonight. And just like his first, this one comes with a command." Elorma rose. "You must keep it from harm."

Something hissed in the darkness. The hair on Asha's arms rose.

This isn't real, she told herself. *This is just a dream.*

But it wasn't a dream. And she wasn't really in a cave, safe below the earth. She was in the Rift, sleeping and exposed.

And she knew before she opened her eyes, something was there with her.

Thirteen

Asha woke. It took a moment for her sight to adjust to the darkness. When it did, there was a single yellow eye, slit through the middle, staring down at her.

Asha's heartbeat quickened with fear. Knowing better than to draw her slayers, Asha reached for her axe. She slid out of her sleeping pack and silently got to her feet.

A series of sharp clicks issued out of the darkness, giving Asha a sense of just how far away this dragon was. She took a slow step back, trying to remember the size of this clearing, and where the trees stopped. But the dark had already descended when she'd made her camp.

The eye disappeared, followed by movement in the trees. Branches snapped. Leaves hissed as a scaly hide brushed past `them. Asha's hand tightened around the handle of her axe, provoking a growl from the dragon.

A heartbeat later, Asha ducked and rolled as a stream of fire lit up the clearing, catching on dried leaves and branches, revealing the biggest dragon she'd ever seen. So big, it could fill Jarek's courtyard.

There was only one dragon that didn't need the power of the old stories to breathe fire: Kozu, the First Dragon. The wellspring of stories.

It had been eight years since they stood face-to-face. Asha had been terrified and trembling then. Nothing more than a child.

Now she was grown and had hundreds of kills to her name.

The First Dragon circled her. In the light of the fires all around her, Asha saw the hideous scar running through his blind eye and down his cheek, hooking just below his jaw. A scar that mirrored her own.

She settled into her fighting stance, ready for this. More than ready. Tonight she would right her wrongs. Tonight, she would put an end to the old ways for good. She would bring back the head of the dragon that had burned her and left her for dead and drop it at her father's feet.

Something whistled fast through the air. With a sickening thud, bright pain lit up Asha's side. She flew sideways with the force of Kozu's pronged tail, now embedded in her ribs.

The breath rushed out of her lungs as she hit the ground. Lying on her back, the world spun around her.

Always know where a dragon's tail is.

It was the first rule of hunting.

Asha brought her axe up and swiftly down. Kozu screamed. The smell of hot, coppery dragon blood made her nostrils flare.

It hurt twice as much when Kozu pulled his tail out.

Blood poured out of her. Asha felt the wool tunic soak it up. She got to her feet to find the fires dying all around her.

Kozu hissed in the darkness, his tail no longer lashing. He was hurt and bleeding, just as she was.

Asha circled, waiting for him to misstep. Her whole right side was soaked. Her head swam. She was losing blood too fast. She needed to stanch it.

Another whoosh and Asha ducked as Kozu's tail sailed over her head, rustling her hair. Drops of hot blood flecked her skin as it went.

Kozu stopped circling. Asha's heart beat loud and sluggish in her ears. Kozu hissed again, but didn't strike.

Three steps. That's all it would take to plunge her axe into his chest. Three steps.

This was her chance.

Asha lunged.

Right before impact, a shadow darted between them, intercepting Asha's killing blow. Her axe edge hit horns instead of flesh and something growled low—but it wasn't Kozu. Asha found herself staring up into pale slitted eyes. Two of them.

She stumbled away.

A second dragon?

The shadow hissed and forced her backward, keeping her from Kozu. Through the darkness, Asha saw its forked tail lashing angrily back and forth.

Red-hot rage flowed through her veins. How dare it come between her and her prey!

Her grip tightened on her axe, but she felt light-headed. The ground dipped and rose. Asha looked down. The right side of her body glistened in the darkness.

The quick, chattering sound of dragon speech echoed through the night. They were talking to each other, Kozu and this shadow dragon. Planning their next move.

Quickly, Asha found her sleeping roll and tore off a wide strip. Gritting her teeth, she wound it around her torso, wrapping that hideous gash in her side. She tied it so tight, the pain made breathing difficult.

A roar made Asha look up, expecting to find both dragons bearing down on her.

Instead, she found them . . . fighting.

Each other.

The shadow dragon was smaller and younger than Kozu, but twice as fast. When Kozu lunged, the younger dragon dodged, circling back to keep itself between the First Dragon and the Iskari. Kozu's tail dripped blood. He swatted and made himself vulnerable. The younger dragon ducked and charged, running circles around the bigger dragon, as if it were a game, as if its plan was to tire the First Dragon out.

If she weren't weak from the blood loss, Asha would have taken advantage of this. She would have struck while the two dragons were occupied.

But she could feel herself losing consciousness. She wanted to put her head down. Needed to close her eyes. . . .

No. Stay awake.

If she didn't get back to the city, if she collapsed right here in the Rift, she would bleed out and die.

Unless a dragon got her first.

Her hands shook as she buckled on her slayers. She left everything she didn't need, including her axe. Asha had plenty of other axes.

Kozu kept charging, trying to get at her, trying to finish what he'd started all those years ago. The shadow dragon blocked, gaining ground, driving Kozu into the trees. Clicking and chattering. Teasing and taunting. It wore the First Dragon down.

Finally, Kozu stopped advancing. Asha felt his slitted gaze on her as she stumbled through the darkness, moving farther away.

A low keening sound split the night, surprising Asha. *A mourning call.* Usually reserved for a dead mate or slain young, the sound was an expression of sadness or grief.

It made Asha shiver. She looked back, following the direction of the sound, but Kozu had disappeared.

The shadow dragon had not.

"Come near me," she growled at it, "and I'll carve out your heart."

The dragon watched her, head cocked, tail thrashing. When she walked, it walked. When she stopped, it stopped. Like a stray pup following her home.

Asha saw Kozu's scar in her mind. Heard the beat of his horrible heart. A moment more and Asha would have dealt a killing blow. This dragon prevented her. The moment it came close enough, she was going to kill it.

But as her rage boiled ever hotter, a voice echoed through her mind:

The Old One bestows his second gift tonight.

Asha stopped walking.

She fixed her gaze on the shadow in the trees.

You must keep it from harm.

This—this *dragon*—was her second gift?

"No. . . ."

As realization sank in, Asha screamed her rage—at Elorma, at the Old One, and at the bloodred moon waning above her. And when she was done screaming, the shadow dragon remained. Head tilted. Eyes fixed on her. As if to say: *Where are you going? Can I come too?*

Fourteen

Asha dragged herself through the temple, then up the dark and dusty stairway. Leaving the flamelit corridors below, her feet tripped on the steps. The slowing thud of her pulse echoed in her ears. Her legs dragged, heavy as chains.

Stay conscious. Just a little longer.

It felt like years passing before she fell against the door, breathing in the sweet cedar. Asha pressed her forehead against the flower carved into the wood, willing it to hold her up.

"Skral!"

Silence answered her. She slammed her palm against the door.

"Please. . . ."

A match struck on the other side. A lock clicked. The door swung in, creaking as it did, and an illuminated face came out of the darkness. Freckled. Sleep smudged.

With her support swinging away from her, Asha struggled to stand and found she couldn't.

"Iskari?"

He caught her, pulling her into him.

"What have you done to yourself?"

But no words formed on Asha's tongue. The skral set down the lantern. He hoisted her up into his arms and kicked the door shut behind them.

Asha woke in the night to a low-burning lamp and the skral bent over her. Someone had changed the yellowing bandages wrapped around his torso. These looked white and fresh.

A sharp pain pricked her side and Asha bolted upright, gasping as the sting flickered through her ribs.

"Hold still," he said, grabbing her shoulder with a warm hand and pushing her back down. His other hand held a needle. It glinted in the lantern light. "I'm almost finished."

She tensed against his touch, but did as he said. He let go of her shoulder. Hunching like a hawk, he frowned in concentration as he gently stitched up her wound—which bled now from the sudden movement.

"Who washed me?" Her blood-soaked tunic was gone and her hair was wet and braided tightly over one shoulder. But that wasn't the worst thing.

She wore a slave's shirt. The linen was thin and plain and rough against Asha's skin.

His shirt, she realized.

She wore *his* shirt and nothing else.

In order to stitch up the gash in her side, he'd pushed the fabric up to her chest and thrown a wool blanket over her waist and legs for modesty. Her entire torso was visible, including her burn scar, which ran down the length of her side, creeping toward her navel.

He met her horrified gaze, saying nothing. He didn't need to. Asha knew in that moment who had washed the blood from her body.

He's just a slave. He's been undressing and bathing his masters all his life. It doesn't matter.

Except it did matter. He'd seen everything. The full extent of her hideousness.

For the first time in a long time, Asha didn't feel proud of her scar.

She felt ashamed of it.

Falling still against the cot, she turned her face away from him.

"Here," he said, lifting a tray from the floor and setting it on her lap. A small plate of olives glistened next to a loaf of bread and olive oil. "You lost a lot of blood. You need to eat something."

"I'm not hungry."

"Iskari."

Asha looked up into his face.

"Please."

Gritting her teeth, Asha propped herself up. She tore off a piece of bread, soaking it in oil before putting it in her mouth.

"What happened?" he asked when the needle went in again.

Asha winced and swallowed the bread. "I found him. Or rather, he found me."

"The dragon you were hunting?"

Asha nodded, tearing off another hunk of bread and dipping it into the olive oil. "This"—she pointed to the gash he was stitching—"is from his tail."

The slave's stitching stopped. "Did you kill him?"

She put the bread in her mouth and shook her head, thinking of the shadow in the trees. The swish of a forked tail.

This is the first time I've come back from a hunt empty-handed.

The fist of her left hand tightened at the thought.

When she remained silent, the slave went back to work. He started humming the tune of a song only to stop, rearrange the notes, then sing them again in a different order. He did this over and over. Like he was testing the song and it kept failing him.

Asha lay back, letting his voice distract her from the teeth-grinding pain of his needle sewing her up.

A story rose to mind, unbidden.

Rayan strode through his mother's orange grove and stopped sharp. Someone was singing. Someone with the voice of a nightingale.

Asha shook the story away. "Can I ask you something, skral?"

The tune halted. Keeping his face tilted toward his work, he raised his eyebrows, peering up at her with just his eyes, making his forehead crinkle.

"Do you believe in the Old One?"

Deciding this only warranted half of his attention, he went back to work. "I have no use for your gods."

"But do you think he's *real*," she said, propping herself up on her elbows to look at him better. The movement sent a sharp pain through her side and she winced. He narrowed his eyes in disapproval.

"He's real to a lot of draksors."

"That's not what I'm asking."

Sighing, he slid the thread out of the needle and tied off the stitching. "*Why* are you asking?" Gently, he ran his fingers across the scarred skin of her side, inspecting his work.

At his touch, a strange warmth bloomed in her belly.

Asha studied him in the orange glow of the lamplight. The silver collar around his throat cast shadows in the hollows of his collarbone. He was a fugitive slave whose life was forfeit. She could tell him everything if she wanted to, and it wouldn't matter.

When she didn't answer, he washed her blood from his fingers in the basin of water on the floor. "I believe in one god," he said, shaking his hands dry. "Death, the Merciful."

She sat up to face him and the linen shirt fell down over her torso, hiding her scar.

He nodded toward her wound, white linen bandages already in his hands. "I still need to wrap it."

"Death is a thief," she said, thinking of an old story. One about Elorma, whose true love was stolen by Death on their wedding night.

The slave took the empty tray off her lap and set it back on the floor. Asha pulled her shirt up again to reveal the freshly stitched gash in her side.

"Maybe for you," he said as he began to bandage her, winding the strips of white around and around her rib cage. More than once, his fingers brushed against her skin. "For some of us, Death is a deliverer."

Asha's gaze lifted. He leaned in so close, she could feel the warmth of him. Like the heat off a fire. When he leaned in farther, to pass the linen from one hand to the other behind her back, his cheek brushed her ear.

Asha's pulse thrummed. He paused and started to turn his face toward her. But something stopped him and his chin straightened. Asha felt him strain to keep his cheek parallel to hers as he continued wrapping, around and around, binding her up.

Asha let out the breath she didn't know she'd been holding.

A windowless room made telling the time of day impossible. So it might have been morning when Asha woke next, or it might have been midnight. But either way, sleep fled, leaving her to stare at shelves full of scrolls in the dim light of the lantern. Her ribs ached when she tried to move, so she didn't move for a long time. When she couldn't take being still anymore, she carefully turned on her side and found someone sleeping on the floor by her cot.

Jarek's slave.

Asleep, he looked like a moonflower whose petals unfurled only at night, rare and beautiful in the starlight. Asha reached down and turned up the lamp so she could better watch the fluttering shadows cast by his eyelashes. She traced the hard, bony lines of him with her eyes. His hair reminded her of the sea in Darmoor: tossed and unruly, full of waves.

She thought of Rayan watching Lillian in the orange grove, then quickly turned on her back, staring up at the ceiling, willing the thoughts in her head to scatter. When they didn't, she pulled the collar of the shirt she wore up over her nose and mouth, breathing in. His smell was there in the linen. A salt musk that made her stomach flutter.

She quickly tugged the shirt down and turned to the shelves full of scrolls on the other side of the cot, trying to distract herself. She touched their wooden handles, running her fingers along the smooth oiled wood. They were new, freshly carved. Asha could tell by the strong smell of thuya wood.

The next thing she knew, she was sitting, fully covered by the slave's shirt. She pulled a scroll down into her lap, ignoring the pain flaring up in her side. It was too dark to see, so she reached for the lamp, bringing it onto the cot with her and turning up the flame.

The moment she started to read was the very same moment she stopped.

It was one of the old stories. The one about the third Namsara, a man who designed the city's aqueducts during a yearlong drought. And just like the handles, the parchment was fresh and crisp. The black ink was bright and gleaming . . . but there was something odd about the strokes. They were shaky and unsure. And some of the words were misspelled.

Asha raised her eyes to the shelf, where hundreds more scrolls were carefully piled. She pulled more down, unrolling them to discover just what she feared: more stories. Each and every one of them forbidden. Stories of the Namsaras—seven of them in total—who rose to defend their people from danger, chasing out enemies and dethroning imposter kings. Stories of the First Dragon, the companion to each Namsara and the living link between the Old One and his people.

Asha pulled scroll after scroll down to her lap, reading one, only to drop it to the floor and reach for another. This was beyond criminal. The old stories had been banished and burned long before Asha was born. Transcribing them and keeping them here was treason.

When she unrolled the next scroll, though, she didn't drop it. Instead, her grip on the handles tightened.

"What does it say?"

Asha glanced up. The slave on the floor yawned and ran his hands through his hair. She looked from him to the wobbly handwriting scrawled across the parchment.

"It's Willa's story," she said. Her mother's voice rose up within her. Or rather, the *echo* of her mother's voice. Despite the years that passed, despite what her mother had done, the memory of her set something glowing in Asha, right beneath her breastbone.

The cot sank in and when Asha looked up again, the slave peered down at the scroll unrolled across her lap. His thigh rested precariously close to her knee, which peeked out from beneath the hem of his shirt. Asha almost told him to move away. But after everything—after he'd bathed her, dressed her wounds—it seemed unnecessary.

"When I was younger," she said, "I had nightmares every night." She hadn't spoken of this in years. "My mother called them *terrors* because even when I opened my eyes, I saw them."

She traced each of the misspelled words on the parchment.

"My mother consulted every physician in the city and they all prescribed something different. Some gave me warm goat's milk before bed. Others hung roots and herbs from my bedposts. One even put the tooth of a dragon beneath my pillow."

She wrinkled her nose.

"Did it work?"

Asha shook her head. "The nightmares grew worse. So my mother tried her own remedy." It didn't matter if she told him. Everyone knew, anyway, because the slaves had stayed to listen at the door. The slaves were the ones who spread the rumor after her death: the dragon queen had told her daughter the old stories to save her, and it was the reason she died so young.

"When she woke to my screaming night after night, my mother left her bed, banished the slaves from my room, and locked herself in with me." Asha glanced up to find him watching her. "She told me the stories until her voice went hoarse and the sun crept in through the windows. They were the only thing that chased the nightmares away."

That was when all the symptoms started: the thinning hair, the lost weight, the shaking and coughing.

And finally, the dying.

Asha rolled up the scroll. She didn't want to talk about this anymore. When she went to drop it with the others, though, she couldn't let go.

"I have nightmares too."

Asha looked to find him staring down at his hands, which

were lying palm up in his lap. She had the strangest urge to touch them. To trace his large palms. To run her fingers along his calluses.

"Ever since I can remember, I've dreamed the same thing, night after night."

"You have the same nightmare *every* night?"

He nodded. "It didn't start out as a nightmare. When I was small, I used to love going to sleep, just so I could see her."

"Her?"

His shoulders rose and fell with the breath he took.

"Yes," he said softly. *"Her."*

He took the scroll from Asha, unrolling it, then rolling it up again. Like his hands needed something to do.

"I used to think she was some kind of goddess. I used to think she was choosing me for some great destiny." His hands tightened on the scroll. When he realized it, he handed it back. "Stupid boy that I was." He forced a crooked smile, one void of lightness. He avoided Asha's eyes as he said, "Now she's a nightmare I can't escape."

His thigh touched her knee. Asha held her breath and looked down, staring at the place where their bodies connected, waiting for him to flinch away.

He didn't.

"Your brother's right, you know. You shouldn't hunt alone."

Those words shattered everything.

Kozu.

Asha didn't know what time of day it was, but she knew one thing for certain: the red moon was thinner than when she'd fallen asleep. Time was slipping away from her.

"I have to go. . . ."

Asha stood. Scrolls clattered to her feet. The white linen shirt she wore fell midway to her knees, leaving her bare legs—one scarred, one smooth—peeking out from beneath the hem.

"Wait," said the slave, pushing off the cot and retrieving something from the floor. "You can't leave like that. Put this on." He handed Asha another plain kaftan made of rough, scratchy fabric. "Maya brought it while you slept."

Her fingers brushed against his as she took it.

She didn't need to ask him to turn around while she dressed; he just did.

After gathering up her armor, Asha reached beneath the cot for her slayers. When she touched the cold marble and nothing else, she dropped to her knees, pain slicing through her side as she searched the floor.

Her slayers weren't there.

But I brought them back with me. I know I did.

She looked around the whole room and . . . nothing. Her slayers were gone.

There was only one other person who'd spent the night in this room. Asha's attention fixed on him like a hunter on her prey. The slave stood at the door, white bandages wrapped around his bare chest, watching her.

"Where are they?"

"I'm not sure what you mean." But his voice said the opposite.

Asha rose and crossed the room, her anger rising in her as

she did. Anger at him for tricking her and anger at herself for letting him.

She slammed him hard into the wood of the door.

The slave hissed through his teeth. His throat arched in pain. It made Asha think of him bound to Jarek's fountain. It made her think of the shaxa shredding his back. She'd probably reopened every one of his wounds.

"Thief," she growled, planting her hands on either side of the door to pin him in place. "Tell me where they are."

His eyes flashed like sharpened steel and his hands grabbed the loose fabric of her kaftan, pulling her in close, reminding Asha that he wasn't innocent. He was a skral. She would need to guard herself much more carefully from now on.

"Tell me how you get past the wall without being seen."

"I don't," she lied.

He stepped in close, stealing her air. So close, the tips of their noses nearly touched. "The soldats let you pass *knowing* you're hunting alone? Your betrothed would never allow it."

"Allow?" Her hands fell to her sides, turning to fists. "Jarek is not *my* master."

"He will be," said the slave.

Asha opened her mouth to snarl at him, except . . . wasn't that what she was afraid of?

Wasn't that why she needed Kozu dead?

Asha lowered her gaze. She stared at his throat, where a frantic pulse betrayed his racing heart.

"You're right," she said in the end. "I don't always use the gate."

"It's only a matter of time before my master finds me," he said. "If I stay here, I'm as good as dead."

Asha's fists uncurled. "Are you asking me to show you the way out?"

He nodded.

What did it matter? He wouldn't survive the Rift on his own.

"Give me back my slayers and I'll show you."

"When?"

"Tonight."

She'd left everything but her armor out in the Rift. She needed to get fresh hunting clothes, a new sleeping pack, and an axe.

"Tonight then," he said.

She looked up to find his eyes softening, his gaze tracing her face.

Asha suddenly felt like a dragon drawn into the thrall of an old story, knowing it was a trap, but drawn nonetheless.

You must take great pains to steel yourself against wickedness.

There had always been something wrong with Asha. Something easily corrupted. Her childhood addiction to the old stories—the very things that killed her mother—was the first sign. The horrible incident with Kozu was the second. And now . . .

This inability to say no to the skral who, for some reason, was important to her brother.

The corner of his mouth lifted, making her pulse quicken.

"I'll be waiting, Iskari."

A Dragon Queen's Betrayal

A realm stood divided by a sea of sand. On one side rose Firgaard, walled and cobbled and refined. On the other sprawled the scrublands, wild and fierce and free. They were old enemies. Bitter rivals.

In the wake of his mother's death, the dragon king wanted peace. Everyone knew it. No one thought he'd win it.

But he did.

In one of the five Great Houses across the sand sea lived Amina—a scrublander girl, and a daughter of the House of Stars. Amina would be his bridge between the old and the new, between a world of cobbled streets and a vast expanse of sand.

The dragon king bound himself to her there in the desert. He brought her home with him to the capital, thinking he was bringing home peace.

Amina was gentle and wise. It didn't matter that she was a scrublander. The people of Firgaard loved her.

Soon, Amina gave birth to two heirs: a boy and a girl. The boy was just like his mother. But the girl was defiant and wild.

"A wicked spirit infects her," the slaves whispered behind closed doors.

"Her scrublander blood has corrupted her," the court said behind their hands.

Amina saw the narrowed eyes. She heard the clucked tongues. But Amina loved her daughter's spirit. Her daughter reminded her of home.

When the nightmares started, when the girl screamed and wept for fear of them, Amina sent for the best physicians in Firgaard. They gave her instructions. They made her remedies. But the nightmares only worsened. And soon the physicians began to look at Amina's daughter the same way everyone else did.

Wicked, Amina saw in their eyes. Infected.

So Amina took matters into her own hands.

When the lanterns turned down and the candles were snuffed and her husband fell to snoring, Amina slipped out of bed and crept down the palace corridors and locked herself in with her daughter.

There, with no one to see her, Amina chased her daughter's nightmares with stories. Old stories. Forbidden stories. She told them aloud, all through the night, until the girl stopped crying and slept.

But every night, as the dragon queen crawled into her daughter's bed and spoke the ancient tales aloud, she grew a little sicker. A little weaker. The stories were poisoning her, just as they'd poisoned the raconteurs before her. The stories were deadly, which is why they were outlawed.

But even as the stories poisoned Amina, they made her daughter stronger. The girl's nightmares stayed away. She slept more soundly than ever.

When the dragon king found out, when he realized the danger his wife had put herself in, he moved to intervene. But it was too late. The stories were draining Amina's life away.

Before the next moon rose, Amina was dead.

It broke the dragon king's heart.

For her treachery—for breaking his own law and putting their daughter in danger—he couldn't give her a proper burning. He couldn't give her the last rites. He could only watch as the guardians abandoned her body outside the gates of the city, to rot in the sun like every other traitor before her.

When the scrublands learned of Amina's death, of her profane funeral, they wept in sorrow and howled in rage. They declared the dragon king a monster and in their fury, took his son and heir—a boy of only twelve, a boy who was a guest in their land—and turned him into a prisoner. He was the heir of a monstrous king who would grow into a monster himself, and they treated him accordingly. In so doing, the scrublanders smashed the dragon king's alliance, scattering its broken shards across the sand.

And Amina, the gentle queen, would never be remembered as the one who cured her daughter's nightmares.

She would always and forever be a traitor.

Fifteen

The problem with returning to the palace four days before her wedding was that the moment Asha stepped through the outer courtyard, she ran the risk of being seen. And if she were seen, she could be summoned.

So Asha was not surprised when she heard someone call, "Iskari!" It was a slave girl. One who worked for the palace seamstresses. "You're late for your fitting."

"What fitting?"

"Your dress fitting."

Asha frowned. Right now she needed fresh hunting clothes, not a fancy dress.

"It's your wedding dress, Iskari."

It was like walking into a trap, one laid just for her. Because at that exact same moment, Jarek stepped directly into her path.

Asha stopped dead.

"I did remind you," the slave said.

Jarek eyed the bundle of armor beneath her arm, then the

kaftan she wore. A kaftan that clearly wasn't hers. She watched him thinking behind his eyes, pondering her strange attire, wondering why she would be carrying dragon-hunting gear but not wearing it. Trying to piece things together but missing bits of the puzzle.

Asha suddenly wanted nothing more than to be hidden away in her room, being measured for a dress. Before he could question her, she brushed past him.

"I'm late for my fitting."

Jarek reached to grab her, but she stepped away quickly.

"Have you seen Safire?" he called.

Asha stopped. She turned to find a smirk marring Jarek's handsome face.

"Neither have I," he said.

Asha turned her back on the commandant. Despite the panic swelling inside her, despite the ice at the base of her spine, she kept her steps measured and calm.

As soon as she turned down the corridor, she started to run.

She didn't go to her room. She went to Safire's, which was empty. The door had been fixed—Asha had asked a slave to swap it with a stronger, newer door from a room down the hall—and there was no sign of any struggle. Everything was in its place.

Asha checked the sickroom next.

Empty. Empty and smelling like fresh-cut limes.

"Please, Iskari, this will go much faster if you hold still."

Her arms ached and the stitched gash in her side bloomed

with pain. She'd been holding still and straight for what seemed like days as the slave girls worked, pinning the delicate fabric where it was too loose and marking it where it was too tight. It was getting harder to keep still with her wound throbbing and her mind humming with worry.

It might be a trick. Jarek knew, better than anyone, how to upset her. He might have mentioned Safire just to unnerve her.

Asha gritted her teeth at the pain in her burned hand. She'd left her fireproof gloves on to keep it hidden. Forcing her outstretched arms to stay perfectly still, she turned her attention back to the slave before her. The one who'd come to fetch her.

"You can lower your arms now, Iskari."

The slave turned away to mark something down. Relieved, Asha did as she said. The other two slaves turned to put away their pins, leaving Asha an unobstructed view of the mirror. Her dress shimmered like sunlight on the sea—which Asha had swum in long ago, on trips to Darmoor with her mother. The port city was surrounded on three sides by a vast expanse of salt water.

The long, petal-shaped sleeves were slit at the elbows and fell past her wrists. Embroidered flowers entwined themselves around her collar. There were two layers: gold underneath and white on top. From the waist down, the wedding dress flared out in shimmering layers of fabric so light, they felt like sea-foam.

It was the prettiest thing she had ever seen.

It did not suit her.

The delicate elegance made her scar stand out even more

than usual. The mottled, discolored skin ran from the right side of her forehead down to her ear and jaw and continued past her throat and shoulders, disappearing beneath the neckline. The rest of it hid beneath the fabric where no one else could see it.

Jarek's slave had seen it, though. He had seen all of her.

The thought sent hot shame rushing through her.

The slave girl returned with a bolt of gold fabric, severing Asha from her reflection. "Can you raise your arms, Iskari?" she asked, holding a soon-to-be sash up to Asha's waist.

Asha raised her arms.

The moment she did, a scream shattered the calm.

Asha and the slave girl looked to the door, where two soldats burst in without knocking, their steel morions askew.

"There's a dragon in the city, Iskari!"

The slaves before her trembled in terror.

Asha slid the top layer of her dress off easily. The bottom layer was another matter. Jarek had this dress made to his exact specifications: the buttons were minuscule, climbing up the back, making it physically impossible for the wearer herself to undo, ensuring that only her husband could get her out of it on their wedding night.

Another show of dominance. Another form of control.

"Get this thing off me!"

Three slaves moved toward Asha at once. Their quaking fingers fumbled the buttons as more screams erupted. The heavy, rhythmic thud of soldat boots echoed down the halls. Asha didn't wait for the slaves to stop their fumbling. She grabbed a hunting knife from where it hung on her wall and placed it in a slave girl's hands. "Cut it off me."

Wide-eyed and terrified, the girl took the knife. Asha turned around. The room fell to silence as the knife ripped through the delicate fabric and the dress loosened around Asha's shoulders and ribs. If they noticed the linen bandages wrapped around her torso, they said nothing.

The moment she was free, Asha pulled on leggings and a thin hunting shirt, then buckled on her armor. She grabbed an axe with a jeweled handle from the wall, given to her by her father on her last birthday. Ornamental until today, but still sharp as the day it was honed. She tucked it into her belt, laced up her boots, and went to find the dragon she thought she'd left behind.

Asha saw it through the arched windows as she ran through the corridors of the palace. Young and lean, the dragon flew into view as the city below descended into screaming chaos. The bright sun silhouetted its form.

The second time it flew into view, she knew its forked red tail and the curve of its head.

As she ran through the outer court, leaving the sun behind, it flew into view a third time. This time, she recognized its pale, slitted eyes. They were the eyes staring down at her last night when her killing blow was intercepted.

Elorma's words rang through her mind:

You must keep it from harm.

Soldats ran past Asha shouting contradictory orders of "Get to the roof!" and "Get to the street!"

In the case of a dragon in Firgaard, a soldat's first priority was to the city. Palace soldats were instructed to abandon their posts and either make for the roof with arrows and spears—things that could take down a dragon—or head to the narrow, winding streets to make order of the chaos.

The street was the most dangerous place to be with a dragon on the loose.

Asha ran with them out of the palace and into the street, where carts lay overturned. Merchant stalls stood abandoned. As people ran in every direction away from the dragon, half trampling one another, soldats tried to keep people calm, corralling them into their homes.

A few braver ones stood on rooftops with the soldats, loading slings with shards of glass, stones, and bits of broken bone. The dragon roared when the projectiles hit. Asha thought he might retaliate, but instead, he rose higher and flew toward the Rift.

Asha followed him to the north gate.

The wall came into view, shielding the mountains beyond. Soldats stood straight as columns along its dusty ramparts, all staring up at the shape in the sky. Jarek had doubled their presence after the last big raid of the slave quarters, when weapons were found hidden in cupboards and pots, shoved beneath mattresses, and tucked into bed frames.

On the ground, half a dozen soldats stood in a line, blocking the gate. Asha slowed at the sight of them.

"You don't need to go out there, Iskari. The commandant already sent out hunters."

Asha's hand tightened on the handle of her axe. What would

happen if Jarek's men killed the beast?

Asha remembered her paralyzed arm—punishment for mis-using the Old One's first gift and disobeying the command that accompanied it.

She needed to stop those hunters.

"Open the gate."

Beneath their steel brims, the soldats exchanged glances.

"We're under orders *not* to open it, Iskari."

Asha frowned. "Orders from who?" Surely not her father.

"From the commandant."

"Do you serve Jarek or do you serve the king?" Asha's thumb slid across the sharpened edge of her axe. "Because it was my father who gave me this task, to hunt down each and every dragon"—she pointed to the shadow in the sky—"including that one."

They didn't answer her. They didn't have to. Their silence was a clear indication they followed the king's orders . . . until those orders conflicted with their commandant's.

Asha prickled with unease. It was just as she feared. "Open the gate."

Over their shoulders, the dragon dived down into the Rift—where hunters waited to kill it.

"*Open it!*"

Nobody moved.

"*Asha,*" growled a voice.

Fire flickered through her. She spun to face Jarek, who was coming at her like a storm. His official crest—two interlaced sabers—blazed across his chest.

"Tell them to open it," she demanded, pointing her axe edge at the gate.

Jarek stepped right up to her, his gaze boring into her. It was one of the reasons people stood in such awe of the commandant: he didn't fear her in the least.

"Tell me where *he* is," he said, "and I'll consider it."

He.

The slave.

Why did he seem so important to everyone around her?

She thought of his callused fingers stitching up her side by candlelight. Thought of his knee, so near her own, as she told him about her nightmares.

Asha shoved all thoughts of him down deep and glared up at Jarek.

"Isn't it *your* duty to find and catch criminals? Perhaps if you stop interfering with my tasks, you will more quickly accomplish your own."

His eyes flashed at her.

"Five hunters have a head start on you, Asha. One of *them* will take it down."

"You and I both know I can kill that dragon long before the others," she growled. *"I am the Iskari."*

He grabbed her arm, squeezing until it hurt, showing just how easily he could overcome her, Iskari or not. He *would* overcome her, once they were bound. Once there was no one to stop him.

She couldn't let that happen.

He leaned in close. "It's my duty to keep you out of danger, *Iskari.*"

Asha's eyes filled with fire. The fire filled up her vision, turning everything red-hot.

Didn't he understand?

"I *am* the danger!" she said.

Jarek nodded to a nearby soldat.

Bristling, Asha watched the soldat slide a ring of keys out of his pocket. Watched him step through a door in the wall. It led up to the ramparts, she knew. Jarek kept a few small cells there, for suspicious travelers seeking passage through the gate.

When the soldat emerged, he had Asha's cousin in tow.

The hood of Safire's mantle crumpled around her shoulders. Her left eye was swollen shut, ringed by a purplish-black bruise, and her lower lip was split down the middle. The hem of her clothing was stained red, and from the way she kept her arm tucked against her hip, it hurt her badly.

The sight of Safire beaten was a knife in Asha's heart.

This was what happened when you didn't give Jarek what he wanted.

The dragon beyond the walls would have to wait.

Sixteen

Asha took her cousin to Dax. As Safire explained everything that had happened, Dax stood there listening, silent and still, his brown eyes hardening under his darkening brow.

Roa wasn't with him.

Good, Asha thought. She hoped her brother had come to his senses and was keeping the scrublanders far away from the king.

While Dax kept watch over their cousin, Asha sharpened her jeweled axe and waited for the sun to set. Beneath the cover of darkness, she'd have a better chance of not being seen by Jarek's soldats. The moment the golden orb slipped below the shoulder of the mountain, she climbed into her arched window, threw her helmet onto the roof, and swung herself up after it.

Asha took the rooftops to the palace orchards, which were abandoned at dusk. The flowering trees filled the air with the sweet scent of blossoms, and the fruit bats' fluttering shapes skimmed the branches. She lowered herself over the palace's outermost wall and dropped to the street below.

Asha zigzagged through the city, away from the singing and drumming of the night market and the coaxing calls of its merchants. She took narrow streets where soldats were least likely to roam, until she arrived at the temple doors and quietly stepped inside.

With her helmet tucked beneath her arm, Asha stood at the cedar door, raised her fist, and knocked.

"Iskari?" The slave boy opened the door, letting her inside. She pushed her way past him. "Are you all right?"

Asha headed for the twin black blades resting on the cot, thinking of Kozu's head dripping blood as she dragged it through Firgaard's streets. Thinking of the look on Jarek's face as the thing he wanted most was taken from him.

"What happened?"

Asha thought about Safire's bruised and battered face.

"I wish I knew how to make him afraid," she said.

A strange silence filled the space between them. Asha looked up to find the slave staring at her. Seeing everything, somehow. Hearing every word she didn't say.

She looked away, her gaze settling on the shelves full of scrolls.

Something flickered in her then. A memory. Her brother in this very room, pulling scrolls off this shelf. Scrolls full of uneven handwriting and misspelled words.

Asha pulled a scroll from the shelf and unrolled it, staring at the shaky letters scrawled across its crisp, white surface. Recently done.

She remembered long-ago lessons with Dax, remembered their tutors' frustration when he couldn't read the words. Remembered the things they muttered under their breath when they thought he couldn't hear.

Stupid. Useless. Worthless.

Everyone assumed Dax had never learned to write.

Unless he did, thought Asha, *and no one noticed.*

She thought of Dax's trembling. Of the lost weight. Of the light that usually shone in his eyes, sapped from him. Asha thought backward. Her mother's symptoms started when she began telling Asha the old stories at night.

What if Dax was writing the old stories on these scrolls?

And if he was, what if writing them down had the same effect as telling them?

"You look like you've seen a ghost, Iskari."

Asha glanced up into the slave's eyes.

"It's my brother," she said. "I think he might be sick."

She thought back to her mother. *What came after the shaking? Coughing.*

She would be alert, watching for the symptom—after she took care of Kozu.

The slave wore Jarek's crimson mantle. With the hood up and the tassels securing it around his throat and shoulders, he was unrecognizable. Not that there was much need for disguise, because as the Iskari led Jarek's slave through the stairways deep below the temple, they didn't pass a single guardian.

"Tell me about those blades strapped to your back," he said.

"Tell me why a house slave knows so much about hunting laws." Now that they were in the crypt, Asha lit the lamp. The orange glow flickered over the rock walls. It cast shadows into long, narrow alcoves, revealing rows upon rows of sacred jars. Jars full of her ancestors' remains.

"Greta was a hunting slave before my master purchased her," he explained.

Greta. The elderly slave. Her name sank inside Asha like a stone. He didn't know Greta was dead, she realized. He had been convalescing here in the temple. In his mind, Greta was safe and sound in the furrow.

"Everything I know about hunting and dragons, Greta taught me." His fingers trailed along the damp, glistening walls, as if caught in memories. "Everything I know about anything, I know because of her. Greta raised me."

Asha thought of that night in Jarek's home. Of the tears in Greta's eyes as she opened the door. She should have been in the furrow, but she'd stayed behind. Because she loved this slave, Asha realized now.

She swallowed. Someone had to tell him.

"Greta is dead."

His footsteps faltered and an icy chill slipped beneath Asha's skin. He was outside the glow of her lamp now and she couldn't see him.

"What?" It was more of a breath than a word.

Asha stood still. "I—I watched her die."

Silence seeped out of the darkness. And then a muffled cry echoed through the crypt as a fist struck stone. Asha's throat constricted at the sound. Very slowly, she walked until her lamplight found him. He'd sunk to the ground with his elbows on his knees and his palms pressed hard into his eyes.

Asha couldn't remember the last time she'd cried. She didn't know what to say to him. But saying nothing felt wrong. Like her rib cage was suddenly too small and getting tighter around her heart.

"The tunnel is there," she said when the silence started to claw at her. Lifting the lantern, she illuminated the slit in the rock. "Now you know. You can escape into the Rift. You don't ever have to return. You're free."

And now Asha could add *liberating a slave* to her list of criminal activities.

He didn't say a word. Didn't even lift his head.

Asha, not knowing what else to do, left him there. She needed to find her shadow dragon. And then she needed to hunt down Kozu. She had only four more days.

She'd done what she'd promised. She showed him the tunnel. It was his own fault if he got caught there, sobbing like a child.

But the higher she climbed, the more she thought. Even if the skral managed to make his way up into the Rift, there were wild creatures, the elements, and of course, Jarek's hunters. What if they caught him?

So Asha turned around and went back.

Seventeen

They hadn't spoken a word since they made their way to the
end of the tunnel. Which was fine with Asha. She didn't need
to talk.

When they stepped out into the moonlight, the soft whoo of
an owl greeted them. Asha breathed in the cool night air just as
the slave abruptly stopped. His arm shot out and Asha walked
right into it. She was about to push it away when, in the cedar
forest ahead, she saw what made him stop: two pale, slitted eyes
peered at them through the darkness.

Asha let out a shaky breath.

Shadow dragon. So the hunters hadn't found it.

"Keep walking," she told him.

"What?"

"You'll see."

Asha moved into the cedars. Out of sight, the dragon crept
along beside them. Above the hush of the wind, Asha could
hear its bulk brushing against the leaves. Could hear the soft

click of its scales rippling as it moved. Asha kept walking until the trees grew thicker and closer together, following the sound of trickling water. At the small stream, Asha stopped. It smelled like wet earth. Crouching down into the grass, she peered into the trees where the dragon stalked, staring back at her, wondering what in all the skies she was supposed to do now.

The slave sat down next to her, his eyes wide, his body shivering.

"I said you can leave," she told him, sitting too and curling her arms around her knees. "I'm not going to stop you."

"Do you know what the punishment is for freeing a slave?"

Asha knew.

"The loss of a hand," he said, in case she didn't.

Asha shrugged. They'd have to prove it was she who did it. And she needed only one hand to kill Kozu.

"Steer clear of the hunting paths," she told him. "They start here, in the lower Rift, and go west, toward the breeding grounds. If you stay east, you *might* make it to Darmoor." But that was a very long walk on foot. And the Rift was a wild, dangerous place. The chances of his making it, alone, were slim.

He must have known this, because he said, "I think I'll stay right here for now."

Asha looked at him.

He reached for a long strand of esparto grass, twisting it around his fingers. "There's a dragon in there." He nodded toward the trees up ahead while plucking two more grass strands. He wove these together, fashioning a kind of braid. "And since you happen to be a dragon hunter, I plan to stick with you until it's either dead or gone."

"Unfortunately for us both," Asha muttered, "neither of those outcomes is forthcoming."

"What?" He looked into the trees where the dragon crouched, then back at Asha. "Why not?"

She sighed. The air heaved out of her in a rush and she fell back into the grass, looking up at the moon: a mere sliver of red in a black sky.

"I can't kill it," she whispered. "I wish I could. But I—" She shot him an embarrassed look. "I'm supposed to protect it."

The slave peered down at her, blocking the sliver of moon. "But you're the Iskari. The king's dragon *hunter*."

"If it dies," she said, looking up into his face, "the Old One will punish me."

"The Old One . . . ?" He raised an eyebrow. There was a hint of mockery in it. "Iskari, you've killed hundreds of dragons. Did he punish you for any of those?" He planted one hand just above her head, leaning in closer.

Too close.

Asha's pulse quickened. She ducked out from under him and rose to her feet. Putting all her focus back on the dragon in the trees, she sloshed through the spring. If she could catch it, maybe she could tame it. And if she could tame it, maybe she could teach it not to follow her into the city.

She felt it in the trees, crouched and ready to spring away. She approached slowly. Cautiously. When she was mere steps away, she slowed even more. Clicking gently, she mimicked the noises dragons made in an attempt to coax it to her.

The dragon vanished into the darkness.

"Great! Go!" she shouted, picking up rocks from the spring bed and, one after another, chucking them into the trees. "I hate the sight of you!"

When she ran out of rocks, she said, without looking at the slave across the stream, "It followed me all the way to the palace, but doesn't let me come closer than that." Turning, she thrashed through the shallow water, kicking her helmet on her way back to the slave. "So how am I supposed to keep it from harm?"

His gaze ran up and down her.

"Honestly? If I were a dragon, I wouldn't come anywhere near you either."

Asha looked where he was looking: from her armor to her boots to the helmet at her feet. She picked up the helmet, studying it. Everything she wore was made from the skins of dragons.

The slave reached for her helmet. Asha's grip on it tightened.

He tugged the helmet out of her hands anyway. "Trust me."

Fear rippled through her as she remembered how it felt as a child to stand armorless before Kozu.

The fire rushing toward her.

The screams trapped in her throat.

Her flesh burning away.

With her helmet tucked under his arm now, he stepped in close. Close enough to reach for the buckles of her breastplate. Holding her gaze, he began to undo them.

Asha's heart raced and her breath came quick.

"Definitely *not*," she said, stepping away.

"Fine." He set down the helmet at her feet. Taking off his

sandals and rolling his pants up to his knees, he sat next to the stream and slid his bare feet into the water. "Maybe by morning you'll have scared it away entirely and I can be safely on my way."

He kicked at the water with his feet while his hands remained planted on the bank.

Asha stood alone in the moonlight, staring down at herself.

What was she afraid of? If the dragon wanted to kill her, it would have done so already. Wouldn't it?

Asha started undoing buckles and taking off pieces of armor. The burn on her axe hand hurt as much as ever. She unbuckled the slayers from her back, then shrugged them off and dropped them next to her armor. The night air rushed up her hunting shirt and across her bare arms. Crouching low, Asha began unlacing her boots. One by one, she slid them off.

In her bare feet, with the esparto grass brushing against her knees, Asha felt . . . unsheathed. The wind tugged at her hair. The night air kissed her scarred skin. She'd thought standing armorless before a watching dragon would make her feel vulnerable and exposed. And she did feel those things. But she felt something else too.

Unfettered.

Wild.

Free.

Without a single thing to protect her, she moved past the slave, through the stream, and back into the trees—toward those slitted eyes. She heard the anxious swish of a forked tail as she approached.

Three steps. Then two. Then . . .

The dragon fled.

Balling her hands into fists, Asha growled. "It didn't work!"

The slave's dark silhouette moved toward her. But Asha walked right past him, back through the cold water of the stream, shivering in the night. What a mistake this had been.

When she stood over her pile of armor, though, she no longer recognized it. It looked more like the discarded skin of a lizard and she couldn't bring herself to buckle any of it back on.

"I'm wasting time," she said, thinking of Kozu prowling the Rift somewhere. She should be hunting him down, not trying to tame this senseless beast. There were only four more days until her binding night. Four more days before Jarek took her to his bed.

Her eyes stung at the thought. Asha pressed her palms against her forehead and crouched down in the grass.

A shadow fell across her. "He's a wild creature, Iskari. And you're a hunter. You can't expect him to come when you call. You have to earn his trust."

Asha looked up at the slave's silhouette. "So what do I do?"

"You wait," he said. "You let him come to you."

The moon was waning. Asha couldn't wait.

But maybe she didn't have to. How many times in the past year had she lured a dragon to her? Too many times. The thought of it made her stomach clench. If she lured *this* one to her, the slave would know she'd been using the old stories. She was still the same corrupted girl who'd brought disaster upon her people.

But then, who cared what the slave knew?

Sinking back on her palms, Asha took a deep breath and began.

Willa's Story

Willa was a farmer's daughter. She was a problem for her parents, who couldn't marry her off, because no one wanted a wife who needed to stop and rest in the middle of a harvest. No one wanted a wife who might not last through childbirth.

Willa had a weak heart and it made her a burden—until the day she went to graze the sheep and never came back.

The Old One appeared to her out in the sand hills. He'd set her apart for his first Namsara. She was to be Elorma's hika—a sacred companion, a perfect match, fashioned for him like the sky fitted the earth. The Old One told her to leave her family behind and seek Elorma out. Willa, who had always been devout, did as she was bidden.

She set out across the desert; and when she arrived in Firgaard weeks later, stepping through the temple doors, Elorma—who'd never seen her before in his life—knew exactly who she was.

It was nine moons before they could marry, though, because Willa was not yet eighteen. In that time, Elorma taught her to read and write so she could help him in the temple. He explained Firgaard customs and taught her the ways of city dwellers, and he never minded, not once, when she needed to stop and rest because of the weakness in her heart. In fact, with every day that passed, Elorma fell a little bit more in love with her.

But Willa did not love him back. She would do as she was bidden, but the Old One could not make her love a man. Elorma tried to win her affection. He brought her gifts, and when they didn't work, he wrote her poems, which didn't work either. So Elorma went to the Old One for guidance, but the Old One kept silent.

One day, the city was set upon by enemies from the west. Elorma himself was captured and held hostage while the invaders established themselves as rulers over the city. It was Willa who herded the people of Firgaard and led them in a revolt. It was Willa who stood before the imposter king with a thousand fists at her back, demanding he hand over her betrothed.

After they'd chased the invaders out, Elorma beseeched the Old One to release Willa from their bond. He didn't want to be responsible for clapping a bird in irons and forcing it into a cage.

This time, the Old One granted his request.

Elorma sought Willa out. He told her to return to her old life and be free.

But Willa refused. The people of Firgaard no longer saw her as a silly peasant girl. She was a hero in their eyes, and the city was her home now. Willa was Elorma's match.

On the night of their binding, Elorma waited in the temple while Willa made her way through the streets. The citizens of Firgaard threw flowers at her feet. They kissed her cheeks and wished her well, and Willa's heart glowed within her. She was a burden no longer.

But Willa never made it to Elorma. She heard Death call her name and her weak and glowing heart faltered.

As Willa collapsed to her knees on the cobbles, the cheers around her went silent.

"My love," she whispered, "I'll wait for you at Death's gate."

The wind carried her words to Elorma, who ran to the girl he loved. But before he could reach her, Willa's heart stopped beating. Death, the thief, stole her away.

When Elorma reached her, Willa's body was still warm. He clung to her, cursing the Old One for not saving her, weeping into her hair.

But when Willa arrived at Death's gate, she planted her feet and looked back to the land of the living. Souls were not permitted to linger at the gate, so Death himself came out to sway her.

She was unmoved.

He sent a sweeping cold to freeze the love in her heart—but Willa didn't budge.

He sent a raging fire to burn away her memories—but Willa held them fast.

He sent a wind as strong as the sea to force her through—but Willa grabbed hold of the bars and wouldn't let go.

So Death gave up and left her alone, thinking time itself would wear her away. But Willa's loyalty never wavered. She waited until Elorma himself stepped up to the gate, a lifetime later, and the moment he did, she let go of the bars.

"What took you so long?" she asked. And then, taking his hand in hers, Willa walked her beloved into death.

Eighteen

After Asha's voice went silent, the old story remained within her, brimming with power. The version on the scroll ended with Elorma walking Willa through the gate. But Asha didn't like that ending. It was Willa's story. Willa withstood cold and fire and wind and time. She should be the one to walk Elorma through. So Asha changed the last line.

When the story released its hold on her, she came back to the woods to find the slave leaning toward her. Asha was once again struck by the gentleness in his gaze. It didn't possess her like Jarek's gaze did. Nor did it fear her, like everyone else's. This slave's gaze was tender and featherlight.

A soft *whuff* broke through the silence. Their eyes snapped upward to the dragon standing over them, its breath hot and rank on their faces, its tail swishing dangerously.

The slitted eyes narrowed. A growl rumbled low.

Asha—still armorless and unarmed—panicked. She scrambled up and away.

"No." Pain flared through her ribs as the slave grabbed her hard around the stomach, swinging her back to face the dragon. "Don't run."

Fire, red and raging. Burning up her skin and sealing off her screams . . .

He withstood her fists and elbows. He held her fast. And all the while the dragon crept closer.

"Hush. Stop fighting."

When it was clear the slave wasn't letting go, Asha gave up. Terrified, she turned into him, waiting for the dragon to strike.

The night stilled around them. Her heart hammered in her ears.

"Iskari." His arms loosened around her waist. "Look."

The dragon sat. Its head cocked, watching them.

The slave clicked at the creature, making Asha wonder if Greta had explained more to him than she realized.

With one arm secure around her waist, he held his other out, clicking softly, trying to coax the dragon to them. Asha held her breath.

It seemed unsure, its gaze moving from the slave's outstretched hand to the Iskari and back. After several heartbeats, it crept forward, watching Asha the entire time. It sniffed at his palm, then nudged it gently. The slave's arm tightened around her, as if fearing she might run. He slid his hand over the dragon's scaly snout, then took Asha's good hand in his and slowly held it out.

It was a long time before the dragon sniffed at her fingers, even longer before it nudged her palm. When it came in close, whuffing at her neck, Asha cautiously took hold of its snout. It had terrible breath. Like rotting meat.

"Explain something to me," he whispered against her cheek. "The stories made your mother sick, right?"

"Yes," said Asha, breathing in the thick, smoky scent of the dragon.

"So why don't they do the same to you?"

"My mother was too soft," she said, following his lead and running her own hand over the dragon's warm snout. "Too good. She couldn't control them. They ate away at her like poison. Just like they did with the raconteurs. I'm—different."

When she looked to see if he understood, there was thunder in his brow.

"It's difficult to explain."

Asha turned back to the dragon, resting her forehead against its rough scales. The moment she did, her mind flickered like a candle flame. Images came in flashes and bursts: *a hooded man riding a black dragon, an army advancing across the desert.*

Asha pulled away and the images flickered out. She eyed the dragon, which darted around her and the slave, circling excitedly. Finally, it settled in a crouch and looked up into her face. As if anticipating some kind of game.

The slave said something, but Asha didn't hear him. She was thinking back. Remembering herself from years before—the girl with the butterfly heart. Asha stepped toward the dragon and took its snout in her hands. Once again, images flared up in her mind.

It was the dragon. It was trying to tell her a story, she realized, in exchange for the one she'd told. Only instead of words strung together in a sequence, it sent flashes of images into Asha's mind. They were like shards of glittering glass, sometimes too sharp to grasp, sometimes out of order.

Eight years had made her forget: dragons liked to tell stories almost as much as they liked to hear them. Asha forced herself to go back, to remember years *with* the dragons rather than against them.

Kozu's storytelling was beautiful. Never hard to decipher. But this dragon chattered like a child who hadn't yet learned how to form proper sentences.

Asha closed her eyes, trying to focus. She struggled to piece the flashes of images together, like assembling a mosaic in her mind.

There was the hooded man—he seemed important. He kept coming up over and over again, riding atop an inky-black dragon. Kozu, Asha realized, before he'd been scarred. But only a Namsara would dare ride the First Dragon. So the man had to be a Namsara.

It was the woman riding next to them, though, who interested Asha most. She wore Asha's father's citrine medallion. And while this woman was young, Asha knew her face. She knew those hard, disapproving eyes. They stared out at her from a tapestry in her father's throne room.

The woman was Asha's grandmother.

And the story was about the last Namsara, she realized. But the dragon's story didn't end where it normally did—with the skral being clapped into irons and turned into slaves. The dragon was telling her the part that came afterward.

The Severing Retold

The Old One granted the dragon queen victory over the skral. He gave her a Namsara who led her straight to the enemy's camp while they slept. He gave her protection against her enemies. And what did she do in return?

She dishonored him.

She did not chase the skral out of the realm as he had commanded. Instead, she enslaved them.

"Draksors don't take slaves," the Namsara told her. "The Old One forbids it."

"Just think of what we can accomplish!" said the dragon queen. "With our enemies forced to serve us, think of how powerful we will be! No one will dare come against us again."

"To defy the Old One's commands will be your undoing," the Namsara warned.

The queen enslaved the skral anyway.

The city's narrow, winding streets filled with slaves being fitted for collars. Gold for the palace. Silver for the wealthy. Iron for the rest.

The Namsara came to the dragon queen with a second warning. "The Old One will show mercy, but you must release the enemy. Break their collars and set them loose."

The queen banished the Namsara from her sight.

The slaves were given roles, and rules were made to govern them: Never look a draksor in the eye or speak their name aloud. Never touch *a draksor other than your master. Never drink out of a draksor's cup or eat off their plate.*

The Namsara came a third and final time. This time, he did not beseech the queen. Nor did he offer mercy. Instead, he declared, for all the city to hear:

"This will be a sign the Old One has left you. Your fiercest allies will turn against you. They will burn down your homes and attack your families, and their fleeing shadows will drive a wedge between all of Firgaard."

And that's exactly what happened.

Nineteen

The dragon was a liar.

Its story was all wrong. The skral were ruthless. They'd pillaged and burned every city they came across. They left only ruin in their wake. If the dragon queen let them go, their horror would continue. Asha's grandmother had been protecting her people and everyone else.

The dragon was twisting the truth. Just like Asha herself had changed the end of her story, this dragon had changed his.

Later that night, Asha woke to the smell of smoke. Ready to yell at the slave reckless enough to make a fire and give their location away, she bolted to her feet. But the words fell silent on her lips in the presence of the man sitting opposite her. A fire roared between them, but it was no campfire. And there was no sign of the skral or the dragon.

Elorma sat across from her instead. "You've done well with your second gift," he said. "The Old One is pleased."

Asha's temper curled around her like smoke. "The Old One can eat sand."

His mouth quirked up at the side. "Let's see how you do with your next gift."

"No," she said. "Please, no more."

"You'll like this one. I promise." He pushed his hood back and his gaze slid to the burn scar running down her face. "I think you'll find it . . . useful."

Asha knew better. She gritted her teeth. Her fists clenched. "No matter how many times the Old One gets in my way, I'm still going to kill his dragon. I swear it."

Elorma sighed, then got to his feet.

"The Old One bestows his third gift," he said wearily. *Fireskin.* You'll need it to fulfill this next command."

Fireskin?

Her fists uncurled.

"You will take the sacred flame from the thief who stole it and return it to where it belongs."

A jolt of panic shot up through her legs. *Her father* took the sacred flame from the caves—where it belonged.

"You want me to commit treason . . . against my own father?"

Elorma's silence confirmed it.

Suddenly she couldn't catch her breath. As if she'd been running.

She felt dizzy. So dizzy, she sank to the ground and put her head on her knees, trying to make the world go still. Trying to force it to make sense again.

She thought of her father in the sickroom, holding her hand through the long, pain-filled nights. Standing fast at her side while her people hissed and spat at her feet. Looking at her with pride whenever she returned from a hunt with a dragon's head on a platter.

Asha couldn't. She wouldn't betray him.

Even if she dared to, there was no way to succeed. A thief couldn't just march in and take the sacred flame. She would be seen and stopped immediately.

"I can't do it," she said. "It's impossible."

"You'll find a way," said Elorma.

When Asha woke, the larks were singing the sky awake and the sun was a haze of gold setting the tops of the trees aglow. Nearby, the red dragon wheezed as it slept.

It was as if the world knew nothing of the wicked task the Old One had set for her.

Asha didn't want to play this game anymore. In three days, she'd be bound to Jarek. She needed to hunt down Kozu. It was the only way to halt the coming tide.

She needed a plan—a way to outwit the Old One.

Asha rubbed the lingering sleep from her eyes, then stopped when she realized her burned hand didn't hurt. She lifted the bandaged hand in front of her face, then started to unwrap it.

When the linen fell away, she stared in shock.

Yesterday her hand was raw and scorched. Today there was the tough skin of a scar. It took up the whole of her palm and some of her fingers. Her burn had healed completely.

Asha sat up. What was it Elorma had said about the Old One's third gift?

Fireskin, he'd called it.

But what does that mean?

She had the tiniest spark of a notion.

Asha reached for the matches next to the lamp and lit one. When it flared to life, she held her breath. Very slowly, she held the quivering flame under her palm and started to count.

One. Two. Three.

Four. Five. Six.

Seven. Eight. Nine . . .

Nothing. No pain.

A slow smile spread across her lips. If she were impervious to fire, how much easier would killing Kozu be?

A hand shot out, knocking the match from her fingers. It hit the earth and died.

"What is wrong with you?" The slave crouched beside her, breathless. On his shoulder perched a hawk as white as mist. It stared at Asha with silvery eyes.

The sight of it startled her. "Is that *Roa's* hawk?"

He reached up to touch its white feathers, as if he'd forgotten it was there. "Her name's Essie." Shaking his head, he returned to the original subject. "Were you just trying to hurt yourself?" He frowned. As if Asha trying to hurt herself was something for him to be concerned about.

"Yes," she said, looking up into his face. She reached for another match and lit it. Keeping her eyes locked on his stormy ones, she raised her hand above the flame and held it there. It tickled. It warmed. But it never burned.

"It's my third gift."

The frown in his brow deepened. "What?"

Asha shook out the match. "He wants me to use it to steal the sacred flame."

"*Who* wants you to use it?" His eyebrows were two hard, dark lines. He seemed exceptionally agitated this morning. Asha looked to the hawk—*Essie*—wondering if its presence was the reason. "What are you talking about?"

Their voices woke the dragon, who sat up.

"The Old One gave me this," she said, raising the scarred hand she'd tried to burn. "Just like he gave me that," she said, nodding to the dragon—now prowling through the grass toward them. "Just like he gave me those." She pointed to the slayers, sheathed on the ground beside her. "And every gift comes with a command."

He reached for her hand. Surprised, Asha let him take it. He frowned as he studied it, his thumb brushing across the rough, discolored skin, sending warmth blooming through her.

"That's not possible," he said. From her perch on his shoulder, Essie peered down too. "I just bandaged this a few days ago. It was completely raw."

Asha watched the smooth sweep of his thumb. Once again, she thought of her mother, of the way she'd reach out and tuck a strand of Asha's hair behind her ear. Or grab Asha as she ran down the corridor and pull her into a hug. Asha always squirmed away—she'd had better things to do.

Now, though, she wondered what those things were.

He let go of her hand, snapping Asha out of her memories.

"What is the command?" His gaze slid to her hair.

She ran her fingers over her braid and found it coming undone. "I have to steal the sacred flame and return it to the caves."

"And you're going to?"

"I don't know." Maybe she could just steal it temporarily. Until she killed Kozu. After that, the flame wouldn't matter anymore. Nothing connected to the old ways would.

The old stories were like the branches of an argan tree and Kozu the thirsty root: cut off the root and the branches withered and died. To silence the First Dragon's heart was to silence the stories forever, and with them, the Old One's link to his people.

The moment Kozu died, the old ways would crumble and turn to dust.

Asha shook out her dark hair, running her fingers through it.

When she looked up, she found the slave staring. He turned his face away so fast, Essie squawked at the sudden movement. She flapped her white wings and flew off his shoulder.

"You need me," he said without looking at her.

"What?"

"You said yourself he follows you." He looked to where the dragon pounced on the hawk, dust-red scales rippling. A blur of white flew out from under him, screeching in annoyance. "As soon as you go back, what's to stop him from flying after you again into the city?"

Essie's flapping wings sounded like the soft hush of

Darmoor's sea. The dragon stared into the sky, contemplating his lost prey, then slunk over to where Asha sat. He walked two circles around her and the slave, then sank to the ground, blocking the sunlight with his folded wings. Lying down, the dragon was roughly the height of a horse.

The slave was right: if she was going to complete this task, she'd need a way to keep the beast in place. She didn't have time to teach it to stay. And she couldn't risk it following her again.

The dragon nudged Asha's arm. She ignored him. When he nudged harder, she moved away.

The slave clicked, dragging his attention from Asha and luring it to himself. He scratched the scaly chin, and the dragon's eyes half closed with pleasure.

"Are you offering to watch the dragon for me?"

"For a price, yes."

Asha's skin prickled. "What price?"

"You promise to fly me to Darmoor when you finish your task."

Asha started at him. Was he *serious*?

"If you fly me to Darmoor," he said, "I can find work aboard a ship sailing far across the sea and you'll never have to see me again."

"I can't just fly you wherever you want."

"Why not?"

She looked to the dragon. "I—I've never ridden one."

That's how links between dragons and draksors were formed: in flight. This creature's attachment was already an inconvenience. Asha didn't want to deepen it.

"How hard can it be? Your ancestors did it."

"The dragons *turned* on my ancestors. Besides, I don't have time to fly you anywhere," she said, looking to the pure blue sky. The daylight had whisked the waning moon away.

"And why's that?"

All these infernal questions! Asha threw up her hands in surrender. "I only have three days left to hunt Kozu."

The quirk in his mouth flattened.

Asha lowered her gaze to the dusty earth. "If I kill Kozu, my father will cancel my wedding."

"What?" His brow furrowed. "Why would he—"

"My father is intent on destroying the old ways." To escape his piercing look, she started tracing symbols in the dirt. The flower pattern from the sickroom tiles began to emerge: elegant, seven-petaled namsaras. "But the Old One keeps sending me 'gifts,' which always come with commands. . . . It seems to be his way of slowing me down." She shook her head. "So you see, I can't help you. I have only so much time."

The slave was quiet a moment. *"After* you kill Kozu," he said, "then you could fly me to Darmoor."

"There's just one problem," Asha growled, smudging the sand-etched flowers. *"I don't ride dragons."*

"If you want me to keep your dragon safe while you go off on your suicide mission, then you'll just have to learn. It's the price I'm asking."

Asha looked to the red dragon. How could she soar through the sky on one of the very creatures she'd sworn to hunt into extinction?

Once she killed the First Dragon, it might not matter. At its death, all trace of the Old One would crumble into dust. This red dragon's attachment to her would probably crumble too.

Asha looked to the slave. *He* didn't know that.

"Fine," she said.

"I need your word. I won't wait here and give you time to change your mind. I need some surety you'll make good on your promise."

Damn it.

Without thinking, Asha touched her mother's ring. The moment she did, she wished she hadn't, because the skral's gaze fixed on it.

"That will do fine."

Asha shook her head. "No."

"Then watch your own dragon." Rising, he headed for the stream.

He shucked off his shirt, giving her a clear sight of the strength in his shoulders and arms. Of the satisfying curve of his torso. Of the linen bandages crisscrossing his back.

Bandages that had been bled through.

Asha frowned. She was fairly certain he hadn't brought fresh ones.

She tried to keep her gaze from skimming him as he rolled his trousers up to his knees, letting the sparkling stream rush around his calves. Cupping his hands, he scooped up water and drank deeply before splashing the rest over his face.

Asha spun her mother's ring around her finger. As long as she made good on her word, he had to give it back. It wasn't like she was giving it to him to keep.

The dragon watched her with lazy, half-lidded eyes as she tugged the band off. Rising, Asha walked to the edge of the stream.

"If you watch the dragon, I promise to fly you wherever you want—*after* I kill Kozu."

He looked up. Water gathered in his eyelashes and dripped from his hair. The sight of him—sparkling in the sunlight— startled her.

When she realized she was staring, Asha shoved the ring toward him.

"Here."

Taking her mother's ring, he slid it onto his smallest finger and studied her. When his mouth tipped up at the side, ever so slightly, Asha felt herself loosen. Whatever was plaguing him receded, leaving something playful in its wake.

And then, before she even knew what was happening, he grabbed the hem of her shirt and pulled her into the stream.

Asha shrieked as cold water splashed up her leggings, soaking her through. When she recovered, she shoved him. He laughed as he staggered back, eyes shining with mirth. And then, as if he weren't afraid—not one bit—he bent down and splashed water into her face.

Enraged, Asha shoved him harder.

This time, he went down. The cold stream swallowed him. When he came up, that crooked smile was gone, replaced by one that curved at both ends. A whole smile.

He rose out of the water and stepped toward her, still

grinning. His eyes burned brightly as he reached to tuck a wet strand of hair behind her ear. "Your hair is pretty when it's down."

Those words lashed like the shaxa.

Pretty?

Was he *mocking* her?

She could have him killed for such a thing.

Asha stepped in close, narrowing her eyes. "Call me that again, skral, and I'll cut out your lying tongue myself."

Dripping with anger, she turned and left him in the stream.

Twenty

Asha was still damp when she stepped out of the stairway and into the temple. Her anger fizzled out when she heard a familiar voice.

"You truly are a useless fool," Jarek growled from somewhere in the maze of corridors. Asha followed his voice until she stood at the bottom of a stairway. The same stairway leading to a locked room, where his slave had been hiding just yesterday.

Her heart leaped into her throat.

The sound of scabbards clanking against belts and buckles made her turn. Two soldats stalked down the corridor, their footsteps echoing off the whitewashed walls.

"The next time you do something illegal, do us all a favor and pick a crime punishable by death."

A second voice rose up, equally familiar and just as fierce. "You know, Jarek, I'm really looking forward to your binding. Specifically the part where my sister cuts off your balls and hoists them high above the walls on your wedding night."

Dax.

His words were followed by a loud *crack!*

Dax swore.

Asha took the steps two at a time, her heart hammering. When she reached the open door, the light of a torch illuminated her brother—who was reeling from the punch Jarek threw, his cheek already swelling.

Flanked by two soldats carrying torches, the commandant stood with a scroll gripped in his fist. More scrolls littered the floor at his feet, while behind him, hidden in darkness, was the cot, its linens folded in what looked like a hurry, then tucked up against the wall.

But far worse than the cot was what lay on the bottom shelf, half hidden in shadow: a worn-looking lute, fashioned out of pale pine. On its flat, pear-shaped face was the elegantly engraved name *Greta*.

Distracted by the scrolls, Jarek hadn't yet noticed this telltale sign of his fugitive slave. But the moment he did . . .

Suddenly, Maya, the temple guardian, stepped into view. She stood inside the room, flanked by a soldat. Her eyes widened at the sight of the Iskari in the doorway. She shook her head almost imperceptibly, telling Asha to go, to escape being implicated in whatever was happening.

Asha ducked back out of the doorway and into the shadows of the stairwell, pressing herself against the wall, out of view.

"I didn't realize you knew how to write," Jarek said. Asha heard the smirk in his voice. Heard the sound of him unrolling one of the scrolls. "Did your scrublander whore teach you? Or did she write it *for* you?"

Asha dared a look around the doorframe just in time to see Dax's fists tighten and his jaw clench.

Jarek ripped the scroll's parchment—once, twice, three times. He picked up another scroll and tore that one too. Dax watched, his eyes sharp as daggers.

With every rip, Asha's chest constricted.

Shame scorched her. She didn't care about torn scrolls. Of course she didn't. The old stories killed her mother. She hated them. She *wanted* them destroyed.

When Jarek turned to the shelves for more, he caught sight of her, frozen in the shadows beyond the doorway. His sneer slid away.

"Asha? What are you doing here?" His hand fell away from the shelves. "Why are you wet?"

She looked to the lute. The moment he turned around, he would see it and recognize it.

She needed to prevent that from happening.

Asha strode into the room, positioning herself between Jarek and the lute while motioning to the crumpled, torn scrolls at their feet. "What happened here?"

"After the news broke this morning, I followed your brother to the temple," Jarek answered. "He led me straight to *this*." He waved a hand around the room, then bent to pick up a scroll, handing it to Asha. She didn't need to unroll it, of course. She knew what it was.

Leave it to Dax to lead the commandant straight to the evidence of his own treachery.

"News?" Asha took the scroll. "What news?"

Jarek's eyes narrowed, suspicious. "No one told you?"

She shook her head. She'd been in the Rift all night.

"The scrublanders took Darmoor last night by force. Your father got word this morning."

Asha thought of Roa and her hawk. Thought of the way Dax always leaned toward her. Like she was a moon and he was a moonflower.

Thought of the way Roa didn't seem to notice him at all.

Asha looked to her brother, who refused to meet her gaze, staring at the floor instead.

Oh, Dax.

The scrublanders had betrayed him twice now.

"Your brother's guests"—Jarek said *guests* like they were something vile—"have disappeared. Their presence here was a ruse. A *distraction* while their army invaded our port." Jarek turned back to Dax, towering over him. "This is further proof he's not fit to rule."

Asha moved to protect her brother from Jarek's ridicule, but Dax met her gaze, then looked sharply and meaningfully to the lute.

Get rid of the evidence, said the look in his eyes.

But how was she supposed to do that, with Jarek standing in the room?

"If Dax is too *foolish* to know the difference between a friend and a foe, how can he protect a kingdom? If he's too *stupid* to notice me tracking him through the streets of Firgaard, how will he notice his enemies plotting against him at his own table?"

Dax's fists uncurled, the fight suddenly sucked out of him. It was no longer Jarek's voice he heard, Asha knew, but the voices of their old tutors.

Foolish. Stupid. Worthless.

"He had one task: to appease the scrublanders and put down their insubordination. Instead, after he spent three months treating with them, they deceived him. I've sent half our army to deal with the insurgents. He's jeopardized the safety of the entire city." Jarek shook his head in disgust. "And now there's *this* to contend with." He gestured to the scrolls. "The old stories, outlawed by your own father."

Jarek's gaze roamed the shelves, then the rest of the room. It was about to settle on the cot behind her when Maya came out of the shadows, snagging Jarek's attention.

"You," he said, "will be removed from your position immediately." Jarek took the torch from one of his soldats, motioning for the man to arrest Maya.

It would be mere heartbeats before he discovered the cot and his slave's lute. If he did, it would surely mean Maya's life.

Asha stepped forward. "Wait."

Everyone looked at her.

"If you arrest her, you'll widen the Rift between the palace and the temple." Which would only weaken the king's rule.

Jarek's gaze wandered along the damp shirt she wore, tracing the shape of her through the thin fabric. Asha backed up against the shelves, putting space between them.

"Force isn't the only way to strike a blow," she said.

A smile stretched across Jarek's face, turning her spine to ice.

"Is that so?" He stepped closer, trapping her against the shelf, his gaze devouring her in the orange glow of his torch. "How about a proposal, then?"

Dax moved to help his sister. The soldats restrained him.

"We could forget this ever happened." Jarek put one big hand on her scarred cheek. "You could offer me something in exchange." His hand moved down her face, then her throat, then ever farther. "If you came with me now, I could overlook the incident with my slave. . . ."

Asha's eyes stung. She felt vile. Repulsive. Jarek's touch made her hate herself more than she'd ever hated anything. More than the old stories and the First Dragon and the Old One, she hated her own heart for being desirable to someone so despicable.

It was further proof of her wickedness.

"Tell me how we should proceed." His voice turned husky. Full of desire. "My fearsome Iskari."

Asha's fingers itched for her axe. But there was no axe to reach for.

So Asha reached for something else.

"Has anyone told you about Moria and the fourth king of Firgaard?" Her angry gaze met his. "It's an old story about a man who took what wasn't his and the girl who put an end to him. Shall I tell it to you?"

Something shifted, then. Jarek's grip on her loosened.

Asha pushed away from the shelves and he stumbled back.

"Give me the torch."

She didn't wait for him to hand it to her. She snatched it from him.

Before anyone could stop her, Asha set the scrolls on fire.

Maya cried out, covering her mouth with her hands as the flames licked the parchment and the wood. Dax, released from the soldat's hold, opened the door and held the guardian back, out of the way of the fire, while smoke filled the room. Asha watched the parchment crumple and burn.

"The stories killed our mother." Asha didn't look at her brother. "They must be destroyed."

She tried to remember her mother's voice chasing her nightmares away, those soft arms pulling her into a hug. But they were only memories of memories and too far gone.

Asha hugged herself tight as she watched the ravenous flames devour the shelves, and with them, any evidence of her brother's treason. Now, if Jarek went to the king, it would be his word against Dax's.

But that wasn't the only evidence the fire destroyed.

As she listened to the strings of the lute—warping, bending, snapping—the skral's freckled face flared up in her mind, drenched and smiling brightly as he tucked her hair behind her ear.

There are plenty of other lutes in the city, she told herself, pulling her hunting shirt up over her mouth to stop from breathing in the smoke. *I will bring him one of those.*

Moria and the Fourth King of Firgaard

The fourth king of Firgaard was not a kind man. Some called him cruel. Others called him wicked. Still others, power starved. He built a palace that towered over the temple. He taxed his people into poverty. And he took a different girl to bed every night.

If the fourth king of Firgaard came to your home and asked for your daughter, you gave her up to him. If you didn't, he would take her anyway and your family would be dead come sunrise.

Moria was the daughter of the priestess. Raised in the temple, she lived a devout and sheltered life. She went to bed early and got up long before the sun to pray. She visited the poor and sick and held fast to the Old One's laws.

Until the king took her dearest friend.

On that night, Moria did not go to sleep early. She did not get up before the sun. She spent the long, cold stretch of moon kneeling on the stone floor of the temple, speaking to the Old One.

"I can't save her," Moria told him. "But I can save the next girl."

"To take the life of another is a monstrous act," the Old One told her. "Even the life of the wickedest among you is sacred."

"If I must become a monster to stop a monster," said Moria, "then that is what I will do."

And the Old One said, "The killing price of a king is death."

And Moria said, "So be it."

She got up from the floor. She grabbed the ceremonial knife off the altar. Its blade scraped against the stone.

That evening, Moria combed her hair until it shone. She smudged her eyes with kohl and doused her skin in rose water. She put on her prettiest kaftan and set out for the palace.

The guards took her straight to the king.

Moria bowed low to the king of Firgaard. She did not meet his gaze for fear he would see the raging fire in her eyes. She did not speak her name for fear he would hear the sharpened edge of her voice.

The dragon king dismissed his guards.

The flame in Moria flickered. Who was she, to pit herself against a king? She was nothing more than a girl. Not yet eighteen. And he was twice her size.

When the king reached for her, Moria froze.

When he undid the buttons of her kaftan, she trembled.

When he slid the kaftan off her shoulders and down her arms, when he let it fall to the floor, Moria thought of her dearest friend. She thought of all the girls who'd stood right here, trembling and afraid. With her clothes crumpled around her feet, Moria reached for the knife strapped to her thigh.

Seeing it, the king's eyes widened in surprise.

And Moria cut open his throat.

The guards found her standing over the body, blood dripping from the ceremonial blade in her hand. When her gaze fell upon them, they shivered. As if it were the gaze of Iskari herself.

Taking life was forbidden. The king's life, especially. Elorma himself instated the law against regicide. It was as old as the founding of Firgaard.

Ancient laws needed to be upheld.

So, three days later, they marched Moria to the bloodstained block in the center square, where a man holding a saber waited. All of Firgaard came to watch. Every girl who'd ever been taken by the king lined the streets, with their families at their backs.

But as the guards marched Moria past them, her people raised a fist over their hearts. And Moria held her head high all the way to the chopping block.

Unafraid.

Twenty-One

Beneath the watchful gaze of the soldats, Asha bided her time, waiting for her moment to steal the flame.

Beneath the blazing sun, Asha and Dax walked side by side. Jarek marched six paces ahead while soldats surrounded them, their gazes cast like spears up and down the green-walled streets of the new quarter. The visiting scrublanders were missing and Jarek's fugitive slave hadn't been found. The city was on high alert.

"No one is allowed in or out," Asha heard Jarek tell his second-in-command, "until the missing scrublanders are found."

While her brother brooded beside her, Asha set her thoughts on her task. She needed to take the sacred flame from her father's throne room without getting caught.

Up ahead, Jarek took off his mantle—useful in the early morning chill but stifling now in the increasing heat of the rising sun. A dagger hung at his hip, the ivory hilt polished and shining. Beside Asha, Dax's gaze burned a hole in the back of Jarek's shirt.

"You didn't have to torch them," said Dax. His brown curls were damp against his skin, where sweat beaded from the sun's heat.

"You didn't exactly give me a choice," she said.

If she hadn't shown up, what would Dax have done? How would he have hidden the evidence of Jarek's rogue slave? She loved her brother, but he was too much of a dreamer. Expert at coming up with lofty plans, unskilled at carrying them out.

Like the scrolls.

What in all the skies was he *thinking*?

"Where's Torwin?" Dax kept his voice low. He didn't look at her.

"The slave?" Asha shook her head, whispering back. "You led Jarek straight to that room. Why would I tell you where he is now?"

Dax opened his mouth to respond, but instead of words, a fit of coughing erupted out of him. The harsh, ragged sound made Asha go rigid. Dax doubled over, pressing his hands to his knees at the force of it.

Asha stared at her brother. For a moment, it wasn't Dax standing before her in the middle of the street. It was her mother, standing at the window of the sickroom, gripping the ledge with her sapped strength, willing it to bear her up as the same harsh cough racked her body.

No, thought Asha.

Jarek turned to see why the soldats stopped, but by then, Dax's coughing subsided. The heir wiped his mouth and Asha looked for blood on the gold sleeve of his tunic. He tucked it out of sight before she could see.

When they arrived at the towering door set into the caramel-colored wall of the palace, Jarek issued an order to the soldats on the other side. Before Asha could pass through the arching doorway next to Dax, Jarek grabbed her arm, forcing her to face him.

"My offer still stands," he said, his voice a low rumble. "I *will* find that slave and finish him. Or you could accept, and I'll forget about him."

Asha twisted free and caught up with her brother. "Hunt him to your heart's content," she said over her shoulder.

"The moon wanes, Asha!" Jarek called after her. "Why prolong the inescapable?"

But her father had given Asha an escape. Jarek just didn't know it.

Once she and Dax were both through the gateway, Asha moved quickly through the shaded arcades, leaving her brother behind. The sound of cascading water chimed from the fountains as mist evaporated in the heat of the sun.

"Asha," Dax said, jogging to catch up with her. "Talk to me. Please."

"Talk to *you*?" She stopped walking and spun to face him. "You who put those scrolls in that room? Who brought enemies into our home? I'm not telling you anything. Jarek's right. You've put us all in jeopardy."

Slaves going about their daily tasks stopped to eavesdrop on the two royal siblings in the middle of the arcade. When Asha shot them warning glances, they quickly moved on.

She thought of the old stories, written in Dax's handwriting.

She lowered her voice. "The stories on those scrolls. Did you write them?"

His eyebrows shot upward. "I'm surprised you think me capable."

That wasn't an answer.

She studied him. His cheekbones jutted out too far. His clothes hung too loosely. As exasperating as her brother was, she couldn't bear to lose him.

"You look just like *she* did," said Asha. "Right before she died."

A wild emotion flickered across his face. But it was gone as soon as it arrived.

"Not everything is as it appears, Asha." His gaze flicked over her shoulders, checking for soldats and slaves. Satisfied that they were alone and unwatched, he stepped in close and lowered his voice. *"When darkness falls, the Old One lights a flame."*

Asha stepped back. "What?"

"It's what Roa says."

Roa? The girl who betrayed him?

Was he serious?

Asha didn't have time for this. Her brother was a lost cause. She needed to steal the sacred flame so she could get back to hunting Kozu.

She moved past her brother, heading deeper into the palace.

Dax's footsteps rang out behind her.

"The realm is divided against itself!"

She ignored him and kept walking—through shady galleries

and bright courtyards, through gardens full of date palms and vines of white jasmine creeping up the walls.

Dax followed her.

"You don't see it," he persisted, "because you're forever in the Rift, doing Father's bidding. Things are bad and getting worse. A reckoning is coming."

When they reached the throne room, Asha turned to him.

"What does that have to do with you?" she demanded. "Since when do you care, Dax? About *anything*?"

He stepped back. As if she'd shoved him. Beneath the wounded look in his eyes she could see a war waging. Could see the reckless, careless Dax fighting to come out. To hide the truer, softer Dax and his myriad of hurts.

She shouldn't have said that. Of course he cared. About too many things.

They were just the *wrong things*.

"The Old One hasn't abandoned us." He stared her straight in the face as he said it, forcing her to look him in the eye. "He's as powerful as ever, waiting for the right moment and the right *person*. He's waiting for the next Namsara to make things right."

Asha froze just beyond the throne room's archway, out of sight of the soldats within.

Did he realize how he sounded?

Insane. Traitorous. Just like a scrublander.

Asha stared at her brother. Dax had always been recklessly heroic. Like Namsara and Iskari, he was the tenderhearted hero and Asha was the destroyer.

But unlike Namsara and Iskari, Asha had never hated her

brother, only worried about him.

Enough of this. I'm running out of time.

Turning from Dax, Asha looked to the bright, eternal flame. She watched it burn in an iron bowl on the black pedestal.

Even though the dragon king's throne sat empty, his guards held their positions all around the walls. Asha counted sixteen of them. Sixteen pairs of eyes all watching her as she stepped through the archway and into the enclosed space, her footsteps echoing up to the domed ceiling. Her gaze swept over the room. There was no balcony level and only one doorway from which to enter and exit. The only other opening was through the sky-light in the roof. The soldats and their watching eyes guarded the throne all day and night, changing their posts at dawn and dusk. Yet Asha was supposed to steal the flame and not be seen.

At a loss, she stared at the sacred flame itself, which twisted eerily, bright white and making no sound. The flame didn't need to be fed; it simply burned on and on, ever since Elorma brought it here from the desert a thousand years ago.

No, she thought. *Not here.* Elorma brought it to the caves beneath the temple.

You will take the sacred flame from the thief who stole it and return it to where it belongs.

Asha pressed her palms to her temples, trying to crush the command out of her head.

What should she do?

Her father would want her to focus on her hunt. Once Kozu was dead, it wouldn't matter where the flame burned. Kozu's death would end the Old One's regime once and for all. With their god proven false, the scrublanders would come to heel and her brother's yammering about the Namsara would cease.

But if she ignored Elorma's task—what price would she pay?

She thought of her paralyzed arm—the cost for using her slayers unwisely.

To ensure her strength was not diminished, she would have to steal the flame. And *then* she would end Kozu. Once and for all.

But she couldn't complete this task alone.

Asha needed an accomplice.

A large, fire-breathing one.

Twenty-Two

Asha took her mare, Oleander, and raced down narrow, cobbled alleyways through the city's largest market. Lengths of freshly dyed silk hung across the space between buildings, forming a canopy of indigo and saffron above her. Open-fronted stalls lined the walls, spilling their wares into the street.

As carts and horses hurried to get out of the Iskari's way, Asha looked for one stall in particular. In her rushing, she nearly passed it. Oleander reared as Asha drew her to a halt, turning back to the display of wooden musical instruments.

The market fell silent. Slaves and shoppers gathered to whisper and stare as the Iskari bought an elegant lute made of burnished mahogany. They kept a wary distance as the craftsman buckled the lute into a hard leather case and the king's fearsome daughter tossed the merchant her payment.

Scattering the watchers, she galloped toward the gate. The soldats didn't stop the Iskari, despite their commandant's order to disallow anyone in or out of the city. Her father had issued a direct order. One they couldn't ignore, despite their loyalty to Jarek.

She rode hard. But when she got to the babbling, sparkling stream, no one waited for her. Asha halted Oleander, glancing around the clearing. Except for the bush chats and the wind rustling the pines, everything was silent. There were no signs anyone had ever been here. Asha couldn't even find the armor she'd shed the night before.

Fear sliced through her.

Please, no. . . .

Dismounting, she tied the mare up in the shade and grabbed the lute case.

"Skral?"

No one answered her.

She moved deeper into the pines, ready to call up an old story. It was the fastest way to know for sure. Before she could, the sound of voices broke through the hush of trees and Asha stilled, listening.

Careful not to make a sound, she followed the muffled voices, moving ever closer, silent as a snake.

A twig cracked behind her.

Asha froze.

Someone was following her. She could feel the warmth of them at her back. Asha reached for an axe that wasn't there, then quickly spun, ready to batter her stalker with the lute case if necessary.

The skral stared down at her. Freckles like stars. Tendrils of hair falling into sharp eyes. Just behind him crouched the dusty-red dragon, its slitted gaze intent on her face. Asha lowered the case. Despite her racing heart, the sight of them safe made her breathe easier.

The slave glanced over her shoulder, in the direction of the voices. Asha reached for his shirt, bringing his attention back to her. Her lips formed a question: *Who?*

Jarek's men.

The slave motioned with his head back the way they'd come. Asha followed him through the thinning trees and out into the bright clearing.

Suddenly voices echoed from ahead *and* behind.

And then, as if he'd done it a thousand times before, the slave reached for the dragon's wing bone, stepped into the crook behind its knee, and mounted. Straddling the dragon's back, he reached down for her.

Asha gaped at him in shock and horror.

Another twig snapped in the trees. It broke through her shock. Asha took his hand and he pulled her up behind him.

"Hold on," he whispered.

But there was nothing to hold on to—other than him.

The slave made a sharp click in the back of his throat and the dragon stretched its wings. The slave clicked twice more, then dug in his heels.

The dragon launched.

Asha panicked and looped her arms around his torso.

A wall of trees rose directly ahead. The dragon soared straight for it. Asha's heart thundered in her chest. Closing her eyes, she buried her face in the slave's neck. But the crash never came.

The slave flinched beneath her viselike grip, reminding her of the lacerations beneath his shirt.

"Sorry," she managed, yet couldn't bring herself to loosen her hold.

"It's . . . okay," he said through gritted teeth.

Asha opened her eyes—which was another mistake. At the sight of the treetops whipping by, she slammed them shut again. In the darkness behind her eyelids, all she could think was: *I'm riding a dragon.*

Which made everything worse.

Branches cracked beneath them, and when Asha looked, she found the dragon flying too low. Its tail and wings kept catching on trees. So the slave issued a series of clicked commands, and the dragon banked out over the river.

Finally, with nothing but blue sky before them and water below, Asha let herself relax. She looked back over her shoulder and couldn't even see the city wall in the distance.

Suddenly, the tree line broke, turning into rock. Asha looked ahead to find the river disappearing.

Or rather, *falling.*

A waterfall roared below them. And then, without any warning, the dragon dived.

Asha bit down on a terrified scream as they dropped with the water. She felt herself lift, felt her stomach tumble over itself. Her arms tightened hard around the slave and she pressed her cheek against his shoulder. His hands came around hers, lacing firmly through her fingers as they flew straight into engulfing mist.

And then into darkness.

The dragon rocked as it landed hard on solid ground, nearly throwing Asha from its back. The slave reached for her waist to steady her as the dragon shook itself, spraying water droplets everywhere. The only light came from behind them, where water rushed off the cliff.

Asha stayed perfectly still, willing herself not to be sick.

The slave dismounted. His footsteps echoed on rock, and a moment later, she heard a struck match, then the smell of a flame flaring to life. Soon a bright glow illuminated the glistening cavern.

"Sorry. I probably should have told you. We spent the day practicing." He cupped the back of his neck with his hand. "I thought—"

"Practicing?" Asha trembled as she dismounted, her limbs shaking with shock. "*Practicing?* Do you have any idea what you've done?"

Links were formed in flight. They deepened each time a rider and his dragon flew. As Asha shouted, the dragon cowered behind the slave. It slipped its flat, scaly head beneath its rider's hand, seeking comfort, and the slave rubbed his thumb across the crown of its head, as if to say *I'll protect you*.

Asha threw up her hands and stalked closer to the mouth of the cave, where the waterfall rushed and water ran in rivulets down the rock, making the ground shiny and slick. But as she stared into the glistening, thunderous waterfall, a quiet question slipped through a crack in her wall of anger.

Why wait for me?

The dragon could have flown this slave to freedom, as he wished. Why risk the danger and wait for her in the woods?

Asha turned back to find both of them staring at her, like mirror images, even though the dragon sat at almost twice the height of the slave.

The sight made her soften—just a little.

"You could have left," she said. "You could have flown far away from here."

"We had a deal," he said simply, then turned and headed deeper into the cave. "Come on. I want to show you something."

"All right," she said, "but first I need your help."

At sunset they would put everything in motion. Asha told him the plan as she followed him down slick rock-hewn steps.

When her foot slipped on the stone in front of her, she pitched forward.

He caught her around the waist.

"Careful," he said, mindful of the stitches in her side. He was warm and steady beneath her hands, and for the merest of heartbeats, neither of them stepped away.

An odd silence rose up. And then, quite suddenly, he ducked his chin and released her, continuing on down the steps, following the click-click-click of dragon talons below.

Asha broke the quiet. "How did you find this place?"

"Redwing found it."

"Who's Redwing?"

"Your dragon."

"You *named* him?"

He shrugged in the darkness. "I had to call him something. He's reddish. He has wings."

She shook her head. The next time Elorma called her unimaginative, Asha would send the slave his way.

There was light, suddenly, breaking up the darkness. When the stairway ended, a round chamber lay before them, with a deep pool at its center. A natural skylight high above let in a solitary pillar of light and water that flowed gently down the walls.

Asha walked the perimeter of the pool, looking upward.

"What is this place?" Her words echoed up the walls.

"I thought you would know," said the slave, his gaze fixed on the dragon.

It seemed like some kind of ancient, sacred space.

Whatever it had been, it was now a perfect place to hide.

"I think his wing is torn. . . ."

"What?" Asha spun, looking where he looked: at the dragon staring into the water, his head cocked, watching the fish swim in circles.

She needed this dragon to aid her in her plan. He couldn't help if he had a torn wing. Slowly, Asha approached from one side. The slave approached from the other.

"He doesn't need a name," she said as they closed in on him.

"And why's that?"

"Naming a thing endears you to it."

Like slaves. The moment you started calling them by their names was the moment you started losing power over them. Better to keep them nameless than to be risen up against.

"Kozu has a name," he pointed out.

"Yes, and soon he'll be dead." Asha crept ever closer to the dragon perching on the side of the pool. She could see exactly which wing it was. Black blood dripped from the thin membrane.

Slowly, she reached for the wing. The dragon darted away, quick as the wind, and jumped to the other side of the pool. His forked tail lashed playfully.

"You hate Kozu that much?"

The question broke her concentration. Asha whirled on the slave.

"Have you seen my face, skral?" She stepped toward him. "Do you know what Kozu did to the city right after he did this to me?"

He didn't flinch, just met her gaze. "Have you seen the collar around my neck, Iskari?" It was the calm of a gathering storm. "Your own betrothed sends us to kill one another in the pit while you stand by, placing bets." His eyes were colder than steel. "For that, maybe I should hunt *you* down."

"I'd like to see you try," Asha muttered, turning back to the dragon. The sooner she tended that wing, the sooner she could carry out her plan.

"There's something I've never understood," he called after her. "Why did Kozu turn on you *then*? On that day, and not before?"

The dragon before her braced himself, crouching low on his front legs, tail swishing, eyes daring Asha. Slowly, she started closing the gap between them.

"Something else I don't understand? *You should have died.* Dragon burns are deadly, Iskari, and a burn like that?" His voice softened suddenly. "You were just a little girl."

A fire sparked in her belly. He hadn't been there. He didn't know the first thing about it.

In her pause, the dragon broke his stance and slithered to the other side of the pool, closer to the slave, who was more friend than foe. He left behind a black spot of blood.

Asha rose to face the slave.

"I was alone," she said, thinking of the sickroom. Of her father filling in the gaps in her memory. "I'd gone to end things. To tell Kozu I was done with the old stories. He kept pressing me, getting angrier and angrier, and when I refused for the last time, he flew into a rage, burning me and leaving me to die while he attacked the city. If Jarek hadn't found me in time . . ."

She rarely told this story aloud because she didn't like to think about it. But now, hearing it on her own lips, something didn't make sense. The slave was right. A burn as severe as the one Kozu gave her would have to be treated immediately.

There must be a detail she was forgetting. She needed to pay more attention when her father told the story next.

Asha fixed her attention once more on the dragon, who stood behind the slave now, using him as a shield. She stalked him down.

The slave held out his arm, stopping her.

"Why did you need to end things?" he asked.

Because the stories killed my mother.

Asha remembered that last night. Her mother could no

longer speak; it took strength she didn't have. Asha sat with her in the dark, stroking her beautiful hair, only her fingers kept catching and the hair kept coming out in clumps. She remembered trying to get her mother to drink, and how the water dribbled down her chin. She remembered lying down beside her and covering her face in kisses.

Asha remembered falling asleep to the beat of her mother's heart. . . .

And waking up to a body cold as ice.

She squeezed her eyes shut.

"You don't know," she whispered, pushing past the slave. "You have no idea the kinds of wicked things the old stories are capable of."

He caught her arm, stopping her. "Not Willa's story. It seemed . . . the opposite of wicked."

So naïve, thought Asha. The old stories were like jewels: dazzling, beguiling, luring you in. "They're dangerous," she whispered, staring over his shoulder at the dragon staring back.

"Well then," he said softly. "I guess I'm drawn to dangerous things."

Asha felt her cheeks burn. She looked back into his face.

"I've been thinking," he went on quickly, his gaze holding hers, "about the first time I ever saw you. You were eight—or maybe nine. My mistress invited your mother for tea, and you came along. While Greta served them in the gardens, you wandered into the library."

Strangely, Asha remembered that day. Remembered the enormous dragon head mounted on the library wall. The lifeless glass eyes, the pale gold scales, the open mouth showing off a multitude of knifelike teeth . . .

"I was dusting the shelves," he said. "I saw you enter, and I knew I was supposed to leave, to give you privacy, but"—he swallowed—"I didn't. You were wearing a blue kaftan and your hair was loose around your shoulders. You reminded me of someone."

Behind him, realizing their game was over, the dragon huffed a sigh and stalked off.

"I watched you trail your fingers along the wooden handles of the scrolls until you found the one you wanted. I watched you pull it down, then sit on the cushions and read it to the end. And then I watched you go back for more."

The scrolls were the reason I wandered in there in the first place, she remembered. *I was looking for stories.*

That thought surprised Asha. Was she remembering that right? Had she been drawn to the stories *before* the Old One corrupted her?

"You came dangerously close to the shelf I hid behind. And I knew if you looked, you'd be able to see me through the space above the scrolls."

Asha thought backward, trying to remember a skral boy in the library that day.

"I didn't move." The reflected light from the pool danced across his face. "I . . . wanted you to see me."

"But I didn't," she whispered.

Asha felt suddenly exposed. Like when she stripped off her armor with a dragon lurking nearby. She turned quickly away from the skral, moving toward that same dragon now.

"Iskari."

She stopped but didn't look back.

"The day I found you in the sickroom, I knew things were about to change. And before they did"—he paused—"I needed you to see me. Just once."

When Asha turned, there was no longer any steel in his eyes.

He lowered his gaze, as if suddenly shy, then gestured to the dragon. "Come on. I'll help you tend him."

Twenty-Three

Asha told the first story to lure the dragon to her. She told the second to keep the dragon calm as she cleaned the tear in his wing, and then the third as the slave stitched up the tear. As each story emptied out of her, the dragon filled her up with new ones. And each time, with Asha's help, the creature's stories were stronger. Less fragmented and clearer.

"Good boy," she said when they finished, scratching his chin.

The slave—who'd been humming a half-finished song while he worked—looked up at them and smiled.

When the wing was mended and they flew Asha back to the clearing, the sun was well on its way to setting.

Asha fetched the lute case from where she'd dropped it in the trees.

"There's just one thing," she said, handing over the case.

"Oh?" he said, taking it.

"You can't name him Redwing."

He crouched down to unbuckle the case. "Do you have a better suggestion?"

"I do, actually."

He stopped unbuckling to look up at her.

"Shadow is better."

"Shadow." He paused to consider it, then looked at the dragon stretching in the sunlight. "Shadow is . . . acceptable."

His eyes crinkled as he smiled. But when he pushed back the lid of the case, the smile slid away.

He stared at the lute, but didn't reach for it.

"This isn't mine," he said. His voice sounded strange. Cracked at the edges.

"I know," said Asha. "I bought it this morning to replace your other one."

"Replace my other one? What happened to—"

"I burned it."

"You . . ." Very slowly, he rose to his feet. "You . . . what?"

Asha raised her palms. "Jarek found the room you were hiding in, so I did the only thing I could think of: I burned the scrolls, the cot, the lute. All of it."

He grabbed her wrist, startling her. His eyes were a storm as he said, "Do you realize how heartless you are?"

The words scorched her. They shouldn't have, because of course she knew. She was worse than heartless. Her heart was a withered husk.

She could have easily slammed her elbow down on his forearm, forcing his fingers to release her. But she didn't. She wanted him to believe her. "I was trying to protect you."

"You were protecting *yourself*," he said. And then, like she was a monster he could no longer bear to touch, he let go, turning away, running his hands roughly through his hair. "Greta gave me that lute."

The image of the gray-haired slave flashed in Asha's mind.

"She was the closest thing I had to a mother. And now she's gone, along with the only thing I had to remember her by."

Asha felt herself unravel. As if she were a carpet or a tapestry, and his words were claws tearing out all her threads.

"I didn't . . ."

"And you don't care, do you? It's why you won't speak the name of any slave. It's the same reason you didn't want to name that dragon." He stepped toward her, closer than ever. "If you name us, you might *start* to care. And if you care, you might not be able to kill us when it suits you."

Gone was the slave who hummed songs while he worked. In his place stood a stranger. An enemy. A part of her said to be afraid. But another part said: *Look at the way his hands shake. Look at the ghosts in his eyes.* Asha had lost her mother, but he'd lost so much more than that. And she'd just destroyed what was probably his most precious possession. Likely his only possession.

Her chest felt like someone had sunk an axe into it.

She didn't realize what she was doing, or that she was doing it, until it was done. All she knew was, just like he'd bandaged her burn and stitched up her side, she wanted to dress this wound. She wanted to soothe this hurt.

Pressing her scarred palm to his chest, Asha broke her own rule.

"Torwin."

His lips parted. He stared at her mouth as if he didn't understand. As if she'd spoken another language entirely.

"I'm sorry."

Very slowly, his fingers rose to touch her hand, checking to see if it was really there, really pressed against his chest.

She looked to the new lute, still in its case. "I'll get it out of your sight."

Her hand fell away from him.

"No." He caught her wrist, stopping her. They both went still as his thumb trailed a circle around the bump of her wrist bone. "That wasn't fair of me. You didn't know."

She stared up at him in the disappearing sunlight.

He dropped his hand to his side.

"You're not heartless," he said, staring into her eyes. "I hate myself for saying that."

Asha looked away. "I should go."

She gathered up her armor and buckled it on. After sheathing her slayers across her back, she reached for her axe, lying in the grass. Instead of putting it in her belt, though, she turned around.

"If they find you," she said, holding the axe out to him, "don't think. Just strike."

He took the jeweled handle, his fingers brushing against hers.

Before making her way into the trees, she stopped, pausing

in the spot where the sunlight ended and the darkness of the canopy began, still warm from where he'd touched her.

"Torwin?" she said, not daring to look back.

"Yes?"

"You could call me Asha. If you wanted to."

Twenty-Four

A pair of soldats walked the street below. Asha held her breath and waited for them to turn the corner before jumping. Her boots landed with a soft thud, raising dust.

She avoided the main streets. When Asha heard footsteps or felt eyes in the darkness, she backtracked. The longer she could go without being seen, the better.

Getting up onto the palace roof was more difficult than getting down off it. But if Asha managed it as a child, she could certainly manage it now. She found the lowest wall and hoisted herself up and over. She ran across rooftops, past slaves rolling couscous and bringing in laundry, past the butcher preparing for his evening slaughter. No one saw her.

She went to her room, where yet another silver-lidded box sat waiting. Jarek's gifts were starting to pile up: a kaftan, a ruby-studded necklace, and now a bolt of bright red sabra silk. She pushed them into a corner and got what she needed: a lantern made of copper, inset with colored glass. She unbuckled her slayers from her back and hid them under the bed, tucking them up into the frame, then stripped off the armor that made her immediately recognizable. She didn't need these things to kill Kozu. All she needed was her fireskin and her axe—which was presently in the slave's care.

No. Not *the slave.*

Torwin.

Asha unbraided her hair, donned her plainest mantle, and went to the window. With the lantern gripped tight in her fist, she waited. Watching the horizon.

The red moon rose.

Two more days until my wedding.

The sky turned from blue to purple.

Two more days to hunt down Kozu.

The sun set over the Rift, and as it did . . .

The screams began. Soldats shouted: *Dragon in the city!*

If she hadn't been so nervous, Asha might have smiled.

Torwin had impeccable timing.

A dragon in the city meant all the soldats would abandon their posts and, once the king was safe, head for the rooftops or the streets.

With the hood of her mantle flipped up, cloaking her face in shadow, Asha moved quickly through the chaos of running soldats.

As the archway of the throne room came into view, the hallways quieted. In the distance, Asha could hear the screams in the street, the shout of soldats keeping order; but here, deep in the palace, all was quiet.

As she stepped into the throne room, Asha's palms were sweaty and her grip on the lantern handle was slick.

She moved swiftly toward the pedestal, her footsteps echoing loudly through the empty chamber. Peering down into the iron basin, she found the white flame burning silently. Mysteriously.

As a child, the wonder of it had mesmerized her. But no wonder filled her now. Only fear.

Asha unhooked the latch of her lantern. Sweat beaded on her temples and dripped down her back. She had no idea how Elorma brought the flame from the desert all the way to the city, but the lantern was all she had. She hoped it would be enough.

Asha reached into the shallow basin. Her hand closed around something smooth and heavy as a stone. The moment she touched the heart of the flame, it seared her—not her skin, though. Something far deeper. Perhaps her soul.

A thousand whispering voices rose in her mind, each one telling a sacred story. As if the voices of all the raconteurs from the beginning of time dwelled within.

Asha shoved the flame inside her lantern and locked it back up.

The voices went silent.

"You there!"

Asha spun, her heart skittering.

In the archway, a single soldat stood staring at her. Young. Maybe Dax's age. His hand was on his hilt, but his morion was missing. It had probably fallen in the chaos.

"What do you think you're . . . ?" He looked from the brightly lit lantern in her hand to the empty basin behind her. Realizing what she'd just done, he drew his saber.

Asha reached for an axe that wasn't there and winced.

"Put it back, thief."

He stepped through the archway, his brow furrowed, his blade pointed at her chest.

Asha had two choices: bolt and risk getting run through, or push back her hood and hope his fear of the Iskari would override all other sense. She was about to choose the latter when her brother entered the room.

"Well, *this* is interesting."

"My lord," said the soldat, who hadn't recognized Asha yet. "She's stolen the flame."

When she didn't move, Dax held out his hand. "Give me your sword. I'll hold the thief here, you get help."

The soldat nodded. Asha watched the young man run, shouting the alarm. Telling the entire palace about the thief in the throne room.

The moment he left, Dax lowered the blade.

"I don't know what you're doing, little sister"—he glanced over his shoulder—"but you'd better scurry."

Asha's eyes pricked with tears of relief.

"Go!"

Nodding, she ran past him, hiding the lantern in the folds of her mantle, snuffing out its unnatural glow.

As soon as she could turn the corner, she did. As soon as she could start to run without drawing attention, she ran. And as soon as there was an arching glassless window, she climbed out of it and onto the roof.

Which was when shouts of alarm rose up behind her.

The thief had been spotted.

Twenty-Five

Asha ran.

She ran across twilight-soaked rooftops and scrambled over plaster walls. She ran through crowded alleys and across chaotic squares.

But the sky was empty now. No dragon soared. Torwin had moved on to the second part of their plan. She needed to meet him at the temple.

She ducked into doorways and shop fronts when one or more soldats came into view. She stayed there until they passed, listened to them describe the cloaked thief from the palace.

Asha raced all the way to the temple, not even trying to keep to the shadows now. Beneath a pomegranate tree's bright orange flowers, Asha buckled the lantern to her belt, then grabbed the lowest branch and hoisted herself up. She launched herself at the first-floor window and pulled herself inside, the lantern knocking loudly against the sill.

Asha flinched, waiting for the Old One to strike her down

for being so careless with his sacred flame.

Mercifully, he stayed his hand.

Asha flew down the vaulted stairway and into the darkness of the temple crypt. She needed to get in, get to Torwin, and get out. As quickly as possible.

She passed the alcove that hid the entrance to her secret tunnel, but Torwin wasn't there.

Asha moved deeper in, her heart racing, the blazing light of her lantern illuminating the rock walls.

What if he didn't make it?

As if in answer to her unvoiced question, a glow flickered in the distance.

Asha's pace quickened. She passed through the empty outer caves, their walls glistening with moisture. The air was damp and cool here, like a cellar. At the doorway to the inner sanctum, Asha stopped, thinking of the one and only time she'd been here before. The day her mother died. The day the Old One corrupted her for good.

Torwin stared up at the walls, her hunting axe tucked in his belt. Except for the glow of his lamp, keeping him alight, the sanctum was veiled in darkness.

Her racing heart slowed at the sight of him.

"Where is Shadow?" she asked.

"Waiting near the tunnel entrance." He glanced over his shoulder at her. "Come look at this."

Asha didn't want to look. She was here for one thing, and she needed to get it over with. Breathing deeply, Asha stepped across the threshold and moved toward the center of the sanctum, where a star with nine points had long ago been cut into the floor. Asha crouched over it, setting the lantern down. She unhooked the clasp and reached into the bright light within. Cupping her hands around the cool, stone-like heart, Asha drew the flame out.

The whispers filled her mind, louder and stronger than before. A powerful energy pulsed through her, setting her whole body tingling from the soles of her feet to the palms of her hands. It surged so powerfully, it made her head throb and her teeth ache.

Quickly, she set the flame inside the star.

The Old One's sacred flame blazed up so brightly, the cave around them glistened. Golden words shone in the darkness, written on the walls, the ceiling, the floor. Stories burned like fire all around her. Hundreds of them.

Asha knew them all.

Her fingers reached to touch the words. Her mouth ached to read them aloud. A spark flared within her, growing into a thirsty blaze.

On the wall behind Torwin was the colorful mosaic of the man who'd visited her three times in the past four days. She would know that smile anywhere. It said: *Look at the trouble I've gotten you in now.*

Asha now stood face-to-face with Elorma's portrait. Elorma, the first of seven Namsaras—sacred heroes who rose up in times of trouble. The Old One's holy flames, burning in the night. As she stared into those dark eyes, the voices returned. Only this time, they weren't telling stories.

Namsara, they whispered, like the wind sighing across the sand.

Torwin grabbed her arm, swinging her around to face him. "Someone's coming."

The moment broke like a severed string. Asha looked back the way she'd come to see a light farther up the crypt, dim but growing.

Asha grabbed Torwin's hand. They ran back through the caves, leaving the sacred flame behind to burn in its rightful place.

"It's a dead end," said a voice in the distance. "And your soldats are everywhere. If she were here, she would have been seen."

The closer Asha and Torwin came to the outer cave entrance, the closer the torchlight came to them. They couldn't reach her secret tunnel in time. So Asha stopped at the narrow lip of a small fissure and shoved Torwin inside. When he realized what she was doing, he seized her wrist, to pull her in after him. But there wasn't enough room for two. The light of the torch would flicker in, illuminating Asha, and they'd both be caught.

She shook her head, trying to wrench away.

Torwin's arm came around her waist, pulling her into him. Their hips collided, sealing up the space between them as the light of Jarek's torch filtered past her shoulder and onto the rock wall beyond.

Torwin's hand cupped her head, tucking it beneath his chin. Asha squeezed her eyes shut, her thoughts a flurry of curses.

Jarek's voice drew nearer, then quieted. With her temple

pressed against Torwin's throat, Asha tried to imagine what the commandant saw. The sacred caves, yawning open. The blazing brightness that was the Old One's holy flame burning the stories into his mind.

Asha's heart hammered in her ears. Torwin must have heard it, because he stroked the back of her head, trying to soothe her. When his thumb brushed her ear, disfigured from Kozu's fire, he paused.

I know, she thought. *It's hideous.*

But instead of dropping in disgust, his fingers continued on, tracing its bumps the same way his eyes liked to trace her scar— with gentle curiosity.

Asha relaxed against him.

How can I be growing accustomed to the touch of a slave?

More than accustomed. Her body lit up at the feel of his arm securely around her, keeping her pressed against him. Asha breathed in the smell of him. All salt and sand. All boy and earth.

Was it possible to love the smell of someone so much, you wanted to taste them just to see if it was the same?

You are corrupted, said a voice in her head. *Look at you, lusting after a slave.*

Asha should have pulled away right then. She should have listened to that voice.

Instead, with danger lurking just beyond the darkness, she slid her arms around Torwin's waist, pressing him tighter against her. His tracing fingers stopped. He went completely still. After several heartbeats, he tilted his face to hers.

Ever so slowly, he dragged the bridge of his nose along her cheekbone, asking a silent question. Sparks skittered through her. Her blood turned to fire. She arched her neck in answer, brushing her cheek across his.

He turned, leaning his forehead against hers. Their noses touched as his hands slid through her hair, cradling her face.

"She's here," Jarek's voice rang out.

Torwin went rigid. Asha's arms tightened around him.

"See the lantern? She's hiding somewhere. Get me some kindling."

"Yes, commandant." The sound of booted footsteps echoed off the walls.

"If she wants to play with fire," muttered Jarek, "I'll beat her at her own game."

He's going to smoke us out, Asha realized.

She couldn't let that happen. She couldn't let Torwin get caught. If Jarek found him, he was as good as dead. Maybe worse than dead.

There was only one way out of this.

Breaking Torwin's grip on her, Asha pushed herself up onto her toes and whispered against his cheek, "I'll come for you at nightfall. Be ready to fly."

Before he could stop her, she took a deep breath and stepped out of the fissure, into the light of Jarek's torch.

Twenty-Six

Cool air rushed against her skin, its chill replacing Torwin's warmth. Jarek stood at the entrance to the caves, his back to her, as if afraid to set foot inside.

"Your thief is right here," she said.

Jarek spun. His eyes narrowed as he took in her mantle, her unbraided hair.

"You've committed a crime against the king," he said. "Against your own father. Why?"

Footsteps echoed through the caves. They belonged to one of his soldats, carrying a bundle of kindling in both arms. The soldat stopped, staring into the inner sanctum. "The sacred flame," he whispered, eyes widening.

Jarek's eyes sliced into Asha, waiting for the answer to his question. When she didn't supply it, he grabbed her arm and marched her through the narrow crypt passages, toward the vaulted stairway that led up into the temple.

Asha didn't fight him. The sooner he dragged her out of here, the sooner Torwin could get to the tunnel and escape.

◆ ◆ ◆

Jarek searched her for weapons and found none, so he took her mantle instead. In the archway of the throne room, his fingers yanked at the tassels around her throat. He stripped it off her and threw Asha to the cold stone floor before the pedestal holding the empty basin.

The floor connected with her knees and she bit down an angry cry.

"What is this?" Her father's slippered footsteps echoed softly through the room.

"Here's your thief," said Jarek.

Her father stood over her. She didn't raise her eyes from his finely stitched slippers protruding beneath the golden hem of his robe.

"Asha? Surely there's been some mistake. Asha, get up."

She didn't. How could she face him? She kept her forehead pressed into the tile work.

"I found her beneath the temple, and the sacred flame in the inner cave."

"Impossible."

She imagined Jarek shaking his head.

"One of my soldats saw her take it, my lord."

She imagined the look dawning on her father's face.

"Asha? Can you explain this?"

She tried to imagine herself through her father's eyes. When he'd first proposed his deal, she was the fiercest of dragon hunters, willing to do anything to get out of her binding. Now? If her father knew just how deep his oldest enemy's claws were in his daughter, what would he do? Would he realize she was beyond saving? Would he cast her away? Find someone else to kill Kozu?

"Tell me why you did this, Asha."

Her voice shook "I—I'm sorry. . . ."

"I don't want an apology!" His voice boomed, echoing through the throne room, empty save him, his commandant, and a handful of soldats. "I want your answer."

She swallowed, staring hard at the blue and green tiles beneath her hands. She needed to be careful what she said. Jarek couldn't know about her deal with her father. And her father couldn't know about the Old One's commands.

"I did it for . . . my hunt." She glanced at Jarek, whose arms were crossed hard over his chest. "This particular dragon is . . . more evasive than the rest. I needed something to bait him."

"So you stole the flame?"

"This dragon cannot resist it."

Liar, she thought, then dared a glance upward. Her father's face darkened as their eyes met.

"Please," she whispered. "I need you to trust me."

His gaze softened at those words.

"My king," interrupted Jarek as he stepped forward. "You can't allow her to escape punishment just because she's your daughter. It sets a precedent. Do you want to be remembered as the kind of king who upholds the law only when it suits him?"

Silence echoed in the throne room as the dragon king looked from his Iskari to his commandant.

"Have I not done everything you've ever asked of me, my king? Have I not defended your walls? Put down your revolts? Kept your secrets?"

At this last question, the dragon king's face darkened like the sky before a storm. Asha wondered what kind of secrets her father entrusted Jarek with. The thought made her jealous. They must have been large ones. Ones strong enough to make him buckle under pressure, because that's exactly what he did.

"What are you asking me for?" said the dragon king, looking back to his daughter kneeling at his feet.

"Something is amiss here." Jarek started to pace. His heavy footsteps echoed through the domed room. "First, my slave goes missing. Next, our supposed allies steal away in the night and the next morning take Darmoor. And now? The sacred flame is stolen by your own daughter." He shook his head. "I want her to stay where I can see her. All I'm asking is that you uphold your own law. Punish her like the criminal she is by locking her in the dungeon until our binding day."

Her father wouldn't allow it. He wanted Kozu dead, and Asha was the only one who could bring the First Dragon down.

Her father hesitated, though.

It made Asha's stomach knot up.

He looked from her to Jarek, as if trying to choose. As if this were a game of strategy and he needed to decide which piece would cost him more: his commandant or his Iskari?

Her father's chest rose and fell with the breath he took.

"All right," the dragon king said carefully.

The air fled Asha's lungs.

"Father . . ."

The king lifted his hand.

"Get up, Asha."

It wasn't a request. She pushed herself onto her knees and rose, keeping her eyes on the floor. The dragon king reached for her chin, forcing her to meet his gaze. It shocked Asha. The dragon king never touched his Iskari. His eyebrows formed a vicious vale and his normally warm eyes were wary. Distant.

"Have I misplaced my faith in you?"

Yes. I'm more corrupted than you ever thought.

Asha wanted to close her eyes against that disappointed gaze.

"No, Father."

"How can I be sure?"

"If you let me return to the Rift, I'll do what you asked. I'll bring you this dragon's head before dawn tomorrow."

There was nothing in her way now. No more commands. No more gifts that were actually curses.

"I can't just let you go without punishment." His forehead creased in a frown. He needed her to hunt down Kozu, yes, but he also needed to uphold his law. "You've committed a serious crime. A crime against your *king*."

He studied her for a long time before releasing his grip on her chin.

"So you *shall* return to the Rift."

Asha sighed in relief.

"In two days' time."

Asha went rigid. An icy chill swept through her. "But that's . . ."

"The morning of your binding." The look in his eyes told Asha he knew what he was asking of her, but she'd given him no choice.

Twenty-Seven

On the morning of her binding day, the cell door opened.

It wasn't Jarek who stepped through. As Asha's eyes adjusted to the torchlight, she found two soldats standing in the rectangular glow.

"You're to come with us, Iskari."

Asha rose. She hugged herself to keep the damp chill from sinking farther into her bones.

"I've served my sentence. My father said I could return to the Rift on the morning of my binding."

"There's a dress in your room," said one of the soldats, ignoring her. "You're to put it on and follow us. Your father commands it."

What?

She thought of escape, but six more of Jarek's men waited in the hallway.

When they arrived at her room, the first things Asha noticed were the bolts fixed to the outsides of her doors.

The second things she noticed were the heavy iron bars running crisscross over her window, sealing her in.

And the third: her empty wall. They'd taken all her weapons.

"Did Jarek do this?"

No one answered her.

Asha slammed the door on them, then sank to her knees before her bed and felt up inside the frame where she'd hidden her slayers.

Still there.

She drew them out.

A dress was carefully laid out on the bed. It wasn't her wedding dress, but Asha could see Jarek's mark all over it—the heavy beading, the plunging neckline, the creamy gold silk.

The soldats knocked on the door, giving her a warning.

Asha didn't put on the dress.

Instead, she went to the chest at the foot of her bed. Inside, her armor remained untouched. Setting down her slayers, Asha pulled each piece out and put it on, from her breastplate all the way down to her boots. The moment she got the chance, she would head straight to the Rift.

In her armor, Asha felt safe—hidden from Jarek's ravenous gaze.

After braiding her hair into a simple plait over one shoulder, she strapped her slayers onto her back, then slid on her helmet.

The door was opening.

Asha grabbed her gifts from Jarek—the indigo kaftan, the ruby necklace, the bolt of sabra silk—and threw them into the hearth along with some kindling. Quickly, she found a match and struck it. The moment a flame flared up, she threw it onto the pile. The bolt of silk caught fire first.

The sound of booted footsteps filled her ears.

They were in her room.

"Enough! Just grab her!"

Asha spun, reaching for the gold dress, needing it to burn too. But a soldat seized her, twisting her away, pulling her toward the door. "We're going to be late, Iskari."

Asha looked back over her shoulder, watching the fire crackle and spit. Watching her gifts blaze—all except one.

The soldats looked warily at one another before marching her down the corridor.

Safire met them at the gate to the pit, which was strangely devoid of protesters.

Asha's heart leaped at the sight of her cousin. She almost didn't recognize her, dressed as she was in a deep turquoise kaftan. Her chin-length black hair was braided back and pinned at the nape of her neck.

"Asha. Where have you *been*?"

Surrounded by shouting draksors, Asha's first instinct was to keep her cousin close. But soldats flanked her, and she couldn't reach Safire.

"What is this?" Asha asked through her line of escorts. "Why am I here?"

All around her were rows and rows of wooden benches, half full of spectators, circling the pit.

On either side of her, draksors stood at tables, pitching their voices loudly, jangling bags of money, placing their bets. But it was the pit itself that held her attention the longest.

Normally the iron stakes rimming the pit were turned up to the sky, keeping criminals from climbing out and spectators from falling in. Today, though, they were lowered so they fell across the top, crisscrossing themselves.

"It's the morning of your binding," Safire said, moving through the crowd in an attempt to keep up with Asha. "You're supposed to exchange betrothal gifts with Jarek today."

Asha didn't have a gift. And even if she did, the idea of giving one to Jarek was ridiculous.

But why the arena? Usually betrothal gifts were exchanged in the city's largest square, to build public anticipation for the binding, which always happened at moonrise. She looked around, thinking hard, searching for an escape.

Men dressed in silk tunics and women in elaborately stitched kaftans sat on benches ringing the pit. But for such an important occasion—the exchanging of gifts—the arena seemed emptier than ever. Even if Asha *could* get free of her escort and grab Safire . . . there was no crowd to get lost in. No way they'd make it to the exit undetected.

The Iskari was all too easy to identify. Even now, the crowd parted for her. Their fearful eyes fixed on her.

When she reached the crimson canopy, the highest point in the arena with the clearest sight of the fights below, she saw Jarek. His usual black tunic, emblazoned with his crest—two crossed sabers—was gone. Instead he wore a white one with gold edging. Betrothal colors. The dress in her room would have matched it.

Jarek pulled her to him. Asha tensed.

"I have the perfect gift for you," he said, his body humming with a strange energy. He didn't seem to notice her attire.

The dragon king sat with his back straight and his citrine medallion on his chest. His fingers glittered with rings. Beside him stood a slave holding a platter of nougat and dried apricots. The king nodded to Jarek, giving him permission to begin.

Jarek raised the hand that held Asha's into the air. Silence descended. All the eyes in the arena were on them in an instant.

"Tonight, the Iskari and I will be bound! Let this gift of mine be a testament to our formidable union!"

Applause roared in Asha's ears. When silence fell again, it was her turn. She looked to Safire outside the tent, remembering a joke she'd made not so long ago.

I hear dragon hearts are in fashion these days, for betrothal gifts especially.

The Iskari turned to face her people. She knew what she had to do.

"Tonight, the commandant and I will be bound." Her voice was neither loud nor confident. "Let this gift of mine be a testament to our long-lasting union!"

The applause this time was much more subdued. But Asha wasn't finished. She pulled herself free of Jarek and stepped in front of him.

"Today I hunt the First Dragon!"

The applause deadened.

"Today I strike the final blow to the old ways and carve the evil out of my own soul!" A cold silence reared up as she turned to her betrothed. "As a sign of my devotion, I will bring you Kozu's *heart*. That will be my gift."

No one clapped. No one breathed. All the eyes in the arena turned to the dragon king. When Asha herself turned to face her father, he raised his golden wine cup. Toasting her. *Well played,* his eyes seemed to say.

The arena erupted. But the reaction was divided: some draksors whooped and yelled; others spoke under their breaths, exchanging nervous glances.

Her hunt was out in the open now. They'd have to let Asha leave, so she could make good on her declaration.

"Let the fighting commence!" Jarek commanded, twining his fingers through Asha's and drawing her down onto his lap.

Asha flinched. She wanted to rise. But she was playing a part now.

If she didn't kill Kozu, she'd be playing it for the rest of her life.

A group of draksors below turned to the pit. They began to chant, pumping their fists in the air, awaiting the arrival of the fighters. More and more draksors took up the chant until the sound buzzed in Asha's ears, drowning out everything else.

The interior of the pit was dark. The torches hadn't been lit yet. All she could see were hordes of spectators—sitting or standing or betting at tables. Cheering and whooping. Waiting for the match to begin.

A sudden roar rippled through the crowd, disrupting the chanters and rattling Asha.

Jarek looped an arm around her waist, keeping her locked against him.

A dragon? She looked to the skies. *Here?*

But the sky was flawless cobalt blue. Nothing flew above them.

Unseated draksors made their way toward the benches. Jarek held tight, his body crackling with energy.

"I found something of yours," he said above the noise. "You must have left it below the temple."

He reached down beneath the bench. When his hand re-surfaced, it held a jeweled axe. The axe she'd given to Torwin.

Asha's heart frosted over.

Instinctively, she reached for it. The moment her hands closed around the handle, all the torches lit at once.

Asha looked up in time to see heavily armored soldats herding a dragon into the pit. They wielded long steel lances and rectangular shields running the length of their bodies. They prodded the dragon, again and again, sticking their sharp lances deep into its dust-red hide.

The axe clattered to the ground at her feet.

"Shadow . . ."

The dragon had no choice but to move farther in, howling and snapping his jaws. He had no place to go, no place to hide. The lowered bars prevented him from flying out.

But worse than all of this?

In the center of the pit knelt Torwin.

He swayed, as if barely conscious, and a jagged knife rested across his palms. It was all he had to defend himself against the dragon so tortured and frightened, ready to kill anything that looked like a threat.

After one hard jab from a soldat's spear, Shadow gave a ferocious, heartrending howl. The armored soldats rushed out of the ring.

Just before the dragon charged across the pit, Torwin raised his face to the horde of draksors cheering on his death. His gaze slid right over them, moving ever upward, until it came to rest on Asha herself.

Twenty-Eight

Shadow charged, kicking up red sand. Torwin rolled out of the way—but only just in time. Blood streamed down his back. His old wounds had reopened and he seemed to be in a great deal of pain. It was going to slow him down. Shadow's forked tail lashed, catching the slave in the side and throwing him onto his back.

Asha pressed her fist to her mouth to stop herself from crying out.

Shadow was also in pain. Blood gushed out of long cuts in his side and he was favoring his right leg. Trapped and hurt, he didn't recognize the slave before him. The dragon's terror overrode the link he shared with Torwin. It was new, after all—weak and untested.

They're going to kill each other, Asha thought.

And she was going to be forced to watch.

"I remembered how much you loved the dragon fights," Jarek said, his arms locked around her. "I thought I'd try to resurrect them for you."

Asha swallowed down bile. She stared at Shadow, who circled the skral, getting ready to strike. The sun glinted off Torwin's knife.

If Torwin killed Shadow, Asha would fail to uphold Elorma's command to protect the dragon. The Old One would pour out his wrath. And this time, whatever punishment he struck her down with might never be undone.

And if Shadow killed Torwin . . .

Fire swelled in Asha's belly and her hands tightened around Jarek's arms. Her fingers dug into flesh and then muscle, driving for bone.

He yelped and his grip on her loosened. Asha leaped from his lap.

She'd taken three steps into the crowd when he grabbed her arm. From the murderous look in his eyes, he planned to never let go. In a single heartbeat, Asha unbuckled the plate of armor sheathing the arm he held and slid away, moving swiftly down to the pit.

When she reached the bars, she crouched. Shadow had charged Torwin, who dropped to the sand at the last moment. The belly was the easiest place to put a knife in. He could have struck a killing blow—but he didn't.

His lips moved now. And if Asha strained, she could hear his voice. Trying to soothe Shadow. Trying to coax him.

Only this time, Torwin was using a story to do it.

"No. . . ."

The old stories strengthened dragons. They made it possible for them to breathe fire.

"Torwin, don't!"

Shadow stopped himself just before hitting the wall and turned around, slitted nostrils flaring, red scales rippling. Torwin got to his feet, his lips still moving.

Shadow planted himself on all fours and reared back his head. His chest heaved. His belly glowed.

"No!" Asha screamed.

Soldats arrived at the edge of the pit. Asha stumbled out across the crisscrossed bars, losing her balance, then gaining it, out of their reach, into the middle. The crowd quieted as Asha clutched the bars beneath her, feet slipping more than once, and finally found a space wide enough to fit herself through.

She lowered herself, dangling above the pit as she realized how far the fall was. It wouldn't break her, but it would hurt.

Shadow's belly turned ember red.

Asha let go.

The air whooshed past her ears as she fell. Pain—bright and stark—rushed up her ankles and legs. She'd landed directly between the dragon and the slave. The crowd above her gasped.

Asha threw up her arms—one shielded with armor, the other bare. She saw her helmeted reflection glistening in those slitted eyes. The reflection of a hunter. An enemy.

The fire was coming and there was nothing she could do to stop it.

Asha turned and ran for Torwin. Dropping to her knees before him, she covered his body with her own, protecting him with her armor. Taking his head in her hands, she pushed it down, shielding his face with her shoulder.

"Stay low." Her voice echoed inside her helmet.

Torwin cried out as the fire rushed past them, the heat searing his skin. He grabbed the lower edge of her breastplate, holding her to him.

Bits of flame flickered and died in the sand.

Asha turned back to the dragon. It crouched low and hissed.

They'd turned her playful Shadow into a predator.

"Shadow," she said, pushing off her helmet. It fell to the sand with a *clunk*. "It's me."

He growled and thrashed his tail.

Asha began stripping off her armor, throwing piece after piece away from her.

"You know me."

Above them sat the hushed crowd, their disbelieving eyes fixed on the Iskari. Their startled murmurs rang in her ears, and above it all came a shout: a command for the soldats to open the gates. To get the Iskari out.

It was her father's command. And worse than the ferocious roar of the dragon king's voice was the chilling gaze he fixed on her. One she could feel even here.

With trembling fingers, Asha worked at the laces of her dragonskin boots, needing to get them off, to convince Shadow she wasn't the enemy.

"He sees you," Torwin said from behind her.

Asha's eyes lifted. Shadow stopped circling. His tail no longer thrashed. He took a hesitant step toward her, cocked his flat and scaly head, and made a small sound. Like a whimper.

Asha had the strangest urge to throw her arms around his neck.

She kicked off both loosened boots and slowly approached, barefoot, with her hands outstretched. Shadow nudged her palm with his snout. He trembled all over.

Asha needed to get him out of here.

Heavy footsteps thudded toward the pit entrance. Both Asha and the dragon looked to find soldats lining the other side of the gate. They were trapped. She may have stopped Shadow and Torwin from killing each other, but she couldn't protect them from her father's army.

"Asha!" Safire's voice rang out. "Fly!"

The sound of metal scraping against metal, the turning of gears, filled Asha's ears. She looked up. The iron bars above started to rise toward the sky.

Safire was in the crank room.

And then: a whistle came from above.

Both their faces turned up in time to see Dax drop two objects, one after the other. Torwin stepped out, catching the bundle of arrows in one hand and a strung bow in the other.

Asha didn't have time to wonder why Dax had a bow and arrows at the ready. She searched the sand for her slayers, which she'd flung off with her armor, while Torwin readied his arrows in his draw hand.

Does he even know how to use those?

As if hearing her thoughts, Torwin met her gaze, and Asha noticed his split and swollen lip. Then the welt across his cheek. Then the purple-black bruise along his cheekbone.

Someone had struck him. More than once.

A searing-hot rage flared up in her.

"Get behind me." She grabbed her hilts from the sand. The sacred blades came free of their sheaths with a ring. "I'll defend you until Shadow has a clear path out of here."

Torwin did as she said, nocking an arrow just as the gates opened and soldats flooded in.

Asha spun her slayers, her whole body humming and alive. She took the front while Shadow defended their backs.

"Shoot left!" Asha pointed with her slayer as the first of Jarek's men swarmed the pit.

The soldat fell before the words left her lips, an arrow embedded in his heart.

She marveled as Torwin nocked his next arrow, letting it fly before she could point out the next advancing enemy. Behind them, Shadow struck with his tail, taking out three soldats at once, flinging them into the walls.

"Where did you learn to shoot like that?"

Another soldat got an arrow through the heart.

"Why? Are you impressed?"

From the crank room, Safire's voice bellowed at whoever was trying to break down the door. She'd locked herself in.

"Greta taught me," Torwin said as another arrow flew, whooshing past Asha's hair. "And I taught your brother."

My brother?

Asha thought of callused fingers—Torwin's and her brother's. But there was no time to ask the questions swirling through her.

"As soon as those bars are up," she said, "get on Shadow and fly."

At the gate, soldats parted to let someone through. Someone dressed in white and gold.

The commandant stepped into the pit, heading straight for them, his saber in hand.

As Jarek advanced, Asha gripped her hilts hard. Everything Safire ever told her about fighting a bigger, stronger opponent ran through her head. Strike fast. Go for the legs. Get in and out. Never linger.

Halfway to her, though, Jarek stopped dead. The soldats around him all lowered their weapons, staring over Asha's shoulder. Wondering at the reason, Asha herself turned to look.

Torwin had drawn his last arrow. It was nocked in his bow, the bowstring pulled taut, and pointed directly at Asha's chest.

No soldat would advance with his arrow trained on the daughter of the dragon king.

"You get on first."

"What?"

"Asha."

He'd never said her name before. The sound of it clanged like a bell inside her, filling up her hollow places.

"Do as I say."

Asha stared at him. "You're mad," she whispered.

Above them the gates creaked. Just a little longer and the way for Shadow would be clear.

"Am I?" Keeping his arrowhead pointed at her chest, he motioned with his chin to the spectators above, their faces crammed together at the bars, staring down at the Iskari they hated and feared. "How many of them want me to put this arrow in your heart?"

Asha swallowed. *All of them.*

"And your father?"

Asha burned at this question, thinking of the king beneath the crimson canopy. Her father would have seen everything. Would have realized the truth: his daughter was corrupted.

At that thought, she stepped away from the slave.

"Please," she said. *"Go."*

Torwin's gaze trailed over her face. "No one is going to forgive you for this."

Not at first, no. But her father needed her to hunt down Kozu. Her father and everyone else would forgive her as soon as she brought back Kozu's head. That one act would absolve her of all her crimes.

"I need to make things right," she said. *"You* need to take care of Shadow. That was our deal."

The bars shrieked in protest, then stopped rising. From the crank room above, Safire cried out. The bars started to lower.

Fear flared hot and bright inside Asha. If those bars lowered completely with Torwin and Shadow still beneath them, there'd be no saving them again.

"If you die here, after I've just saved your life, I will hunt you past Death's gates and kill you a second time."

"You can kill me a hundred times," he said, raising his last arrow over her shoulder, taking aim at his master. "If I can't free you from him, I'm not leaving him alive."

Asha stared at him.

He was trying to protect *her*?

Madness.

"Torwin." Above them, his chance of escape was slipping away. "I still owe you a dance, remember? You can't dance with me if you're dead."

He glanced at her, surprised..

"Promise me you won't bind yourself to him," he said, muscles straining against the pull of the bow. "Being owned by him"—his eyes were suddenly feverish—"it will kill you, Asha."

She stared at his knuckles, clenched hard from his grip on the bow. He still wore her mother's ring.

"I'm not leaving until you promise me."

"I promise," she whispered.

Accepting this, he clicked to Shadow, then threw himself up between the dragon's wings.

Released from the threat of Torwin's arrow, Jarek advanced swiftly now. Like a sandstorm sweeping across the desert. His gaze locked on his slave, who was about to escape him a second time.

From the crank room, Safire screamed, turning Asha's blood to ice.

The gust of Shadow's wingbeats snatched at loose strands of her hair. She didn't look. Didn't dare take her eyes off the commandant. All she had time for was a silent prayer, begging the Old One to get them safely out.

Jarek raised his hands to signal his soldats. But he never finished the command, because Asha charged him first—disregarding every rule Safire ever drilled into her.

He caught her blades easily. But when he tried to cast her off, Asha held her ground. She didn't have to beat him in combat. All she had to do was hold him back.

"Out of my way, Iskari. Or I will make you regret it."

Asha gritted her teeth, holding off the strength and weight of his saber. Her body screamed. Her legs buckled. Jarek roared in her face.

Asha roared right back. Screaming out her fury.

Holding fast.

When he looked up over her head, whatever he saw made his mouth contort with rage. The force of him lifted as he stepped back, casting his saber into the sand.

Asha turned and looked skyward just as the bars clanked closed. Beyond the crisscrossed bars, the empty sky stretched cloudless and blue above her.

They're gone.

And with that thought came a loneliness so sharp and cruel, it felt like an axe cleaving her heart in two.

Twenty-Nine

Above the bars, the crowd hissed at Asha, cursing her name.
Shame crept around her heart like a poisonous vine.

She didn't resist when Jarek took her slayers, then gave the
order to empty the arena. She didn't meet the gazes of the soldats pulling arrows from their fallen comrades' chests, all of
them looking like they wanted to put a dozen arrows in *her*.

Under the weight of what she'd done, Asha sank to her
knees in the sand.

Somewhere in the arena above, her father was making his
way down to the pit. She should be thinking about what she
needed to tell him.

Instead, she thought of Torwin saying her name.

Asha. The name her mother gave her. Not *Iskari*, the name
of a corrupted god.

What if I never see him again?

It shouldn't have mattered.

At the sound of Safire's moan, Asha looked to find two

soldats dragging her into the pit. Asha went to rise, but three soldats moved toward her at once, and the look of pure hatred on their faces stopped her.

Jarek dragged Safire to Asha, throwing her into the sand, where she collapsed in a battered heap.

"Asha!" Her father's roar rumbled through the empty arena as he entered the pit. Sand scattered as he walked toward his Iskari. "You've made me into a fool!"

Asha kept her eyes lowered as he closed the distance between them.

"Look at me."

Obediently, her gaze trailed up his golden robe, past his royal crest, and settled on his stormy face.

"For years, I believed in you. *For years*, I've been on your side when no one else was. And in a single morning, you have undone all of it. *All our hard work*. Why?"

A voice rose from behind the king.

"Leave her alone."

Dax stepped casually through the gate, tossing a knife, undecorated and roughly forged, from one hand to the other. As if it were a ball. His gaze locked on their father, and in her brother's eyes Asha caught a glimpse of something dangerous.

Her father grimaced and motioned to a soldat to his left. "Get him out of here."

But Dax kept walking, heading straight for the king, his chin tilted high, his brown eyes the clearest they had been in days.

When the soldat arrived at his side, Dax lifted his knife.

Scrublander made, Asha realized.

"Touch me," said Dax, "and I'll open your throat."

The soldat paused, looking to Jarek. Jarek looked to the king, waiting for the order.

Dax didn't wait.

"Five days ago"—his voice echoed through the empty arena as he moved toward their father—"I begged my sister to save the life of a slave."

The king narrowed his eyes.

"Naturally, Asha refused. So I blackmailed her." Arriving at Asha's side, Dax stepped in front of his sister, cutting her off from sight. "Just like I blackmailed her into stealing your precious flame and intercepting the fight down in the pit."

What?

Confused, Asha looked to Safire. But Safire's eyes were cast down at her hands, planted in the sand. Her body trembled from the beating she'd taken.

Her father studied Dax with caution. "And why, my son, would you do that?"

"Isn't it obvious?" Dax's eyes gleamed. "I hate you. And what better way to strike at the one you hate than use his own pet monster against him?"

Pet monster. Those words stung worse than if Dax had cut Asha with his knife.

But he'd lied about blackmailing her. Maybe he was still lying.

"Take my *son* out of my sight." The king's voice was measured and calm, but beneath it, Asha heard a fault line. "Put him in the dungeon and wait for me. I want to interrogate him myself."

As the soldats moved in, Dax crouched down before Asha, his gaze softening on her scarred face.

"When darkness falls, little sister, the Old One lights a flame."

As they grabbed his arms and pulled him away, Dax winked at her. There was no fear in him as they hauled him off. As if this was just a small part in a much bigger game he was playing.

They heaved Safire out of the pit after him. She glanced back at Asha, her face full of worry.

Worry for *Asha*. Not herself.

Asha frowned, remembering something Torwin had told her.

The day I found you in the sickroom, I knew things were about to change.

What things? she wondered now, thinking of the bow and arrows. *What is my brother up to?*

"Now that we've swept out the riffraff . . ." Jarek handed something to the dragon king. It was Asha's leather arm piece. The one she'd unbuckled to escape him. "Her arm was unprotected when the dragon breathed its fire." He stepped toward Asha, grabbing her bare arm and holding it up. "So why isn't she scorched?"

Her father held up the armor, asking her a silent question.

"I can't be burned," she whispered to the sand.

"Speak up."

Raising her chin, Asha said it louder: "I can't be burned by dragonfire. Or any fire. It's a . . . gift. From the Old One." She couldn't meet his eyes. "I wasn't allowed to refuse it."

Jarek and her father exchanged a look. Together, they turned their backs on Asha, speaking quietly.

Asha watched them: her father and his commandant, surrounded by soldats. The arena was empty. The Iskari knelt weaponless in the sand, while the king's heir was being marched to the dungeons. If Jarek really were planning to take the throne, what was stopping him? Why wasn't he overcoming her father right now?

Her father turned back to her, his grip on her arm piece tightening. "Has the Old One given you other gifts?"

Asha looked away, her shame scattering her thoughts. "Yes."

"And? What are they?"

"The slayers," she said. "And . . . the dragon."

A stony silence solidified between them.

"You mean to tell me, all this time, you've been dealing with the Old One?"

Tears stung her eyes. She squeezed them shut. "If I don't do what he says, he takes away my strength and keeps me from"— she darted a glance at Jarek—"from hunting."

He'll denounce me now. He'll realize I'm a lost cause and cut me loose.

Her eyes opened. She looked to find her father examining her scarred face with worry in his gaze.

"He wants to use you, Asha. Like he used you eight years ago. You're easily corrupted. A dangerous vessel he can turn against the rest of us." He began to pace, running his hand over his bearded cheeks as he thought. When he stopped, he crouched down before her. "My dear child, why didn't you tell me this before now?"

Asha loosed the breath she'd been holding.

"Because I was ashamed," she said. "Because there is and always has been something dangerous inside me. I was afraid if I told you the truth, you'd think I was beyond saving."

"Look at me."

She did.

Those eyes were warm again.

"I can't help you if you don't tell me when you're in trouble."

Asha stared at her father, dangerously close to crying tears of relief.

"Our initial bargain still stands," her father said softly, so only she would hear. "You have until moonrise tonight."

The commandant reached down to help his king rise. Asha watched the locking of their hands, the strength of their grip.

"She's going to hunt you a dragon," the king said as Jarek pulled him to his feet. "I want you to go with her this time."

Asha froze, too startled to speak. Jarek raised his eyebrows, surprised.

"You saved her once from the Old One's machinations," said the king. "If the Old One seeks to manipulate her now, I want you there, at her side."

Asha stared at her father. Their shared secret hung in his eyes. He wanted her to kill Kozu in front of Jarek. Jarek, who thought Kozu's heart was a pledge, not a severing.

Was this his way of bolstering her? Of saying he knew she could do it?

And then, for the second time in the span of mere days, the king reached out and touched his daughter, gripping her shoulder tight.

He didn't even hesitate.

"I wish I could be there when you strike the final blow," he said. "The moment you do, you will free us all."

Thirty

At midday, the Iskari and the commandant rode into the Rift.

Asha took the lead, atop Oleander, whose hooves thudded the earth in a rhythmic tattoo. Jarek rode on Asha's left; and in their wake a dozen soldats galloped, armed with spears and halberds and armored with shields. Warblers and bush chats chirped out warnings from the trees as they thundered by.

The air felt heavy and charged. As if a storm were rolling in.

Asha raced down hunting paths, taking every shortcut she knew through woods and streams and more treacherous rocky terrain.

Jarek kept pace.

"Something doesn't make sense," he said as their horses waded through a wide creek, splashing cold water. "Why would Dax blackmail you? What does he care about my slave? Or the sacred flame?"

Oleander reached the bank first, clambering up and trying to put distance between herself and Jarek's black stallion. Jarek grabbed Asha's arm. She pulled hard on Oleander's reins before he yanked her backward.

The sunlight sifting through the cedar and argan trees dimmed as the sky darkened above them.

"What is he up to, Asha? What secret are the two of you keeping?" Jarek loomed over her, his grip tightening. "Tell me the real reason you threw yourself into that pit."

Asha thought of Torwin's bruised face and bloody back. She thought of Shadow's belly, glowing red with fire.

There had never been a choice. Asha could never have watched them die.

"How about a trade?" she said, narrowing her eyes. "My secret for the one you're keeping for my father."

Asha didn't expect him to let go of her.

Nor did she expect the fearful look in his eye.

When the soldats galloped into the stream, Asha tore away from Jarek, through the pines, then burst into the meadow beyond. The clouds hung low. Swollen and dark, like a purple-black bruise.

Jarek came through behind her, followed by his soldats, the pine boughs rustling in their wake.

"Stay where you are," Asha told them as she dismounted, then waded into the esparto grass. The storm clouds turned the meadow silver and gray.

This was where everything started.

At the edges, a familiar presence lurked. She smelled the faint scent of smoke and ash. But Elorma couldn't stop her now. It had been eight years since Kozu burned her. Eight years since the city went up in flames and people lost their lives—because of her.

Asha was here to set things right.

"Well?" called Jarek. "Where is he?"

"He'll come," she said, reaching deep inside for the story buried in the darkness. "Tell the soldats to hide themselves."

The soldats took up their positions in the trees, keeping out of sight. A memory flickered in Asha's mind. One from eight years ago. The last time she'd stood in this meadow.

She shut it out.

"Asha?" Jarek sounded uneasy.

There was no way around it. She was going to have to tell the story right in front of her father's commandant, and in doing so, reveal the truth: she'd never succeeded in overcoming her nature. She'd only succeeded at hiding it.

But it wouldn't matter in the end. Not once Kozu was dead.

Staring up at the clouded sky, Asha threw her voice out as far as it could go. It wasn't an old story she told—not exactly.

"Once there was a girl who was drawn to wicked things!" The wind snatched up her voice and threw it across the field. The grass rattled and hissed all around her.

"It didn't matter that the old stories killed her mother. It didn't matter that they'd killed many more before her. The girl let the stories in. Let them eat away at her heart and turn her wicked. The girl didn't care."

The air crackled around Asha. In the distance, she saw a black shape launch itself from a jagged, mountainous ridge into the dark clouds.

"Under the cloak of night, she crept over rooftops and

snaked through abandoned streets. She sneaked out of the city and into the Rift, where she told the dragons story after story. She told so many stories, she woke the deadliest dragon of all: one as dark as a moonless night. One as old as time itself. Kozu, the First Dragon."

"Asha . . ." Jarek's voice sounded strange. Frightened.

She walked farther into the tall grass. The sound of wing-beats reverberated on the air. The wind rose, howling. It tugged her hair out of its braid and whipped it across her face.

"Kozu wanted the girl for himself! Wanted to hoard the deadly power spilling from her lips! Wanted her to tell stories for him and him alone. Forever!"

A shadow fell across her. She looked up to see a dragon circling. Black as ink. Black as a still pool on a moonless night. Black as Asha's eyes.

She drew the axe at her hip.

Kozu landed with a thud. The earth trembled beneath him. His shadow shot over her, cloaking her in darkness. His scales gleamed and his slitted yellow eye drank her in. Asha's eyes did the same, fixing on his scar. A mirror image of hers, it ran down his serpentine face, cutting through his eye, marring those inky scales. Two horns twisted out of his head, perfect for goring prey; and on each foot were five talons, sharp as knives. As wide as a courtyard, his wings remained outspread—a show of just how large he was, how easily he could crush her.

Like a story himself, Kozu was formidable and fierce, beautiful and powerful.

The thought of him dead suddenly struck Asha with a piercing sadness.

She gripped her axe harder.

Someone moved behind her. Kozu's gaze darted to him, slitted nostrils flaring. But whoever it was, the First Dragon hadn't come for him. He'd come for Asha.

Like the predator he was, he circled her, the grass rustling as he moved.

Asha raised her axe. Her eyes fixed on the place where his heart beat out its ancient song. It was her or that song; they couldn't coexist. If Asha didn't silence it, she would be forced to go to Jarek tonight.

Kozu's chest glowed like a simmering coal in the center of a fire. Her fingers tightened around her axe, waiting for the perfect moment.

She waited too long.

Kozu's tail lashed, hitting her in the stomach—not with the spiked end this time, but with the strength of the middle. The force of the blow knocked the axe from Asha's hand. It landed in the grass as she staggered back.

Asha reached to draw her slayers, but Kozu's tail came again, wrapping around her chest, pinning her arms to her sides and squeezing the breath from her lungs. She gasped for air as Kozu lifted her off her feet and drew her to him.

His breath was hot on her face. His teeth were hundreds of yellowed spikes.

No. . . .

How could she have come this close, only to fail?

Death's gate rose up in her mind. In a moment, she'd be walking the path to those gates. The same path Willa walked all those years ago. . . .

Suddenly, a story flickered through Asha's mind, like a flame in the darkness. It brought her back to the meadow and the dragon and the soldats surrounding them. But the story wasn't hers.

Another flicker.

This story belonged to Kozu.

She'd told him one. And now, just like they used to do, he would tell her one in return.

Right before he killed her.

Kozu's Story

He was waiting in the trees, waiting for the girl to come out of the rock. It was dark and he was waiting. Craving the voice thrumming with ancient power. Wanting the girl speaking the stories aloud.

The sun rose, and still, she didn't come. He thrashed his tail. His wings ached to fly. His hunger needed slaking.

But he wanted the stories more than his wings wanted air and his belly wanted meat, so he stayed. She would come. She always came.

When he heard her voice, it was in the wrong place.

He launched himself out of the trees and into the air. The heat of the sun coursed through him. The strength of the wind bore him up. He saw her alone, far from the wretched city, far from the eyes and teeth on the wall.

He didn't think why. Why here, when it was always there—at the rock, higher up on the mountainside. Kozu needed, so Kozu went.

She was all he saw. He watched her face turn up to him, the story of Elorma pouring out of her mouth. He circled, landed, sending up red dust. When it settled, he started toward her, needing to tell her a tale of his own, needing her to put a voice to all the stories inside him so the Old One could live on.

Fixated on his dark jewel, he didn't see the glint of sun on metal. Didn't see until all of them were stepping out of the trees with blades that stopped the hearts of dragons.

He looked from the girl to her kin swarming out of the woods. They smelled like iron and hate. Their gazes devoured him, hungry for his hide.

With her story finished, she reached for him. It was his turn to tell.

But Kozu stepped back. She had brought her kin, armored and afraid. She had tricked him into flying to this unsheltered place. There was nowhere to hide.

Fire sizzled in his veins. Thunder rumbled in his blood.

He lashed his tail as the circle of metal tightened around him. He roared a warning to keep back.

They didn't heed him. They followed the orders of one man only: a king with power in him. It was this king who Kozu would destroy.

The fire in his chest grew, big and bright and hot.

The circle tightened, its teeth sharp and ravenous.

The king called the name of Kozu's jewel. She went, scared now, crying for Kozu to stop. But the fire was too big and too bright inside him.

The armored men stepped closer, metal raised, ready to pierce Kozu's heart. A heart that beat too fast and loud.

Kozu lunged. His tail and claws came down on metal. A claw-sharp point ripped down his face. Bright burning pain exploded in his eye, followed by darkness.

Kozu screamed as hot blood spilled out.

The fire in him rushed across the armored men whose blades were tearing down his face. It rushed across those beyond, stopping their ascent.

It rushed toward his dark jewel.

Kozu couldn't stop it. Kozu could only watch.

He watched the king raise his shield. Watched him step away from his daughter, leaving her to face the fire alone.

Her scream pierced the sky.

That scream.

It chased him as he leaped into the air. Lived inside him as he spilled his rage over the king's city. With the city burning behind him, Kozu flew fast and hard and far. Out of the Rift, across the endless desert, to the other side of the world, half blind and aching for the girl with the ancient voice.

The girl who betrayed him.

Thirty-One

"Liar!"

Kozu dropped her into the grass. The moment she touched the ground, she drew her slayers.

Lies. Wasn't that what all stories were? Wasn't that what made them so dangerous?

Suddenly, a familiar voice rose up in her.

Dragon burns are deadly, Iskari, and a burn like that?

Asha tried to shake Torwin's voice loose. But it lodged inside her.

You were just a little girl.

If the story she believed was true—that she was alone when Kozu burned her—how had the toxins been drawn out in time?

Asha remembered the burn Torwin helped treat. Her hands shook so hard. The poison set in so fast. . . .

Kozu stood stone still, watching her. The glow of his belly dimmed.

"What are you waiting for!" Jarek yelled. "Strike!"

Asha stared at the commandant. The one who found her that day and raced her back to the city.

Have I not done everything you've ever asked of me, my king?

Jarek drew his saber—which shimmered against the angry sky. He motioned to his soldats, who swarmed the field like cockroaches.

Have I not defended your walls? Put down your revolts?

Kept your secrets?

Kozu stood at Asha's back. Those great wings spread wide as he eyed the armored men around them. Asha could have turned and plunged her sacred blades into his breast. It would have been easy. It would have ended everything right here.

Instead, she fixed her gaze on Jarek, like a hunter on its prey. "Tell me: how long did it take you to find me, the day Kozu burned me?"

Jarek turned to face her. There it was again: the fear in his eyes.

Kozu's story blazed inside her, weaving with her own memories of a fire burning away her skin and the screams trapped inside her throat.

"How long!" she demanded.

She watched him bury his fear the way she buried her shame. Watched him look to the dragon at her back, then change his mind about the saber. He called out to a soldat behind him and the man tossed him a spear.

"Truly, you're as foolish as your brother," he said, his grip tightening on the shaft as he waded into the tall, rattling grass. "The enemy stands behind you, Asha. Everything you've ever wanted lies at the edge of your blade, and yet you *hesitate*."

A soldat holding a body-length shield waded out with him.

Everything I've ever wanted . . .

She wanted deliverance from Jarek. She wanted redemption for her crimes. She wanted revenge on the one who'd burned her and brought destruction to Firgaard.

But what if the crime was never hers?

What if the enemy was not the one she'd always thought?

Jarek crept closer. At her back, Kozu growled again, louder this time. The commandant stopped short, fifteen steps away. The soldat at his side trembled.

Asha stepped closer to Kozu's beating heart. Kozu, who could have killed her mere moments ago if he'd wanted to. Kozu, who didn't take to the skies even as the soldats closed in around him.

If Kozu were truly her enemy, she wouldn't be alive.

"Dragonfire is deadly." This was one truth she knew. "Even the smallest of burns must be tended immediately, to draw out the toxins."

"I'm the one who discovered your treachery." Jarek's gaze darted to the soldats moving closer in, checking their positions as he kept her distracted. "Eight years ago, *I* followed you. I saw you telling the old stories aloud. I saw the First Dragon come to you."

Asha lowered her slayers. "You *followed* me?"

"I told your father," he said. "And he put a stop to it."

Asha felt light-headed.

She thought back to the sickroom after the burning. When she couldn't remember what happened, her father filled in the gaps. It was all her fault, he said. Together they would make it right, he said. He would use her scar to show the world how dangerous the old ways were.

While everyone else looked away from her scar in revulsion or fear, her father looked on with pride. As if it were his crowning achievement. His magnificent creation.

His creation . . .

Asha wanted to shut off her thoughts, to stop herself from following them to their most logical conclusion. But they were like a scroll unraveling. She had to read to the end.

Asha's father had always wanted to rid the realm of the old ways. He used Asha to hunt down Kozu. And when she was burned, he turned her into a tool—a cautionary tale. A living piece of propaganda.

A monster.

Asha didn't want to believe it. She wanted to believe Kozu's story was the wicked, twisted thing. But there was the burn, and here she was—still alive.

Her father had been there when it happened, along with his soldats and—she realized now—his healers.

Asha looked to her betrothed. *This* was the secret Jarek kept for the king. All those years ago, her father stepped aside and let Asha burn. And Jarek knew. *This* was why Asha had been promised to him—in exchange for compliance and secrecy.

All her life, she'd thought of herself as wicked, corrupted, in need of redemption.

A shocking thought occurred to her. *What if I'm not any of those things?*

A low growl shook the earth at her feet. Asha turned to find the soldats advancing on Kozu's back.

"Kill it now!" Jarek shouted, looking over Asha's shoulder. "Strike! Before it flies!"

Asha lifted her slayers. But Kozu's tail came around her, stopping her from charging, pulling her back against the searing-hot scales of his chest.

Asha felt his acid lungs filling up with air. Felt the beat of his ancient heart.

Jarek ducked behind the soldat's shield.

Kozu breathed, streaming flames in an arc. Red and orange filled Asha's vision, swallowing the advancing soldats. The air shimmered with heat.

When the fire stopped streaming, the whole field was ablaze. And it wasn't the only thing on fire.

In the distance, beyond the trees, beyond the lower Rift and the wall, the city rooftops were going up in flames.

"Firgaard!" she screamed, pointing.

Jarek—unburned behind his shield—turned to see.

"The city is under attack!"

Asha's hands clenched as the smoke billowed into the sky. Dax and Safire were in there.

When darkness falls, little sister, the Old One lights a flame.

It was the last thing her brother said to her.

Asha's hands unclenched as she remembered the look on his face as they hauled him away to the dungeon. Like it was all a part of his plan.

No, she thought. *Dax wouldn't destroy his own home.*

"The skral are revolting!" called one of the soldats. "We need to go back!"

Every skral in the city would have heard of what happened in the pit. That the Iskari saved a doomed slave. It would have bolstered their courage. And with half the army on its way to Darmoor, and the commandant here in the field . . .

It was the perfect opportunity.

While the soldats around her paused, caught between their burning city, their homes and families, and their loyalty to their commandant, Asha turned to Kozu.

She thought of the pit and Torwin's arrow pointed at her chest. Thought of what he'd say if he were here right now.

It was the same thing her heart said.

Get on the dragon, Asha.

Kozu looked at her. If she sealed the link, it would mean they were allies. And allying herself to her oldest enemy made Asha hesitate.

No, she thought, staring into his slitted yellow eye. *You and I were never enemies.*

Asha reached for his wing bone the way Torwin had reached for Shadow's that day. Stepping into the crook of Kozu's knee, she hoisted herself up onto the First Dragon's back.

From this high up, Asha felt invincible. Lightning flashed above her. The blazing field sprawled out before her. And in the midst of the chaos, Jarek stared up at her, his eyes wide and afraid.

"Fly," she told Kozu. "Fly far away from here."

Jarek shouted orders to stop them, to kill the dragon. Kozu

stretched out his wings the way night stretches over the desert. But just as he leaped into the air, there came a sickening thud. Kozu roared and swooped sideways.

Asha slid but clung on. She looked down to find Jarek's spear lodged in Kozu's side.

No. . . .

Thunder cracked as Asha reached for it, her hands gripping the smooth wood of the shaft. As she pulled, the pain of it made Kozu lurch. The earth surged toward them. The spear came out at the same time Kozu staggered, then lost his balance. They hit the ground and the force of Kozu's momentum made him roll, pitching Asha from his back.

She heard a loud *crack!* Smelled the earthy scent of esparto grass. And then: pain, bleeding through her.

The world went ink black.

Thirty-Two

Asha woke in a cell deep below her father's palace.

She didn't know how much time had passed. Didn't know how much of the city had burned in the revolt.

Didn't know if Kozu was dead or alive.

He can't be dead, she told herself, *or the stories would be too.*

Chains streamed from her wrists and food came only occasionally. She gleaned information from her guards' whispered conversations.

The revolt started in the furrow, they said. The furrow burned and the fire caught and spread through a quarter of the city. Hundreds of slaves escaped. Hundreds more draksors were missing too. The most notable among them were Dax and Safire. Witnesses said the heir and his cousin led both skral and draksors through the streets. Together, they overtook the gate, which allowed for so many to escape.

Days passed before the soldats came for her, unlocking her shackles and marching her up through the palace. By now, the new moon had come and gone. Three slaves waited in her room, their ankles chained together. The soldats stood at the door while the slaves washed away the dirt and grime from Asha's body. She stared straight into the mirror, wondering how she'd ever been proud of the scar marring her skin.

The oldest slave stepped in front of her, severing the sight of her reflection and holding out the first layer of her dress. The gold piece. Asha didn't step into it.

"If you refuse," she whispered, her eyes averting Asha's, "we will be punished."

So Asha stepped into the gown—which had been resewn after her last fitting, when they'd cut her out of it—and threaded her arms through the slender sleeves. When they held up the white outer piece, she stepped into that too.

Half the night slipped away as they did up the multitude of tiny buttons at the back. When they finished the arduous work, they laced up the sash, pulling it tight. Last of all, they rimmed her eyes with kohl and smeared honey across her lips.

Just before midnight the soldats led her through the palace and out the gates. Asha halted at the palace entrance, looking out. Watchers crowded the city streets. Candles illuminated their faces. Their flames were as numerous as the grains of sand scattered across the desert.

Here were the people who hated and feared her. What would they say if they found out the truth—that Asha wasn't the one responsible for their burned homes, their dead loved ones? What would they do?

The soldats escorted Asha down the steps to the latticed litter made of fragrant thuya wood. Asha climbed onto the silk pillows. She gripped the holes in the wooden frame as the litter tipped, then righted itself while soldats hoisted it onto their shoulders.

Marching footsteps rang through the streets. The wind scuttled across the rooftops. Asha watched the sea of faces through the latticework as they passed.

She thought of Elorma waiting in the temple—like Jarek waited now—while his bride made her way to him through the streets. Willa might have died too young, but she'd found her place. She'd been loved and esteemed.

If Asha were to die tonight, how would her story get told?

The streets bordering the temple were packed wall to wall with draksors holding candles. Soldats lined the temple steps. The doors of the front archway were swung wide, keeping the symbol of the Old One out of view.

The soldats carved through the crowd and lowered the litter. A hush fell as Asha climbed out. The cut stones were cold against her slippered feet. The night air was even colder.

They took her into the temple corridor—lit by candles perched in alcoves, lined with soldats. When they marched her through the doors of the central chamber, Asha halted.

It had been years since she set foot here.

The chamber floors were laid with slabs of marble hewn from the mountains of the Rift. Columns rose ever upward, supporting the domed roof. Not so long ago, draksors would have knelt in this chamber, singing prayers or exultations, facing the low altar where hundreds of half-burned candles dribbled wax onto the floor. Asha remembered hearing their voices all the way from the market. Asha remembered joining them.

No candles burned now. No voices whispered.

Instead, huge red banners hung down the walls, all bearing her father's emblem: the dragon with the sword through its heart. Behind the banners, Asha knew, were dazzling scenes from the old stories cut out of colored glass: the First Dragon, hatching from his embers; the sacred flame, burning bright in the night for Elorma to find; the building of Firgaard and the raising of the temple.

The central window held the likeness of the Old One—a black dragon with a heart of flame—and was itself as wide as a dragon. It too was blotted out by her father's banners.

In the middle of the chamber, a ring of torches burned. Inside the firelit circle stood Jarek, the dragon king, and a robed temple guardian. Outside the circle, stationed along each column, stood a ring of six more guardians, there to bear witness.

In a ceremonial white tunic with gold embroidery, Jarek matched his betrothed. The flames of the torches caught in the hollows beneath his eyes and, despite lines of exhaustion bordering his mouth, desire flickered across his face as his gaze ran up and down Asha.

The dragon king stood a little beyond the commandant, shimmering in a golden robe. At the sight of him, all the hurt buried inside Asha swarmed to the surface.

"Why?" she demanded. "First, you turn me into a killer. And now, you'll give me to someone I hate. Someone you yourself fear. Why are you doing this?"

Jarek looked to the king, confused. "Someone you fear?"

She turned to her betrothed. "He knows what you're planning."

Jarek frowned at her, his confusion deepening. "What am I planning?"

Her father stepped into the light of the torches. "That you intend to take my army and rise against me."

Jarek shook his head. "Why would I rise against the man I owe everything to?"

What?

Her voice shook as she said, "Your parents are dead because of him!"

Jarek reached for her, his fingers clamping around her arm. Asha didn't even try to twist free. Where would she go? Soldats lurked down every hallway. And beyond them was a city full of people who reviled her.

"My mother loved my father more than she ever loved me," Jarek explained. "And my father loved his army more than both of us combined. I was an afterthought, if I was that much." Jarek brought her hand to his mouth, kissing her palm. Asha shivered. "Were their deaths a terrible accident? Yes. But look at me, Asha. I wouldn't be where I am today if they were alive. Their death was my glory."

Asha stared at him.

Was everything she knew a lie?

And if Jarek wasn't really a threat to her father, why would he offer to cancel the wedding?

"You never intended to cancel the wedding," she realized

aloud, hardly daring to believe it, wanting him to refute it. It was so twisted. So cruel. "You only told me that so I would kill Kozu."

And in doing so, destroy the old stories. And with the stories went all trace of the Old One. Any resistance to her father's reign would die off.

"Look at you, Asha. Look at your *brother*. What am I supposed to do with a fool for a son and a disgrace for a daughter? How could either of you rule a kingdom?" He shook his head at the disappointing sight of her. For so long, she'd craved this man's approval that, in spite of everything, she still felt shamed by that look. "Jarek is the heir I always wanted. He's the heir I shall have."

Her father motioned for the temple guardian to begin. The young woman trembled at the closeness of the Iskari—the death bringer. What her father had turned her into.

"Tomorrow morning, once your marriage is consummated, I will revoke Dax's birthright. As an enemy of Firgaard, he will forfeit any claim to my throne. Instead, Jarek will be king after me."

In his eyes Asha saw only cold, honed hate.

"Guardians!" The young guardian's voice rose up, a little shakily, to replace the dragon king's. "We gather here tonight to bear witness. To bind this couple together for life. What is bound here tonight can never be unbound."

Asha looked from the young woman to the silent, robed guardians beyond. Their hoods were pushed back. Asha glanced at each of them, until she came to the last one: Maya, the guardian who hid Torwin in the room with the scrolls.

Their gazes met and held.

"By the power given to me by the dragon king himself . . ."

Those weren't the binding words. The power to bind a pair together came from the Old One, not the king.

Maybe her father didn't need Kozu's death to usher in his new era. Maybe he could simply seize it for himself.

"I weave these lives together as one! Only death can break my threads and tear them asunder!"

Normally the bride and groom refuted this last line by reciting vows taken from Willa's story. Because the line was wrong. Willa had proven that Death *couldn't* break the bond between her and her beloved. Love was stronger than death.

"Only Death himself," Jarek recited, "can tear this bond asunder."

Those weren't the vows. They were butchering Willa's words.

She stared at the guardian, wanting her to protest. But the young woman simply stood there, waiting for Asha to repeat the words.

Jarek reached for Asha's arm and drew her in close. His grip tightened. Always tightened. "What do you think will happen to you if you don't say the words, Asha?"

My father will give me to you anyway. It was the worst punishment she could think of.

"Say them."

She never would. Not to Jarek. The words belonged to Willa. Saying them to Jarek was a desecration. A mockery of

Willa's fierce, unyielding love.

Asha looked to the guardians beyond the circle of flame. Six sets of eyes looked back at her, watching. As if she were nothing more than a slave being sold and locked in a collar.

She thought of the people gathered outside. Thought of how, before her mother died, she could hear the chant of prayers all the way from the market.

Asha didn't have any prayers. But she had something else.

"Once there was a king, rotting from the inside out!" Asha threw her voice so hard and so high, she imagined it reaching beyond the stained-glass windows hidden behind her father's banners. Imagined it reaching all the way to the sky. "He tricked his own daughter into betraying the First Dragon! He turned Kozu against her, *letting* her burn, all so he could *use* her! So he could twist her into a tool for his own dark purposes!"

Beyond the circle of flames, the guardians exchanged startled glances.

"The dragon king convinced his daughter it was her fault; she burned because *she* was the rotten one. He showered on her false kindnesses, to make her feel indebted to him. To use her to usher in a new era—one without dissent."

"Silence!" her father commanded.

Jarek squeezed, crushing her bones.

But Asha didn't stop.

"She believed the lies he told. She hunted down monsters because he asked her to, never realizing the most wicked monster of all stood right behind her."

From outside, Asha thought she heard murmurs turn to shouts. Thought she heard the crash of lanterns dropped on the stones.

"Bind them," commanded the dragon king.

"But, my king, she hasn't said the—"

"BIND THEM!"

The temple guardian stepped forward, her hands trembling as she did. She took the white silk and, as Jarek laced his fingers with Asha's, tied it around their wrists.

"Your worst fear has come true, Father." Asha stared down the dragon king. "I am corrupted. The Old One owns your Iskari. You have nothing left to use against her, nothing to make her do what you want."

The guardian said the binding words. A moment later, Jarek ripped off the silk. It fluttered to the stones at their feet. He grabbed Asha and yanked her out of the circle of torches.

The sound of shattered glass erupted from above.

A thousand colored shards rained down on them.

Jarek let go. Asha raised her arms over her head, protecting herself from the falling pieces. She looked up, watching her father's torn banner flutter to the floor.

A fierce wind howled through the broken window—or maybe that was the dragon.

With outstretched wings, the dust-red dragon swooped, circling downward, as out in the street, the screaming started. Asha could hear people pushing and shoving, running for cover.

Shadow landed clumsily on the stone floor before Asha.

Gasps rose from the guardians behind her. Two of them fell to their knees.

Righting himself, Shadow's pale slitted eyes flickered over her, checking for injury, before narrowing on the commandant and the king at her back. Shadow roared, and the temple shook with the sound. As if the Old One himself had woken from a too-long slumber, angry, ready to take back what belonged to him.

Atop Shadow sat Torwin, a bow slung over his shoulder and a knife tucked into his boot. Steely eyes met Asha's. He wore a strange fitted coat and gloves, with a dark green sandscarf pulled up over his face, covering his nose and mouth.

You're supposed to be gone, she thought. *You're supposed to be safe.*

And yet her hope ignited at the sight of him.

Shadow hissed. Jarek stepped back, out of the circle of fire and away from Asha, his hands raised.

Her father yelled for the soldats. But the doors to the chamber were shut tight. Maya and a few of the other temple guardians were shoved up against them.

With Shadow's gaze pinning Jarek in place, Torwin held one hand down to Asha. She rose and seized it, letting him pull her up. Asha hiked up the hem of her dress to straddle Shadow's back. Torwin's arm slid around her waist, keeping her tight against him. He clicked to Shadow, who hissed another warning and stretched his wings wide.

"Are you ready?"

Her heart thudded at the sound of his voice at her ear, slightly muffled by the fabric of the sandskarf. He smelled like dragon-fire and smoke.

"I've never been more ready," she said.

His eyes crinkled. She knew beneath the sandskarf he was smiling the smile she loved best. One that involved his whole mouth.

"Hold on." His arm tightened as Shadow beat his wings, shifting from foot to foot.

Asha's stomach lurched as they sprang into the air.

In his leap for the window, Shadow knocked over a torch and her father's crumpled banner caught fire. As they rose toward the window, Asha looked back to the flames, past Jarek, to the dragon king. Smoke twisted around him.

His eyes raged at her. But underneath the surface, Asha thought she saw the seed of a great fear.

Be afraid, Father. I'll make you regret everything you've ever done to me.

Shadow soared out through the broken window and into the night.

Asha laughed—softly at first. And then deliriously.

She'd just escaped her own wedding on the back of a dragon.

They soared over rooftops, then over the wall. Asha turned and looked back, watching the city fall away, marveling at how different the streets and rooftops looked from so high up. Like a winding web. Shadow sailed higher, beyond the wall and out into the Rift.

The higher they rose, though, the colder it got. Soon Asha's teeth chattered. Torwin pulled her closer, trying to use his heat to stave off her chill.

Asha curled into him. With the lower half of her face pressed into his shoulder, she watched her home shrink into the distance before turning her eyes to the sky.

The stars shone like crystals above them and the moon had bled out. It was waxing instead of waning now.

It would be pale and slivered and new.

Thirty-Three

Asha woke with her cheek against a bony shoulder. Torwin unlatched her hands from their grip on his arm and Shadow fidgeted beneath her, waiting patiently for his riders to dismount.

They'd landed on some kind of precipice. The Rift surrounded them, snakelike and silhouetted beneath the stars. Somewhere in the distance stood the city, but they were so high and far, Asha couldn't even make out the wall. Below them sprawled thick, scrubby forest.

Torwin dismounted first, sliding effortlessly down Shadow's side. Asha swung her leg over so she could follow and found Torwin already turned to catch her, his hands taking hold of her waist as he guided her down to the earth.

When her slippered feet touched the stony ground, she looked up to find his worried gaze tracing her scar. Remembering the sight of herself in the mirror, she turned her face, keeping the scar out of his sight.

"I'm fine."

Torwin's hands slid up her cheeks. Gently, he turned her to face him.

"Are you?"

The breath rushed out of Asha. She nodded.

With his hands still cradling her face, his gaze continued to search her.

Asha grabbed hold of his wrists, stopping his searching gaze. "No one hurt me," she said, willing him to hear what she wasn't saying: *Jarek didn't hurt me.* "I promise."

He lingered over her, trying to decipher if this was the truth or her attempt to protect him. Finally, he nodded.

Shadow whuffed. Torwin and Asha both looked up, over her shoulder, at the hulking dark form. Torwin's hands fell away from her face. Whistling to the dragon, he reached out a palm and Shadow nuzzled it before turning and launching himself into the sky.

Torwin motioned Asha toward the thick woods. "This way."

She stood for a moment, watching him. He seemed different here, so far from the city. Dressed in his strange jacket and gloves, with a bow slung over his shoulder and a knife tucked in his boot.

He seemed free.

The trees clustered so closely together, their boughs blocked out the starlight. The wind rustled the crisp leaves of eucalyptus trees. This part of the Rift was unfamiliar to Asha, and she had difficulty keeping up. She stumbled through the darkness, her dress catching on branches, her feet snagging in root systems. Pine needles crunched beneath her footsteps, echoing loudly in her ears.

"Some hunter you are." Torwin smiled in the darkness. His fingers brushed against Asha's, making warmth bloom through her. "You'll alert the entire camp to our arrival."

"Camp?" she whispered, distracted by the back-and-forth movement of his knuckles across hers, soft and hesitant. "What camp?"

"It's not much farther now," he said.

But Asha didn't want to leave this wood. She wanted to stay right here, alone in the darkness with him.

Torwin seemed to want that too, because his footsteps slowed. He laced his warm fingers through hers. "Asha?"

"Hmm?"

"There's . . . something I need to tell you." His thumb ran nervously across her skin. "Before we go down there. In case I lose my nerve."

Asha paused, suddenly nervous too. "All right."

In the darkness, she heard the soft sound of him swallowing. "I'm leaving."

The words sliced the air, cold and abrupt.

"Leaving?" Asha frowned. "What do you mean?"

Torwin took a deep breath. "Your brother gave me enough coin to buy passage aboard a ship in Darmoor. From there, I'm heading north. Across the sea."

It shouldn't have surprised her. This was what he'd wanted ever since he'd stolen her slayers that night in the temple and made her show him the way out of the city.

He wanted to escape. To be far, far away from everything that had ever hurt him.

Asha didn't blame him.

Still, her footsteps halted. The thought of him, gone . . .

Torwin stopped too, turning to face her in the dark. He still smelled like dragon musk and smoke. "You could come with me. If you wanted to."

Asha fell into silence, thinking of the last time he'd made her this offer. She'd turned him down then, and that had been a huge mistake.

"Just think of it, Asha: freedom, adventure, the salty sea air on your face. . . ." She could hear his excited smile. "I've never even *seen* the sea."

He leaned in, pressing his forehead to hers.

She tried to smile, tried to catch his excitement. But her heart suddenly felt so heavy.

"When?" she asked, even as she dreaded the answer. "When do you leave?"

Before he could respond, though, the light of a lamp flashed across their faces.

Asha didn't think; she reacted. Her hand slid out of Torwin's. Grabbing the knife in his boot, she pushed him behind her, positioning herself between him and the intruder.

But all she could see was a light in the trees.

"It's all right." The heat of Torwin rushed up her back as he closed the distance between them. "It's only the patrol."

"Actually," came a voice with a honeyed accent, "it's just me."

"Jas?" Torwin asked.

Asha squinted through the bright orange glow of the lamp, her blade lowering. The bearer of the lamp lowered it to his side, illuminating him.

The intruder was a young man, maybe a year younger than Asha. The horn hilts of two huge knives gleamed at his hips, and a maroon sandskarf was wrapped loosely around his shoulders.

Everything about him said scrublander.

Enemy.

Asha lifted the knife again. The boy's smile slid away.

"This is Jas," said Torwin, stepping out from behind Asha and resting his hand on hers before peeling his knife from her fingers. "Roa's brother. He's a friend."

Roa. The girl who betrayed Dax.

"What's he doing here?" she demanded.

Jas smiled nervously, looking to Torwin for rescue.

"He's here to help," Torwin said, tucking the knife back into his boot on the side farthest from Asha. "Jas, meet Asha."

At her name, Jas's eyes went wide. He glanced at her scar. "The Iskari," he whispered. Her reputation apparently preceded her, because Torwin didn't say anything more. "I've heard . . . a great many things about you." He lifted his fist to his heart, and then—as if addressing Asha a moment more might make her reach for the knife again—he turned to Torwin.

"You haven't seen my sister, have you?"

Torwin shook his head. "We only just arrived."

Jas worried his lip with his teeth. "She and Dax quarreled, and now she's disappeared."

Asha frowned in confusion.

Dax was here? With *Roa*?

Asha looked to Torwin. "What's going on?"

"There's . . . a lot you don't know," he said. "Come on. I'll show you." He looked to Jas. "Coming?"

The boy shook his head. "I need to find my sister." Glancing to the Iskari, he said, "It was nice to meet you, Asha."

She nodded, then followed Torwin through the trees.

When the woods grew sparse, voices mingled with the sound of the wind in the leaves. When the trees disappeared completely, Asha found herself standing atop a hill covered in pinecones, looking down over a camp of thousands. Dozens of bonfires burned, surrounded by groups of people sitting and drinking. Canvas tents of all sizes were pitched around them.

"Welcome to New Haven," said Torwin, motioning to the bowled-out valley below. "The name was your brother's idea. This is where he's assembling his army."

My brother, she thought, her heart racing, *is plotting a war.*

Was Dax even capable of such a thing?

Suddenly, two forms approached. When they stopped, Asha saw they were draksors. Draksors studying Asha with the same wary look she directed at them. They nodded to Torwin, then stepped back.

Torwin held his hand out to her, but Asha—all too aware of the patrols watching—didn't take it. Instead, she headed down the hill, toward the tents and the bonfires.

The moment she set foot in the camp, hundreds of eyes looked up, first to the Iskari, then to the slave at her side. Asha couldn't help staring back. Around every fire were not just draksors and skral but scrublanders too.

Enemies . . . united.

Dax did this?

"Asha," Torwin said from behind her. The moment he did, a hushed silence descended. Asha halted on the trodden-down path and looked back. Torwin clearly wanted her to follow.

Asha looked past Torwin, to the faces lit up by firelight. Draksor and skral. They sat side by side, sharing jugs of wine. But collars still hung around skral necks. And skral eyes didn't quite meet draksor ones. And every gaze narrowed on one young man. The slave who said the Iskari's name. Out loud. As if he had a right.

The hair on Asha's arms rose. She went to Torwin's side, her fingers moving to an axe that wasn't there. She stayed close as he led her to a tent guarded by two scrublanders, their double-edged sickle-like swords sheathed in leather scabbards. They nodded to Torwin, who stepped inside the tent.

Asha followed him in.

Thirty-Four

A map lay unrolled across a roughly made table, and over it leaned Dax, his finger tracing some boundary Asha couldn't see. Next to him, looking where he looked with her arms crossed over her chest, stood Safire, the bruises on her face receding. Around them stood a hastily pitched tent, the fawn canvas kept aloft by roughly hewn columns made of thick branches.

Asha's heart jolted at the sight of them.

When Torwin cleared his throat, Dax and Safire looked up, their mouths opening at the same time.

Safire moved first, hopping the table and lifting Asha up in a hug. No one would punish her for touching Asha now, and she took full advantage of the freedom, squeezing her cousin until it hurt.

"Saf," Asha managed. "I'm so sorry."

Safire pulled away, frowning hard. "For what? This?" She pointed to her bruised face and grinned. "You should've seen what I did to *their* faces." Letting go of Asha, she looked to Torwin. "When the red moon bled out and you hadn't returned . . ."

"They had her in the dungeon," Torwin explained. "I couldn't get in alone. I had to wait."

Asha looked from Safire to Torwin to Dax. The three of them had planned her rescue together.

"The day of the revolt, we searched for you," said Dax, coming out from behind the table. His hands no longer shook. He was still reed thin and tired, but his eyes were clear and earnest. "But you weren't anywhere." He looked away. "So we left you behind." She heard what he didn't say: *with a monster. He thinks he abandoned me*, she realized.

"I never would have forgiven myself if—"

Asha shook her head. "I'm here now."

"Yes," said Safire, her eyes narrowing. "Which means Jarek is already looking for you." She glanced at Dax. "We need to double our patrol."

He nodded. "Go do it."

Safire hugged Asha one more time before leaving the tent. In her absence, Asha looked to her brother. Though his golden tunic was wrinkled and smudged with dirt, he seemed to shine in it.

"Tell me what all of this is," she said, motioning to the map, the tent, the door leading out to a camp full of rogues.

"We're going to invade Firgaard and overthrow the dragon king," said Dax. "But we need more men, women, and weapons in order to stand any kind of chance. So Roa made me a deal: the scrublanders will lend us what we need *if* I make her my queen."

Asha felt like her heart had just fallen out of her chest. It was Roa's household that turned against Dax all those years ago. "But . . ."

"It was Roa's idea to take Darmoor," he explained, anticipating her objection. "Roa gave us the distraction we needed. She knew Jarek would send the army there, which would cut the number of Firgaard's soldats in half."

Which was why the revolt had been so successful.

Asha marveled. Roa was a mastermind.

"But *queen of Firgaard*? Are you sure you can trust her?"

He sighed, not quite meeting her eyes, and ran a hand through his brown curls. "I don't have much choice. Without the scrublander army, our father will tear this realm apart, piece by piece."

Piece by piece. Until he found Asha.

She looked at Torwin, silhouetted in the opening of the tent.

Until he found them both.

Just think of it, Asha, Torwin's voice echoed through her mind. *Freedom, adventure, the salty sea air on your face. . . .*

It was a delusion. A fantasy. As long as her father held the throne, Torwin would be hunted. It wouldn't matter how far away he got.

The thought hit her like an arrow to the chest.

Asha couldn't run. She had to stay and fight.

"A caravan bringing weapons is due in three days," Dax went on. "Once it arrives, there will be a wedding. And then we go to war."

"I want to help," she said.

Only Asha knew what her father was truly capable of. The way he'd lied to her, twisting her into a horrifying tool to do his bidding. The way he handed her over to Jarek, like she was worthless. Like what she wanted didn't matter. Like her heart and *soul* didn't matter.

Dax smiled at her. "I was hoping you'd say that."

"What? No." Torwin stepped farther into the tent, glaring at Dax. "You said if I brought her to you, you'd keep her safe."

"This is her fight too."

Torwin swung to face Asha, his eyes full of anguish. "You've only just escaped. You can't march right back—"

"Who are you to say what I can and can't do? You plotted a revolution with my own brother and told me *nothing*."

Torwin's jaw clenched, his hands curled into fists. "I *plotted* a slave rebellion. I *plotted* the freedom of my people. I want no part in this grasp at power." His eyes slid to Dax for the briefest moment and his voice dropped to something softer. "Asha, you're *free*. What if this fails? What if you fall into their hands again?"

Asha saw the fear in his eyes. He'd risked so much to save her tonight. And here she was, throwing it in his face by marching back to the city alongside her brother.

"Asha." Torwin's voice was strained, his eyes pleading. "You don't have to do this."

But she did. She wanted—no, *needed*—her father brought to his knees.

My father must pay for what he's done to me.

Asha turned to face her brother. "Whatever you need me to do, I'll do it."

From behind her, Torwin said, very softly, "Then I guess this is good-bye."

When she spun to face him, he was already gone.

Thirty-Five

Asha tracked Torwin through the camp and up into the blue-black darkness of the woods, where she promptly lost him. Why hadn't she brought a torch? Her heart pounded. She needed to find him.

She would not let that be their good-bye.

When starlight filtered through the cedars, Asha followed it to where the trees ended, giving way to the precipice Shadow had landed on. Asha stared out over the realm before her. The jagged ridges of the Rift slowly collapsed into desert, and beyond it: stars forever.

Asha stood at the edge, shivering in the cold night air, searching the skies for a dust-red dragon and its rider. With the Rift sprawled out before her and the camp nestled in the valley at her back, Asha did the only thing she could think of: she spoke an old story into the wind. One meant for the dragon darker than a starless night.

She heard his wingbeats in the distance. Saw the silhouette

of his form fly across the face of the moon. Asha hugged herself to stay warm, waiting.

Finally, Kozu landed in a spiral of dirt and leaves, tucking in his wings. Asha traced the scabbed wound in his side from the spear, remembering how he'd stumbled and hit the earth. Remembering how she'd been pitched from his back.

She was afraid to try again.

Kozu swung his head around to face her. They stared at each other, the Iskari and the First Dragon, until finally Asha took a deep breath.

Slowly, her fingers felt for the bump of his shoulder bone. After grabbing hold, she swung herself up onto his back, hiking her dress up to her thighs. His scales were warm and smooth beneath her palms. She breathed in his smell: all smoke and ash.

If she let herself think of what she was about to do, she might climb down. So she didn't think. With her tongue against her teeth, Asha clicked the way Torwin had with Shadow.

Kozu leaped off the precipice and into the sky.

Asha's stomach lurched as the wind rushed past her face and rocky ridges rose up to meet them. She gripped Kozu's neck and held on tight until he leveled out.

This time, something locked into place deep inside her. Something that was always meant to be.

Asha sat up, looking out over craggy outcroppings, over meadows flecked with oleander. She felt Kozu not just beneath her, a dangerous creature moving from wind current to wind current, but in her mind too. Like a dark shadow. An ancient presence. Fixed and fierce and *hers*.

The wind smacked her bare legs and face. It whipped her hair and stung her eyes. When her teeth started to chatter, she pressed herself against Kozu to keep from freezing. But she didn't turn him back; she needed to find Torwin.

She needed to persuade him to stay. To fight with them against her father.

As Kozu flew, Asha searched the sky. Shivering, she watched the smoky clouds pass overhead, depriving her of light from the stars. When the clouds fled, she scanned the peaks and ridges they flew past. But there was no sign of any other dragon.

As her shivers turned more violent, Asha understood the reason for Torwin's fitted coat and gloves. If she didn't find him soon, she would have to head back—or she'd freeze.

It was when she looked down again that she saw a familiar shape, flying below. Asha clicked to Kozu and he dropped, making her stomach flutter. A heartbeat later, both dragons flew side by side.

Shadow's rider looked over at Asha. His sandskarf covered his nose and mouth.

Don't make me say good-bye to you, she thought.

Asha pitched her voice above the wind. "Where are you going?"

He didn't answer.

Squinting into the distance, just past two rocky peaks, she saw the glassy surface of a lake, silver in the moonlight.

"There's water down there!"

Again, he kept silent.

"I'll race you to it!" she shouted.

Torwin didn't have time to respond. Asha leaned close to Kozu, who knew exactly what she wanted, and together they plunged into the wind.

A feeling rushed through her as they fell: excitement, fear, exhilaration, all snarled up together and lodged in her belly. Soon, though, a sharper feeling replaced it. Asha looked from side to side, searching for Torwin and Shadow. They hadn't followed. She and Kozu were alone.

Asha swallowed disappointment. Sensing it, Kozu started to level out, and, just as he did, a dust-red dragon and its rider plunged past them. For a moment, Asha watched them: Torwin keeping low to Shadow's back while Shadow tucked his wings in—falling, falling. As if they'd done this thousands of times. As if it was their favorite game.

A moment later, she was falling too.

Asha clutched Kozu's neck as the wind whipped her hair. When they righted again, Kozu was head-to-head with Shadow.

Torwin glanced their way, then clicked. Shadow sped up.

A moment later, almost lazily, Kozu caught up with them.

Above his sandskarf, Torwin's eyes narrowed. He clicked once more. But this was the fastest Shadow could go. He was smaller and more agile, but Kozu was stronger and had more weight to thrust them forward.

Torwin and Shadow fell back. Asha turned her attention to the lake.

She thought Kozu would land *beside* the water. Kozu did not. As Asha focused on the bank, the dragon headed straight for the water. Asha clicked frantically, then tried to pull up on his neck, then his wings, wanting him to slow down. To stop before—

The surface of the lake broke as Kozu hit. Asha held her breath just before the water rushed up to swallow them.

Underwater, she slid from Kozu's back. When her feet touched the bottom, she pushed up, then broke the surface. Asha spluttered and gasped. She splashed at Kozu in retaliation, but the dragon was deep underwater, swimming away from her. The lake was warmer than the night air and Asha stayed a moment, her dress floating around her as she tilted her face back to the jeweled sky above.

On the shore, Shadow landed.

Asha swam for the lake's edge as Torwin dismounted, but the layers of her dress made kicking hard, and it took her twice as long as it normally would. She lost both her slippers. When her feet finally touched stone, Asha made her way toward the place where Torwin stood. Her bare feet slipped on the under-water rocks.

"You win," he said, reaching down from his dry overhang.

Asha made a face as he grabbed hold of her hands and pulled her out of the water. The wet dress stuck to her body and weighed her down. Shivering, she picked up the hem and wrung it out.

"Here." He slid off his strange coat and tucked it over her shoulders. "There are dry clothes in my tent, if you want them." She did want them—and along with them, an escape from this gown. Torwin pointed up the shore to an angu-lar shape hunched on the sand. "I'll make a fire while you change."

Asha nodded, shivering, then made her way toward it.

Halfway up the shore, though, her feet fell still as she remembered the tiny buttons dotting the back of the underlayer of her dress.

I can't take it off without help.

Her face flamed at the thought. Jarek had her gown made for exactly this reason: so she would need her new husband to undress her.

At that thought, Asha pulled Torwin's coat tighter around her. She looked back, to where the skral knelt before his crackling kindling, blowing on the fragile flames. The silver collar around his throat caught the light.

Not so long ago, she'd thought they were nothing alike, her and this boy. Now she knew the only difference between them was he wore his bondage around his throat while hers was invisible to the eye. She'd thought her title, Iskari, was her greatest power. She'd thought hunting dragons in the Rift was her fiercest freedom. But the truth was: these things had never been anything more than a collar around her throat.

And now that they were both free, he was escaping the horror while Asha was marching right back into it.

How can I ask him to stay and fight? she thought. *This isn't his war.*

Torwin had suffered enough. He deserved to be free.

She looked away from him. She didn't dare ask for his help with the dress. Not after everything back in the camp. But with the sun gone, the temperature would drop. It was dangerous to be inadequately dressed in the Rift at night.

Trembling with cold, Asha made her way toward the fire, hoping the heat of the flames would be enough to dry her. Otherwise . . .

She didn't want to think about the second option.

Thirty-Six

Asha sank down onto the log next to the struggling fire, shivering in her soaking-wet dress. Just beyond the firelight, Shadow stalked a sleeping Kozu. His forked tail thrashed. He lowered himself on his front legs, ready to pounce. Kozu opened one yellow eye, saw the dragon readying himself, and closed it again.

"Why are you sleeping out here?" Asha asked as Torwin fed more wood into the flames. "So far away from New Haven?"

A loud growl startled them. Asha peered into the darkness beyond the fire. Kozu's scales rippled in the firelight as he pinned Shadow on his back. Kozu's tail was in the younger dragon's mouth as Shadow's own thrashed happily.

Asha turned back to Torwin, her teeth chattering. She held her trembling palms out to the fire, letting the heat lick her clammy skin, trying to get warm. "There isn't enough room in the camp?"

"I've spent my whole life in cramped quarters," said Torwin, blowing into the flames, making them spread. "I prefer the open sky."

Asha wanted to say she understood. Sleeping under the sky was one of the best parts of hunting. But her teeth clattered so hard, she could only clamp them together and hunch farther toward the fire.

Torwin fed it two more logs, and only when these caught and burned did he sink back on his heels and look up at Asha. His hands were streaked with ash.

An immediate frown creased his forehead.

"You're still in your binding dress."

She didn't meet his gaze. Just waved her hand. "I'm fine." Her whole body shook with shivers. "Really."

"I promise the clothes are clean. They might not fit well, but you won't freeze to death."

When she said nothing in response, he rose a bit huffily. "Fine. Do what you want. That's what you always do anyway."

Asha threw him a look and found him struggling to pull her mother's ring off his smallest finger. When it finally came free, he held it out to her. "Here. This belongs to you."

Asha stared at the white circle of bone on his palm.

All those days ago in the Rift, she didn't want to give it to him. So much had changed since then. Now that he held it out to her, she didn't want to take it back. As if taking it back meant taking back everything else.

"I'm leaving in the morning," he said. "I'll probably never see you again. Take it."

At those words, Asha pulled her hands away from the fire

and placed them firmly on the damp log beneath her. "I can't take it back." She kept the scarred side of her face turned away from him. "We had a deal. I promised to fly you to Darmoor, and I didn't. The ring belongs to you now."

"I don't care about that," he said, stepping closer, holding it farther away from himself. "It was your mother's, Asha. I think she'd want you to have it instead of *some slave*."

Anger sparked in her then. How dare he say that—to her, of all people? Asha had risked her life for him. She'd risked even more than her life.

Rising, she narrowed her eyes on him. "I said, *I can't take it back*."

He reached for her hand and pressed the ring into her clammy palm. But when he pulled away, Asha's fingers didn't close around the band, and it fell into the sand at their feet.

For several heartbeats, both of them stared at it.

Torwin turned away.

Fire coursed through Asha's veins. "Don't you dare walk away."

He kept walking.

"Take it back!"

He stopped then, almost out of reach of the firelight. He didn't turn around when he said, very softly, "Is that a *command*, Iskari?"

Her throat burned.

"Torwin . . ."

He turned around. But he didn't look at her. Like a good, obedient skral, he kept his gaze on the sand at her feet. Where the ring had fallen.

"Look at me." Asha's voice shook.

His hands fisted. His shoulders bunched. But he didn't look up.

Anger blazed through her. He didn't get to do this. Not in the Rift, where rules bound no one. Not after everything they'd been through.

She moved like wind.

Right before she shoved him, Torwin looked up. His anguished gaze met Asha's furious one.

And then, beneath the force of her palms, he staggered back. Behind them, both dragons stopped playing and looked up.

"Why are you doing this?" Asha demanded, warmed by the heat of her own fury.

A breath shuddered out of him. "I thought I was getting you *out* of danger."

Asha stopped. Her fists uncurled.

"And then I walked you right back into it."

Asha stared at him. Over his hunched shoulders, the lake shone. The stars' reflections were a rippling silver on black.

"And worst of all, you're *fine* with it. You're happy to be a piece in someone else's game." He ran frustrated hands through his hair. "It's as if you *believe* them when they look at you like all you're good for is being used. Like all you're good for is destroying things."

She frowned at him through her dripping-wet hair.

"That's not what you are, Asha. And it's not how you should be looked at."

All around them was the soft sound of the lake lapping at the shore. Asha crossed her arms. His words struck something soft and exposed. Something she needed to protect at all costs.

Very quietly, she whispered, "How should I be looked at?"

Torwin lowered his gaze to her throat. A breath shuddered out of him.

"Like you're beautiful," he said. "Beautiful and precious and good."

The words cracked her open, tearing that soft, exposed thing out from the safety of her chest. It angered her that he could do it so easily. It infuriated her that he could do it with just his words.

But Asha remembered the sight in the mirror.

She knew what she was.

"I've spent my whole life believing lies."

His gaze rose to meet hers.

"Please," she whispered, "no more."

Torwin no longer hesitated. He stepped toward her. "If *I'd* spent my life believing lies, I wouldn't trust myself to know the truth when it stood staring me in the face."

Asha narrowed her eyes at him, forcing him to look at all of her. She didn't turn her cheek. Didn't hide her scar. She forced him to look his own lie in the face.

"Why is it so hard for you to hear, Asha? You're beautiful."

Asha opened her mouth to refute this obvious untruth, but he interrupted.

"You're precious," he said, softer this time. "You're—"

"Stop it!" She swung her fist, and he caught it. When she tried to free it, his grip tightened, so she elbowed him in the stomach.

The breath went out of him. He put his hands on his knees, breathing unsteadily.

But Torwin never gave up easily.

"It's what I thought the very first time I saw you," he said, recovering. "In my master's library, pulling down scrolls." Asha shoved him again. He staggered back. "It's what I thought after Kozu burned you, when you stood before the entire city. It's what I thought when they shouted at you and turned their backs on you and spat at your feet and you . . . you stood there and took it. I've never, not once, stopped thinking it."

Tears burned in her eyes. Her throat stung with heat.

"You're a liar."

He grabbed her fist, pulling her into him. Asha tried to push him off, but his arms tightened around her. She used her elbows and knees, but Torwin only buried his face in her neck and held on.

When the fight went out of her, she collapsed against him. Her teeth chattered and her body shook. Her arms moved around his neck, hugging him close, surrendering to the warmth of him.

"You're going to freeze to death," Torwin whispered against her neck. "Why didn't you change?"

When she didn't answer, when she only hugged him harder, Torwin pulled away, silent and considering. She could hear the thoughts forming in his head as his gaze ran over her gown.

He was a house slave. House slaves knew these things.

"You can't take it off," he realized.

Asha looked down to the sand, hugging her arms now,

willing her traitorous body to be still, her chattering teeth to be silent.

He held out his hand.

She didn't reach for it. Didn't dare look up at him. She stared at her toes. Toes she was starting to lose feeling in.

"Asha." He said her name like it was something exquisite and exasperating at the same time. Crooking his finger beneath her chin, he tilted her face up, bringing her eyes back to his. "This won't be the first time I've undressed you."

Asha's pulse quickened.

"I've spent my whole life dressing and undressing draksors," he said. "It's just a task. Nothing more."

But his trembling fingers betrayed him. The nervous wobble in his voice matched Asha's own fumbling pulse.

And still, she went with him.

Thirty-Seven

Inside the tent there was darkness, then the sound of a match being struck. The smallest of flames lit up Torwin's hands as he cupped the match and ignited the lantern hanging above. It swung, scattering light across the tent and illuminating a bedroll, a pile of folded clothes, and the lute she'd bought in the marketplace.

They stood face-to-face, Asha chattering and trembling and dripping. Torwin, waiting and silent and still.

Asha had been dressed and undressed by slaves before. But they'd always been female slaves. Torwin was not. And the dress in question was her binding dress, meant to be taken off by her husband.

She needed to turn around so he could undo the buttons. She didn't, though. In case a better option presented itself. Maybe she could call Kozu, fly back to camp, and get Safire to help her instead. But the thought of flying wet, in the freezing wind, made her shiver all the harder.

Torwin touched the knot in her sash. When she didn't resist, he stepped in close. His fingers trembled as they untied the knot. The wet silk slid across her waist when he pulled and the dress loosened, letting her breathe.

The sash fell to the floor.

Torwin pushed the gossamer overlayer off her shoulders. With the slightest of tugs, it joined the sash at their feet.

When Asha still didn't turn, he touched her wrist. His fingers trailed slowly up to her elbow, turning her gently until she faced the rough canvas wall of the tent. With her blood humming, she gathered up her wet hair and pulled it over her shoulder.

His fingers started at the top of her underlayer, sliding the tiny pebble-like buttons out of their corresponding loops.

The silence grew like a storm rolling in.

Soon, Asha couldn't bear it.

"Thank you," she said, breaking the silence.

Her voice startled him. He fumbled, his knuckles brushing across her bare skin. Asha's heart raced like a desert wind.

"*This* is no imposition," he whispered.

As the dress loosened and air rushed against her, Asha felt his gaze trail over her. The bumps of her spine. The wings of her shoulder blades. The curve of her lower back.

"There." He swallowed softly, undoing the last button. "You're free."

Asha turned her back to the tent walls. She kept her arms crossed against her chest, holding the loosened dress up as she looked at him. The light cast by the hanging lamp made his skin glow. The shadows sharpened his cheekbones. Her gaze slid to his mouth, where the line of his lower lip dipped like the mantle of the Rift.

What would it feel like to press her mouth against his? To close the space between them? To claim him right here in his tent?

As if sensing her thoughts, Torwin raised his eyes to her face. Asha turned her scarred cheek away.

"Why do you keep doing that?" His voice hardened around the words.

When she didn't answer, he slid off his shirt.

A feeling rushed through Asha, like plunging through the air with Kozu. Dropping the shirt at their feet, Torwin turned so his lacerated back—scabbed and finally healing—was on full display.

"Do you hate the sight of them?"

Asha sucked in a breath. "*What?* No."

He turned back to her, his eyes cold. "Then why would I hate the sight of yours?"

But Torwin had never been proud of his scars, while Asha had loved her scar—because her father loved it. She'd used it to justify killing dragons. Her father lied to her over and over again while she brought him their heads. That's what Asha saw now when she looked at her scar.

Tears stung her eyes and blurred her vision. Asha pressed her hands to her face, trying to hide them.

"Asha . . . ?"

When she wouldn't look at him, Torwin's arms came around

her, crushing her into his warmth. With his cheek pressed against her hair, he didn't say a word. Just held her as she cried. His warm palm moved in slow circles against her back, trying to soothe her.

"I almost killed Kozu," she whispered into her hands when her hiccups fell silent. "I nearly destroyed the old stories."

"Isn't that what you wanted?"

Asha shook her head. His hand stopped. He reached for her wrists, pulling her hands away from her face.

"Tell me."

She told him everything. The truth about the day Kozu burned her and all the things that came after. All the lies she'd ever believed. All the dragons she'd ever killed. And for what? For a tyrant. For a father who never really loved her at all.

Torwin held her tighter.

After a long while, he turned his face into her wet, glistening hair. "Stay here tonight," he said. "It's quiet and peaceful and you'll get a good rest. Better than you will back at camp."

"Here?" She palmed the tears from her cheeks. "In your tent?"

"Just for tonight." He stepped away to pull his shirt back on. The cool air rushed in, chilling her once more. Grabbing a bundle of dry clothes, he held them out to her. "I'll sleep outside."

Taking them, she said, "Torwin—"

"I prefer the stars." He reached for his lute, ready to leave so she could change. "And besides, I don't sleep much. Nightmares, remember?"

But before stepping out of the tent, he stopped and turned around.

"You don't ever have to go back. Not if you don't want to."

She frowned at him.

He took a shaky step toward her. "We could leave," he said. "We could leave *tonight*."

"Torwin, where would we go?"

His mouth tipped up at the side. "Anywhere. To the edge of the world."

That smile sent the tiniest of thrills rippling through her. Asha tamped it down.

Run away? No.

She understood wanting to run from Jarek, but he would never stop hunting them. And what of the rest? What of Dax and Safire? She couldn't leave them to fight this war alone.

Asha stepped back. "I can't." She shook her head. "Everyone I love is in that camp."

And a lying tyrant ruled over Firgaard.

"Everyone you love," Torwin repeated.

He stood very still. Like he was waiting for something.

But Asha didn't know what else he wanted.

The light in his eyes went out.

"Get some rest," he said, turning to leave. Without glancing back at her, he slipped out of the tent and into the darkness beyond.

Asha stared at the tent flap until the shivering returned. It felt like the time she left him in the clearing. Something lay unfinished between them. Like they were a fraying tapestry in need of a weaver.

She changed out of her sopping-wet dress and dumped it outside in a heap. Torwin's clothes, while far too big, were warm and dry.

Turning down the lantern, she climbed into the bedroll. She tossed and turned in the darkness, her thoughts full of thorns.

It was only when a quiet melody drifted in that she fell still. From outside the tent, Torwin plucked a familiar tune from the strings of his lute. The same tune he'd been humming ever since he'd stitched up her side. There was more of it than the last time, but it still wasn't complete. Torwin kept falling into silence halfway through, only to pick it up again at the beginning.

She imagined those hands, so deft and sure, plucking strings as easily as they'd made a poultice and stitched up her side. As easily as they'd undone the buttons on her dress.

Swallowing, Asha imagined those hands going farther. Sliding off her dress. Moving across her bare skin.

She shut her eyes, trying to escape the thoughts, knowing the danger they put him in. But they only flared up brighter behind her eyelids.

Much later, when Torwin gave up on his song at last and went to sleep, Asha lay awake, thinking of his hands.

Thirty-Eight

The next morning, when Asha entered the meeting tent, she ran straight into Jas. His eyes, rimmed in dark lashes, widened at the sight of her. Recovering, he smiled, fisting his hand over his heart in greeting.

"You look well this morning, Asha."

His kindness startled her. After all, she'd pulled a knife on him just last night. And most people upon meeting the Iskari were not so quick to smile at her.

Torwin stepped in behind them. "Sorry we're late. We . . ." At the sight of what was clearly the middle of a meeting, he stopped.

A dozen people looked up from the roughly hewn log benches. Dax stood in the center, pouring tea.

The sight of it jarred Asha. Serving tea was a slave's task. But here was her brother, the heir to the throne, holding the brass teapot high in the air as liquid gold streamed in an arc, filling the circle of glasses with frothy, steaming tea.

Before the Severing, under the old ways, the master of the house always served the tea.

Dax stopped pouring to stare at Asha's clothes. Which were actually Torwin's clothes. The daughter of the dragon king was wearing the clothes of her husband's slave.

Her face flamed as she realized how it looked. But she was surrounded by strangers—draksors, scrublanders, skral—so she said nothing. She didn't look at Dax, whose stare burned up her skin, just ducked past a wordless Jas and filled the empty spot on the cushions next to Safire, who shot her a curious look.

Dax's stare turned to a wordless question, which he fixed on Torwin. Torwin, who was supposed to be leaving.

Avoiding eye contact, Torwin filled in a gap on the other side of the circle, as far from Asha as he could get, sitting between Roa and a woman Asha recognized: the blacksmith who'd forged her slayers. The blacksmith nodded to her. Asha nodded back.

Safire broke the awkward silence, continuing as if they'd never been interrupted. "Aren't we forgetting something?" She tossed a throwing knife from hand to hand. Its sharpened steel edge broke the light into countless colors that went skittering across the tent. "There's a law against regicide, in both the old age and the new."

Asha thought of the last three scrublander assassins who'd tried to take her father's life. Remembered the blade hacking at their necks beneath the blazing midday sun. Remembered their heads falling to the stones with sickening thuds. Dax had been sitting right next to Asha, watching it happen.

She thought of Moria, centuries earlier, kneeling on those same stones, resting her head on that same bloodstained block.

The law against killing kings was an ancient, sacred law. It couldn't be circumvented.

If Dax killed their father, he too would lay his head on that block.

And Asha would have to watch.

"You can't be thinking of killing the king," she said.

"We can't take the throne if your father lives," Safire said. Essie, Roa's silver-eyed hawk, perched on the leather patch on her shoulder. "Not officially."

Asha stared at her brother. "But if you kill him, your life is forfeit."

"A detail we have yet to work out." Dax set down the tea and served the first cup to Roa. She took it stiffly, not meeting his gaze, as if still vexed from their argument. But the moment Dax turned to pour the next cup, she looked up, watching him with her dark brown eyes.

"Let me help," said Asha.

Dax shook his head. "I don't want you anywhere near Firgaard when this starts."

"I don't need to be near Firgaard."

He gave her a puzzled look.

"We can use the dragons," she said. "The king won't expect an attack from the sky."

A murmur rose around her as everyone exchanged nervous glances.

"If the dragons are on our side," Asha continued, "so is the

Old One. Any draksor in the city still devoted to the old ways will be with us."

Dax shook his head in disbelief. "*You*—the girl who's made it her life's mission to hunt dragons into extinction—now want to *recruit* them? The dragons hate us, Asha. How can you possibly think of bringing them to our side?"

Her eyes fixed on the silver collar resting against Torwin's collarbone. "I know a way."

Dax waited, looking skeptical. He was right to look skeptical. Asha didn't actually know—not for certain. But according to Shadow, the dragons turned on the draksors because they enslaved the skral. So if the draksors set them free . . .

"You'll have to prove your motives are true. Prove you're not just hungry for the throne."

"And how do I do that?"

Asha's gaze cut to Torwin. His attention fixed on the bone ring encircling his smallest finger. His hands shook, ever so slightly, as he twisted it back and forth. He must have retrieved it while she slept.

"Break the collars of every skral in this camp," she said.

Torwin's gaze lifted to her face.

"And the moment you seize the throne, break the collars off those still in the city. It must be the first thing you do."

Her brother looked at her as though he no longer recognized her. She didn't blame him. Not so long ago, she'd thought that if the skral went free, they would finish what they came for.

Asha glanced at Torwin.

She didn't think that anymore.

The blacksmith spoke up suddenly, her voice ringing like a hammer on an anvil. "I can remove every collar in this camp by nightfall."

Asha nodded at her, then turned back to her brother. "All I need are riders, and you can count dragons among your arsenal."

"I'll find them for you," said Torwin.

Asha met his gaze. Very quietly, she said, "Does this mean you're staying?"

He looked away. "Just . . . until the wedding. That will give me enough time to find you riders, and train them so they're flight ready."

Asha bit down on the smile creeping across her lips.

In the silence that followed, Safire's knife flashed as she tossed it one final time, then sheathed it in her boot. "Well," she said, "I guess that's settled."

To aid him in his plan, Asha told Dax about her secret tunnel beneath the temple. They decided the scrublander army would wait outside the city wall with Roa while Dax, Jas, Safire, and a few other Haveners—what Dax called his group of rogues— took the tunnel into the city, then ran to the north gate. There they would hold the gate open long enough to let the army in. Roa's hawk, Essie, was the signal. Dax would take the bird into the city and, once the gate opened, let her fly.

After the city was secured, the dragon king imprisoned, and Dax sat on the throne as regent, things would begin to change. His union with Roa would fix what was broken and bring peace back to draksors and scrublanders. The skral would be free to choose. They could remain in Firgaard or seek out new lives elsewhere.

When the meeting ended and Asha went to follow Safire out of the tent, Dax halted his conversation with a scrublander girl and called for Asha to wait.

The tent emptied, and Dax leaned against a map of Firgaard unrolled across the table. His hands cupped the edge of the rough wood as he looked his sister up and down.

"You disappear with him last night and then reappear wearing his clothes?" He motioned to the shirt and trousers she wore. "Think about how that looks."

Asha crossed her arms over Torwin's shirt and raised her chin. "Would you prefer I still be standing in my binding dress?"

He made a frustrated sound. "You're the daughter of the dragon king." He pushed himself off the table. "And Torwin is . . ."

Beneath me. Forbidden.

"A skral. And while most draksors in this camp are friendly with skral, there are *many* who aren't. And there are just as many skral who won't think twice about hurting him simply because of the way he looks at you."

Asha's arms fell to her sides.

"In this camp and beyond it, if people think you care about him, they'll use him to hurt you. To make you do things you don't want to do."

"I fell in the lake," she said. "Torwin gave me dry clothes. He was just being kind."

"Asha," Dax said. As if he were the adult here and she were the child. As if he'd just caught her in a lie.

Asha scowled. "What."

"You—you of all people—know how these stories end. I don't want *either* of you getting hurt."

Unable to look Dax in the eye, Asha stared over his shoulder at the canvas walls of the tent, lit up by the morning sun.

"Lillian wouldn't have died if Rayan hadn't pursued her," Dax said. "If he'd put her safety first, above his own selfishness, they'd both be alive today."

And Safire wouldn't exist.

The mere thought of it broke her heart.

Dax stepped toward her. "If you want to keep him safe, you must keep him at a distance."

Asha dropped her gaze to her bare feet. Her slippers were probably washed up on the shore by now.

"I know," she whispered. "I'm trying."

Dax sighed. He reached for Asha's shoulder and gently squeezed, making her look up into his face.

Whatever his affliction had been, it was receding, if not gone altogether. His eyes were starry again and he was putting weight back on, easing those sharp edges he'd developed. He was almost back to his regular handsome self.

But there was something still tugging at Asha. This plan of his was a sound one: getting into the city, seizing it with the help of the scrublanders—it could work. But as for the throne . . . as long as their father lived, no one would consider Dax the dragon king. Dax could lock their father in a prison for the rest of his life, but as long as the true king lived, he was the rightful ruler of Firgaard. Not Dax.

Their father had to die. And Dax wouldn't leave a task as dire as this to someone else. He would consider it his responsibility.

Yet the ancient law against regicide was unbendable. If Dax killed the king, Dax too would die. And if that happened, who would rule Firgaard?

Roa was a scrublander. No draksor would submit to her solitary rule.

Asha was the former Iskari, hated and feared by her people.

Safire was half skral and an abomination in the eyes of Firgaard.

That left . . . no one.

Dax couldn't die. He needed to rule. But if he couldn't die, then he couldn't kill the king.

Which meant someone else had to.

Thirty-Nine

Asha spent the days before the weapons caravan arrived calling dragons. Torwin found her a dozen riders—mostly draksors and scrublanders, along with two skral. Asha raised an eyebrow when he brought the skral boys forward and Torwin shrugged. "You asked for riders. I found you the best."

Asha told the old stories aloud and out of earshot, high above the tree line. She didn't want them poisoning those in the camp, the way they poisoned her brother and her mother.

More than this, ever since the night of her binding, she'd noticed Torwin's hands shaking. He was thinner than he had been, and there were dark half-moons under his eyes. When she asked him about it, he attributed it to exhaustion.

But Asha couldn't shake the feeling that it was more than that.

So she called dragons alone, keeping the stories far away from Torwin and the camp, then passed the dragons off.

Torwin paired dragons to riders, showing them how to seal

their links in flight. He recruited Asha's former seamstress, the skral girl whose name was Callie. Her task was to sew coats, gloves, and skarves to protect the riders from the elements. But it was a lot of sewing, and if she was going to finish in time, she needed help.

At dusk on the third day, Asha found Torwin alone in the riders' tent they'd erected high in the valley. He sat hunched in the light of a lamp, sewing the sleeve of a coat. It was still strange to see him without his collar. Her eyes often caught on the scars across his collarbone, hinting at where it used to rest.

But Asha did as Dax suggested. She kept her distance.

There was so much work to do and such limited time to do it in, it made avoiding Torwin easy. Despite spending the day in close proximity, they rarely spoke. And at the end of the day, when Torwin waited to walk her into camp, she shook her head and told him to go on without her. She still had work to do.

At meetings, she wedged herself between Safire and Dax. When Torwin sought her out at dinner, she fell into a conversation with Jas, who was endlessly curious and easy to talk to. When Torwin inserted himself into these conversations and it became clear that Jas valued his opinion, Asha sought out someone—anyone—else.

Sometimes, in the middle of the day, she felt him watching her. Sometimes, when she turned her back on him at dinner, she caught a glimpse of the hurt in his eyes. Like he knew what she was doing, and he was going to make it easy on her.

And why wouldn't he? He was leaving.

Soon he stopped waiting for her. He stopped trying to sit

next to her. He stopped seeking her out.

It hurt Asha's heart.

So when no one was looking, she started watching *him*. From a distance, she saw his hands move with gentle reverence over dragon flanks, showing the riders how to calm their mounts and conquer their fears. He taught them various combinations of clicks that could make a dragon launch or turn or drop on command. He taught them everything he knew, until the spaces beneath his eyes grew even more hollow.

She watched him with Callie, the seamstress, as the two skral bent over her designs. Watched the way Torwin motioned with his hands, pointing out what he thought wouldn't work or what might work better. Whenever he smiled his crooked smile at Callie, something in Asha broke a little more. She found herself comparing Callie's smooth face to her own. The girl was pretty as a desert dawn. She was a skral, just like he was. Maybe Torwin would take Callie with him across the sea instead.

Back at camp, Callie and Torwin played music together with a handful of others. Asha didn't dare follow them, but sometimes she lingered out of sight, sharpening her already sharp axe while she listened to the sounds of Torwin's lute weaving with the sounds of Callie's reed pipe and a scrublander's hand drum, waiting for his unfinished song . . . only it never came.

If you want to keep him safe, you must keep him at a distance.

But now, after days of avoiding him, here she stood, alone with him in the riders' tent.

Taking a deep breath, Asha crossed to the desk piled high with cut leather and carded wool. It was Callie's desk. Her tools—knives, needles, charcoal, thread—were arranged in neat little rows. Beside the desk, on a rough-hewn chair, hung Asha's wool mantle.

"Where's Callie?" she asked, keeping her voice steady as she lifted the mantle and swung it over her shoulders. The walk back to camp was a cold one.

He didn't look up from his work. "That's the first time you've spoken to me in two days."

Asha's fingers paused on her tassels. "What do you mean?"

"Come on, Asha." He glanced up at her. The lamplight caught in his hair, making it gleam. "We both know you're avoiding me."

That might be true. But Asha had watched him introduce Callie to Shadow, showing her where the dragon liked to be scratched—right below the chin. She'd watched Callie linger at the tent entrance two days in a row now, waiting to walk him back to camp, and he always went with her.

"What about you?" she whispered.

He lowered the needle to his lap. "What about me?"

You're giving up on me.

It was ridiculous, of course. She *needed* him to give up.

Asha tied the tassels around her throat. "Never mind."

As she made for the tent entrance, she heard him say, "Safire's right. You're stubborn as a rock."

Asha halted and looked back. Safire was talking about her? To Torwin?

That stung.

"Safire can eat sand."

His mouth quirked up.

She shouldn't have looked. If she hadn't, she might have left.

But if she'd left, she wouldn't have noticed the hunch of his thinning shoulders or the way his hands shook a little too hard as he worked. He looked wasted, there in the lamplight, with a half-sewn coat spread out across his lap and extra needles and thread on the rug beside him. He looked the way her brother had, before the revolt.

Fear gnawed at her insides.

But I've been so careful. Why is this happening?

Asha loosened the tassels around her throat. She stepped back into the tent, letting the mantle fall from her shoulders as she sank down next to him on the woven grass rug. Leaning across his lap, she grabbed a needle and thread, taking stock of his symptoms and trying to match them with her mother's.

Rapid weight loss, unnatural exhaustion, tremors . . .

Maybe she should keep him away from the dragons entirely. Dragons told stories too, in their own silent way. Maybe, somehow, they were the cause. . . .

"Do you even know how to use that?"

His question startled her out of her thoughts. It was the same question she'd asked herself about him and the arrows, down in the pit. Asha met his gaze with a glare.

"How do you think I made all my armor?" she said, threading the needle and setting to work on the other sleeve.

When his knee fell against hers, she looked up to find him smiling. Something sparked inside her. She shouldn't have, but she let her leg relax against his. Just this once.

330

They worked in weary silence. When they finished attaching the sleeves of one coat, they moved on to the next one. Halfway through, Torwin started humming that mysterious tune. But by then, Asha was having trouble keeping her eyes open.

When Torwin noticed, he took the needle from her. "Time to sleep, fiercest of dragon hunters."

Asha was too tired to correct him: she didn't hunt dragons anymore.

She didn't want to be the Iskari anymore.

Asha pressed her palms to the rug, about to rise and make the long trek back through the woods, to the tent she shared with Safire, when Torwyn touched her hand.

"Stay."

She shook her head, avoiding his gaze. "I can't."

"Asha."

Her name tugged at her. She looked up to find his eyes warm and feverish. He looked so fragile tonight. It worried her.

She looked away. "Fine. I'll stay until you finish the coat."

A small smile tugged at his mouth.

"Wake me when you're done," she said, curling up on the rug beside him and closing her eyes. A heartbeat later, he pulled her mantle over her. A heartbeat after that, a dream rose up to claim her. A dream about her namesake, the goddess Iskari.

Much later, Torwyn set aside his needle and thread and stretched out beside her. Asha woke. She turned to find him on his back, elbows crooked, hands cradling his head as he stared up at the canvas tent ceiling.

With her dream echoing in her mind, she forgot about the danger.

"Torwin?" she whispered.

He turned his face toward her.

"Do you think the goddess Iskari hated herself?"

It wasn't the question he expected. She could tell by the way he sucked in a breath, like she'd elbowed him in the stomach.

"I think . . . ," he said after a stretched-out moment, his gaze intent on her face, "I think the goddess Iskari was forced to be something she didn't want to be."

That wasn't any kind of answer. Asha was about to say so when he went on.

"Iskari let others define her because she thought she didn't have a choice. Because she thought she was alone and unloved."

He turned on his side, propping himself on his elbow and looking down at her.

"The first time I heard them call *you* Iskari, I hunted down her story. I didn't care about the danger or the law. I found an old beggar in the market who was willing to tell it to me. And, Asha, when I heard it, it didn't sound like a tragedy to me."

"Of course it's a tragedy." Asha frowned up at him. "She *dies* at the end. She dies all alone."

"But is that the end?" His mouth turned up at the side and Asha felt herself soften beneath him. "I don't think it is. What of Namsara? He goes looking for her. The sky changes seven times before he finds her. And then, when he does find her, he falls to his knees and he weeps. *Because he loves her.* Because she was never as alone as she thought she was. She was never just *life taker.* To him, she was *sister.* She was precious. It's a love story, Asha. A tragic one, to be sure. But a love story, still."

Asha studied his much-thinner face above her. The line of his jaw. The curve of his mouth.

"Does Iskari hate herself?" His voice shifted into something tender. "Of course she does." He said this like he was only just realizing it. Like Asha's question had forced the realization. "I used to get angry with Namsara for letting it all happen. I used to get angry with Iskari too for living out the role she'd been forced into. For never once trying to be something else."

Torwin brushed aside a strand of Asha's hair, tucking it behind her scarred ear.

"I got angry with Iskari for never looking around her. To the ones who loved her. To the ones who could save her."

"But no one can save her."

"How do you know? She never lets anyone try."

That night, Asha had a nightmare.

She dreamed she stood in the shadows of the dungeon and before her loomed an iron door. Horrible sounds came from behind it. Sounds of the shaxa tearing at someone's back. Sounds of bones being snapped. Sounds of a body contorting in terrible ways.

And through it all, she heard a voice, begging.

No . . . please, no. . . .

When the begging turned to screaming, she realized that she knew the owner of the voice. And because she knew him, she threw herself against the door. She pounded it with her fists.

She searched for the key—only there wasn't a keyhole. There was no way to get in.

She couldn't save him. Couldn't free him.

Could only listen while they killed him.

Asha woke in a sweat, breathing hard. Someone stood over her, silhouetted by the sun shining behind him. With the nightmare lingering on the backs of her eyelids, she bolted upright. Panic flared through her. *Jarek*. Jarek was here. She turned to find the carpet empty beside her. Torwin was gone.

"Asha."

Asha scrambled up and away. Her back hit the makeshift desk full of Callie's tools, which scattered and fell. She ran trembling hands along the floor, searching for something to use as a weapon.

"Asha."

That voice.

It made her stop. Her breath scraped out of her lungs, loud and ragged. She looked up. Squinting through the sunlight, she found her brother crouching beside her.

"You're all right. You're safe."

Her surroundings shifted, no longer tainted by the nightmare. Her brother's voice brought clarity and vision. Dax stared down at her, cloaked in a gray mantle with a mud-stained hem. His dark brows drew together over eyes full of concern. Beyond him, the canvas walls were bright with morning sunlight. The still-burning lamp sat on the rug next to a half-finished flight coat.

"Where's Torwin?"

Very carefully, Dax said, "Being tended."

Asha's heart jolted. "Tended?"

"A group of draksors and skral saw you come in here with him."

Asha's mouth went dry.

She remembered when Torwin had first brought her to New Haven, the way the Haveners looked at him when he said her name aloud . . . as if he didn't have the right.

She remembered the warning Dax had given her: *There are just as many skral who won't think twice about hurting him simply because of the way he looks at you.*

She struggled to her feet. Cold morning air rushed against her skin, making her shiver.

"Where is he?"

Dax looked as if the sight of her pained him. "I told you this would happen. I told you to keep your distance."

Safire strode into the tent then, her eyes sweeping the premises before coming to settle on Asha.

"Saf," she pleaded. "What's happened?"

"Come on." Safire slid an arm around her shoulder. "I'll bring you to him."

"When you didn't return to our tent, I went looking for you," Safire explained as they strode through New Haven. "Halfway up the valley, I found a group of Haveners in the woods, cursing someone curled on the ground, feeding kicks into his gut and back."

Safire swept aside the flap of a small tent. From inside, Asha heard raised voices.

"They tried to break his leg, but I stopped them."

Inside the tent, Asha found a row of cots, a dirt floor, and . . . a shirtless Torwin reaching for the bundle of clothes Callie held behind her back.

"The physician said you need to rest!" Callie's index finger sliced the air, pointing to the cot.

"Give me my shirt," Torwin snarled. His hair was damp with sweat and his eyes seemed strangely hollow.

"Get in the cot!"

He was about to shout something back when he noticed the newcomer. At the sight of her, the fight rushed out of him.

"Asha."

Torwin looked her over, as if checking *her* for wounds. When he didn't find any, he shook away the relief in his eyes and turned back to Callie.

"I'll stay if Asha stays with me."

Callie shook her head in disbelief. Giving up, she marched right past Asha and out of the tent, taking his clothes with her.

In spite of everything, Torwin smiled a victorious smile, just for the scarred girl standing in the entrance. It made Asha wonder if he even noticed the way Callie was around him. If he had any inkling at all.

Thinking of Dax's warning, she said, "I just came to make sure you're all right."

Torwin moved toward her, a little stiffly. He was obviously hurt, his leg in particular.

"I can't stay," she said, stepping back. "This is what happens when I'm near you." She forced herself to turn, to head for the entrance. "I'll see you tonight. At the—"

"They gave me a sleeping draught."

Because you need to rest, she thought, fingers reaching for the tent flap.

"Do you know what it's like, being trapped inside nightmares all night?"

Asha faltered.

"Nightmares . . . about you."

She didn't turn back. Just stared at the tent flap, where Safire waited on the other side.

"They're always about you," he whispered.

The words wrapped around her heart and squeezed.

Torwin reached for her wrist, his fingers gentle. Asha let him turn her. Let him draw her in close. When she didn't pull away, his forehead fell against her shoulder, as if Asha—only Asha—was the balm for a hidden wound.

"Over and over again, I watch them hunt you down." He shuddered. "And I can never stop them."

She looped her arms around his neck, holding him tight, the way her mother used to do in the face of her own nightmares.

"I'm right here," she said, pressing her cheek to his. "I'm safe."

Asha ran her fingers through his hair, trying to soothe him. But her fingers caught. And when they came free, a sick feeling coiled like a snake in her belly.

Very slowly, she pulled her hand away. Stepping back, out of his arms, she stared down at her hand.

A thick clump of his hair lay in her palm.

The past rose up before her. Asha suddenly remembered stroking her dying mother's hair. Remembered the way her fingers caught the dark strands coming out in clumps.

Asha choked on a startled sob. She raised her eyes to Torwin's thinning face.

"No . . . ," she whispered. But Torwin only stared at her, confused.

A fierce and desperate anger swept through her.

"Are you telling the old stories?"

He frowned at her, his confusion deepening. "What?"

"The stories!" she demanded, her hand closing around his hair. "Are you telling them?"

He shook his head no. "I don't know them well enough."

"Then it must be the dragons." She started to pace, tried to think. "I'll get someone else to train the riders. You can stay in the camp. . . ."

He reached for her. "What are you talking about?"

Asha let him take her hands in his trembling ones, stopping her pacing footsteps.

She looked down at their interlaced fingers. His were flecked with freckles, hers were hardened with scars. He still wore her mother's ring.

The ring.

It was the same ring Asha's mother wore on her deathbed, carved and given to her by the dragon king. The dragon king was always carving things out of bone for his wife to wear.

It should have been burned with her other possessions, but it wasn't. Her father kept it. And then he gave it to Dax.

Dax, who shared all their mother's symptoms . . .

. . . until he gave it to Asha.

But Asha had only worn it a day before giving it to Torwin as a promise. And Torwin had been wearing it ever since.

Now he too was showing signs.

Father carved it out of bone, she thought. *Why would . . . ?*

A story flickered in her mind. A story about a queen who poisoned her guests with dragon bone ash. The slaves found the guests dead, their bodies like hollow shells.

The horror of it dawned on her. Asha grabbed Torwin's wrist, needing to get the ring off.

"Ouch! Asha, you're—"

She twisted, then pulled hard.

The ring came free.

Asha had spent eight years hunting dragons. She knew how to bring one down. Knew how to skin one. Knew what all the various parts could be used for.

And she knew one thing most of all: when someone was burned by dragonfire, the only thing strong enough to draw the toxins out was the poison of dragon bone. But used alone, in small amounts, it was just as deadly as dragonfire, slowly leaching the body of life.

As she stared down at the ring, Asha thought of the queen who had killed her enemies by putting a pinch of dragon bone ash in their food at night. The ring on Asha's palm—the ring her father made for her mother—was made of that same deadly substance.

"He murdered her," she realized aloud. "And then he tried to kill Dax."

Torwin stared as if she were speaking an unknown language.

"Come with me," she said, taking his hand in hers.

Torwin obliged, letting her lead him out of the tent.

She found Dax and handed him the ring. With Torwin looking on, Asha explained: it wasn't the stories that killed their mother. It was the ring. And maybe more than that. Everything their father ever carved for his wife to wear, Asha was willing to bet, was made out of the poisonous dragon bone. It only *seemed* like the stories killed her, because that's when the symptoms started.

Thanks to the eavesdropping slaves, everyone knew the dragon queen had been telling her daughter the old stories. Everyone knew she was committing a criminal act.

"And what better way to prove the stories were wicked than with the death of a storyteller?"

Dax stared at her, his jaw hardening, his hands turning to fists. She could see the thoughts churning in his eyes. The pieces of a puzzle coming together.

"What if it wasn't just one storyteller?" he whispered, as if to himself.

Asha frowned. "What do you mean?"

"If the old stories were never deadly," he said, looking at her, "what killed the raconteurs?"

Or rather, *who* killed them?

The question unearthed something in Asha.

She thought of a certain tapestry hanging in her father's

throne room. Of the woman who was queen at the time of the Severing. A queen who needed to prove the Old One had turned against her people.

"You think *our grandmother* poisoned the storytellers?"

Dax said nothing. He didn't need to.

The world spun.

If the stories were never poisonous, if they never killed *anyone*, then they were never wicked. Which meant Asha was never wicked for telling them.

Not only had the dragon king turned his daughter against Kozu, the Old One, her own self . . . he had killed her mother. And then he had tried to kill her brother.

He'd tried to strip Asha of everything she ever loved. Which made her new purpose sparklingly clear: she would do the same to him.

Forty

Asha called twelve dragons over a span of five days. By the time
the caravan arrived from the scrublands, she was beyond weary.
She wanted to rest for a month. But the wedding was tonight,
and tomorrow they went to war.

There was no time for rest.

At dusk, Asha and Safire set out for the center of camp,
cleared of tents for the ceremony. Asha wore a dress the color of
blood and fire. It was a simple, modest dress that laced up at the
back and fell to her knees. It had been waiting in their tent. She
asked Safire where it came from.

"Jas, I think. He came by earlier. He says he's hoping to
dance with you."

"I hope you told him I don't dance," she said, looking
around her. New Haven—full of dirty, stinking rogues just that
morning—had transformed into a polished, respectable collection
of scrublanders, skral, and draksors, all waiting for the bride to
make her way to the binding circle. Lanterns were lit and placed

on the ground, forming a circle in the dirt around Dax, who wore what seemed like the only clothes he'd brought with him.

Another crude circle made of cedar benches ringed the lanterns. The logs had been chopped and fastened that morning, and as Asha sat down on one, she breathed in the sweet smell.

From farther down the bench, a conversation caught her ear.

"How could I turn down that offer?" said an elderly skral with short, graying hair. She sat next to a young draksor, sharing her ale jug.

"But you've lived in Firgaard all your life. It's your home."

"Is it?" the old woman leaned toward the girl. "Or is it a cage I've just gotten free of?"

The draksor passed her the jug. "So you'll go to the scrublands after all this is over."

The skral woman took a swig, then wiped her mouth with her wrist. "I reckon most of us will. There's land out there. The scrublanders say if we can work it, we can have it. If we stay in Firgaard, most of us will be homeless and starving by month's end."

"Lord Dax would never let that happen."

"Lord Dax will have plenty more to worry about than us skral. Trust me, girl. I've lived through three uprisings."

"*Failed* uprisings," the draksor pointed out.

The skral woman only shrugged. "Even if Lord Dax wins tomorrow, he could fail the day or the month or the year after. He'll be making a lot of enemies if he takes his father's throne. And those enemies will want to take it out on someone. I've spent my whole life among you. I know exactly who that someone will be." She tapped her chest with her index finger. "No one's going to look out for us. We need to look out for ourselves."

She offered the jug back to the girl, who shook her head.

"It might be worse out there."

"I'll take my chances," said the skral, taking another full swig of ale.

A hush fell over the camp. Roa had left her tent. As the silence descended, Asha watched the scrublander girl move through the parted crowd. She wore a sleeveless cotton dress with a neckline that scooped wide but not low. Her skin gleamed in the lantern light and her eyes shone like dark pools.

The moment she stepped into the circle, something shifted. Asha saw a girl who was already a queen. Roa, daughter of the House of Song, was graceful, dignified, and . . . a little bit fierce.

"What is bound here tonight can never be unbound!" said Jas. There were no guardians present to perform the rites, so Roa's brother had stepped in. "I weave these lives together as one. Only Death can break these threads and tear them asunder."

Roa recited the words first, her voice shining like a blade: "May Death send his worst! Cold to freeze the love in my heart. Fire to burn my memories to ash. Wind to force me through his gate. And time to wear my loyalty away."

Her eyes held Dax's as Willa's words spilled from her lips, ringing with power.

"I'll wait for you, Dax, at Death's gate."

Shivers ran across Asha's skin.

Dax repeated the lines. Where Roa's voice had been steady, his trembled with emotion.

"May Death send his worst! Cold to freeze the love in my heart. Fire to burn my memories to ash. Wind to force me through his gate. And time to wear my loyalty away."

He took her hand in his with a startling gentleness.

"I'll wait for you, Roa, at Death's gate."

After their wrists were bound, they raised their clasped hands for the camp to bear witness. Cheers rose up like waves. Chaos descended as draksors lifted Dax high above their heads. Scrublanders lifted Roa, chanting now, intent on carrying them both to Dax's tent.

Asha watched the couple's eyes meet. Watched her brother smile a little nervously. And then they were gone, whisked out of sight.

Forty-One

After the ceremony, musicians played within the circle of lanterns as draksors and scrublanders danced around them. Asha sat on one of the benches ringing the dancers, waiting for Safire to return with food.

Separated from her by a sea of revelers, a certain lute player kept time in the dirt with his heel while his fingers coaxed song after song from his lute strings. The scrublander beside him, a broad-shouldered man with a round belly and sparkling eyes, beat out a rhythm on his hand drum, striking it with his palm and singing the words, while Callie played the reed pipes on Torwin's other side, dancing as she did.

Suddenly, someone stepped in front of Asha, cutting the musicians off from view.

Asha looked up into kind eyes framed by thick lashes. Jas, in all his handsome glory, smiled down at her. He smelled like cardamom and citrus.

"I don't dance," Asha said before he could ask.

"So I've been told." He pointed to the empty space on the bench beside her. "Can I sit with you?"

By the time she opened her mouth to say it was reserved for Safire, he had already taken it.

They sat in silence a moment, staring at the dancers, who were a blur of color and limbs and faces. Asha watched Callie's dress twirl around her thighs as she spun, barefoot, in the dirt.

"Dax says you love the old stories," Jas said, watching a scrublander girl with gleaming black curls that spilled down her back.

Asha looked at him. "I suppose he's right."

"He also said you burned the only copies in the city."

Asha flinched at the memory.

Seeing her reaction, Jas went on. "I wanted to extend an official invitation to the House of Song." He glanced back at the dancing scrublander girl, and from the affectionate look in his eyes, Asha thought she must be a friend. "So many stories are lost, but our library has a small collection. If you came to visit, you would have access to it. You could transcribe them, if you wanted to."

Asha couldn't remember the last time a stranger had been so kind to her. It made her smile. Just a little.

Seeing it, Jas smiled too. It was a bright, shining thing that lit him up from the inside.

"As for the forgotten ones," he said, "maybe you could find them."

Asha frowned. "Where would I even start looking?"

"You're a hunter, aren't you? Instead of hunting dragons . . ."

He paused, checking to see if he had offended her. "You could hunt down the lost stories and bring them back to us. Restore our traditions. Make our realm whole again."

But stories couldn't save the realm. Only the death of Asha's father could.

Jas was so full of optimism, though, she didn't say this aloud.

"And *now* I think you should dance with me."

Asha looked at him, her lips parting in surprise. She looked to the dancing scrublander, her curls spilling over her shoulders, her face turned up to the stars as she danced with two other girls.

"Why don't you ask your friend?"

Jas looked where Asha looked. "Who? Lirabel?" He bit his lip, as if the thought scared him a little. "She already has two dancing partners." He turned back to Asha. "Besides, I'm asking *you*."

He seemed determined to be her friend. *Her.* A girl he'd been taught to despise. Because he was a scrublander, and she was a draksor.

It made Asha feel . . . strangely honored.

"I don't know how," she admitted.

"Neither do I, really."

Asha bit down on a smile. "All right. *One* dance. But if it ends horribly, it's not my fault. You were warned."

Jas grinned. He rose and pulled her to her feet. But as they moved into the sea of dancers and skirts flared against her legs, Asha's palms started to sweat. She remembered why she never did this: it made her feel clumsy and foolish.

She looked to Callie, her feet moving to the tune of her reed pipe. She looked to Jas's friend, her smile as bright as the moon. Dancing was for other girls. Not death bringers.

Jas slid his arm around her waist.

"Ready?" he asked as the next song started up.

Asha wasn't ready. In fact, she was starting to panic. But even if she could find her voice to say so, the beat of the drum and the chime of the lute and the whisper of reed pipes would have drowned her out.

And then, just as Jas's fingers slid between hers, ready to lead her in the steps, something caught her eye.

Torwin stood at the edge of the dancing circle—where Asha had been sitting just moments ago. He wore a simple white shirt, unlaced at the throat, revealing his sharply defined collarbone.

The sight of him tugged at her heart.

Asha glanced to the musicians. Next to Callie, a gangly draksor boy stood plucking the strings of Torwin's lute.

She looked back to Torwin. He'd caught sight of her and was now watching her and Jas dance, his lips parted in surprise, his eyes full of . . . hurt.

Before she could realize why, he disappeared down the path between tents.

Forty-Two

Asha didn't wait for the song to end. Instead, with her hand still in Jas's, she stopped dancing and pulled him through the crowd.

"What are you . . . ?"

Pulled him all the way up to his friend.

"I'm sorry to interrupt," Asha said when the scrublander girls stopped dancing and turned to face them. Sensing what she was about to do, Jas tried to tug his hand free and escape, but Asha held firm. "I'm afraid I have to rush off, but I don't want to abandon my dancing partner. So I wondered . . ." Asha looked from one to the next, until her eyes fell on the girl Jas had been watching. *Lirabel,* he'd called her. "I was wondering if *you* might want to dance with him?"

Lirabel's big eyes looked from Asha to Jas in surprise. She was a soft-looking girl with a heart-shaped face and a gentle mouth. Lirabel dipped her head shyly, then said, "I would be honored."

And that was that.

Asha smiled. Jas looked terrified. But when Lirabel looked up into his face, he stepped toward her, swallowing.

Asha released his hand. Turning, she pushed out of the crowd, heading in the direction Torwin had disappeared, down the path between tents.

She walked past the noise and the crowds and finally caught sight of him near the outskirts of New Haven.

"Torwin! Wait!"

At the sound of her voice, he slowed. Then turned around.

Asha ran to catch up, stopping just before a leaning structure that smelled like iron. There was no door, just a small opening, and in the starlight Asha could make out the shape of an anvil before everything melted into shadow. The smithy stood on the edge of the camp. Out here, the world was silent and dark and the stars were bright specks of sand, glittering above them.

"What are you doing here?" he asked. "You're supposed to be—"

"Dancing with Jas?"

Torwin looked away from her.

Was he . . . jealous?

"It's rare for someone I've only just met to be *kind* to me instead of afraid of me," she told him, touching the crimson fabric of her dress. It was a little rough, but she never truly belonged in the beautiful sabra silk of her kaftans, and Asha didn't mind it. "He gave me this."

"Did he?" Torwin smiled a shadow smile. A fake. "Well, Jas certainly has fine taste. You look exceedingly pretty tonight."

He looked over his shoulder. "He's probably wondering where you are. Maybe you should—"

"Or maybe you should tell me what's wrong."

Torwin went quiet, looking immediately out over the night-touched tents. Asha studied the shape of him. Already he'd recovered from the effects of the dragon bone. He was lean and tall and strong. Not strong the way Jarek was strong. Torwin's strength was a strength of spirit.

She hadn't forgotten what he'd said in the meeting tent a few days ago. He would stay until the wedding, he told her. And now the wedding was over.

And here they were.

"I heard a rumor tonight." She stepped toward him. "Are the skral planning to leave Firgaard?"

He kept his gaze away from her, nodding. "The skral support your brother, but most intend to leave the city after the invasion." Torwin sighed, running long fingers through his hair. "When this is over, if your brother secures the throne . . . the scrublanders have offered to take us across the desert."

Us. Her heart sank at that word.

But not you, she thought, staring up at him. *You're planning to run even farther.*

"For those who stay behind . . ." He shrugged. "No one knows what their fate will be."

"Dax promised to free every slave."

He nodded.

"So what's the problem?"

"It's easier said than done, Asha."

"You can't think he'll go back on his word."

"When we all go free, who will dress you and cook your meals? Build your temples and labor in your orchards? Your way of life will crumble and in the midst of that crumbling, we're supposed to find our place among you? Be treated as your equals?"

"Yes," she said, angry—but whether it was anger at his doubt, or her own, she wasn't sure.

He shook his head. "Very few draksors will be eager to lose their slaves. And where will we live now that we're free? Who will employ us?" He kicked at the earth beneath his feet. "Things are going to get worse before they get better. Draksors will be angry and skral will be easy targets. It will be dangerous for us to remain in the city."

"So you're leaving," she said.

She wished she didn't sound so angry.

Torwin merely glanced at her.

"When?" she demanded. The question had been burning within her for days now. "Tonight? Tomorrow?"

He swallowed. "When the army heads to Firgaard in the morning, I'll leave for Darmoor. My things are already packed."

Something broke inside her.

"You *should* go." She spat the words like they were bitter. Like she hated the taste of them. She couldn't look at him, thinking instead of what he'd told her. Of what he wanted most: freedom. She stared out at the hundreds of tents scattered across the valley. "You'll be safer far away from here."

Away from *her*.

Torwin went silent. After a moment, he stepped in close. "Safe?" His gaze bore into her. "Is that . . . ?" She could almost hear the thoughts spinning though his mind. "Are you trying to keep me safe, Asha?"

Looking at him would give her away. So, to keep her eyes from meeting his, she stared at his collarbone, noticing how it jutted out just a little, swooping elegantly in toward his throat on both sides.

To stop herself from reaching out to touch it, she curled her fingers into her palms, keeping them firmly at her sides.

"Asha. Look at me."

When she didn't, he reached for her. The backs of his fingers moved across her scarred skin, tracing her hairline, brushing down her cheek and neck.

Asha glanced up. The look in his eyes made her breath catch. It was like looking into the heart of a star: bright and burning.

"Do you know what it feels like to watch you dance with someone else, knowing that someone can never be me?" His hand fell to his side. "Do you know what it feels like to have you *not even consider* the gift waiting in your tent . . . might be from me?"

Asha looked down at her perfectly fitted garment. "The dress?"

He nodded. "I knew you wouldn't have anything to wear. And Callie owed me a favor. I asked her to make it for you."

"Why didn't you just tell me?"

Suddenly, footsteps crunched along the dirt path.

They broke apart. Torwin spun to face the intruder. Așha stepped back.

The musician who'd taken Torwin's spot stood before them, gangly and pimply, barely fifteen. He held the lute in one hand as he looked from the daughter of the dragon king to the skral and back again.

"I came to tell you"—he gaped at Asha's scar—"that they want you back." He thrust the lute at Torwin. "They say I keep throwing them off tune."

Do you know what it feels like . . . ?

Asha knew what it felt like.

Torwin took the instrument. "Tell them I'm coming." The draksor boy nodded, then returned the way he'd come.

"I should get back," Torwin said, "before—"

"It's like watching you with Callie," she told him, "knowing she'll never endanger you just by being near you."

Torwin turned to stare at her. "What?"

"You asked me if I know what it feels like."

Asha suddenly didn't want to care anymore. About any of it. The wedding or the war or the fact that he was a skral and she was a draksor.

She lifted her finger to his collarbone, tracing the tough scars there. Torwin drew in a shaky breath as her touch trailed into the hollow of his throat, stopping where his pulse beat out a frantic rhythm.

"Asha . . ."

She wanted to take him away from here. She wanted to hear him say her name over and over.

"Asha . . ."

Her fingers followed the arch of his throat, running slowly

upward, over his jaw, across his cheekbone.

He dropped the lute and stepped in close. So close, Asha could almost taste the salt on his skin.

He dug his fingers into her hair and tilted her head back. And then, with his eyes burning into hers, he kissed her. Gently at first. Then harder. Like he was hungry and Asha was the only one who could satisfy his craving.

Asha grabbed the collar of his shirt and kissed him back, hungrier and clumsier than he was. Torwin grabbed her waist, pulling her to him.

The smithy lay just behind her. Torwin guided her into the dark mouth of it until her back hit a warm, hard wall. Her palms moved over his chest and shoulders. He buried his hands in her hair, kissing her throat.

Asha made a soft sound. She wanted to hoist herself up, to wrap her legs around his hips, but Torwin grabbed her wrists, stopping her as the sound of footsteps rose up once more.

Asha froze. Torwin pressed his forehead to hers, listening.

"Torwin?" It was the boy again.

Torwin bared his teeth.

More footsteps. "I swear, he was right here. . . ."

A second voice grumbled an answer.

Torwin leaned into Asha, forehead to forehead, keeping her pressed against the heat-soaked wall. Releasing her wrists, he slid his thumb slowly over her bottom lip. When the footsteps got closer, his thumb stopped. When they moved farther away, it started again. Asha leaned forward to kiss him, but he didn't let her, continuing his gentle torment. His thumb brushed along her jaw and down her throat. It trailed over her collarbone and shoulder.

Asha closed her eyes, tilted her head back, letting him explore her.

It felt like forever before the footsteps moved away. When they disappeared completely, Asha exhaled.

Torwin kissed her throat. "When I finish playing . . . Asha, can I come to your tent?"

"My tent?" The thought terrified her. "You'll be seen." Not to mention: she shared a tent with Safire.

"I won't be."

It was too much of a risk. It put him in so much danger.

I'm supposed to be keeping my distance. For his own protection.

"Please," he murmured against her skin. "I'll be so careful."

She thought of all the times she'd put his life at risk before now.

His forehead fell against hers. His hand cupped her neck. "What if you came to me instead?"

Asha squeezed her eyes shut. She thought of his tent on the beach. Of sneaking away in the middle of the night. Of lying next to him under the stars.

In the morning, she would go to war. A war they might not win.

And he would leave. *Leave for good.*

This was their last night together.

Say no.

There was no future here. No way she could ever be with this boy. She needed to cut off whatever feeling was growing inside of her. Kill it at the root. He was leaving and she was staying, and even if things were different . . .

She thought about Safire's parents, one draksor, one skral—how they burned her mother alive, how they forced her father to watch.

The thought of Torwin dead made something crack inside her. But it had the opposite effect. She didn't say no. Instead, she pushed herself up on her toes and kissed him.

Torwin smiled a rare smile. One that involved his whole mouth instead of just half of it.

"Is that a yes?" he whispered, breaking away.

She nodded.

He walked backward, out of the smithy, like he was memorizing the sight of her and taking it with him. "Then I'll see you tonight, fierce one."

Forty-Three

Asha lay in her tent long after the music stopped and the voices died down. Long after New Haven grew silent and still. Her body was on fire, screaming for her to get up and go. Now, while everyone slept. Now, while there was no one to see.

But she had to be sure. So Asha waited longer.

She waited too long.

A shout broke the silence of the camp. It was followed by two more. Warning shouts, frantic and wild. Several heartbeats later, screams broke out as the clang of steel on steel erupted like the first crack of thunder in a storm.

Asha and Safire flew out of their bedrolls at the same time. Safire passed Asha a knife. Together, they stepped out of the tent and into chaos.

Her father's emblem was everywhere, adorning the shields of soldats barreling down on New Haven. Safire threw her knives. Asha shouted old stories into the sky, one after another, calling all the dragons she'd summoned in the past five days.

Most of them were already on their way, the links that had formed between them and their riders telling them something was wrong.

At the sight of the dark shapes circling above, the soldats faltered. More Haveners woke and armed themselves. Roa was at the forefront of the fighting. Her half-moon blade hacked and bit while her white hawk, Essie, flew at the enemy, screeching and diving. With every advance, Roa shouted a command, and a heartbeat later, fiery arrows flew from somewhere behind her, catching the soldats by surprise.

By the time Asha reached the edge of the camp, the soldats were retreating into the trees, chased by Safire and Jas, who were flanked by hundreds of Haveners.

Asha looked around her at the fallen, of which there were only a few. She saw Dax crouch to help a man who was bleeding badly from a wound in his leg. Asha ducked under the man's other arm and together they walked him to his tent, where his friend waited to cut the leg of his trousers and check the wound.

Asha heard Safire shout in the distance, organizing a search of the woods.

"What was that?"

"I don't know." Dax halted when he saw Jas moving toward them. He sheathed his knives.

"He knows everything now," said Jas. "Our numbers. Our location. He probably has a weapon count." He pointed at the shadows perched on the precipices high above them. "Not to mention a dragon count."

Dax frowned. "Call a meeting. We'll assess the damage,

then decide what to do."

Jas nodded. Before he left, Asha grabbed his arm. "Have you seen Torwin?"

He shook his head. "He sleeps away from New Haven," he said before leaving to do as her brother commanded. "He's safer than anyone."

"I'll send him a message with Essie," Dax said, seeing the worry etched into her face. "Go to the meeting tent. I won't be long."

As the bell clanged, Haveners made their way to the meeting tent. Asha was one of the first to arrive. One after another, people trickled in. Safire and Jas. The blacksmith. A scrublander girl with five gold earrings in one ear. Dax and Roa were the second to last to arrive.

The only one missing was Torwin.

The moment her brother stepped into the tent, the questions rose up like birdcalls at sunrise, loud and all at once. As Dax started taking one at a time, Asha stared at the canvas tent flaps, willing Torwin to walk through. It would take him longer than everyone else. He not only had to get the message, he had to fly to the woods' edge and walk down to the camp.

That's why he isn't here yet.

"We should strike quickly," Safire said. "The dragon king won't expect an immediate attack, he'll expect us to hesitate. We should chase them down and attack *now*."

The tent flaps rustled and Asha's heart leaped—but it was only Essie, flying in and settling on Roa's shoulder. Asha watched the hawk nip at the girl's ear.

"Did she find him?" Asha asked.

Roa untied Dax's message from the bird's leg. "It doesn't seem so."

The bird flew off Roa's shoulder to land on Dax's, where she squawked loudly, interrupting his response to Safire. Rising, Roa called Essie away from the heir and took her out of the tent.

Asha should have fetched Torwin herself.

"We still have the tunnel," Dax said. "We'll just have to take extra care."

The tent flaps rustled again and were shoved aside. But it was only Jas who stepped through, flanked by two scrublander soldiers, one of whom held out a roll of parchment, sealed with wax.

"For the Iskari."

All the eyes in the tent settled on Asha, who rose to her feet. She took the parchment and broke the seal. A seal she recognized as the commandant's. Her fingers shook as she unrolled it and read:

If you want him alive, you'll hand yourself over tonight.

It was signed: *Your beloved husband.*

The parchment fell to the dirt at her feet.

"Asha?"

She moved for the tent opening. Dax stopped her, forcing her to look into his eyes. "What is it?"

"Let go of me."

From behind her, Safire picked up the message and read it. "He has Torwin. . . ."

The words rocked her. Asha knew, better than anyone, what they meant.

She pushed past Dax and ran. Jas reached, trying to stop her, but she was too fast. Asha ran hard to the edge of the camp and up through the woods. Safire was behind her; she knew the steady thump of those footsteps by heart. But Asha ran faster, calling Kozu to her as she did.

She knew her way through the woods now. And by the time she reached the other side of the trees, the First Dragon waited, glimmering in the starlight. Asha launched herself onto his back.

Safire stumbled out of the woods behind her.

"Asha!"

Asha paused.

"Please. Don't go down there alone."

Asha looked back. Safire's face tilted upward. The starlight gleamed on her skin and her eyebrows knit together with worry.

At a movement in the trees, both their heads turned. Reaching down, Asha grabbed her cousin's arm and pulled her up.

"Hold on tight."

Safire's arms came around Asha's waist just as Kozu leaped into the air.

Forty-Four

The moment the lake came into view, shimmering beneath the pale light of the moon, Asha saw the scorched rock. There'd been a fire. Torwin's tent was in tatters.

But that wasn't the worst of it.

Kozu landed and Asha dropped to the rock, with Safire following her, both of them staring at the hump in the darkness.

"Shadow?" Asha called softly. The hump didn't move.

Safire stayed back while Asha moved closer. She stepped in blood. It glistened on the rock all around her, pooling from some deep gash. The dust-red dragon curled tightly around himself. His eyes were closed.

"Shadow?" Asha's voice sounded tinny in her ears.

Those pale eyes opened slowly and only halfway.

Asha let out a shuddering breath. "Oh Shadow . . ."

She sank to her knees, reaching for his snout. His eyes closed again.

"No," she said. She needed to figure out how deep the

wound was. *Where* the wound was. So she could tend it. "Come on. Get up."

Pale eyes flickered open. He didn't raise his head, just looked at her. Like he was too tired. Like his playful spark had gone out. His stare made her think of Torwin, walking away, trying to soak up the sight of her before he was gone.

"Get up!" Her voice shook. Her hands trembled. She got to her feet and walked around him. His chest rose and fell slowly. Hardly at all.

"Asha . . . ," Safire said softly from behind her.

Ignoring her cousin, Asha pushed on his haunches. She sharpened her voice. "Get up, Shadow."

This time, he tried. He raised his head and several heartbeats later, he pushed up on his front legs, but his claws slipped in blood and he fell with a terrible thud.

Asha saw the gash in his chest then. It was so deep. Right next to his heart, which slowed with each thump.

Asha's eyes blurred with tears.

She could feel him straining, feel him trying—because she wanted him to. Because he loved her and it was the very last thing he could do for her.

"Good, Shadow," Asha whispered, pressing her hand over his heart. It beat so faintly now. Like a dying echo across the Rift. "That's so good, Shadow. You can lie down now. Just lie back down. . . ."

Shadow collapsed. Asha sank to her knees. The dragon's black blood soaked her dress.

Safire came to sit beside her.

As the star in him faded, Asha pulled Shadow's warm snout into her lap. As his eyes closed, she told him one last story. The story of a girl who hunted dragons to soothe the hurt in her heart. The story of the dragon who changed her.

By the time she finished telling it, there was no rise and fall of his chest. No flicker of pale eyes trying to open.

Shadow had stopped breathing.

He was gone.

"Oh, Asha," whispered Safire.

While Asha sobbed out her rage and grief, Safire's arm came around her, pulling her in, cradling her while she cried.

Kozu came out of the shadows then. He nudged the younger dragon with his snout. He nudged twice. When Shadow didn't respond, a sound split the night in two, joining with Asha's sobs. A low, keening wail.

A dragon song for the dead.

Forty-Five

"I'm going to kill him."

Safire dragged Asha out of the pool of dragon blood and brought her to the lake edge, trying to wash it from her knees and legs.

"I'm going to gut him with my bare hands and use his entrails for dragon bait."

Her dress was ruined. Soaked in blood. When Safire finished washing her, Asha headed for Kozu. She would fly to the city this very night and carve out Jarek's heart.

"Asha." Safire caught her hard. "No."

Asha struggled against her cousin. *"Let me go."*

"You need to be calm." Safire held on. Safire had always been stronger. "You need to outthink them, not play right into their hands."

Two dragons flew above them. Asha stopped struggling to watch them circle the lake. Kozu watched them too. When they landed, the First Dragon melted into the darkness.

Both of these dragons were young. Half the size of Kozu. The one on the left had earth-brown scales and black horns. The one on the right had pale horns—one of them, broken—and was charcoal gray in color. Their wings folded back like crumpled leaves as they waited for their riders to dismount.

"If I don't go, Jarek will kill him."

Four riders dismounted. Two stayed with the dragons. The other two—Dax and Jas—moved toward them.

"Jarek needs Torwin alive to lure you in," Safire said, resting her head against Asha's as Dax approached. "He expects you to come. He wants you angry and reckless. Don't give him what he wants."

Illuminated by the lamp in Jas's hand, Dax looked like he'd aged ten years in a single night. His words echoed Safire's.

"As soon as you set foot inside the city walls," Dax told her, "he'll have no reason to keep Torwin alive. The longer you stay away, the longer Torwin lives."

Asha shook her head, remembering the sound of the shaxa on his back. She thought of the one god Torwin believed in.

Death, the Merciful.

"There are worse things than death," she whispered.

Safire's arms loosened around her. Asha looked to Shadow's form.

If Torwin had left for Darmoor when he first wanted to, he'd be on a ship right now, sailing far away. He would be *safe*.

To stop the floodgate inside her from breaking, Asha curled her hands into vicious fists.

"If I had just *been* here!"

"If you'd been here, Jarek would have cut Torwin down before your eyes and taken you instead," Dax said gently, carefully. "They were outnumbered. There's nothing you could have done."

"No. There's nothing *you* could have done. *I* am the Iskari." She glared at her brother, daring him to contradict her. He didn't.

Instead, he took her shoulders in his hands. "We are going to get him out. I'll think of something, Asha. Just don't do anything rash. Promise me you won't."

Asha couldn't promise that. She knew Dax was right—Jarek would expect her to come. He would set a trap for her. But if she didn't go . . .

Asha scanned the darkness for Kozu. She could sense him in her mind, restless in the presence of enemies. If he wouldn't come to her, she'd go to him.

Asha moved to step around her brother. He blocked her.

"Get out of my way."

"If I get out of your way, you'll fly to Firgaard and put everyone here at risk," said Dax. "I'm sorry, but I can't let you do that."

All of New Haven moved out the next morning. They couldn't stay—the commandant knew their exact location. So they packed the tents and readied the dragons. It should have been Asha who led the dragons and their riders down into the lower Rift, close to the entrance of her secret tunnel. But Dax forbade her from flying—in case she decided to fly straight to the palace. So Asha chose the best rider and put her in the lead.

Once they reassembled in the lower Rift, Dax called a meeting. They gathered in a makeshift tent where he and Jas outlined the plan. Dax would go in alone, as a decoy. While he entered through the north gate, Jas and Safire and a handful of other Haveners would make their way through the tunnel below the temple. While Dax negotiated with the dragon king, Jas and Saf would take over the gate and hold it open long enough for the army waiting just beyond the wall. Essie was still the signal to advance. Jas would bring the hawk. The moment the gate opened, he would send her skyward.

Asha would not be setting foot anywhere near the city. She had too much at stake, and no one trusted her to stick with the plan.

"I know it seems unfair," Dax said after everyone but he, Asha, and Safire had left the tent. Asha sat in the dirt, with her lower back against a wooden tent post and her forehead pressed into her drawn-up knees. Safire sat next to her, sharpening her knives. Dax sank down between them. "But I need you to wait here with the army until it's safe."

Without looking at her brother, Asha said, "You mean, until you've killed the king."

Silence descended. When Asha looked up into her brother's warm eyes, she found them shining with tears.

"I have to, Asha."

Safire paused her sharpening.

"No," said Asha. "What you need to do is *stay alive*, so you can be a better king than he is."

Dax shook his head. "So long as our father draws breath, no one will consider me king."

"Think of Roa, then. You'll leave a scrublander to hold the throne alone? Firgaard will devour her."

"Trust me," he said, his jaw tight. "Roa can take care of herself."

"What about what I want?" Safire demanded. "What about what Asha wants?"

Dax wiped his eyes with the hem of his sleeve.

"I want you to live," said Safire, a little angrily.

"And I want you to rule," said Asha.

He pulled away from them both. Asha let him go. Let him get to his feet.

"This is what good leaders do," he said, not daring to look either of them in the eye. He seemed every bit a hero in his dirty scrublander clothes and his tearstained cheeks. "They make sacrifices for their people."

Asha thought of the day she burned the scrolls, when Dax told her the Old One hadn't abandoned them. He was just waiting for the right moment. The right person.

He's waiting for the next Namsara to make things right.

Asha thought Dax a fool that day. Now, though, as her brother turned and left the tent, she thought something very different.

There. There is our Namsara.

Safire stayed behind, continuing to sharpen her throwing knives while she waited for the signal.

"You have to stop him," said Asha the moment Dax left the tent.

Without looking up from her work, Safire said, "I'm planning on it."

Asha leaned her head back against the wood post, listening to the drawn-out *hiss* of steel on the whetstone.

Safire stopped suddenly, lowering the sharpened knife in her lap. "Whatever happens, I want you to know I love you."

Asha looked into her cousin's eyes. "What?"

"As much as I want you at my side in there"—she nodded toward the tent entrance, toward the city—"I can't bear the thought of what Jarek will do to you if this all goes completely wrong."

Asha stared at her cousin, horrified. "What he'll do to *me*? Think of what he's already done to *you*, Saf."

Her cousin held up the knife edge, examining it. "All I need is one clear shot."

Asha didn't like this thought. She looked away, angry. They should be going in together. But as the tent darkened around her and Safire's departure crept closer, Asha let her head fall against her cousin's shoulder.

They sat in silence for a long time, both of them thinking of what would happen if it *did* all go wrong. They were still sitting there, with Asha's head on Safire's shoulder and Safire's knife lowered in her lap, when footsteps crunched on the hard, dry earth.

"Safire?" Jas entered the tent. "It's time."

Just before she rose, Safire leaned in close. "Don't you dare do anything reckless."

Asha stared as her cousin pushed herself to her feet, tucking the sharpened knife into her belt.

"Don't *you* do anything reckless," Asha countered as Safire walked past Jas, who held up the tent flaps for her to step through. When she did, Jas turned to Asha, solemnly fisted his hand over his heart, then dropped the tent flaps, cutting them both off from view.

Reaching for the whetstone her cousin left behind, Asha drew the axe at her hip. She'd taken it from the weapons caravan almost as soon as it arrived in New Haven. Made of acacia wood, the unadorned handle was worn and smooth.

Slowly, carefully, Asha started to sharpen it.

Forty-Six

Asha couldn't tell how much time had passed. Only that it grew dark shortly after Safire left with Jas, and it was still dark.

Too dark.

And too quiet.

Footsteps rose up, crunching the dry pine needles littering the ground outside the tent. Asha rose from the dirt floor and tucked her axe into her belt.

This is it. They've secured the gate.

The tent flaps whispered open. Roa stood in the entrance, alone, with a torch in her hand. The tent flaps fell shut behind her, sealing them in together.

"Something's wrong." Her dark gaze sliced into Asha. "Essie's returned, but the gates are shut tight."

"What?"

"I think they've been captured."

Fear spiked in Asha. Everyone she loved was in the city. They couldn't be captured. Because that meant everyone she loved was in the hands of the two people who wouldn't think twice about hurting them—in order to hurt *her.*

"Maybe there are too many soldats guarding the gate," Asha said, wishing she was still leaning against the tent pole. Wishing she had something to bear her up. "Maybe they're regrouping."

"They've had all night to return and collect more soldiers. It's almost dawn." Roa lifted the tent flap, waiting for Asha. "We're going in."

They couldn't go in on dragonback—not with the commandant in possession of so many hostages. Roa feared the sight of dragons would push Jarek to start taking lives, beginning with the least important.

Asha didn't like to think about who the least important would be.

"The tunnel, then?"

Roa nodded, her eyes glittering in the torchlight.

A familiar craving curled like smoke in Asha's belly. She wanted to hunt. Not a dragon, though. Never again would she hunt a dragon. Tonight she would hunt her own husband.

Roa whistled, holding up the torch. Out of the darkness two young women materialized. Asha recognized both of them from the night of Dax and Roa's binding.

"This is Lirabel," said Roa, touching the shoulder of Jas's friend and then the girl beside her. "And Saba."

Lirabel wore her gleaming black curls bound in a thick braid over her shoulder; Saba wore her hair in two plaits running down each side of her head. Judging by their belt quivers and the bows slung over their shoulders, they were archers.

Three armed scrublanders against troops of soldats seemed like bad odds to Asha. She kept this thought to herself, though, too afraid Roa would change her mind and leave her behind. Taking the torch, Asha led them into the tunnel.

Roa's white hawk swooped in after them.

The orange flame pierced the darkness as they walked deeper into rock. When they neared the tunnel opening, Lirabel touched Asha's shoulder, stopping her. Taking an arrow from her quiver, the girl held it to the torch. The tip was wrapped in cloth and Asha could smell the alcohol it had been dipped in. The arrow lit and burned, bright and furious. Lirabel shot the arrow through the crypt, lighting up a much larger path than the torch would have, allowing them to see if anyone waited in the darkness.

Deciding the way was clear, Lirabel stepped out first. Asha followed her, leading them through the crypt, up the vaulted stairway, and into the temple. And all the while, Lirabel shot her arrows tipped with fire, making sure no enemies lurked ahead.

They should have run into someone by the time they reached the front doors. A guardian. Or a soldat. But the temple was silent and empty. It made the hair on Asha's arms rise.

Roa pressed both hands against one of the front doors, ready to push it open, when Asha stepped on something.

"Wait," she hissed, lifting her foot and crouching down to the floor. The glow of her torch illuminated a knife with a hilt made of ivory and mother-of-pearl.

Safire's knife. The one she'd been sharpening in the tent.

Asha picked it up. The hilt was cold.

Safire never dropped her weapons—not by accident, not even in a fight. Which meant she'd left it here on purpose.

Asha's eyes lifted to where the knife pointed: the temple entrance. Roa's palms were still pressed against the door, ready to push. Her gaze met Asha's, who shook her head. Rising, she motioned for the three scrublanders to follow her. Whatever Safire's reason, Asha needed to put as much space as possible between them and the entrance.

She led them to the window that opened out to the pomegranate tree. The street below was just as empty as the temple. No torches burned in the narrow laneways. The only light came from the stars.

Where were the soldats?

"Do you know how to get to the gate from here?"

Roa tapped her head. "Your brother's map is in here."

Asha shook her head. "Don't take the main streets." She sank to a crouch, holding the glow of her torch just above the floor while she drew a rough map in the dust. "This way will take more time, but more streets branch off it." Roa crouched with her, watching silently as she drew. "You'll have more escape routes this way, if you need them. And no one will expect you to take the most cumbersome way."

Roa's eyes memorized the path made by Asha's fingertip.

Asha handed over the torch. "You'll need it for your arrows."

Dipping her head in the barest of nods, Roa said, "May the Old One guide your steps."

Asha climbed out the window and into the branches of the pomegranate tree, then quickly glanced back.

"Roa?"

The girl in the window paused.

"Don't break my brother's heart."

Roa smiled a small smile. "Is that a threat, Iskari?" And then she raised her fist over her own heart in a silent salute.

Asha dropped to the street below. Gathering the darkness around her like a cloak, she crept through the shadows, making her way to the palace alone. And all the while, she felt Kozu in her mind. Restless. Pacing. Wondering where she was.

Forty-Seven

Devoid of marching soldats and the sounds and smells of the night market, the city seemed lifeless. No donkeys brayed. No beggars sat with outstretched palms. No water sellers wandered or called. The night was silent around Asha. The thud of her own boots on dusty streets and tiled rooftops echoed loudly in her ears, so she took them off and left them behind, continuing barefoot.

It felt like walking into a trap.

Asha had walked into a trap once before. She'd been hunting down a very old dragon and, after two days, found herself going in circles. It was on the third day that she realized the dragon was leading her in those circles. *It* was tracking *her*, keeping to the shadows, just out of sight.

The only reason Asha defeated it was because she pretended not to know. She played its game, walked into its trap, and when the dragon had her cornered and alone, Asha revealed just how unoblivious she was . . . and how sharp her claws were.

The trap waiting for her now was not so different from that dragon's. The only thing to do was step right into it.

Swinging herself down from the roof and into one of the palace's covered walkways, Asha paused in the arched window to scan the shadows. She was about to jump down when the sound of voices stopped her.

Asha heard Dax's voice first, followed by her father's. She lowered her bare feet to the marble floor, following their voices in the direction of her father's largest courtyard. The same courtyard where Elorma first called her.

"I won't," Dax said.

"Then I'll start killing them, one by one. Starting with this one."

Asha stepped into the archway. The walls were lit with torches burning in their sconces. Their light glinted off a familiar black blade, gripped in the dragon king's hand. It was one of her slayers. The last time she'd seen them, she'd been defending Kozu in the meadow.

Her father pressed its edge to a throat.

Torwin's throat.

"Stop!"

The dragon king looked to the archway. "There you are." Her father sounded strangely relieved. As if, in spite of everything, the sight of his Iskari was a salve for his soul.

Dax turned. His hands were tied behind his back and the two soldats guarding him had his weapons.

"Asha," Dax said, "I told you not to—"

"Roa sends her love," she said, silencing him with a

look—one she hoped conveyed the truth: *Roa's on her way.*

But where were Safire and Jas? Asha glanced around the courtyard.

Empty.

Her gaze fixed on Torwin. He didn't look broken. He didn't even look afraid as his eyes met hers from across the court. As if he'd resigned himself to this. As if he knew what was coming and he was going to face it, unwavering.

The distance across the courtyard had never felt as vast and uncrossable as it did now.

"It seems I'm in possession of something you want, my dear."

"And what's that?" She tried to sound calm as she moved toward her father, letting her hunting instincts guide her.

Go slowly. No sudden movements.

Sensing what she was doing, her father began to slide the edge of her slayer across Torwin's throat. Blood gathered and spilled. Torwin's body clenched.

Asha halted, throwing up her hands.

"No! Please. I won't come any closer."

Her father eased up on the blade, smiling a slow smile. If he was uncertain before, he was uncertain no longer. He did indeed have what she wanted.

Asha's heart beat out a frantic rhythm as she stared at the blood staining the collar of Torwin's shirt. The same shirt she'd kissed him in.

This was not going as planned.

Think, Asha.

In the back of her mind, a shadow moved.

Restless. Worried.

No, she thought. Her father knew they had dragons. Which meant he would be prepared for them.

Asha couldn't let Kozu come here. They would kill him.

So she did the only thing she could think of. Pinning her hopes on Roa, she stalled for time.

"You tried to poison Dax with dragon bone. You tried to kill your own *son.*" She looked from her brother to her father. "Why?"

Their father smiled a cruel smile.

"You figured that out, did you? You always were the smarter one. You and I both know, my dear, your brother could never be king. I've always thought his affection for our enemies was a threat to the throne. And look: tonight he's proved me right."

He narrowed his eyes on Dax. "I'd hoped the ring would kill him out there. It would have been the perfect reason to start a war with the scrublanders . . . and finally subdue them."

"You would kill your own heir . . . to start a war?" asked Dax, sensing what Asha was doing. Helping her stall.

"A dead heir is more useful than a traitorous one."

Anger blazed through Asha at those words. "Is the same true of a dead wife?"

For half a heartbeat, a strange emotion flickered across her father's face. Surprise, maybe. Or remorse. Whatever it was, he recovered quickly, his hand tightening on the hilt of his daughter's slayer.

"Your mother disobeyed the law, Asha. She undermined my rule. I needed to make an example of her."

"She was my *mother*."

"She was corrupting you."

Asha's fingers itched for her axe.

The dragon king looked over her shoulder at something behind her.

"Ah," said a voice that sent an icy chill down Asha's spine. "I see you've found my wife."

Asha spun to find Jarek standing in the archway. He wore a very fine kaftan the color of midnight. But while its threads glinted and gleamed in the moonlight, Jarek's ravenous gaze turned what might have been a beautiful sight into a terrifying one.

Beyond him, a sound rang out: marching footsteps and clanging metal, getting louder and closer. Soldats who'd been nonexistent just moments ago were now bleeding out of the darkness behind him, pouring through doorways and into the courtyard.

The edge of her vision flared orange. Startled, Asha looked to the rooftops, where hundreds of soldats wielding freshly lit torches stared down at her.

"It's time to fulfill your end of our bargain, my dear. It's too late to cancel the binding, of course. But I'm willing to let Jarek's slave live *if* you call the First Dragon and end this."

The moment her father said the words, Asha felt it again: a dark presence, there in her mind. Kozu knew exactly where she was and the danger she was in. He'd known the moment she stepped into it.

And he was getting closer.

No, thought Asha, thinking of the soldats on the rooftops, all of them armed with bows and arrows. One archer against a dragon was nothing. But dozens? Asha's hunting slaves had helped her take down plenty of dragons using only arrows.

"What's it going to be?" Her father pressed the blade a little harder into Torwin's throat, forcing the skral's chin up. "The dragon or the slave?"

Asha didn't take her eyes off Torwin.

"He's coming," she whispered. Hating that, after everything, her father still had the power to make her do what he wanted.

The dragon king narrowed his eyes at his daughter. "Don't think you can fool me, Asha."

"He knows where I am. He knew the moment I stepped into this courtyard." She stared the dragon king down. "Because I'm his rider."

Her father's face darkened.

The black steel of her slayer shimmered as the dragon king motioned to Jarek. All around the walls, archers took up their positions. Halberds and spearheads glittered at the ready.

"If you want this slave alive, you'll strike Kozu down the moment he arrives," said the dragon king. "If you don't, I'll cut his throat open in front of you."

Asha knew better than to believe a liar. If she did as he said, Torwin would die anyway. Her father would have what he wanted. There'd be no reason to keep him alive. And if she chose Kozu and let Torwin die, the soldats would kill Kozu before he could escape.

She was going to lose them both.

"May Death send his worst," Torwin said softly, interrupting her thoughts. Asha's gaze snapped to him. He kept his eyes on her, like she was the one steady point in a world spinning out of control.

"Cold to freeze the love in my heart . . ."

"Silence," hissed the king.

"Fire to burn my memories to ash . . ."

The dragon king pressed the blade harder, trying to choke off Torwin's voice. But if he pressed too hard, he would kill him. And he couldn't kill him—not before Kozu arrived.

"Wind to force me through the gates . . ."

They were Willa's words he spoke. Binding vows. And they were something else too.

Death is a release, he'd told her once.

"Time to wear my loyalty away . . ."

"No." Asha moved toward him.

"Stay back," her father warned.

Asha halted. Her gaze locked with Torwin's. "Don't you dare."

Torwin's gaze never left her face. His eyes were silver sad. "I'll wait for you, Asha, at Death's gate."

Asha thought of Death calling Willa's name.

Her hands fisted. "Death is *not* your god."

A shadow passed overhead, making the stars wink out. The soldats shifted uneasily as her father looked to the sky. There was a sound like a rushing of sighs and Asha felt a familiar wind on her face.

A blazing fire shot across the sky, lighting up half her father's archers on the rooftops. They screamed and thrashed their arms, burning brightly before falling to their deaths.

Kozu landed next to his rider. The ground shook with his weight. His black scales glittered in the torchlight, and his yellow eye narrowed on the dragon king while his body curled protectively around Asha.

"Now!" Jarek commanded.

Arrows rained down.

"No!" Asha screamed.

Kozu roared as arrowheads sank into his flesh and tore through his wings.

"Strike," said the dragon king.

Kozu hissed and thrashed. Arrow shafts stuck out of his hide. He didn't know who to attack first. Were the archers the bigger threat, or the king?

"Strike now!"

Asha looked from Torwin to Kozu and back, frozen.

More arrows flew. Kozu roared with pain and rage. Blood dripped from his wings and ran down his flanks.

The First Dragon made up his mind. He rounded on Asha's father, leaving Asha undefended.

From the corner of her eye, she saw Jarek draw his saber. She felt him move toward her.

In his panic, the dragon king turned, keeping the slave between him and the fire-breathing monster, using the slave as a shield.

Asha's gaze fixed on her father's back. In one single heartbeat, the past, present, and future wove together like a tapestry.

Her mother ice-cold in her bed.

Her brother failing to win his people's loyalty.

The boy she loved, walking through the gate of the dead. Alone.

This king had to die.

Her fingers wrapped around the handle of her hunting axe. Lifting it from her belt, Asha drew the axe back. She knew the punishment for regicide. She knew the moment her axe left her hand that her life was forfeit.

And still, she threw it.

"No!" Dax screamed.

Asha's axe sailed toward the dragon king, whistling through the air before carving easily through flesh and bone. A sickening silence descended.

Jarek stopped mere steps from Asha. His shining saber fell to his side as he stared at his king.

Dark red blood seeped across the dragon king's golden robe. Asha's slayer clattered to the stones as he staggered, releasing the skral, and turned to face his daughter. The tip of her axe stuck through the front of his chest, where it sliced through his heart.

Her father touched his crest, blotted with his own blood. He gulped and gulped. Blood spread and spread.

"Asha . . . ?"

His voice echoed against the walls of the court, but not as loudly as it echoed inside her own rib cage, catching there to haunt her heart.

The dragon king fell to the ground at her feet, his body contorted, blood pooling all around him. Just like every dragon Asha had ever killed. His sightless eyes stared up at her. Asha stared back, unable to look away.

Darkness enveloped her then. Torwin pressed her face into his chest, blocking out the sight of her father's corpse. He cupped her head, holding her tight as she shook, her hands bunching the fabric of his shirt.

"Get away from her, skral," Jarek growled.

Torwin held her tighter.

And then: the piercing cry of a hawk filled the air.

Torwin loosed Asha as a flurry of flaming arrows sailed through the air above them. Each and every arrow met its mark, sinking into the chests of the archers on the walls.

The courtyard erupted into motion as the scrublander army poured into the court, its ranks joined by draksors and skral, all of them armed to the teeth. Roa led them. The curve of her double-edged blade already shone with blood as her gaze searched the crowd. At her side stood Safire, her eyes blazing.

Roa gave a command. Her hawk flew to Dax.

"Kill them!" Jarek screamed at his soldats. "Kill them all!"

But the soldats were outnumbered and the dragon king was dead. The next time arrows rained down, there were only half as many.

Asha turned to Kozu, who was bleeding and studded with arrows. The First Dragon watched her with a calm, slitted eye. His body arched around her as she pulled the arrows out, thinking of Shadow. Of the blood streaming from the gash in his chest.

But Kozu's wounds were minor. Kozu was going to live.

Torwin grabbed a dead archer's bow and caught arrows as

they sailed past, quickly shooting back, picking the rest of the balcony archers off, one by one. The clash of metal on metal rose as soldats charged. Asha heard the sickening sound of bodies connecting with blows.

Dax was at Roa's side. They fought back to back as Essie flew in a tight, protective circle above.

And in the distance was the sound of a multitude of wings.

A moment later, the rooftops lit up with fire, breathed from the bellies of dragons swarming like storm clouds above them. Any archers still on the rooftops were there no longer. The gust of dragon wings rushed through the courtyard as they landed. When the rooftops became too crowded, the others flew in circles above.

The courtyard went silent and still. Overpowered and surrounded, soldats began laying down their weapons and surrendering. All except Jarek, who stared down Dax, both hands gripping his saber.

Dax approached, his footsteps ringing with victory. "You're finished."

Jarek spat at Dax's feet. "If I'm to die, I'll die defending the true king."

"So be it," a voice rang out. A knife hissed through the air, followed by two more. They sailed from Safire's hands and sank into Jarek's chest.

His saber fell, clanging against the marble floor. He reached for the hilts, trying to pull them out. Scrublander soldiers rushed in, tackling him to the floor and fastening irons around his wrists and ankles.

Safire stood over him, breathing hard, her last throwing knife gripped in her hand. "I should have done this a long time ago."

She stabbed the knife in his heart.

Forty-Eight

They burned the dragon king's body on a pyre. Asha didn't see it, chained as she was to the damp dungeon walls. But afterward, Safire told her how the fire consumed his body. How the smoke clotted the air. How all Firgaard came to mourn while Kozu watched from the wall.

Safire visited Asha's cell as often as she could, but when Dax promoted her to commandant, her visits stopped almost entirely. Not everyone was happy with Dax taking the throne. They were less happy with his scrublander wife. So when Dax presented his skral-blooded commandant, there were riots. Draksors took out their aggression on the skral, who began fleeing the city in droves. And when there weren't any skral left to scapegoat, draksors turned on draksors.

Which kept Safire more than a little occupied.

The dragons helped. They and their riders acted as peace-keepers, watching from the rooftops. But they could only see so much.

Asha was all but forgotten about as Dax, Safire, and Roa tried to keep control of a capital falling apart at the seams. Asha learned to tell time by the changing of the guards. She gleaned information by eavesdropping. She learned that soldats refusing to obey the orders of the new commandant were banished from their positions, effectively cutting the army in half. She learned that the loss of slave labor meant people were struggling to subsist.

Most important of all, she learned her execution was three days away.

The day before they sent Asha to the chopping block, they made Dax king.

Normally, when a new ruler took the throne, he or she was paraded through the streets, followed by trumpets and the steady beat of drums, while the citizens of Firgaard threw rose petals and sang coronation songs. Dax's coronation was nothing like that. It was a much more modest affair, set in the smallest of the palace courts, near the olive groves. The rains came in the afternoon and by evening the palace smelled of cool, damp plaster.

It was the only time they allowed Asha out of her cell. She was kept under guard, her ankles shackled with heavy chains, and confined to the upper terraces, away from the crowds who—upon seeing her—began to whisper and point.

"Life taker," they said.

"Death bringer."

"Iskari."

Their stares made Asha want to walk herself back to her cell and lock the door behind her. She'd saved them from a monster, and still they feared her. There had never been any hope of redeeming herself. In her people's eyes, she would always be Iskari.

Well, it wouldn't be long before they never had to look upon her face again. Very soon, Asha would be dead.

Torwin too was nowhere to be found. Feeling his absence, she gripped the balustrade. Asha didn't know if Torwin was dead or alive, living in the city or long gone to the scrublands. Over the past few weeks, whenever her guards mentioned yet another skral attack, Asha found her chest constricting. Her hands tightening on her chains. She hadn't seen Torwin since the night her brother led her to the dungeons and, with tears streaming down his cheeks, locked his own sister in a cell.

No matter how many times her gaze scanned the courtyard, there was no sign of him.

Above the din of conversation, just beyond the walls, the trilling birdcalls announced the approach of the night. Asha leaned over the balustrade, letting the hard, cold marble bear her up as she stared out across the lantern-lit court, still searching for Torwin. But all she found amid the potted kumquats and hibiscus hedges were colorfully clad scrublanders and collarless skral all mingling peaceably with draksors. It was a vision of the future. Of what Firgaard was capable of becoming.

Dax stood on the white-tiled terrace. At his side, Roa gleamed in a blue and gold kaftan that belted high at the waist and moved like water even when she stood still. A crimson flower sat tucked behind her ear. One with seven petals. She looked like a girl born to be queen, outshining even Dax, who stood at her side, matching her blue and gold. Their father's medallion hung across his chest. Dax looked tired and a little sad, but the set of his shoulders and the rise of his chest said these feelings were inconsequential to the work that lay ahead.

When he spotted Asha, his smile broke. A shimmering grief fell over him as their gazes met and held. He raised his fist to his heart in a solemn scrublander salute. Asha returned it.

The courtyard fell silent, looking where their new king looked. A chill crept up Asha's spine as the eyes of every scrublander, draksor, and skral fixed on her. In their sparkling kaftans and silk tunics, they gawked at Asha's chains and dirt-streaked garments.

She still didn't belong here. Would never belong here.

Asha was a blemish on her brother's new reign.

A soft shadow fell over her then. When she turned her back on the courtyard, she found her eldest guard standing before her. He had a perpetually wrinkled brow and a graying beard in need of a trim.

"Time to leave, Iskari."

Asha nodded, letting him take her arm.

As the other guards fanned out, ahead and behind, he led her down the stairwell and into the court below.

Whispered voices rose up as the guards walked through the arcades, keeping their charge away from the staring revelers. Asha fixed her attention on the towering entrance, its archway bordered by yellow and red mosaic tiles.

Halfway there, her guards halted, forcing Asha to halt too. In the space between the guards ahead, her gaze caught on slippered feet, then trailed up a shimmering blue and gold kaftan all the way to the dragon queen's face.

Roa stood directly in their path, blocking the way out of the courtyard.

The guards bowed their heads.

"Step away," said Roa.

The two guards standing between Asha and the queen exchanged glances. "My queen . . . she's dangerous."

Roa arched one elegant brow. "Shall I repeat myself?"

Both guards paused, not sure how much they could test their new queen. Finally, they shook their heads and stepped aside.

"And you." Roa nodded to the graying guard at Asha's side.

Obediently, he let go of Asha's arm and moved away. A heartbeat later, Asha stood alone before Roa.

With every pair of eyes watching her, the dragon queen bowed to the criminal before her.

"Kozu circles the city, night after night, searching for you. Yearning for his Namsara."

Murmurs and gasps rippled across the courtyard. The hair on Asha's arms rose.

Her? The *Namsara*? The life *bringer*?

Impossible.

Asha had spent her life killing things. She was hated and feared. She was the *Iskari*. The very opposite of what Roa thought.

"You're mistaken," said Asha, staring down at the bowing queen. "My brother—"

"*Your brother* says you know the old stories better than any of us." Roa rose from her bow. "Which means you know *who* the Old One sends to mark his Namsara."

Asha's lips parted. The stories glittered in her mind. She sifted through them.

The Old One sent Kozu to Nishran. Just like he sent Kozu to Elorma. Just like he sent Kozu to . . . *Asha*. All those years ago.

She'd thought it was her wickedness that called to Kozu as a child. Just like her wickedness allowed her to tell the old stories without being poisoned by them.

But the stories weren't wicked. And neither was Asha.

The proof was right there in the stories: Kozu was the mark of a Namsara. And Asha was Kozu's rider. She had the link to prove it.

Even if all of that were true, Asha had spent her life hunting dragons and trying to eradicate the old ways. She was no Namsara.

Roa took a step closer, and the court hushed.

"There are other marks, are there not?"

Asha thought of Nishran. The Old One gave him the ability to see in the dark so he could find the enemy's camp. Just like the Old One gave Elorma the gift of a hika—a girl who saved the city from an imposter king.

Just like the Old One gave Asha gifts to accomplish the tasks he set before her: slayers, a dragon, the ability to be unburned by fire.

She'd been trying so hard to suppress the stories, she'd been so consumed with her hunt for Kozu, she hadn't put it together. All those years ago, when she'd gone into the innermost cave after her mother's burning . . .

"The Old One was *choosing* me?" she whispered, staring into Roa's eyes.

But what of Elorma? If she was the Namsara, Elorma would have told her.

Except . . . wasn't that what he'd been doing all along?

I am the Namsara.

She hardly dared to believe it.

Roa's eyes shone as she lifted the fire-like flower from behind her ear. Seven bloodred petals curled back on themselves as a yellow stamen dropped pollen, flecking the petals with orange. It was the same flower mosaicked into the sickroom's floors. The same flower carved into a temple door.

A flower so rare, it was almost a myth.

Roa stepped forward. Tucking the stem behind Asha's ear, she whispered, "The old stories say Namsara is a needle sewing the world together."

Asha was too startled to respond.

"And our world is in dire need of sewing."

Then Roa was gone, putting space between them as she nodded to Asha's guards. They resumed their positions, severing Asha from her queen. With the entire courtyard still looking on, Roa returned to her husband's side. Dax looked the most shocked of anyone.

Silence rang out in her wake. When the guards recovered, they reached for Asha's arms and moved her through the scandalized court. They marched her through archways and down corridors, all the way back to her dungeon cell.

And their footsteps seemed less certain this time.

Forty-Nine

Asha couldn't sleep that night. She sat in the dark, on the cold, damp floor of her cell, with Roa's words running over and over in her mind. But even if what Roa said was true, what did it matter? There was still the law to contend with: Asha had killed a king, and the punishment for that was death.

She might be the Namsara, but she was about to become the *dead* Namsara.

Dawn was coming. And with it, the long lonely walk to the square.

How had Moria walked so bravely to her own beheading?

Trembling, Asha hugged herself and closed her eyes. She thought of the Rift, hoping this would calm her. She thought of the chattering bush chats and the wind whistling in the pines. She thought of the stars, like words on a scroll rolled out across the sky, and the bright, fierce sun.

She thought of the ones she loved best.

Safire.

Tears welled in her eyes.

And Dax.

Her vision blurred.

And—

The sound of footsteps echoed in the distance, crashing through her thoughts. Asha turned her face to listen. Someone was bringing her breakfast.

The last meal she'd ever eat.

It seemed like forever before the guard shuffled his keys, sliding one into the lock. Forever before it turned and clicked and the heavy iron door slid open, letting orange torchlight sweep into her cell.

In the rectangle of light stood a kitchen servant, cloaked in a wool mantle. His face was hidden deep beneath its hood, concealing him from the Iskari's deadly gaze. The lidded silver tray in his hands shone in the torchlight.

The guard withdrew the key. "She's all yours."

The moment the words were out of his mouth, the servant hit him hard across the face with the tray. The ringing sound ricocheted off the walls. The keys fell to the floor a mere heartbeat before the guard did.

No food tumbled from the tray. Only a flutter of cloth.

With his comrade down, the second guard drew his saber. He thrust it at the servant, who blocked with the silver lid, kicked him in the groin, then slammed the lid down on his head.

The man dropped like a stone.

With both guards lying unconscious on the floor, the kitchen servant bent to pick up the keys and stepped into the cell.

From the floor, Asha slid back against the cold, damp wall, the shackles on her wrists and ankles clanking, her heart pounding like a drum.

"Who are you?"

In three strides, he closed the space between them and crouched down. Reaching for her wrist, he slid his thumb over the bump of her bone. His fingers were callused but gentle.

Warmth flickered through Asha. She knew that touch. Peering up into the darkness of the hood, she knew the face behind it even if she couldn't see it.

He thumbed through the keys until he found the one that fitted her wrist shackles. It slid into the lock. With a swift click the heavy chains fell away, snaking to the floor. As he turned his attention to the chains around her ankles, Asha grabbed his wool mantle. With trembling fingers, she pushed back the hood.

The torchlight illuminated his hair and lit up his skin, revealing a multitude of freckles and eyes soft with worry.

"Torwin . . ."

At the sound of his name, he looked up. When their gazes met, he let go of her chains—just for a moment—and pulled her to him, breathing her in and burying his face in her hair. Asha curled her arms around his shoulders, squeezing him hard, not wanting to let go.

He went back to work trying several keys before finding the right one, desperate to get her unchained. The click came. The weight of her chains fell off for good. When the cold dungeon air brushed against her bare ankles, Asha let go of him.

Torwin remained, crouching over her, staring into her eyes. "Asha . . ."

In that one word, she heard so much more than just her name.

She heard all the sleepless nights he'd spent pacing the ramparts, wondering what was happening to her. She heard all the shouted arguments he'd had with her brother, who was bound by an ancient law to sentence his own sister to death. She heard all the things that led him here, to the belly of the palace, with two unconscious guards at his back and the keys to her cell in his hand.

"You're mad," she whispered.

Smiling her favorite smile, Torwin slid both hands around her neck and kissed her.

Asha, who'd become accustomed to the harsh chill of the dungeon, dug her fingers into his hair. She pulled him into her, craving his warmth.

"Maybe I am," he whispered back, breaking away. "Come on."

He grabbed her hand and pulled her to her feet, then bent to pick something up off the floor. It was the garment that had fallen from the dinner tray—a pine-green mantle. Stepping in close, he flung it around Asha's shoulders, tying the tassels at her throat, then flipped up the hood to conceal her face.

Together, they walked out into the torchlit bays of the dungeon. Through the long shadows stretching from wall to wall, Asha saw more unconscious guards. Some lying in the dirt, others half propped against the walls. One of them was already coming to, groaning softly.

"You did this?"

"I had help."

They moved quickly through the shadow and torchlight and took the stairs up into the palace. They ran through sleepy corridors and silhouetted gardens. Past soldats making their nightly rounds. By the time the soldats realized who they were, Asha and Torwin were already down the hall or across the court or through the garden.

Frantic shouts and thudding boots rang out behind them. Asha thought they were making for the front gate, but when Torwin turned down hallways that led farther into the heart of the palace, she halted, thinking he didn't know where he was going, and tried to drag him in the opposite direction.

"No," he said. "This way."

As three soldats careened into each other not twenty paces behind them, Asha decided to trust him.

Just when they hit a dead end, Torwin tugged her through a plain wooden door. Shutting it behind them, Asha found herself in a narrow, dusty passageway that smelled of mildew.

A secret passage.

Asha had grown up with rumors of the palace's secret passageways, but she'd never found any, and had always thought that's all they were: rumors.

"How did you find this?"

"Dax showed me."

Asha marveled. What other secrets had her brother been

keeping from her all these years?

"Come on."

He pulled her onward, through the stone-flagged darkness to another, older, door. One with rusted hinges and weak, rotting wood. Torwin pressed his eye to the sliver of light carving a line through the dark, peering into the room beyond, checking to see if it were occupied.

Asha leaned against the cold, damp wall. As her heart slowed and her breath came easier, reason came crashing down around her. They were surrounded; every soldat in the city was looking for them now; and once caught, she would lose him all over again.

"Torwin, there's nowhere to go."

Didn't he realize that? They were deep in the palace, with every soldat alert and looking for them.

Keeping his eye pressed to the slit, Torwin said nothing.

"Even if we manage to elude them, even if there were someplace safe to escape to, my brother would be obligated to hunt me down. He can't just let me go."

Torwin whirled on her then.

"Listen to me." He took her shoulders in his hands. "We're in this together now. So we can give up and hand ourselves over, or we can run. But whatever we do, we're doing it together."

Asha looked up into his shadowed face. Lifting her fingers, she traced his cheekbone and jaw.

"Okay," she said. "I guess we're running."

He grabbed her wrist and kissed her palm, then turned back to the door.

"Ready?" he asked, sliding the rusty pins out of the hinges, then dropping them to the floor.

"Ready for what?"

"The door's locked. We have to break it open."

Asha froze. "What?"

"On the count of three," he said, coming to join her against the wall.

"One . . ."

"Torwin—"

"Two . . ." He twined his fingers through hers.

"I don't think—"

"Three!"

They ran at the door, charging it with their shoulders. It broke open on the first try. The rusted hinges gave and the rotten wood cracked away from the lock. The door fell flat to the floor with Asha on top of it and Torwin on top of her.

"By the skies, did you *crawl* here?"

A familiar, silhouetted form leaned against the wall. Arms crossed. Knee bent.

"I left you in that dungeon *ages* ago."

Torwin grinned up at Safire as he hopped to his feet, grabbed Asha's hand, and hauled her up.

"Come on." The new commandant pushed away from the wall. "We need to hurry."

They were in one of the orchards. Safire led them through the silhouetted trees, their twisted branches reaching for the lightening sky.

Dawn had arrived.

"Roa convinced the scrublanders you're the new Namsara," Safire explained as they approached a door on the other side of the orchard. She slid the key into the lock. The lock clicked. The door creaked open. "They've offered you sanctuary. You'll be safe there . . . for a little while, at least."

Torwin stepped into the stairway first. Asha went after him, followed by Safire, who locked the door behind them. Together, they climbed the steps to a dark room, where Torwin grabbed some kind of pack and hoisted it over his shoulder.

When they walked out onto a rooftop terrace, a night-black dragon with one yellow eye prowled before them. Waiting. Waiting for a long time. Black talons gleamed in the dawn's light.

"Kozu."

A rumbled growl answered her.

Torwin opened the pack and pulled out two flight coats, two pairs of gloves, and two sandskarves.

Asha turned back to her cousin.

"Torwin has everything you need," Safire said, then pulled her into a hug, squeezing the breath out of her. Asha squeezed back, her vision blurring with tears.

"I miss you already," Asha whispered. Safire squeezed even harder.

Sounds in the distance wrenched them apart. They turned to look over the city, where torches floated through the streets, gripped in the fists of soldats, already searching for the escaped Iskari.

"I have to go," Safire said. "Before they realize I'm helping you."

Asha turned to find Torwin already dressed for flying and holding out a coat for her. She threaded her arms through the sleeves, then quickly did up the clasps and wrapped the cotton sandskarf around her neck, pulling it over her head. Asha mounted Kozu first, with Torwin following.

"Don't do anything reckless, Namsara," Safire said from the ground.

Asha didn't know whether to smile or cry.

"Don't *you* do anything reckless."

A shout rang out from much too close. Safire turned to look as Torwin slid an arm around Asha's waist.

"I have to go . . . ," said Safire, catching sight of her soldats below.

Not ready to let her go yet, Asha reached for Safire. Despite her fear, Safire reached back, clasping Asha's hand hard.

"I love you," said Asha.

When Torwin clicked to Kozu, their fingers slid apart. Kozu spread his wings. Safire stepped back into the terrace archway, concealing herself. Kozu took a running start and dived into the air. Asha lurched forward as the wind whistled past, then quickly looked back, but the shadows had swallowed Safire. Asha looked beyond her, to the flat rooftops and copper domes of the palace, then to the royal quarters. A lamp burned in one of its windows. If Asha squinted, she could see someone standing there, looking out into the night, watching as a criminal and a skral escaped into the early morning sky.

Fifty

They didn't stop flying until the sky darkened again that night and the stars clustered above them. Even then, Torwin seemed agitated. Like he wanted to fly straight to the scrublands without stopping. Despite the creases of exhaustion next to his mouth, despite the dark smudges beneath his eyes, despite the way he hunched over a paltry meal of nuts and too-hard bread, he wanted to keep going, to put as much distance between them and the horrors they'd left behind.

As Asha watched him, she thought of Shadow. Torwin would have seen Jarek strike that killing blow. He would have felt the moment Shadow's life winked out. He would be feeling the absence of his dust-red companion even now.

Asha didn't know how to soothe such a hurt. Didn't know if it *could* be soothed.

She sat close to him while they ate. Let her thigh fall against his. Smiled at him when he looked at her.

But even when he laced his fingers through hers or brushed

his thumb across her cheek or stared at her like he couldn't believe they were free, the silence still shimmered. And the space between them felt littered with loose threads. Threads streaming from an unfinished tapestry.

"I'll stay up and watch," she said after they set up the tent.

Torwin shook his head. "I won't sleep anyway. You get some rest." He grabbed his lute, then kissed her scarred cheek before heading toward a grassy dune. "Tomorrow will be another long day."

Asha watched him walk away until the darkness swallowed him up.

She climbed into the tent.

After a moment, she heard a familiar sound. The glossy, golden sound of his lute. Asha sat perfectly still, listening. And then exhaustion overcame her.

Lying down, she closed her eyes and let Torwin's song lull her to sleep.

The smell of smoke and ash woke her. When she sat up, Elorma crouched over a fire just big enough to illuminate his face.

Too tired to protest whatever it was he wanted from her now, she went to sit next to him.

"Aren't you done with me yet?" Curling her knees up to her chest, she hugged them hard to keep from shivering. "I did what the Old One wanted. What else is there?"

Elorma smiled, his eyes reflecting the fire. The hollow places of his face were darkened by shadow. "Much more, I'm afraid. Your work is just beginning, Namsara."

Namsara.

That name. It would take some getting used to.

Elorma cracked his knuckles and rose to his feet. "I'm here to bestow your final gift. The gift of a hika."

Asha's grip on her knees loosened. A hika. Like Willa was to Elorma.

"W-what?" she stammered.

Elorma ignored her. "A hika is formed just for you. Like your slayers were formed for your hands. Like the sky was formed for the earth. Come and look upon his face."

But Asha stayed where she was, hugging her legs harder. "I'm an outlaw," she said. "I'm guilty of regicide. Whoever you choose will be sentenced to a life of danger. I'd rather you leave him be."

Beneath all these things, though, lay a deeper truth: Asha loved someone else.

She rose to her feet.

She never meant to look into the fire. She only meant to walk away.

But her gaze snagged on a face in the flames.

Asha stepped closer. A boy peered out at her. He had stars etched into his skin. He had eyes as sharp as her own two slayers.

Asha's heart slammed against her ribs.

She stepped back.

The Old One knew just as well as she what happened when draksors coupled with skral. Those kinds of stories only ever ended in tragedy.

"You can't do this to him." Asha looked to Elorma. "It's a death sentence."

Being with Asha meant putting his life at risk.

"Death is no stranger to this one." Elorma rose to face her. "And doesn't he get a choice in the matter?"

He has no choice, she thought. *If the Old One commands it, there isn't a choice.*

And Torwin had spent his whole life being forbidden from making his own choices.

"I can't," she whispered. "I won't be another master he has to submit to."

She turned away, her footsteps sinking into the cold sand.

"Ask him who he dreams of at night," Elorma called after her. "Ask him who he's dreamed of every night for the past eighteen years of his life."

Asha stopped walking.

Torwin's voice rose up in her mind. *I used to think she was some kind of goddess*, he'd told her in the temple room, explaining his recurring nightmare. *I used to think she appeared to me because she was choosing me for some great destiny.*

And then, again, in her brother's war camp: *They're always about you.*

Elorma stood behind her now. She could feel his shadow stretch across her back.

"Do you know why I recognized Willa the first time I saw her?"

Asha turned and looked up into the First Namsara's eyes.

"Because I'd spent my life dreaming of her."

410

When he smiled, it was as if two suns burned warm and bright out of his eyes. "Willa chose love in the end." Very gently, he placed one strong hand on Asha's shoulder. "Now it's time for you to choose. Because, despite what you think, you do have a choice. And so does he."

Asha thought of something her brother told her once. If Rayan hadn't been selfish, Dax said, if he hadn't pursued Lillian, they'd both be alive today. But saying that denied Lillian's choice in the matter. It denied Lillian her power. And what's more: saying that meant the only thing to be learned from their story was that death is stronger than love.

Asha didn't believe that.

"And afterward," Elorma said, "there's more work to be done. Stories to be hunted down. A realm to be made whole again."

The fire roared behind Elorma as he smiled tenderly down on Asha.

"You and I will see each other again soon, Namsara."

The fire went out, plunging Asha into darkness.

She stood still for a long time, lost in the swirling storm of her thoughts.

Namsara.

The rare desert flower that could heal any ailment.

That's what Asha was.

Fifty-One

Asha woke to the sound of a song swelling in the air. She lay still for several heartbeats, letting the sound melt inside her, filling her up with longing.

With the First Namsara's words in her heart, she rose and followed the song.

Asha found the lute player in the sand, a silhouette against a sky so full of stars, it looked silver. She watched the roll of his shoulders, the dip of his head.

The sight of him held her transfixed.

He must have sensed someone watching, because the song stopped and he looked up from his strings, casting his gaze into the darkness.

"Asha? Is that you?"

Asha remained where she was.

He started to play again. A different song. Its familiar tune jolted her. It was the same unfinished song he'd been humming in the Rift. The same song he'd been trying to work out while

Asha fell asleep in his tent.

At some point, he'd finished it and he was playing it now. As he played, Asha could feel him staring into the spot where she stood.

"Greta used to say," he said as he played, "that every one of us is born with a song buried deep in our hearts. A song all our own. And our mission in life is to find that song."

His song was sharp like a knife and tender as his fingers stitching up her wounds. It dived into darkness, then soared toward the light. It was itself a kind of story—one that lured Asha out of the shadows.

Slowly, Torwin moved toward her.

"Tell me again about your nightmares," she said.

Fingers still plucking strings, he took another step and obliged her.

"They weren't always nightmares. They were just dreams, once." She felt him smile in the darkness, thinking about them. "Dreams about a scarred girl who rode a black dragon."

The music stopped as he lowered his lute. It fell to the sand with a soft thud.

"And then you got burned. That's when I knew, for certain, the girl I'd been dreaming about was you. That's when the dreams turned into nightmares."

Asha swallowed.

"I know what it means," he said. "I've always known what it means."

Asha felt her eyes burn with tears.

"I'll put you in danger," she said, admitting her deepest fear.

"Haven't we been through this? I *love* danger."

"Torwin."

"Asha." His voice went soft and careful. "I've only ever wanted three things. A lute of my own, to make music with. A life of my own, to do what I want with. And the girl I've been dreaming about for as long as I can remember. A girl who was always out of reach. . . ."

He reached for her, his fingers curling around her arms, closing the gap between them, tying up their loose and fraying threads.

"You could die," she whispered.

"Everything dies," he whispered back. "I'm afraid of so much more than dying."

A lump gathered in her throat. Thinking of Willa, she said, "Then may Death send his worst."

Torwin cupped her neck with his hand, touching his forehead to hers.

"Cold to freeze the love in my heart."

His thumb, warm from playing, brushed along her jaw.

"Fire to burn my memories to ash."

He pressed his mouth against her throat, making Asha fumble her words.

"W-wind to force me through the gates."

He trailed kisses up her neck, and Asha had to close her eyes against the pull of him.

"Time to wear my loyalty away."

The kisses stopped.

"I'll wait for you, Torwin—"

The final words were lost in the softness of his mouth.

Several heartbeats later, Asha broke away, needing to finish. "I'll wait for you at Death's gate."

And there was the tapestry: its threads no longer fraying.

There was the tapestry: finished, whole.

"Do you promise?" he whispered, seizing her wrists and pulling her close.

She nodded.

"Ah, but you made me another promise once and you never came through on it. So how can I trust you?"

Asha frowned. "What promise?"

He placed her hands around his neck, then slid his arms around her waist as a honeyed hum rose up from the depths of his throat. It was the song he'd just been playing. While he hummed, he led her in the steps of a slow, three-beat dance.

"Torwin?"

"Mmm?"

"What are you doing?"

"Dancing with you."

"I don't know how."

"Well, you're about to learn, aren't you."

Asha smiled as his song filled the air around them. She laughed as she tripped over him when he tried to lead her in the steps. Soon though, her feet found the rhythm. Soon, she was twirling through the sand.

He pulled her back.

"You're beautiful and precious and good," he whispered. "And I love you."

Asha looked up at him, there beneath the stars, and found herself starting to believe these things were true.

Maybe Greta was right. Maybe everyone did have a song in them—or a story. One all their own. If that were so, Asha had found hers.

And here she stood at the beginning of it.

Acknowledgments

I started writing this book when I was seventeen. Back then I was enamored of girls like Mulan, Eowyn, Xena, and Princess Mononoke. I desperately craved stories in which young women got to wield weapons or go to war or be fierce. I didn't realize it then, but what I was looking for were girls breaking out of a cultural script that dictated who and what they could be. I was tired of the narrative that said women were inherently weaker, inherently victims. I didn't see myself that way, nor did I see the women around me that way.

I wanted something different. So I started writing this story.

But writing the story is just the beginning. Something you don't see when you pick up a book from the shelf is just how many people were involved in getting it onto that shelf. Though my name might be on the cover, *The Last Namsara* was by no means a solitary feat. These are the people who helped me make it what it is today. . . .

First and foremost: Heather Flaherty, my world brightener and fiercely optimistic agent. Thank you for fighting so hard for me and this book. I think we were waiting for you.

Kristen Pettit, my sweet and inimitable editor. I adore you.

Thank you not only for making my books better, but for being so supportive of me.

The amazing team at the Bent Agency, including Jenny Bent (for making so many dreams come true), Victoria Cappello (for having endless patience with me and my pesky questions), and most especially my UK agent, Gemma Cooper, for finding my books the perfect UK home.

A big huge thank-you to the entire team at HarperTeen who helped turn this book into a beautiful reality, most especially: Renée Cafiero, Allison Brown, Martha Schwartz, Megan Gendell, Vincent Cusenza, Audrey Diestelkamp, Olivia Russo, Michelle Taormina (I can't even count the hours I've spent staring adoringly at my cover), and Elizabeth Lynch (for being all-around amazing, but especially for writing jacket copy so beautiful it made me cry).

The entire team at Gollancz, but especially Gillian Redfearn and Rachel Winterbottom. I'm ridiculously excited and proud to be part of the Gollancz family.

My international coagents and foreign publishers: Never in my wildest dreams did I imagine my stories would be translated into other languages and sold in countries so far from my own. Thank you for believing in this book.

My early readers (of various drafts): Cassandra Roach, Kayli Kinnear, Shannon Thomson, Leslie Morgenson, Amber Sundy, Andrea Brame, Rachel Stark, Emily Gref, Franny Billingsley, Traci Chee, Renée Ahdieh, Chris Cabena, Joan He, Michella Domenici, Hope Cook, Merrill Wyatt, Kamerhe Lane, Heather Smith, Amy Mathers, Tomi Adeyemi, Isabel Ibañez, Kit Grant,

Leila Siddiqui, and Geoff Martin. I'm probably forgetting someone. If I am, I'm so sorry!

Extraspecial thanks go to:

Franny Billingsley, for teaching me everything I know about storytelling.

Leila Siddiqui, for your honest feedback and kind help at the eleventh hour.

Art and Myrna Bauman, for letting me use the cottage whenever I need to escape the world and just write.

Leslie Morgenson, for telling me all those years ago that I am, in fact, a writer. You gave me the courage to go rogue.

Heather Smith and Nan Forler, for coffee, friendship, and general mischief-making.

My Pitch Wars cohort: I never expected to fall so hard in love with you all, but I did. It is a joy to be journeying with you.

My Pitch Wars mentors, Traci Chee and Renée Ahdieh: Thank you for dragging me out of the hole I'd dug myself into, then believing in and championing this book. Your mentorship was one of the best things to ever happen to me. Far better than book deals.

Brenda Drake: Thank you for working so tirelessly, thanklessly, and invisibly behind the scenes of Pitch Wars. You are a life changer.

Michella Domenici and Joan He, for your friendship and fangirling and willingness to drop everything when I need fresh eyes and another perspective. *squishes you both*

Isabel Ibañez, for backseat conversations from Charleston to

Orlando. For devouring this book "like a starving wolf." But most of all for your love and support. Sweet friend: you are beautiful.

Hope Cook, for always being just a text away whenever I need to a) melt into a puddle of self-pity or b) go on an angry rampage. I love you, O wise one.

Chris Cabena, for chess games and SAGA reminders and patiently listening to me ramble through all my plot snags. I cherish you more than you know.

Tomi Adeyemi, for your friendship, wisdom, and support. For talking me off ledges and bringing me back to the heart of things. But most of all for being so proud of me.

Joanna Hathaway, I don't know how I would have survived this year without you. You make me braver than I am on my own.

Asnake Dabala, brother and dearest friend, for letting me abuse all your printing privileges. Nilimuuliza Mungu kwa ajili ya rafiki na akakuleta wewe. Thank you for always being there for me.

My entire Cesar family: I wouldn't be who I am today without you all. Thank you especially to Nancy McLauchlin, Mary Dejonge, and Sylvia Cesar, for teaching me everything I know about love and bravery and being true to yourself; Larry Dejonge, Brian Baldoni, and Jim McLauchlin, for making my childhood one happy adventure; Pa, for carrying me to bed every night for almost a decade (we miss you); Bobbi, for making my lunches, driving me to appointments, teaching me how to braid my hair . . . you've always been so much more than a grandmother. Belonging to all of you is one of the greatest joys of my life. Thank you for raising me.

Jordan Dejonge, for being my coconspirator in all things growing up, but mostly: writing, adventuring, and figuring out how to be human together. I love you.

Dad, for always supporting and defending me. I'm so proud to be your daughter. Jolene, for always being proud of my art-making. Nathan and Graeme, for being two beacons of light in my life.

Mum, you're the best thing that's ever happened to me. Your love is a bright, fierce thing and the most precious gift I've ever been given.

Joe, for never thinking to doubt me. For talking me through this and everything else. For always, *always* bringing me back to myself. Now let's go chase your dream, my love.

Last of all, thank you, dear reader, for making it this far. Never forget: you are not what you've been told you are, you are what lies within you.

Turn the page for a sneak peek at the
next novel in the Iskari series

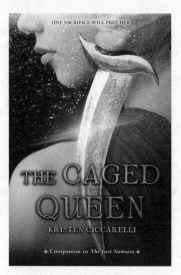

ONE SACRIFICE WILL FREE HER

THE CAGED
QUEEN

KRISTEN CICCARELLI

Companion to *The Last Namsara*

The Skyweaver's Knife

Once there lived a man named Sunder who loved everything about his life. He rose every day with the dawn and walked out into his fields. He marveled at the rain that nourished his crops and the sun that made them grow. He cherished the strength of his own two hands—hands that planted and threshed and built his house. Hands that rocked his child to sleep.

He loved his life so much that when Death came for him, Sunder hid.

Death searched Sunder's house and did not find him.

Death called out over his fields, but Sunder did not come.

So, giving up, Death took someone else instead.

When Sunder came out of his hiding place, he smiled at his own cleverness. He strode down the dirt roads toward home, whistling happily. But as he approached the door of his house, a sound made him pause.

Someone was wailing.

Sunder opened the door and found his wife kneeling on the kitchen floor, clutching their child to her breast. When Sunder fell to his knees beside her, he found his small daughter's eyes lifeless. Her body cold.

Sunder cursed his cleverness. He wept and gnashed his teeth.

After that day, Sunder no longer rose with the dawn. No longer marveled at the rain or the sun. And when he looked around the house he built, he saw only what he'd lost.

He begged Death to give his daughter back. But Death could do no such thing. Her soul was with the Skyweaver.

So Sunder set out to make it right.

He found the goddess of souls at her loom. Skyweaver's warp was fashioned from the dreams of the living, her weft from the memories of the dead. At the sound of Sunder's intrusion, her shuttle stopped. She put down her threads.

Sunder fell at her feet and he begged.

"There is a price for what you're asking," she said.

"Whatever it is, I'll pay it."

Skyweaver rose from her loom. "It's your soul that is owed. Your death that was cheated."

Sunder closed his eyes, thinking of the rain that nourished his crops and the sun that made them grow and the strength of his own two hands.

"I can give back your daughter's soul. I can restore her life." Skyweaver picked up her weaving knife. "But only you can pay the price."

On his knees, Sunder looked up at the faceless god and said, "Take it, then."

So Skyweaver lifted her knife . . .

and cut his soul loose from its mooring.

One

Her sister said it would take a year to raise an army, bring down a tyrant, and marry a king.

Roa had done it in just three months.

And now here she sat, at the carved acacia table polished to a sheen, in the smallest pavilion of her father's house. It smelled smoky-sweet from the heart-fire, and Essie was perched on her shoulder, her talons clenching and unclenching, while Roa's bare feet tapped the woven rug impatiently.

Five days of negotiating peace terms was starting to get to the both of them.

The ceremonial weapons of every man and woman present were piled in the middle of the table—long and short knives, elegantly carved maces, gleaming scythes—laid out of reach as a show of trust. Only three chairs sat empty. They belonged to representatives from the House of Sky, and they'd been empty all week—a fact no one was talking about. Least of all Roa.

She stared at the empty chair on the left, imagining the

young man who normally sat there. Strong shoulders. Wheat-gold eyes. Dark-brown hair pulled back from his handsome face.

Theo, heir to the House of Sky.

Roa's former betrothed.

He's always been stubborn. Essie's thoughts flooded Roa's mind as her claws dug into Roa's shoulder. *But never this stubborn.*

Roa traced the delicate wing bone of the white hawk on her shoulder. The bond they shared—something Essie called *the hum*—glowed bright and warm between them.

I betrayed him, thought Roa. *I won't be surprised if he never speaks to me again.*

Their silent conversation was suddenly interrupted by the sound of someone snoring.

The new queen and her hawk looked sharply away from Theo's chair to the young man seated beside her. The warm afternoon sunlight pooled in through the windows, alighting on his unruly brown curls. His elbow was propped on the table, his cheek rested on his fist, and those long black lashes fluttered softly against his cheeks.

This was the dragon king. Asleep in an important treaty meeting.

This . . . *waste* . . . was the person for which Roa had given up everything.

She bristled at the sound of his snores and glanced up to the dozen men and women gathered around the table, all of them representatives of Great Houses in the scrublands. All were men and women Roa deeply admired.

She prayed they didn't notice the snoring.

It was a useless prayer. Of course they noticed. Dax had been falling asleep in treaty meetings all week, revealing the truth to everyone: he didn't care that his father's sanctions hadn't been lifted or that Roa's people were still going hungry.

These were not the kinds of things Dax cared about.

Which was why Roa was here. She'd insisted on traveling across the sand sea and drawing up an official treaty document herself. With a signed treaty, Dax couldn't continue to break his promises. Not without consequences.

It was why they were all here, in Roa's childhood home, with their heads bowed over a scroll.

Roa looked past the sleeping king, past the pile of weapons, to find her father studying her. A man of almost fifty, his curly black hair was speckled with gray now, and he looked thinner and more tired than she remembered. Was that possible? In just the two months she'd been gone? He wore a cotton tunic, split at the throat, with the pattern of Song fading around the collar. It matched Roa's own garment.

A proper dragon queen would have worn a brightly colored kaftan, finely stitched slippers, and a gold circlet on her head. But Roa was a scrublander first and foremost. She wore an undyed linen dress sewn by her mother and a necklace of pale blue beryl beads.

Her father's eyes held Roa's, then glanced to the young man snoring beside her. The look on his face was unmistakable.

He pitied her.

Roa's stomach tightened like a fist.

She would *not* be pitied. Certainly not by her own father.

Beneath the table Roa elbowed her new husband hard in the ribs. Surprised by the movement, Essie flexed her wings to stay balanced on her shoulder. Dax jolted awake, eyes widening as he let out a soft *oof!* But instead of sitting up and paying attention, instead of showing any sign of remorse, he yawned loudly, then stretched—drawing full attention to the fact that he'd fallen asleep.

As if he wanted everyone to know how little he cared.

More men and women around the table glanced at Roa. When she looked from one face to the next, each and every one of them averted their gaze. As if humiliated on Roa's behalf.

These were the same people who'd put their trust in her when she asked for an army to help Dax dethrone his father. And here they were, watching her now with shame in their eyes.

Daughter of Song, she could hear them all thinking, *what have you done?*

Their stares scorched her. Roa's fists clenched in her linen dress. She desperately wanted this meeting to be over. But the treaty scroll was still collecting signatures.

Roa looked to Dax, who was yawning again.

"Do we bore you, my king?" She didn't even try to keep the bitterness out of her voice.

"Not at all," he drawled, his attention snagging on something across the table. "I didn't sleep much last night."

Essie shifted restlessly from claw to claw as Roa looked where Dax did: to the young woman who'd just entered the pavilion. It was Roa's cousin, Sara, a tray balanced on her hip. Her long hair was tucked in a bun and held in place with an ivory comb. On her wrists were three bracelets made of shiny white nerita shells.

As Sara collected cups of cold tea from the table, she smiled brightly beneath the king's gaze.

Roa reluctantly remembered the night previous. After a round of drinking games with her brother and cousins, Dax had openly flirted with the women of her household, Sara among them. It was something she'd had to get used to: Dax's flirting.

Roa was pretty sure he'd flirt with a dragon if he were drunk enough.

She looked away from the king and her cousin. She didn't want to see the smiles passing between them. Didn't want to know how far the game had gone.

But there were only two other places to look: the embarrassed faces of the house representatives or that empty chair.

It was an unbearable choice.

In the end, Roa chose the consequence of her broken promise. She stared at Theo's chair as if he were in it, staring back at her.

Sometimes she let herself wonder what her life would be like if she'd kept her promise to him. There would certainly be no king in her father's house flirting with Roa's cousins and humiliating her in front of the people she loved most.

And there would be no one keeping the scrublands safe. Essie's voice rang through her mind. Those talons squeezed Roa's shoulder affectionately. *Dax's father would have bled us dry.*

Essie was right, of course.

You did what you needed to do, Essie told her, brushing the top of her feathered head against Roa's cheek. *They all know that.*

Truly, Roa had done it for every scrublander, Theo included. She would not allow another Firgaardian king to take whatever he wanted from them. He'd already taken enough.

Roa looked to Dax as she stroked Essie's soft feathers. When the scroll came to the king, he signed it, then took a pinch of sand from the bowl in front of them and sprinkled it across the wet ink. After it dried, he blew off the sand, rolled up the scroll, and gave it to Roa.

The relief in the room was palpable. The king was now bound to his promises. They would finally be free of Firgaard's tyranny.

Voices rose, talking and laughing easily now that it was done.

When a jug of wine was brought in, Roa frowned. It had been years since her father served wine to his guests. Few people in the scrublands could afford it anymore. She wondered what her family would give up this month in order to compensate for the indulgence.

Oblivious, Dax poured the wine into two red clay cups, then looped his arm lazily around the back of Roa's chair. Startled at his closeness, Essie flew off Roa's shoulder.

Roa, who was more used to the weight of her sister's imprisoned form than the absence of it—whose shoulders bore eight years of tiny scars from Essie's claws, went immediately cold at the loss of her.

Dax bent toward Roa, holding out a full cup.

"To peace," he said softly, the peppermint smell of him enveloping her.

Roa didn't dare look at him. She knew the kinds of spells those warm brown eyes cast. The kinds of things that curve of a mouth promised. She'd seen enough girls fall for Dax's charms to know she needed to protect herself against them.

Staring at his throat instead, she watched the steady beat of his pulse. Taking the cup from him, she said, "To kings who keep their promises."

Her gaze flickered to his. For the briefest of heartbeats, she thought she saw amusement in his eyes. But then it was gone, hidden behind a smooth smile.

She hated that smile. Hated the effect it had on her.

Roa set down the cup and quickly rose.

"If we're finished," she said, catching her father's gaze as she reached across the table toward the pile of earned weapons, "then you must excuse me. There's somewhere I need to be."

Taking her scythe from the top of the pile, Roa didn't wait for her father's answer. Just turned away from the table, left through the open door, and didn't look back.

Essie followed her out.

Roa rode hard across the border of Song. Poppy's hooves pummeled the hot, cracked earth, putting distance between her and her father's house. Between her and the boy-king.

It was as if the wide-open world Roa once knew—as open as the sunset sky above—had become a prison. She might have walked willingly into it, but her bonds still chafed.

Halfway to her destination, Roa felt a familiar *hum* flare up inside her. Instinctively, she looked to find a white hawk soaring above.

Essie.

Even with so much distance between them, Roa could sense her sister's uneasiness.

Where are you going? her sister called. *You'll miss the Gleaning.*

Poppy slowed to a trot as Roa leaned back in the saddle. She'd forgotten that tonight was the Gleaning.

Once a week, the House of Song made dinner for those who were hardest hit by Firgaard's sanctions. On Gleaning nights, it was normal for the house to be full to the brim. The very poorest would eat—and take home anything extra that could be spared.

You should be there, said Essie, still trying to catch up. *You give them hope, Roa.*

But going back to the House of Song meant facing Dax. It meant watching him drink her father's wine while he flirted with every girl in her home.

Roa gritted her teeth.

I sat obediently next to him for days now. Her thoughts burned into her twin's mind. *If I have to stand by his side one more moment, I'll . . .* Her grip tightened on the reins. *I'll take it all back.*

She *could* take it back. The marriage was unconsummated. Which meant it could still be annulled.

And who will protect us if you do? came Essie's reply.

That was just it. This was the decision she'd made. It was up to Roa to keep her people safe.

She'd thought it would be easier, trading in her freedom for the protection of the scrublands. She hadn't realized it would cost her so much more than freedom.

Her sister's voice had gone soft and quiet in her mind: *Roa, you should be more careful. People are starting to notice your nightly absences.*

Roa had been absent every night since they'd arrived home six days ago.

Let them notice, she thought, urging Poppy into a gallop.

In the distance, the red-brown earth shifted into a smudge of green forest. Roa headed straight for the hidden path through the acacias. They were entering the shadow precinct, where the fifth Great House had once stood proud . . . and then fallen into ruin.

A sharp jab of her sister's frustration shot through her. Roa ignored it.

Roa. Essie's voice flickered into her mind as she struggled to keep up. Her elegant white wings fought with a wind that kept battering her back. *You can't just run away!*

I'm queen, she thought. *I can do as I wish.*

You're not acting like a queen. Essie's thoughts were getting fainter. *You're acting like a . . . scared . . . selfish . . . child.*

That stung.

In answer, Roa sent a stab of cold at her sister's hawk form. Essie sent her version of the same feeling back—only sharper.

Just before Poppy halted and stepped into the trees, the white hawk screeched. Roa felt a painful tug and stopped them both, frowning hard. She looked over her shoulder to see Essie—a speck of white in a carnelian sky—still battling the wind, try-ing to get to her.

A second, sharper tug came. Roa sucked in a pained breath. She squeezed Poppy's reins in her fists and sent her thoughts into her sister's mind: *If you're trying to hurt me, it's working.*

Essie didn't respond.

Roa had thought Essie would understand. Essie knew better than anyone what it was like to be trapped. But just like Roa's friend, Lirabel, Essie seemed to side with Dax more and more these days. As if his ridiculous charms were working on them, too.

A little angrily, Roa turned away from her sister. She didn't wait for Essie to catch up, just retreated into the trees without her.

Essie would find her. She always did. The bond hummed between them, bright and strong, keeping them linked. Roa could always sense her sister—could feel the shape of her soul. Even if a desert lay between them.

Jacarandas bloomed here. Their purple flowers carpeted the ground, more beautiful than any palace rug. Roa breathed in the sweet smell of them as Poppy rode up to the entrance of the House of Shade.

Corrupted, people called this place. A man had died here, a long time ago now, and his loved ones hadn't performed the proper rites. They hadn't broken the bonds between the living and the dead. So, on the last night of the Relinquishing—the longest night of the year—the man's soul became corrupted and he slaughtered his entire household.

Or so the story went.

Corrupted spirits were dangerous things. It was why the rules for relinquishing needed to be upheld.

But even if the story was true, the man's spirit had long since moved on.

After dismounting and tying Poppy to a branch outside, Roa stepped through the crumbled entrance of the ruined house. As she walked through the roofless halls, Roa thought of that empty chair. It was an obvious insult. But Theo had been insulted first. Sky was the only Great House who voted *against* Roa helping Dax in the revolt. And in the scrublands, a unanimous vote was needed before anyone could march an army across the sand sea. Roa had broken scrublander law to do what she'd done.

And then she'd broken Theo's heart.

Roa checked every room in the ruined house. All were empty. She checked them again.

He didn't come, she thought, her heart sinking.

Theo hadn't wanted her to help Dax. He told her that if she left, she wouldn't come back.

You were wrong, she thought now. *I did come back.*

She was here now, wasn't she? She'd been here in this ruin— their usual meeting place—waiting for him for five nights straight.

And for five nights straight, he didn't come. Because Roa married Dax. Because Roa was queen now.

It was too late for her and Theo.

As the wind rattled the canopy above, she climbed up onto

...ne windowsill of a half-crumbled wall. Leaning back against the cool and dusty stone, she pressed her face into her hands.

You're queen now, she told herself. *Queens don't cry.*

It was something Essie would say. If Essie were here.

As she waited for her sister to arrive, Roa thought of the shame in her father's eyes. In all their eyes.

Maybe it was better this way. She wasn't sure she could bear that same look on Theo's face.

When a hundred-hundred heartbeats passed and Essie still hadn't shown herself, Roa looked up to the canopy. To the patch of darkening sky beyond it.

Instinctively, her gaze found Essie's two favorite stars. *Twin stars,* Essie liked to call them. Essie loved stars. The stories she most loved were ones about the Skyweaver, a goddess who spun souls into stars and wove them into the sky.

Roa thought of Skyweaver spinning Essie's soul into a star, then putting it up there, all alone, without Roa.

A cold feeling knotted her insides.

What was taking her sister so long?

Roa reached for that normally bright hum. Even before Essie's accident, the hum had always been there, warm and glowing inside them both.

This time when Roa reached for it, she found it dim and weak. Like a too-quiet pulse.

Essie?

No answer came.

Roa pushed herself down from the sill and walked back through the empty, ruined rooms.

"Essie?" she called, her voice echoing. "Where are you?"

Silence answered her.

Roa's pace quickened, thinking of the way her sister's thoughts had flickered strangely. At how distant she'd felt earlier.

Essie, if this is a joke, it isn't funny.

At the entrance, Roa untied Poppy and quickly mounted, nudging her back toward the tree line. When they got there, the sun was long gone and the sky was blue-black. She couldn't see any sign of a white bird in its depths.

Roa cupped her hands and called her sister's name.

"Essie!"

Her voice echoed and died. The wind rustled the leaves at her back.

It was something the two sisters never spoke about, as if speaking it would make it come true: an uncrossed soul couldn't exist forever in the world of the living. Eventually, the death call of the Relinquishing became too strong.

Essie had been resisting her death call for eight years now.

Looking up to the stars, Roa whispered, "Essie, where are you?"

EXPLORE THE LUSH AND DANGEROUS ISKARI SERIES.

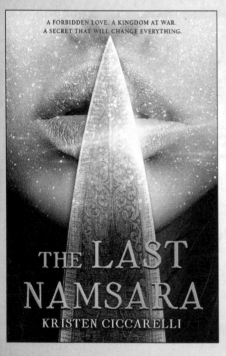

A FORBIDDEN LOVE. A KINGDOM AT WAR.
A SECRET THAT WILL CHANGE EVERYTHING.

THE LAST NAMSARA
KRISTEN CICCARELLI

ONE SACRIFICE WILL FREE HER

THE CAGED QUEEN
KRISTEN CICCARELLI
❖ Companion to The Last Namsara ❖

THE
Epic Reads
COMMUNITY